THE DOOMED EARTH
DESTINY'S WAY

ALSO BY JACK CAMPBELL
AND AVAILABLE FROM TITAN BOOKS

THE DOOMED EARTH
In Our Stars

THE LOST FLEET SERIES
Dauntless
Fearless
Courageous
Valiant
Relentless
Victorious
Beyond the Frontier: Dreadnaught
Beyond the Frontier: Invincible
Beyond the Frontier: Guardian
Beyond the Frontier: Steadfast
Beyond the Frontier: Leviathan
Outlands: Boundless
Outlands: Resolute
Outlands: Implacable

THE LOST STARS SERIES
Tarnished Knight
Perilous Shield
Imperfect Sword
Shattered Spear

THE GENESIS FLEET SERIES
Vanguard
Ascendant
Triumphant

THE STARK'S WAR SERIES *(as John G. Hemry)*
Stark's War
Stark's Command
Stark's Crusade

JAG IN SPACE *(as John G. Hemry)*
A Just Determination
Burden of Proof
Rule of Evidence
Against All Enemies

JACK CAMPBELL

THE *NEW YORK TIMES* BESTSELLER

THE DOOMED EARTH
DESTINY'S WAY

TITAN BOOKS

The Doomed Earth: Destiny's Way
Print edition ISBN: 9781803367286
E-book edition ISBN: 9781803367293

Published by Titan Books
A division of Titan Publishing Group Ltd
144 Southwark Street, London SE1 0UP
www.titanbooks.com

First Titan edition: February 2025
10 9 8 7 6 5 4 3 2 1

This book is a work of fiction. All of the characters, organizations, and events portrayed in this novel are either products of the author's imagination or are used fictitiously. Any resemblance to actual persons, living or dead (except for satirical purposes), is entirely coincidental.

Copyright © 2025 John G. Hemry writing as Jack Campbell.

The right of John G. Hemry to be identified as the author of this work has been asserted by him in accordance with the Copyright, Designs and Patents Act of 1988.

This is a work of fiction. All of the characters, organizations, and events portrayed in this novel are either products of the author's imagination or are used fictitiously.

No part of this publication may be reproduced, stored in a retrieval system, or transmitted, in any form or by any means without the prior written permission of the publisher, nor be otherwise circulated in any form of binding or cover other than that in which it is published and without a similar condition being imposed on the subsequent purchaser.

A CIP catalogue record for this title is available from the British Library.

EU RP
eucomply OÜ Pärnu mnt 139b-14 11317
Tallinn, Estonia
hello@eucompliancepartner.com
+3375690241

Typeset in Bembo 11/13pt.

Printed and bound by CPI Group (UK) Ltd, Croydon, CR0 4YY.

To Danielle Ackley-McPhail and Mike McPhail, the finest of people, and strong creative voices who have worked tirelessly to support other creative voices as well

For S., as always

1

8 July 2140

THE VIEW FROM THE lunar shuttle heading for a landing on the east coast of North America still felt unreal to Selene Genji. Born in 2158, a lieutenant in a fleet that wouldn't exist until 2171, veteran of the multiple conflicts known as the Universal War that would rage through the 2170s, and witness to the death of the planet Earth on the twelfth of June, 2180, she had trouble at times believing that Earth still existed. That somehow the massive forces unleashed by the destruction of Earth had warped space and time itself to hurl her back to the year 2140, giving her a chance to try to alter the past that had led to that awful event.

If, that is, she could survive long enough to make enough changes while not knowing which changes were needed, her eyes and glossy skin betraying the fact that she was a genetically engineered "alloy" containing alien DNA in her mostly human genome. Alloys weren't supposed to exist until the late 2150s. But to some humans in 2140, the mere fact of her being partly alien was enough to mark her as a horrible threat that had to be eliminated.

A lot of those humans would be waiting when the shuttle landed.

Lieutenant Kayl Owen of Earth Guard, one of his hands tightly grasping hers, shook his head as the panel "window" in their compartment went blank, preventing any more outside views. In place of that, the window displayed warnings to cooperate with the security personnel waiting to screen all passengers when the shuttle returned to Earth at the minor spaceport named Wallops. "How do you suppose they figured out we're aboard this shuttle?"

"I'm more worried at the moment about getting off it without being killed. We have to assume shoot-on-sight orders are still in place when it comes to me," Genji said.

"They've targeted me as well," Kayl said.

"What if you put on your uniform?" she suggested. "Wouldn't they hesitate to fire at you if they knew you were an Earth Guard officer?"

He shook his head once more. "No. Whoever is waiting for us down there won't be Earth Guard. Probably soldiers and spaceport security. Soldiers fired on me while we were on Mars, remember? They know I'm officially a renegade Earth Guard officer, helping the dangerous alien scout they think is laying the groundwork for an invasion by the Tramontine."

"How long do the Tramontine have to demonstrate peaceful intent?" Genji asked in frustration. "Since their ship arrived in orbit about Mars, they haven't done anything aggressive."

"You haven't done anything aggressive, either," Kayl said. "That hasn't stopped some people from thinking you're a deadly threat."

Genji felt the shuttle shudder slightly as it entered thicker atmosphere. They were probably only a few more minutes from landing. "If I'm trapped here, Kayl, you need to move on. Find a way to remain free and try to carry out the mission."

"I'm not leaving you," he said.

"We may not have a choice! It's not just about trying to save the Earth! I love you, and I don't want you to die."

Kayl nodded to her, his expression solemn. "And I love you, and you're not going to die. Not as long as I'm around."

"The mission, Kayl! We have to save the Earth!"

"I understand," Kayl said. "When we land, let's scope out the security and see what options we have." He turned to speak to the fourteen-year-old girl sharing their compartment. "Krysta, remember what you promised Lieutenant Genji. When we tell you to drop, you get on the ground fast, and stay there until police come along. We don't want you hurt."

"Why do they want to hurt you?" Krysta asked, her voice plaintive.

"That's complicated," Genji said. Why had they yielded to Krysta's pleas to bring her with them to Earth? After rescuing Krysta from the abusive "husband" who'd bought her when she was eleven, they should have turned her over to a child welfare organization at the lunar colony named Hamilton. "Just do as we say so you'll be safe."

What would they be facing when the shuttle landed? How many foes, how much backup, how many bots and drones?

Her primary specialty in the Unified Fleet had been, or would be, close combat. She'd chosen that so she could battle the fanatics of the Spear of Humanity, trying to kill as many as possible of the sort of people who'd murdered her mother. But she'd never been able to kill enough, and eventually the Spear had won, if destroying the world could be considered winning.

An eye for an eye hadn't worked to win the future. It wouldn't work now to convince people in 2140 that she was trying to save the Earth and everyone who lived on it.

But, if she died here, only Kayl would be left to try to carry on, to try to complete the mission she'd given herself and he had agreed to give everything to try to accomplish. And if Kayl died as well . . .

One way or another, one of them would have to survive.

"Five minutes until landing at Wallops," the cheerful voice of the shuttle's announcing system informed them. "The security level at Wallops is Code Red One. Please comply with all security instructions to ensure the safety of you and your fellow passengers. Local time at landing will be 1700. The weather is comfortable with scattered clouds and light winds. Everyone is reminded that failure to cooperate with all security instructions could unnecessarily endanger you or your fellow passengers."

/ / / / /

LIEUTENANT KAYL OWEN HADN'T exactly turned his back on a successful career in Earth Guard. Before encountering Lieutenant Selene Genji, he had been on a one-way road to nonpromotion and dismissal from the service, not because he couldn't do his job, but because senior officers in Earth Guard had tarred his father with responsibility for the loss of the cruiser *Sentinel* ten years ago. Since his father had died along with most of *Sentinel*'s crew, and an independent investigation had absolved him of responsibility for the disaster, those senior officers had to be content with blaming Kayl in his place.

But then he had been sent to investigate a piece of wreckage that had mysteriously appeared out of nowhere, and he'd found a living survivor aboard it. A survivor named Selene Genji, who had turned out to have alien DNA among her genome. Suddenly, Selene Genji officially ceased to exist, all contact with her forbidden. Worried for her, Kayl had found means to communicate with Genji, convincing the stunned refugee from the future destruction of Earth that it was 2140.

He still didn't know what he would have ended up doing if he and Lieutenant Genji hadn't both been put on a sabotaged ship on its way to a catastrophic entry into Earth's atmosphere. After two more attempts to kill them both, he'd thrown himself wholeheartedly into helping her.

And ended up falling in love with the part-alien woman from the future who was trying to save a world that kept trying to kill her.

But the path they'd been on to try to save the planet looked like it might have hit a dead end. If the security forces at Wallops were expecting them and prepared for them, managing another escape might be impossible. And with shoot-on-sight orders still in effect, no one would listen to them before opening fire once they'd been identified.

The shuttle grounded. In other passenger compartments and the main passenger deck where hundreds of people were seated, the rest of those aboard the shuttle would be grumbling about diversions and delays as they prepared to debark.

Owen stood up, gazing at Selene. "We'll make it through somehow."

"Sure we will," she said, smiling.

They both knew they were lying.

He kissed her for what might be the last time.

"Stay close, Krysta," Selene said as they paused at the door to their compartment so Owen could figure out how many passengers had already left.

"Looks like about half are off. We should go now," Owen said.

He was in civilian clothing, hopefully looking unremarkable in every way. Selene, due to the unusual shape and size of her eyes, and the gleaming skin that came with her genetic makeup, had once again donned the sort of clothes worn by UV Aversives, who tried to avoid any exposure to the sun: a sun jacket covering her arms and neck, light gloves on her hands, large sunglasses, and a broad-brimmed hat with a flap hanging down along the sides and back of her head and neck. The outfit wouldn't normally attract much attention, however, the authorities knew about Selene's skin and eyes, and would be watching for anyone concealing those things. But there wasn't any alternative to wearing it except instantly giving herself away.

The three of them merged with the flow of passengers going out the accesses. The shuttle was parked well away from the terminal, so instead of entering the building, stairs were leading the passengers onto the surface of the spaceport. Kayl could see a ring of portable security fences already in position. The portable fences had a total of four gates in them, and each gate was occupied by multiple sentries with DNA scanners positioned. Beyond the fences, there were numerous security vehicles, groups of soldiers and security personnel, drones hovering, and a couple of warbirds making slow passes overhead.

Beyond the immediate area, a perimeter fence surrounded Wallops, a large number of buildings visible along with rows of grounded aircraft, hangars, orbital lifters, and a variety of military defensive equipment.

"It looks like they're ready to fight an army," one of the passengers close to Owen grumbled. "How long is this going to take?"

"Why were we diverted from Tanegashima?" another complained. "I have a meeting in Nagasaki in six hours! Even a suborbital taxi won't get me there in time!"

Once on the concrete of the spaceport field, the mass of passengers opened up a bit, some crowding forward to try to get through the security screening first. The air was hot and muggy, the slight breeze offering little relief, a far cry from the comfortable weather predicted before they landed.

Selene looked around them, slowly appraising everything that could be seen. "Kayl, I know we talked about no more suicidal plans, but I don't see any way both of us are getting out of this. We could try surrendering."

"Selene, I can tell from here that the soldiers have charged energy weapons and mag rifles. You can see how pumped up they all are, nervous and edgy. The moment they know who you are, they'll kill you."

"I know."

"I'll do the diversion, then," Owen said, trying not to get too rattled thinking about what that meant. "They may not kill me right off. You get free while I'm distracting them."

"*I'll* do the diversion," Selene said. "*You'll* get free. You know they're going to come after me the moment they realize it's you and not me."

"They're going to kill you," Owen repeated.

"If it has to be one of us—"

"You don't get to decide that, Selene."

"You're talking like we have a choice," Selene said. "We can't afford to take too long to decide this. The fewer passengers left unscreened, the less cover we have. Krysta, get ready to—"

"No," Krysta abruptly said. She'd been passive and quiet up to that point. "You saved me. I'm going to save you."

With no more warning than that, before either Owen or Selene could react, Krysta yanked the UV Aversive hat off Selene and bolted toward the far side of the security perimeter.

"Krysta!" Selene gasped, horrified. Both she and Owen stood, frozen, for a few precious seconds. As the entire security apparatus focused on the fleeing figure of Krysta, her large hat easily visible, Selene spun about, grabbing Owen's hand and yanking him in the opposite direction. "Damn that girl!" she sobbed.

"Why did she—?" Owen began, feeling sick as he heard the first shots being fired. Not the snap of stunners, but the thunder of energy bolts and the crack of bullets fired from mag pistols and rifles.

"We have to make sure it's not in vain," Selene said, her voice ragged with emotion. "Damn her! She was supposed to live."

Most of those in the crowd were surging away from where the security forces were converging on Krysta's path. Selene and Owen moved with them, coming up against one of the security checkpoints, the two guards remaining there craning their heads to try to see what was happening.

Selene hit them before either knew their target was here instead of somewhere out there.

Owen grabbed the mag rifle one of the guards had dropped as she fell, following Selene as she ran across the concrete to a nearby tactical vehicle with a single security officer standing by it.

The officer tried to get out his sidearm, but Selene was moving as quickly as if possessed by a demon, one hand knocking him down while the other grabbed the ID / key card off the officer.

"Swap!" Selene told Owen, tossing the key card to him.

Owen tossed her the rifle, jumping into the driver's seat and bringing the engine online.

Selene slammed her door as Owen gunned the engine, producing a sudden roar as the backup power immediately kicked in. The vehicle tore off down the field, guards scattering away before turning to fire.

"She's down!" Selene shouted, sounding torn between sorrow and rage. "Krysta is down!" She lowered the window, aiming her mag rifle at the swarm of drones starting to head for the vehicle.

Owen swung the vehicle past a parked service van, thinking that Selene could never score a hit manually aiming from a car moving like this.

He heard the crack of the bullet, moving at supersonic speed, and in the rearview saw the nearest drone shatter.

Crack. Crack. Crack. Three more drones either fell from the sky or fluttered erratically off to the side.

Bullets were impacting the armored rear and back window of the tactical vehicle. Kayl felt it lurch as something important took a hit. Looking ahead and around, he saw security forces and vehicles gathering at the exits. The perimeter fence was too high and too strong to punch through. "We can't get out on the ground!"

"Find something that can fly!" Selene yelled back. She steadied her aim again, dropping a drone that was about to fire a missile into their vehicle.

Owen spotted an aircraft idling among the rows of parked jump craft. Swinging the vehicle around so hard it tilted dangerously up on one side, he aimed for the aircraft, skidding the vehicle to a halt next to it.

The pilot was frantically running through takeoff preps when Owen ran toward her. She paused to haul out a pistol, but before she could bring it to bear, Selene hit her and, with one swift motion, popped the pilot's seat harness and tossed her onto the field.

Owen jumped into the aircraft, seeing drones and security vehicles swarming toward them. "Hang on!"

The aircraft's engines screamed in protest as he yanked the bird into the air, bullets pattering off the armored sides. Swinging it about, Owen shot down the field, keeping low, jerking the bird from side to side.

As they cleared the perimeter fence, guards and sentry bots firing up at the bottom of the aircraft, Owen felt the aircraft jolt alarmingly as something large hit it. Danger lights all over the controls were blinking like a Christmas display.

Selene shot again, taking out another drone zooming toward them from the side. "We're on fire."

"Where?" Owen called.

"Looks like the entire back of the bird. The good news is, we're putting out so much smoke they can't see to target us visually."

"You can swim, right?" Owen asked as he angled the crippled bird along a watercourse.

"Of course I can swim. We're still pretty close to the spaceport to be abandoning this bird."

"Selene," Owen said, feeling the controls grow increasingly sluggish and stiff, "we either abandon it soon or we ride it down, crash, burn, and die."

He took the risk of going lower despite the aircraft's wavering flight. Glancing back, he saw smoke billowing out from the rear of the bird. "Stand by to jump."

Selene put down the rifle. "I'll go out my side when you go out yours."

"I'm not the one who comes up with suicidal plans," Owen said. He hastily entered some flight instructions into the autopilot. He wouldn't have to tell the autopilot to jink along the flight path since the controls were badly enough damaged that the aircraft could no longer hold a straight course.

A stream flashed by below, a larger watercourse visible

ahead. A river? The Atlantic? The Chesapeake Bay? No time to look. "Stand by. Go!"

Owen rolled out of his side as Selene did the same on hers.

He hit the water, went under, and stayed under as long as he could, able to see dark shapes flashing by overhead as a swarm of drones pursued the crippled aircraft, followed by a few larger shapes as other aircraft raced past.

Finally, unable to hold his breath any longer, Owen went to the surface and gasped in air. He didn't need to fight to keep from floating too high since his clothing was trying to drag him down.

Someone grabbed him and started towing him toward the shore.

Owen and Selene stumbled out of the water, scrambling into the high grass near the swampy shoreline before collapsing to the ground, both breathing heavily.

"Can *I* swim?" Selene finally got enough air to gasp. "I should've asked you that."

Kayl saw a wavering track of smoke marking the path of their former aircraft. He heard the distant whomp of an explosion in the same direction the smoke led. "There went our bird. Hopefully they think we're still in it."

"As soon as they get a bot on-site, they can send it in even if the wrecked bird is still burning and tell we're not inside," Selene said. "Where the hell are we?"

"I have no idea. Which direction were we going?" Owen tasted the water on his lips. "Salt. We're on the shore of the Chesapeake Bay. Or the Atlantic."

Selene raised herself cautiously to look around. "Which direction is that from Wallops?"

"South. East. West. And north."

"That's very helpful. We need to get off the direct path that bird flew. Which way?"

"North looks harder."

"North it is," Selene said. She got up, limping slightly the first few steps, angling toward a patch of trees on a hummock rising above the salt marsh. "Damn that girl."

"Yeah," Owen said, remembering his last glimpse of Krysta bolting through the crowd. "Maybe she's okay."

"I saw her go down, Kayl," Selene said, her gaze fixed ahead of them. "She was definitely hit at least once. But if they didn't kill her, they won't finish her off when they see she's not me. We can hope for that."

"I keep telling myself it's not our fault," Owen said, nearly twisting his ankle as a marshy bit of soil gave way under his foot. "And then I tell myself, yes, it was."

"We should have left her at Hamilton," Selene said. "Handed her off to Yolanda Thanh."

"Yeah."

"Did she give us any hint she was planning that? Something we missed?"

"I'm not sure she planned it," Owen said. "I think we didn't get any warning because Krysta acted on the spur of the moment. Which doesn't make me feel the least bit better." It didn't help to realize that if not for Krysta's impulsive sacrifice, neither he nor Selene probably would have made it out of Wallops alive. They might still get run to ground soon, but they had a chance. And that made him feel guilty as hell. "We didn't save her from that guy so she could die for us."

"No, we didn't. I hear sirens that way and that way," Selene said, pointing across the landscape. "That's Wallops back there. Is that a town over in that direction?"

Owen squinted to look. "Some of the buildings have collapsed. I'm guessing it's an old subdivision flooded by sea level rise."

"Good place to hide?"

"What are your feelings about mosquitoes?"

"You haven't cleared out mosquitoes yet in 2140?" Selene demanded.

"No," Kayl said. "It's a difficult problem."

"Why— Cover! Now!"

They'd almost reached the low trees on the hummock of land, so Owen followed Selene in a dash to lie down under that protection.

He finally heard the faint whine of the drone motors moments before a loose line of searchers tore past overhead. He waited, unmoving, until the drones were well past. "Good thing your ears are so much better than mine."

"Yeah," Selene said. "Being an alloy is so great. Let me know if you want to swap bodies. That search line looked too spread out and was moving too fast."

"I had the same impression," Owen said. "They don't seem to have had a backup plan if we made it off the spaceport, and now they're improvising and trying to run us down fast instead of taking time to organize a tight search."

"Which gives us a chance," Selene said. "Krysta sacrificed herself for us. We have to do our best to ensure that sacrifice wasn't in vain. Do you feel as guilty about that as I do?"

"Yeah," Owen said. "It's late afternoon, the sun should be in the southwest. That means we're headed roughly north."

"If we power up our burner phones, they might spot them," Selene said. "Do you have any idea what the geography is like around here? Which way should we be going?"

"I think we're on a big peninsula named the Eastern Shore. A lot of it has been turned into salt marshes by sea level rise." Owen looked about him. "It's a trap. We need to either break out to the north, which is a long hike, or head west and hope we can find an unguarded boat to carry us across the Chesapeake Bay."

Selene twisted and rose up a bit to look around. "They're going to assume the shore to our west is a barrier we can't cross. Same for the shore to our east. The search is going to focus on the north as soon as they figure that out."

"So we go west?"

"I think we should. We might get pinned on the coast, but that's still our best chance."

"Okay," Owen said. "Do we risk moving now?"

"Wait until the drones come back. I bet they'll run them out a dozen kilometers and then bring them back over this area on the return to Wallops."

Despite their precautions, they were still far too close to Wallops and the center of the search. They would surely have been pinned down, Owen thought, if the Earth itself hadn't come to their aid.

Heavy clouds marshalling to the southwest swept closer and then overhead, the sky rapidly darkening. A flash of brilliant light and the crash of thunder seemed to trigger the deluge that followed, rain coming down in torrents.

Owen and Selene did their best to drink the rainwater as it fell, cupping their hands for it. There might not be any other source of fresh water available to them. With lightning tearing open the sky and the rain so heavy it pounded on their shoulders, Owen and Selene took the chance of racing as fast as they could across the marshy landscape, at one point crossing over a raised road still in use, the sporadic vehicle traffic on it slowed and nearly blinded by the weather.

By the time the rain let up, they'd covered a good distance west, and sunset wasn't far off.

OWEN WOKE WITH A groan he barely managed to stifle. Selene had advised against hiding during daylight in any of the abandoned buildings or towns, pointing out that they would attract searchers. And from their hidden vantage point, it had indeed been possible to see bot, drone, and human searchers going through any standing structures within sight.

Their hiding place was a mound of wood that had once been a barn before collapsing and decaying and settling. There had been barely enough room beneath it for them to wriggle inside when dawn approached.

What had woken him? Moving his head cautiously in the

limited space, Owen saw a large black snake, close to two meters long, thrashing out the end of its life near Selene. "Was it poisonous?" he whispered.

She shook her head slightly. "No. It's food."

"Food? You think we can risk trying to make a fire?"

"No, I don't think we can risk that." As the snake's struggles ebbed, Selene held up a rusty nail she'd found amid the broken wood. "Have you ever had snake sashimi?"

"No. Never wanted to," Owen said.

"We need the food, and its blood will provide moisture we also need," Selene said, working to peel off the snake's skin. "Survival, Evasion, Resistance, and Escape training taught me a few useful skills I haven't forgotten."

"Did you eat raw snake when you were doing that?"

"Maybe Earth Guard should be giving you guys SERE training," she suggested.

"Is it like what we've been doing for the last day or so?"

"Pretty much."

"Then, no." He watched, appalled, as Selene peeled off strips of raw meat and offered him one. "We're really going to do this?"

"Our bodies need fuel, Kayl." She held up a strip of snake meat. "Thank you for the food." Dropping it in her mouth, she swallowed.

He did the same, grimacing. "At least it doesn't need salt."

"Yeah, that's one advantage of having blood on it."

"I hope the Earth appreciates what we're going through to try to save it," Owen grumbled.

"If it does," Selene suggested, "maybe it'll give us some more storms for cover."

As it turned out, another intense thunderstorm hit during the early afternoon, giving them enough cover to move quickly. As it eased, they took shelter in a partial structure that showed signs of having been searched recently. A second thunderstorm marched through perhaps an hour later, letting them make more progress west, and providing some more fresh water to help them cope with thirst that was once again becoming agonizing.

The sea grass that had been planted all over the region as the water levels rose, a genetically modified strain designed to prevent erosion by holding the land with dense fields of vegetation, provided more and more cover the closer they got to the coast.

Soon after sunset they reached a tidal stream with the remains of a dock on one bank, the waterlogged remnants of a wooden boat still visible next to it.

"What do we do when we reach the coast?" Selene asked. "Swim?"

Owen fought down an urge to snap back at her. "This was the best option."

"It still sucks."

"I never claimed it didn't!" Pointing out that she'd been the one to suggest heading west wouldn't accomplish anything except elevating the temperature of the debate they were having. He took the risk of rising up enough to gaze out across the night-shrouded bay. "There are a lot of lights out there."

"People searching for us," Selene said.

"There's normally a lot of other traffic on the water. You remember my former juvenile delinquent friend Edourd?"

"The guy from Mars."

"Yeah," Owen said. "We did some sailing together. He loves anything to do with the water. Surfing, sailing, you name it. As long as he could be on or in an ocean, a sea, or a river, or a lake."

"Sure," Selene said. "He grew up with oceans that were expanses of dirt and rock. I'm trying not to be negative, Kayl. But we thought they wouldn't expect us to head west because they would think the coast would be a trap. We and they might both be right."

"Anything else we did would have put us in worse trouble," Owen insisted.

Selene rubbed her face wearily. "What do we do when we reach the coast and there aren't any convenient boats lying around? We'll have to head either north or south at that point."

Owen looked south, fighting a sense of despair. "If I remember right, the land to the south necks down and ends in a point. We'd have less and less room to hide in. We'll have to work our way north. Eventually we'll hit a community that's still unflooded. They'll have boats. We'll borrow one."

She lowered her hands, looking dejected. "I can tell you know how desperate that plan is. But there isn't anything else that offers even a small chance. I'd just like to point out that this time you're the one proposing what is essentially a suicidal plan." Selene looked up. "Drones coming. Let's get in the grass."

After the search line of drones passed, they made their way cautiously through water of varying depth toward the soggy coastline. Not because they still had much hope, but simply because neither one of them was willing to give up.

It was probably near midnight when they reached the bay, huddled in the high grass near the water, gazing at the lights of boats and ships moving through the cloaked-in-darkness waters of the Chesapeake. The drones moving overhead, tirelessly searching for signs of Owen and Selene, were almost invisible and nearly silent. But they occasionally heard the sounds of vehicles crunching or splashing across the landscape farther inland, and sometimes the purr of a larger aircraft moving past overhead.

The net around them was tightening.

"There's a lot of search activity to the north," Selene said. "They know we have to head that way."

"Swimming out into the bay would be crazy, but it may be our last option," Owen said. "If we can avoid the boats searching for us. But we'd still be out there on the water when the sun came out."

"Ducks sitting in a barrel," Selene grumbled. "That boat is

close," she murmured to Owen, gesturing to a light on the water just offshore which was moving slowly along the coast.

He nodded. "It's not too big. Looks like a sailboat with one mast."

"It has two masts. There's a much smaller one behind the tall one."

"I think that's a yawl, then," Owen said. He didn't question her statement, having long ago learned that Selene's night vision was better than that of full humans. "Really old design. Strange it'd be out here so close to shore at night."

"A sailboat." Selene shook her head. "Are they really hunting us with sailboats? If I can get aboard, there's a chance I can take out the crew. There can't be too many people on something that size."

"Maybe if I distract them?" Owen said, knowing he was grasping at straws. But when he tried to say something else, Selene raised a hand to quiet him.

"Someone on the boat is calling something."

Owen had learned early on that Selene's hearing was also better than his, better, in fact, than most full humans'. He waited, despite the growing sense that time was quickly running out.

Then he heard it, too.

2

SELENE GENJI? SELENE GENJI?" The voice was pitched low, trying to carry without carrying too far. "We're friends. If you're out there, please let us know. Selene Genji?"

"It seems a little too obvious for a trap," Owen said.

"Should we risk it?" Selene asked him.

"We're out of options," he said. "If we don't get clear of this area soon, they're going to find us."

"So that's a yes."

"That's a yes," Owen reluctantly agreed.

The boat had continued moving slowly along the coast, a little ways out, navigation lights shining, but no other lights visible above deck except that of the binnacle near the helm. It was almost opposite them now, and Kayl could see that the yawl seemed to be about ten meters from bow to stern.

"Selene Genji?" the voice called again. It sounded like a young woman.

"Here," Selene called back. "I'm here."

"Selene Genji?"

Owen waited, wondering what they could do if this did turn out to be a trap. If they ran, the drones overhead would spot them in no time.

"Yes," Selene called again. "I am Lieutenant Selene Genji. Are you friends?"

"Yes! Yes! Can you swim out to us? We can't risk getting any closer to shore without grounding."

Selene waded out carefully, trying to make as little noise as possible, while Owen did the same behind her. Despite the darkness, he felt fearfully exposed walking slowly through the water.

The bottom shoaled slowly before suddenly dropping away, leaving Owen and Selene swimming the last part of the journey to the boat.

A rope ladder dropped over the side. "Can you make it up?" the young woman called.

"No problem," Selene said. She went up carefully, the water dripping off her sounding tremendously loud to Owen as it hit the surface of the bay.

He followed as soon as she was on deck.

"She's already below," a young man said. "Get down there with her in case someone checks us out."

The boat's crew didn't look anything like security personnel. Owen let willing hands urge him along a brief stretch of deck and down a short ladder into the boat's cabin, where a blackout sheet at the foot of the ladder prevented light from shining upward.

Past that was a small but efficient cabin, with multiple fold-down cots toward the bow and some fixed berths along the sides that could also serve as seats.

Selene, sitting on one of the berths, waved him over. She'd already drained half of a glass of water, offering him the rest.

Owen sat next to her, drinking greedily and gratefully, acutely aware of their dripping wet clothes.

Also in the cabin were two women and a man, all of whom seemed a little younger than twenty-two-year-old Selene. "We've got more," one of them hastened to say, bringing out additional water. "Are you guys hungry?"

"Very hungry," Owen said.

"I hope you like trail mix and jerky," one of the women said, offering them bags.

"Thank you," Owen said, feeling dizzy from the sudden shift in their fortunes. "It's a lot better than our last meal." He ripped open a package of jerky, offering some to Selene.

The young woman sat down on the berth opposite them. "We might get asked questions about people, so we're not going to ask what your names are, and for tonight our names are Pandora, Alera, and Gus. We just picked up a couple of people, that's all. And we're going to drop them off where they want to go. We're assuming that's the coast across the bay from here."

"As long as it's not too far," the young man going by Gus said. "We're not supposed to be out too long."

"It's not your boat?" Owen asked.

"Nah. It belongs to the college. St. Mary's. We're just out doing a night sail." He grinned. "A lot of people with boats are out there right now. Just in case someone needed a lift off the Eastern Shore. Everybody knows something happened at Wallops. There are a lot of rumors about who was involved. We figured they might need help."

"You haven't done anything," the young woman called Alera said. "Except good things. We wanted to help."

"It's been hairy out here with all the people and things looking for whoever escaped from Wallops," Gus added. "But we don't know anything about that! We've already turned to head back west across the bay, sort of easing along like people with no special place to be."

"Quiet!" someone called down from on deck.

Owen and Selene stopped eating and drinking, trying not to make any noise. The small group sat, listening to the water running along the hull, until an amplified voice suddenly sounded. "This area is temporarily restricted. Move offshore a minimum of ten kilometers. Do not approach this close to the shore again until notified that the navigational restriction has been lifted."

"Okay, man! You can see we're heading out already!" a man called from on deck.

"Why are you out here?" the amplified voice demanded.

"We're just doing a night sail! Pleasure cruise! Is that, like, a crime now?"

"Have you seen anyone near the coast?"

"Huh? Is someone lost?"

"Just get away from the coast," the voice ordered. "A minimum of ten kilometers. Understand?"

"We got it," the student on deck said. "Fine. See? We're heading out into the bay. Happy?"

Silence fell except for the creaking of the boat's hull and the rush of water.

After a couple of minutes, someone on deck spoke again. "Okay, they've moved off toward the coast."

"Let me see what happened," Gus said, dodging through the blackout curtain. He was back in about a minute. "A military bird was up there. They scanned our deck when they ordered us out of here, but didn't notice anything."

"Why are you helping us?" Owen asked.

Pandora looked at Selene. "Because so much of what's going on seems wrong. We've all seen what you said on Mars. What was wrong with that? But they tried to kill you! And whenever we ask exactly what it is you've done that's so terrible, we either get told it's classified or that you're still preparing to do something."

"Some of us have ancestors who got that treatment," Alera said. "Locked up because they might do something because they weren't like everybody else."

"Supposedly they're trying to capture you guys," Gus said. "But then at Wallops they had some sort of major battle. What was that? How do you capture people by blowing up everything?"

"I fired a few shots there," Selene said. "But only at drones. Everything else was aimed at us, or at . . ." She swallowed, looking toward one side. "Have you . . . have you heard anything about Krysta?"

"Is that the girl at Wallops?" Gus said. "The one who got hurt?"

Selene's eyes fixed on him. "Hurt?"

"Yeah. There are reports a girl got shot a few times. But sources are saying she'll be okay."

"She's alive?" Selene stared at the others, her eyes wide. "Krysta's alive?"

"Yeah," Pandora said. "I guess you couldn't check any news or rumor sources while trying to maintain a low electronic profile. Most of them are saying she got shot up pretty bad. No one's explaining how that happened, but she's supposedly out of danger."

"She's alive." Selene buried her face in her hands, shaking with reaction. "She's alive. Kayl, she's alive."

"Yeah," Owen said, putting one arm about Selene, blinking to stop his own tears. "Someday we'll get to yell at her for not doing what she promised to do."

"I am going to have a long talk with that girl." Selene stopped herself, looking up as she lowered her hands and wiped away tears. "She's really alive?"

"She's really alive," Pandora said, smiling and looking as if she, too, was about to cry. "What happened?"

"She was supposed to go to ground when we told her to," Owen explained. "So she'd be safe. Instead, she took off on her own to distract everyone. She was trying to protect us. But the last thing we wanted was for her to get hurt."

"Why was she with you?" Alera asked.

Owen looked at Selene, who was still trying to control her breathing. "We ran into her on the Moon. She was with a guy, much older, who'd bought her as a bride when Krysta was eleven."

Several seconds of silence followed. "That still happens?" Pandora whispered.

"It still happens," Owen said. "I'm learning that a lot is still happening that never shows up in the official databases."

"Did you do anything to the guy?" Gus asked, his voice gone hostile.

"He's dead," Selene said.

"We didn't kill him," Owen added quickly. "We wanted to get Krysta to an organization that would help her. She really wanted to get back to Earth first, though."

"We shouldn't have caved on that," Selene said. "It was too dangerous for her. Sorry that I lost it back there. Thank you so much for letting us know about Krysta."

"You didn't react much like a heartless alien monster," Pandora replied. "Are you . . . are you really an alien?"

Selene inhaled deeply, still calming herself. "I'm part alien, mostly human. Some of my genome is Tramontine DNA."

"That's true?" Pandora said in amazement. "So humans and these aliens can reproduce?"

"No," Selene said. "They can't. I mean, they could sort of have intercourse, but nothing would come of it. I'm the product of genetic engineering."

"Who did the engineering?"

"Humans," Selene said. "And that is all I can say about it."

"Your skin, um, is that what the Tramontine look like, too? None of the images we've seen seem to show that."

Selene shook her head. "No, Tramontine skin doesn't look like this. The shiny aspect to the skin is an unexpected side effect of the Tramontine DNA interacting with my human DNA. The size and shape of my eyes are a direct result of the Tramontine DNA, though."

"And the eyes work okay?"

"Yeah," Selene said. "They work fine."

Owen wasn't surprised that Selene didn't elaborate on that. She'd told him that in her experience, a lot of full humans got uncomfortable when told about ways in which alloys had slight advantages over them.

"What are the Tramontine like?" Gus asked. "I mean, physically. You said sort of intercourse?"

Pandora rolled her eyes. "Trust a guy to want to know if he can screw one of them."

Selene smiled, clearly feeling much better after the news about Krysta, as well as the food and water. "The onemales and twomales are recognizably male to humans, but neither are built in ways that would be comfortable for human females.

It would hurt. A lot. A Tramontine female could accept a human male, but I don't think either party would get any enjoyment out of it. I guess you could say the parts are compatible, but they don't really fit."

"Onemales?" Alera asked. "Twomales?"

"The Tramontine have two and a half sexes," Selene explained. "Two types of males, and one type of female. All mutually fertile, so it doesn't matter whether a female shares her life with a onemale or a twomale, and their offspring might be either female, onemale, or twomale."

"That is so amazing!" Pandora said. "I'm a biology major and . . . is this a secret? Do the Tramontine want stuff like that kept private?"

"No," Selene said. "To the Tramontine, it's just biology. And they recognize that if they want other species to share information about themselves, then the Tramontine have to be willing to share information about their physical nature."

"So the aliens are not here after our women," Gus said. "I did hear someone warning about that, believe it or not."

Selene shook her head. "No. Some Tramontine have kinks just like some humans, but to the Tramontine, everything about the bodies of human females is built wrong, and we don't smell right. There are no biological cues attracting them to us. I don't think there's enough beer in the universe to get the average Tramontine onemale or twomale attracted to a human female."

"And the same is true in reverse of human males and Tramontine females?" Pandora asked. "No attraction?"

"Right," Selene said. "I mean, I'm sure someone has . . . will someday . . . experiment that way, because that's humans, right? But I don't think it'll ever be a thing, because it won't be fun, it'll just be weird."

"Right," Pandora echoed. "So, are you—?" Both hands went to her mouth. "I'm sorry. I didn't mean to ask that."

Selene looked at Owen. "Do you want to answer that, Kayl?"

"Do I want to answer what?" Owen asked.

"I didn't ask!" Pandora said, embarrassed. "It's none of my business!"

"She wants to know if I'm physically a human female," Selene told Owen.

He realized that his mouth had fallen open as he stared at her. "That's . . . that's between you and me and nobody else."

"Kayl," Selene said, "do you have any idea what kinds of stories were told about alloys? About me? About what we're like physically? I'd rather, this time around, the truth be told up front."

"But that's such a private thing!"

"I don't mind, Kayl." She grimaced. "Actually, I do mind. But it needs to be said. Just please tell them. So the truth can start fighting against the . . . strange rumors."

Owen looked at the deck, trying to get the words out. "I don't talk about my partners. I don't do that. But, since she has asked me to, Selene Genji is . . . physically . . . a human female."

"Okay," Pandora said, still looking horribly embarrassed. "I really didn't mean to ask."

"There are stupid rumors going around," Gus said. "Sorry."

"I'm not posting any pictures," Selene said. "So anyone who isn't convinced by Kayl's statement can believe what they want to."

"You're so amazing," Alera said.

"Excuse me?"

"You're so amazing, Selene Genji," Alera repeated. "Being willing to talk about that. Standing up for everyone. Helping so much with First Contact. Lots of people think you're great."

"I'm an alloy," Selene said, "a Human-Tramontine alloy."

"Yeah. And you're amazing! That's why we came out here. That's why a lot of boats are out here, looking to help you if we could."

Owen saw the baffled look appear in Selene's eyes, the expression she got when confronted with things in 2140 that dramatically differed from her experiences growing up in the 2160s and 2170s, when alloys would be tolerated at best and often shunned.

As Owen expected, facing what were for her strange attitudes, Selene changed the subject. "Everything we've spoken of here is about me," Selene said. She pointed to Owen. "Don't forget this guy. Without this guy, I wouldn't be here. Without this guy, my mission to protect the Earth and its people would have already failed."

"Right," Gus said, nodding and smiling at Owen. "The Earth Guard guy who stood up to the whole corrupt system. Man, that must have taken some guts. Now they're trying to kill you, too!"

"Everybody's seen those images of you standing by her on Mars, guarding her with your life," Alera said. "It is so cool that you're doing that. And so cool that you two are together despite your differences. I'm sorry. People are saying that, but I don't know. You are *together* together, aren't you?"

Selene smiled and reached to take Owen's hand. "We are one."

"You know that's freaking out some people, right?" Gus asked. "The whole alien and a human thing. I don't personally think it's anyone's business but yours, but there are people warning about humans being replaced by alien/human mixes."

"People have always worried about that," Alera said, her disgust clear. "Only they were usually talking about different humans replacing them. They just have a new target now."

"There have always been aliens," Pandora said. "Always outsiders. Now we have real aliens, and some people are acting like humans always have. But we don't have to be afraid! Do we?"

"No," Selene said. "Not of me, and not of the Tramontine. What people need to fear is what has always posed the greatest danger to people, and that is other people."

She paused as the students took that in.

"But," Selene added, "as you three and everyone else aboard this boat prove, other people are also the source of our greatest hope. We're the problem, and we're the solution."

"We," Pandora said. "You do consider yourself human, too."

"Yes," Selene said.

"She's human in every way that matters," Owen said.

"But how can you be so sure humans are also the solution?" Alera asked. "We're so screwed up."

Selene paused before answering. "Yes, we're screwed up, but we have to be the answer. Because, if we're not, Earth is doomed. I have to believe there's a chance to save the Earth."

The silence following her words stretched across several seconds.

"You sounded really certain when you said that," Pandora said, worried eyes on Selene.

"I am," she said. "That's why I need the help of people like you. It's impossible for me to thank you enough for helping us tonight. But, in the days and weeks and months to come, it is important that things work. Everything you take for granted. If those things work, people won't turn to reasons to blame others for why things don't work."

"What . . . things?"

"The things we count on," Owen said. "Like the Earth Cooperation Council, and Earth Guard, and everything else."

"Earth Cooperation Council is useless," Gus said. "When's the last time they did something important? And, Earth Guard, look what they did to you! Why get involved with something that messed up?"

"Because if people like you don't," Owen said, "it leaves important jobs to people who don't care or can't do the jobs. I admit, it's tough to beat your head against some of those walls. But Selene has reminded me that we have to. Otherwise the things we need get weaker and weaker, and then . . ."

"A lot of people end up dying in senseless wars," Selene said.

"It doesn't sound like you're *guessing* what will happen," Alera said, shaken.

"I'm sorry," Selene said. "This is my burden. Not yours."

"Our burden," Owen said.

"It sounds like it's everyone's burden," Pandora said. She looked at the other students, exchanging nods with them. "We won't forget what you said. But we need to talk about where you're going. Not long-term. Just tonight. We can't go too far astray to drop you off. That would attract more attention."

"And get us in trouble," Gus said.

The woman projected a chart between them, pointing to spots on it. "So, we can let you ashore where we dock, but that's down here at the end of a peninsula. There's only one major road still certain to be unflooded that'll get you north from there. I don't know if you want to risk that. If we drop you up here, you can reach one of these towns and get a car pretty easily, with a number of roads north and west. Oh." She dug in a pocket, producing some IDs. "I don't know if you need them, but these are fake IDs. The great thing about these is they'll show you as a local resident, so they won't attract any extra attention."

"College students with fake IDs?" Owen said. "I am shocked."

Gus grinned. "That never happened when you were in college, huh?"

"Not unless we got caught," Owen said. Thinking about it now, he wondered why he hadn't seen the significance of how easily college students could get fake IDs good enough to pass any examination. If college students could get them, at reasonable prices, why couldn't anyone? The more IDs had been made mandatory, the more carefully they'd been crafted to avoid counterfeiting. Yet, in retrospect, since they were required to do just about anything, the more incentive there had been for clever people to create and sell fakes.

"Maybe we should drop them on the other side of the

Potomac," Alera suggested. "That'll give them a lot more room to move in different directions."

"Yeah," Pandora said. "See?" she added, pointing to areas on the coast. "It's not that much farther for us, but it'll make sure you're not stuck on a peninsula that can be sealed off."

Selene looked at Owen for his appraisal. He studied the chart, then nodded. "I think that sounds good."

"Great!" Pandora looked at both of them, concerned. "You guys look terrible. It's been a tough few days, huh?"

"Yes," Selene said.

"Eat and drink as much as you want. You can draw the curtain screening those berths near the bow and sleep as much as you can. We'll wake you when we're getting close to the place where we'll drop you off."

"We owe you more than we can ever repay," Owen said.

"It sounds like we owe you guys more than we thought," Alera said.

The students went on deck to give them some privacy, but both Owen and Selene were too tired to do anything but slam down jerky and trail mix, accompanied by plenty of water.

Owen wasn't sure he'd be able to sleep, but exhaustion did the trick for him. He passed out in the dimness offered by the forward berths, looking across at the berth where Selene lay looking back at him.

THE GIRL LYING IN the emergency treatment bed looked dismayingly small and frail, numerous tubes and lines leading into and out of her body, heal packs over the three places where mag rifle bullets had hit, a burn pack over another where an energy bolt had clipped her. She was sealed into a quarantine room, the attending nurse bots the only moving presence with her.

"It's a miracle she's alive," Dr. Bortnick told Special Representative Cerise Camacho.

"Will she recover?" Camacho asked.

"She should. That's one lucky girl. Two of those bullets would have killed her if she hadn't received immediate medical care." The doctor frowned at his readouts. "She wasn't carrying any ID, but we got a hit on her DNA. Krysta Fogorais. The last verified status on her was three years ago when she was eleven. Since then there have been sporadic DNA hits on her at screening sites such as airfields and spaceports, but she's never been reported missing."

"How does an eleven-year-old girl fall through the cracks like that?" Camacho asked.

"Nobody reported her," Dr. Bortnick repeated.

"There's nothing else on her in the last three years?" Camacho turned toward one of the men beside her. "Congratulations, General Molstad. You nearly killed a teenage girl with no charges against her."

"What was she doing there in the first place?" Molstad replied. "Why didn't the databases alert us to her presence among the passengers?"

"Are you asking me that question?" Camacho said. "Or are you asking yourself?"

"*My* job isn't to oversee databases, it's to protect human lives and the Earth itself," General Molstad insisted.

"How do you do that job if your data isn't accurate?" Camacho asked him. She pointed toward the images of Krysta. "That girl effectively disappeared for more than three years. How many other people aren't being tracked? Is that alien you're unsuccessfully hunting using special alien skills to move around, or is she exploiting holes in our system that we've allowed to develop while assuring ourselves that everything was working fine? Holes that many other people may be using as well."

"That's . . . a leap from what we know," Molstad said, but he was plainly discomfited by the idea. "I will concede that we need to take a good look at how the alien has been able to move around so effectively. It may indicate systemic problems that need to be addressed. But it should not distract from the need to identify and stop the alien."

Colonel Kalibangan, head of Wallops Security, made an angry noise. "Identify the alien? I was told there was a positive ID on the target before I approved the shoot-to-kill order. Why was I told that when this is obviously not the alien?"

Molstad shook his head. "You're familiar with the chaos of a battle situation, Colonel."

"I was told there was a positive ID," Kalibangan repeated. "My people came this close to killing a young girl with no warrants against her."

"We couldn't take any chances," General Molstad said. "The alien is too dangerous."

"Dangerous?" Cerise Camacho said. "I keep hearing that. Exactly how many humans has this alien killed, General?"

"We have no idea what that number is," Molstad replied.

"Is it more than one, General? Is it even one? Can you give me one name of one person we know that alien woman has killed?"

"She could have killed some of my people," Colonel Kalibangan said. "She didn't. She used disabling blows."

"But you think she could've used lethal blows instead?" Camacho asked.

"I have no doubt of it," Kalibangan answered.

"That's pure speculation," General Molstad said in a scoffing tone.

"Anyone who knows how to strike disabling blows also knows how to strike killing blows!" the colonel said. "They have to know what not to hit! There's nothing speculative about that."

"What about this girl, then?" Molstad demanded. "Using her as a decoy! How cold-blooded is that? You're trying to blame me for this? Who sent her out to draw fire?"

Cerise Camacho turned to the doctor. "Can she answer any questions?"

"Maybe a few," Dr. Bortnick said cautiously.

Camacho tapped the comm link. "Hello? Can you hear me?"

After a long moment, the girl's eyes opened partway. "Hel . . . lo?" Her voice was a raspy near-whisper.

"Krysta? Is your name Krysta?" Camacho asked.

"Y . . . yes."

"You're going to be all right, Krysta. Were you with the alien, Krysta?"

"A . . . li . . . en?"

"The female alien. Were you with her?"

"Yes."

"Did she send you out as a decoy?"

The girl didn't answer for a moment. "No."

"Why did you run across the field, Krysta? Was the alien chasing you?"

"No." Krysta struggled weakly for a moment against the restraints holding her in place, the doctor watching the medical readouts with a concerned expression. "Gen . . . ji . . . nice. Saved . . . me. Want . . . help . . . her."

"Are you saying you acted as a decoy on your own?"

"Yes."

"It's all right, Krysta. Relax."

"No!" the girl said with more force. "Why? Why . . . try . . . hurt . . . her? Why?"

"I have to halt this and give her some sedation," Dr. Bortnick said, worried. "She's getting too agitated."

"Are . . . they . . . o . . . kay? Saved . . . me. Are . . . they . . . o . . . kay?" The girl's voice faded into a murmur as the sedation took hold.

Cerise Camacho looked at General Molstad. "All she cares about is whether *they* are all right. I'm assuming that means the alien and Lieutenant Owen. She doesn't sound like an escaped hostage to me."

"Classic hostage syndrome," Molstad said dismissively.

Camacho didn't bother replying to the general. "I want to be notified as soon as Krysta is able to speak with us without risking her health," she told the doctor.

"Hold on," General Molstad said. "This is a security situation, she is an important witness and apparent collaborator, and we're still gathering information. The alien is still out there, on Earth. Until we've taken out the alien scout, this girl needs to be interrogated only by military personnel able to acquire the information we need."

"Taken out?" Cerise Camacho said. "I thought the intent was to capture the alien if at all possible, General."

Molstad hesitated. "That's what I meant. Captured if possible. But if it is necessary to eliminate the alien in order to neutralize the threat to humanity, we can't have our hands tied."

"I see. General, I am a special representative of the Security Committee of the Earth Cooperation Council. Don't try to pull rank on me. I'll speak to this girl whenever I want to. Colonel?"

"Yes?" Kalibangan said.

"I want to be certain she's safe. Please post some of your personnel as guards to keep an eye on her. I want continuous protection."

"Certainly." Kalibangan eyed Molstad for a moment, apparently waiting to see if the general would object to the implication that local security forces were more reliable than those answering to the general. "I'll get it set up immediately."

Molstad turned a critical look on Camacho. "If you have some problem with how I'm doing my job . . ."

"Let's speak privately, General." Camacho waited until the doctor and Colonel Kalibangan had left. "I want some straight answers, General. Why are we being told this alien is a threat? Why are the official assessments of the Tramontine aliens and their ship still stressing the danger they pose?"

"Planetary defense and Earth Guard are tasked with

protecting lives," Molstad said. "The Earth Cooperation Council gave us that job, and has rightly deferred to us in deciding how we have to carry it out."

"I was reviewing the history of the ECC's relationship with the mutual defense forces," Cerise Camacho said. "In early decades, the Earth Cooperation Council exercised a lot more oversight of the defense forces. In recent decades, though, the Council has deferred more and more to the defense forces to make decisions on policy as well as pure defense issues."

"Because it works best that way," General Molstad said.

"Or because it's easier for the Council that way?" Camacho said. "We don't have to get our hands dirty. Let the professionals make those decisions."

"Which is a wise policy."

"Is it?" Cerise Camacho gestured around her. "We've been informed that this alien scout has somehow traveled around on Earth's surface, made it to Mars untracked and undetected, carried out a wide variety of actions on Mars, escaped to the Tramontine ship, escaped from the Tramontine ship, managing to avoid Earth Guard at every turn, before reaching the Moon, and from there managing to get to Earth's surface again. And now she is once more free out there somewhere. How do you explain that, General? How do you explain the failure of our security forces to stop that alien, or even keep track of where she is?"

General Molstad breathed in and out a few times like a bull trying to decide whether or not to charge. "First, the alien possesses inhuman capabilities. Secondly, the alien has been aided at every step by a renegade Earth Guard officer."

"Oh, yes," Camacho said. "The renegade Earth Guard officer. The one who was declared officially dead after being placed on a ship that had been sabotaged to cause his death."

"That report is not true. It's typical slander of the defense forces by those who want humanity to be helpless in the face of threats to our existence."

"General," Cerise Camacho said, "I talked to the Earth Guard safety officer who produced that report. He stands by it and is willing to testify publicly under oath. Why was Lieutenant Owen targeted for death *before* he turned renegade, General?"

"I can't comment on such wild accusations," Molstad replied. "I do know that particular officer has always had a bad reputation."

"Lieutenant Owen," Camacho said. "Marginal at best, according to his evaluations, which the Security Committee has reviewed. Yet now we're being told that this officer usually rated borderline incompetent by his superiors has somehow become remarkably resourceful and capable, managing to evade every attempt by Earth Guard and other security forces to capture or kill him."

General Molstad shrugged. "Obviously, that lieutenant engaged in a long-term deception to hide his true abilities from Earth Guard, allowing him freedom to act when he most needed it to betray his oath."

"His oath," Cerise Camacho repeated. "What is the oath of Earth Guard, General Molstad?"

"I am not an Earth Guard officer."

"Then I'll help you out, General. The oath taken by Earth Guard officers states that they will protect and render aid to all people. Exactly how, to date, has Lieutenant Owen violated that oath?"

"These are classified matters—" Molstad began.

"That 'explanation' is getting very tired, General. Either produce some actual examples, or stop making claims that you cannot or will not back up. As for both Lieutenant Owen and the alien, I am bringing you orders from the Earth Cooperation Council. The Council wants that alien to be captured alive. And for Lieutenant Owen to be captured alive. The Tramontine are expressing concern for the safety of both of them, and we cannot afford to create rifts between us and the Tramontine unless we have solid reasons for them."

"You're going to let these aliens dictate our actions against the agent they sent to undermine our defenses?" General Molstad demanded.

"No one is going to dictate the actions of the Earth Cooperation Council, General. Not aliens. And not anyone else." *The implication of that should be clear enough to the general*, she thought. "All shoot-to-kill orders are to be canceled *immediately*, and no new ones are to be issued. Lethal force is not permitted under any circumstances. These orders have already been sent to every organization participating in the search for Genji and Owen, but I wanted to ensure that you were personally informed of them."

"Just how many humans do you want to die trying to capture that thing alive?"

"You have your orders from the Council, General. Catch that alien alive. Catch Lieutenant Owen alive. Do you understand?"

"Yes," Molstad said. "I understand."

Special Representative Cerise Camacho stayed a little while longer after General Molstad left, gazing at the small body of Krysta lying in the large bed festooned with medical equipment. Thinking that even though the general had acknowledged the new orders, she had no confidence that he would abide by them. General Molstad would surely issue those new orders, surely cancel the shoot-on-sight commands, but Camacho had no doubt those would be accompanied by wink-wink-nudge-nudge signals letting all of those hunting Genji and Owen know that any "accidental" deaths would be at least overlooked and possibly still rewarded.

The Council had spent more and more time in recent years arguing over smaller and smaller issues, leaving big decisions to others. Such as letting the defense forces pretty much run themselves. Cerise had been working to convince the Council that had been a mistake. Hopefully it wouldn't take the deaths of Genji and Owen to prove her argument.

3

THE STUDENTS HAD SAILED their yawl past the mouth of the St. Mary's River where they would normally have gone up, on west and north through the wide waters of the Potomac, before coming in to the coast of Virginia and alongside a floating pier. Dawn had long since passed, the rising sun lighting up the salt marshes where low-lying land had been inundated by rising waters in the last century.

Genji hopped down from the deck onto the pier, wearing a newly acquired St. Mary's Seahawks sweatshirt covering her upper body, and a Seahawks bucket hat that, along with wearing her hair down, did a decent job of concealing her head and face. Kayl came after her, wearing his regular clothing but with the addition of a ball cap advertising a bar somewhere in the region. "You look just like locals!" one of the students called to them. Their backpacks hadn't entirely dried out, but weren't as soggy as they had been. "Just head west and you'll hit some big roads and plenty of towns."

"Thank you," Genji called in reply. "We owe you so much."

"Save the Earth!" another of the students called as they all waved and the yawl moved back out onto the river.

"Maybe we actually can," Genji said to Kayl as they watched the yawl head back east.

But a moment later her sight of the boat on the water and the beautiful day were obscured. The glare of the rising sun flashed into a field of hideous blue-tinged light, her memory supplying a vision of annihilation as everyone and everything vanished in a wave of unleashed energy. She stared into the future, seeing Earth being destroyed before her eyes, knowing her own death must be only seconds away.

"There's something beautiful about a boat under sail," Kayl said, glancing at her with a smile that faded when he saw her expression. "What's the matter?"

"I just saw it again," she said, gasping for breath, knowing her feelings were written on her face. "My memory of June twelfth, 2180. Seeing that horrible light when the Spear detonated their Sigma bomb, everything exploding in seconds, billions dying in the blink of an eye, the waters vanishing along with everything and everyone. Knowing in what seemed the last moments left to me that the Spear of Humanity had won, had 'cleansed' the Earth by destroying it."

Kayl stared at her, momentarily wordless. "Selene . . . you've already changed a lot of things. We'll change enough to ensure that future doesn't happen."

"We have to," Genji said, struggling to control her breathing, trying to banish the images of destruction. "Kayl, I couldn't sleep while we were on the boat. That's probably why I . . . am sort of stressed. More than usual."

"Why couldn't you sleep?"

She closed her eyes, not wanting to confess the truth, knowing how much it would distress him. "I . . . kept thinking I might vanish at any moment."

"That's back?" he asked, anguished.

"It never fully went away," she said. "Wondering if all the changes we've made have canceled out my own birth in the future, which they must have already, if at some point that's going to catch up with me, and I'll cease to have ever been." Genji inhaled slowly before looking at him, working to calm herself. "Wondering if you'd remember me. Or if me never having existed meant no one remembered I'd ever been."

"Nothing could make me forget you," Kayl said. "Those Tramontine scientists think you have to exist, right? Because you're the cause of all these things that are happening in this year. The universe needs you to exist in 2140 to justify everything you're making happen even if you don't get born in 2158."

"That's a theory, Kayl. They don't know for certain. No one does." She looked away, then back at him. "If I'm not there some morning, and if you remember me, I want to be sure you know I didn't leave you. If I'm not there, it will be because I'm not anywhere."

She blinked at the sun, its brilliant light mocking the darkness of her thoughts.

"Selene," Kayl said, "I'll find you. If you vanish, I'll find you. Even if you're nowhere, I'll find you."

"That's . . . ridiculous," Genji said, fighting off an absurd urge to laugh. "Do you know how ridiculous that sounds?"

"I mean it," Kayl said.

She felt a smile slowly forming as she looked at him. "You do. Okay. Even if I'm nowhere, I'll be trying to find you."

"That's a deal, then," Kayl said, nodding to her. "We'd better start walking."

"Right." Genji reached to grasp his hand as they walked, the sun at their backs now, their shadows stretching out in front.

"Is there any chance we can save the entire world except for the mosquitoes?" Kayl asked, swiping at one, his tone obviously a little too light considering what they'd been talking about.

"Sorry I dragged you down," she said.

"I want you to share those things with me," he said. "I wouldn't be much of a partner if I only wanted you to share fun things, would I?" He looked ahead as if not really seeing the landscape. "It would hurt so much if you were gone. But I tell myself that's because of how happy knowing you has made me. And, don't worry, no matter what, I'll still do my best to get the mission done. To save the world from the fate you saw. I promised you that and I'll do it."

"Thanks for making that the hill you'll die on." She squeezed his hand a little tighter. "Now, let's focus on staying alive for at least one more day. Do you know where we are?"

He pulled out one of their burner phones, checking the map data. "Way up that way is Fredericksburg and Quantico.

We probably want to avoid those places."

"Quantico? Really?" She twisted her head to look.

"What happens to it?" Kayl asked.

"I didn't say anything happened to it."

"When you say something like that, it means something will happen."

Genji made a defeated gesture. "Okay. It becomes Quantico Bay in 2170. A small crater. The bay fills it."

"Why?" Kayl said.

"The strike will take out a major military facility and severely disrupt transportation along the East Coast of this continent," Genji said.

"Why . . . ?" Kayl shook his head, searching for words. "Why will the Spear of Humanity do that?"

"That won't be the Spear," Genji said. "It will be part of the Sanctions War. But the retaliatory strikes after Quantico is destroyed will build a lot of support for the Spear in the places that will be hit." She looked around her. "This whole region will be devastated. A lot of places will be devastated."

"The Sanctions War will be part of the Universal War?"

"Yes."

"So we're trying to stop it from happening, too?"

"Right." Genji made a face, trying to remember facts she'd once attempted to forget. "Most people talk about Karachi in 2169 being the opening salvo in the Universal War, even though that will be supposedly a limited conflict. I never understood how you could call something 'limited' when it led to the destruction of a city the size of Karachi."

"And turning the Moon's Free Zone into the Dead Zone," Kayl said.

"Right. Which will be done by an ad hoc alliance pursuing those responsible for Karachi because the Earth Cooperation Council won't do anything. I was . . . will be only eleven when Karachi is destroyed, but I remember the shock everyone felt. My mother told me before Karachi the whole world had been sort of sleepwalking forward, thinking nothing like that could happen even though everything meant to stop it was falling apart. The failure to act after Karachi leads to the final dissolution of the Earth Cooperation Council and the widespread abandonment of treaties between governments, which leads to the Sanctions War, which leads to other conflicts, all of which combine into the Universal War."

"Which leads to the destruction of the entire planet," Kayl said.

"On the twelfth of June 2180," Genji said. "Forty years from now. If we can't make enough changes to the history I know, Earth is doomed to die in forty years."

Kayl nodded, his face shadowed by worry. "How do we prevent something like Karachi?"

"I don't know," Genji admitted. "I don't think I ever knew all the details that led to that. We have to try to change the things that will lead to Earth Guard's slow collapse, and the failure of the Earth Cooperation Council, and similar problems."

"Okay. So how do we prevent the Earth Cooperation Council from coming apart?" Kayl asked. "That seems like a pretty big job for two people, even if one of them is Selene Genji."

"I don't know," Genji repeated. "It was like with Earth Guard. Internal rot that led to more and more problems until the remnants quit pretending they were still accomplishing anything. But . . . I'm pretty sure one of the triggers was First Contact. I think the worries around that, arguments about how dangerous the Tramontine were and how to respond to them, played a big role in setting off the events that led to the final collapse of the Earth Cooperation Council. As best I remember, arguments over how to respond to the Tramontine will soon lead to the Council deciding to postpone its next full meeting. Committees will keep meeting for a couple of decades, but the full Council won't ever meet again. Not until it formally dissolves. Hopefully, helping to fix First Contact will have some influence on what's going to happen to the Council."

Kayl made a face, his foot moving to avoid trampling a single brave flower trying to brighten the dirt path. "Why is First Contact causing all of these institutions to fail?"

"It's not," Genji said. "The structure of the institutions should be able to withstand the force of First Contact. But they have growing cracks in their foundations, cracks that have been papered over. It's those cracks that First Contact is widening."

Kayl frowned. "The cracks being institutional problems? What if we ripped off the paper covering them? Caused people to see them?"

"How do we do that?" Genji asked. She really liked these kinds of conversations with him, where they both encouraged each other to think through problems and find answers.

"Maybe we are doing it," Kayl suggested. "Earth Guard has very publicly failed to catch us or kill us."

"And the fact that Earth Guard is trying to kill us in the first place?" Genji said. "People have to be asking themselves why that is happening. Those students were. If we get enough people asking that, maybe it will help trigger reform inside Earth Guard. Oh. That whole thing about the courier ship they tried to kill us both on. And the safety office report of the malware that caused it. And that report being canceled without a reason being given. We've seen news reports that all of that was leaked."

"People are noticing," Kayl agreed. "Selene, it's possible us staying free and alive isn't just keeping us alive, it might also be exposing problems that need to be exposed."

"Let's hope you're right," she said. "You don't want to go north, then. Where should we head? I don't know all that much about the East Coast of this continent."

"Nothing goes straight west except aircraft," Kayl said. "The terrain is too rough. If we don't head north, we'll need to go south. Once they realize we've made it off the Eastern Shore, they can flood both directions with security and make it very hard to get any farther away. I wonder . . . There's an Earth Guard spaceport at Fort Walker."

"Which we should avoid," Genji said.

"Maybe. Let's see how it looks as we get to places that offer better transportation options than our feet."

The land had been slowly rising as they walked inland, leaving the marsh behind them. Off to their left, fenced-in pastures held animals of some kind that were grazing.

Genji picked up the scent of the creatures as the wind blew from the south.

She sneezed violently.

And again. And again.

Kayl watched her, alarmed. "What's the matter?"

"I don't— Achoo! Know! Achoo! I can't—" Genji turned to stare to the south. "Are those llamas?"

Kayl shaded his eyes to look that way. "I think so."

"Damn! We have to get away from them! Come on!" Running while sneezing frequently was a unique form of discomfort. By the time they were no longer downwind of the llamas, her chest, nose, and throat were all aching and sore. She had a headache, her skin itched, and it took every ounce of her self-control to keep from lashing out at Kayl, who as a full human didn't have to worry about the llama allergy shared by every alloy.

This was shaping up to be another long, difficult day, and they hadn't even encountered any police or other security forces yet.

KRYSTA STILL LAY IN the bed, as before, attended solely by nursing bots.

"How is she doing?" Special Representative Cerise Camacho asked as she viewed the image through the room's panel.

"She's doing well," Dr. Bortnick said. "Using the latest treatments, we can accelerate healing to up to seven times typical rates. She has effectively undergone a week and a half of healing since the last time you saw her."

"Why is she still in medical isolation?" Camacho asked.

"Because of exposure to the alien," Dr. Bortnick said, his tone gone flat. Clearly, this wasn't a decision he approved of.

"What about the rest of the passengers on the lunar shuttle?" Camacho said. "Are they also isolated?" A prolonged silence answered her question. "Has the compartment Krysta and the alien stayed in on the shuttle been carefully examined?"

"Yes," Dr. Bortnick said.

"What was found? Anything unusual?"

Bortnick spread his hands. "Nothing like that. All normal for any area occupied by humans."

"No space cooties?" Investigator Jamie Costanza asked.

"No," Dr. Bortnick said.

"Is there any medical reason," Camacho said, "anything detected, that would justify keeping that girl isolated from human contact?"

"No," Dr. Bortnick said more firmly. "We were told the matter was not up to us to decide."

"Let me guess who told you that," Camacho said. "If there's no medical reason to keep her in there, I want her out of isolation as soon as you and the other doctors involved sign off on the necessary approval."

Bortnick smiled. "I'll get it rolling as soon as we're done here. She's getting all the technical medical care she needs, but direct human interaction is critical to a healthy recovery."

"Good. Jamie, see if you can get Krysta to answer your questions."

Costanza sat down at the panel, adjusting the volume. He leaned forward slightly to activate the microphone. "Krysta? Can you hear me? Can you see me?"

The front of the bed had been raised, elevating Krysta's

upper body and head. She still looked weak, but nodded. "Yes. Am I in prison?"

"No, Krysta," Costanza said. "You're not in prison. There have been some medical concerns. We wanted to be sure you'd be okay. And you will be okay. You're going to get all of the medical treatment you need. Are you having any trouble understanding me?"

"No."

"I work for the Earth Cooperation Council. We want to know what happened to you. Were you a prisoner of the alien? Was she holding you captive?"

Krysta seemed puzzled by the question. "Do you mean Lieutenant Genji? Why would Lieutenant Genji hold me captive?"

"Did she?"

"No. Of course not. She and Lieutenant Owen wanted me to go to someone at Hamilton who would take care of me, but I insisted I wanted to go to Earth with them."

"Why, Krysta?"

"Because they saved me from Ivan. Ivan would have taken my oxygen and killed me. But Lieutenant Genji made him stop hitting me, and Lieutenant Owen protected me, and when Ivan attacked Lieutenant Genji, she defended herself and me."

"Who is Ivan?" Costanza asked.

"The man who bought me."

Costanza sat back, startled, looking at Cerise Camacho. She nodded to him to continue speaking.

"Ivan bought you?" Costanza asked.

"When I was eleven. My parents sold me to Ivan. I had to marry him. Lieutenant Owen told me that wasn't legal or real, though. You're not going to send me back to my parents, are you? They'd sell me again."

Jamie Costanza sat back once more, rubbing his face.

Camacho looked at Dr. Bortnick, who was checking some medical files and nodding with a grim expression.

"Krysta has been sexually active."

"Can we be sure the alien or Owen didn't do that?" Costanza asked.

"Ask her," Camacho said.

Costanza leaned forward again. "Krysta, did either the alien or Lieutenant Owen ever force you to engage in sexual activity with them? Did you ever willingly engage in sexual activity with either of them?"

Krysta looked startled. "No! They'd never do that. Ivan was the only one who . . . Do I have to tell you what he did? What he made me do?"

"Not right now, Krysta," Costanza said. "Where is Ivan now?"

"He's dead." She squinted as if trying to read Costanza's expression. "He fought Lieutenant Genji. She protected me."

"The alien killed Ivan?"

"No! He had a knife, and when she knocked him down, he cut his own suit with it and the air came out and he died. Are you the police?" Krysta asked. "Lieutenant Genji told me to tell the police the truth. And I am. That's what happened."

"She told you what to tell the police about what happened to Ivan?" Costanza asked.

"No! Lieutenant Genji told me to tell the truth. Why would she have to tell me what to say? Ivan would do that when he wanted me to lie. Lieutenant Genji never wanted me to lie."

Costanza leaned back again, shaking his head. "I don't think any jury would convict the alien for killing Ivan. Krysta certainly seems to be speaking truthfully about it."

"Ask some more general questions," Camacho said.

"Sure. Krysta, did the alien ever hurt you?"

"No. She'd never hurt me. She's nice."

"What about Lieutenant Owen?"

"Lieutenant Owen is also nice. They saved me! They protected me! They got me . . . What happened to my clothes?

They got me new clothes at Hamilton. I've never had new clothes. Where are they?"

Costanza sighed. "Your clothes got damaged when you were hurt. You'll get new clothes, Krysta."

"But these were special! Lieutenant Genji and Lieutenant Owen got them for me!"

"Krysta, we need you to answer this question. We need the truth. What happened at the spaceport? Why did you run with that hat on?"

Krysta looked as though she was about to cry. "Lieutenant Genji made me promise if things got dangerous I'd lie down and stay safe until the police came and then tell them the truth. But she and Lieutenant Owen were really worried about all of the soldiers at the spaceport. I heard them arguing over which one would try to distract the soldiers long enough for the other to get away. They were talking like the one who did the distracting would die! I didn't really think much about it, I just thought they saved me, so now I have to save them. And I grabbed Lieutenant Genji's hat and ran and put it on and kept running until . . . it really hurt, and I fell, and . . ."

Costanza rubbed his face again before speaking. "It was your idea? The alien and Lieutenant Owen didn't suggest it?"

"No! They told me not to!" Krysta did start crying. She couldn't move her arms because of the medical restraints, so the tears simply ran down her face. "Do you think Lieutenant Genji will be mad at me because I did that? She took such good care of me. And I took her hat and that's gone. She and Lieutenant Owen were so good to me. I didn't know people could be that good. Do you know if they're mad at me because I didn't lie down and stay safe like I promised? Are they okay? I need to know if they're okay!"

Dr. Bortnick tapped some commands into his panel. "I'm giving her a mild sedative. She's getting very agitated. She should be able to speak to you for another minute or so before the sedative knocks her out."

"Krysta, please calm down," Costanza said. "Everything is all right."

"Are they okay?"

"As far as we know, yes, Krysta, they are okay. Now, please, can you answer a few more questions? You say the alien never hurt you. Did the alien ever make you unhappy?"

"Why do you keep calling her 'the alien'?" Krysta demanded tearfully. "Don't you know her name? I've told you her name. Her name is Lieutenant Genji."

"Krysta, did the alien ever make you unhappy?"

"I'm not going to answer you unless you call her by her name! She's a person!"

Costanza looked at Cerise Camacho, who nodded. "All right, Krysta. Did Lieutenant Genji ever make you unhappy?"

"Ummm." Krysta blinked away tears, looking uncomfortable. "One time."

"What did she do to you?"

"Well, I wanted more coffee, and Lieutenant Genji said no, I should drink some water instead, and that made me kind of unhappy," Krysta said. "But then she got me more French fries, so it was okay."

"How much coffee had you already had?"

"Three cups."

Costanza sat back, spreading his arms. "Acting like a slightly indulgent mother. That appears to be the sum total of atrocities committed by the alien against this girl."

Cerise Camacho looked at Krysta. Her eyes had closed and she seemed to have fallen asleep. "I want your professional opinion, Jamie. Is this girl displaying some kind of hostage syndrome? Or is she reacting to genuinely kind treatment by Genji and Owen?"

"I'd say kind treatment," Costanza said. "But this girl's life seems to have been hell since at least when she was sold to that Ivan guy. It wouldn't take much kindness to make her feel a huge amount of gratitude."

"Do you think she was telling the truth about everything?"

"She doesn't show any signs of lying. Mind you, it sounds like this Ivan taught her to lie. But, I think, if she was doing that, she'd appear older, more in control. This feels more like someone who is still close to eleven emotionally and letting it all out." Costanza eyed Camacho. "What are you planning to do with her? Returning her to her parents is not an option."

"No. The fact that they never reported her missing is proof enough that they're unfit. I want a report filed, an investigation launched, and those parents held to account." Cerise Camacho sighed. "I suppose we'll have to see which child welfare organization is willing to take her once she's well enough. But with the publicity surrounding her, and the connection to Genji, that might be a hard sell."

"Excuse me," Dr. Bortnick said. "When we removed her clothing to treat her injuries, I was able to image this before the military investigators took it. Perhaps this is someone who could help?" He displayed a picture of a piece of paper with a name and contact information handwritten on it.

Jamie Costanza tapped out a query. "Hmm. That's Lieutenant Owen's aunt in Albuquerque. He must have given Krysta that so she'd have someone to contact if they got separated. If there's nothing negative on her, maybe she should be contacted about Krysta. Of course, then we'd be doing what Lieutenant Owen wanted, and presumably what Genji wanted."

"Is there any reason not to?" Camacho asked.

"Honestly? I don't know of any. The aunt's home has been under constant watch, just like Owen's mother's place and his sister's home, in case either Genji or Owen tried to visit or contact any of them. That'll also ensure Krysta's safety if she's there. And as long as we know where Krysta is, we can ask her more questions at any time and make sure she's being treated well. But the military won't like it. They'll want to keep Krysta locked up in protective custody."

"The military doesn't make decisions on the fates of fourteen-year-old civilian girls," Cerise Camacho said. "Look into this aunt. If she's clean, I'll contact her about Krysta and see if she's willing to take the girl. Have you heard anything new about the search for Genji and Owen?"

Costanza shrugged. "They haven't got them yet. Last I heard, every available person was being lined up along with bots and drones to form a north cordon and a south cordon. They're going to be marched toward each other, and, if Genji and Owen are still on the Eastern Shore, they won't be able to avoid being spotted."

"Do you think they still are on the Eastern Shore?"

Another shrug. "Maybe. But if they were, I'd think they'd already have been spotted. If it was me running this search, I'd be telling people to stop concentrating on searching every blade of grass on the Eastern Shore and instead expand the search out to try to catch them if they've made it to the other side of the bay."

"How could they have gotten to the other side of the bay?" Camacho asked.

"There have been an awful lot of boats out on the bay the last couple of nights," Costanza said. "Many more than usual ever since rumors said Genji might be on the Eastern Shore after escaping Wallops. Some want the reward. A whole bunch of them think Genji is some kind of hero, though, because of what happened on Mars and everything else. In my opinion, not nearly enough resources have been devoted to watching the coast because that would mean diverting assets from the search on the Eastern Shore itself. I suggested they might want to rethink that approach, and was told my input was not required. Do you want me to bring it up again?"

Cerise Camacho didn't quite suppress a smile. "We don't want to try to tell the military how to do their job, do we? Let me know if the search of the Eastern Shore turns up anything. Are you going to stay around here?"

"Yes," Jamie Costanza said. "I'm assigned to Krysta's case, so I'm not going anywhere until that's resolved."

"I have to go back north. Please keep an eye on her for me as well. I'd appreciate it."

"No problem. Is the Earth Cooperation Council finally starting to stir from its hibernation?"

"I hope so," Camacho said.

THERE WERE A LOT of ways to get north or south along the coast, but Cerise Camacho always preferred using a car when possible. The distance was too short for a suborbital hop, but the trains were faster. So were aircraft. None of them offered the privacy and isolation of a car gliding along one of the main highways. Even delays due to heavy traffic were just a means to gain more time to think and work while the autopilot handled the driving.

Her phone was blinking urgently, though. One of the Security Committee's press officers trying to get in contact with her, a priority signal accompanying the alert. Sighing, Camacho accepted the call. "Hello, Denis. What is it?"

Senior Press Officer Denis Raymound looked pained. "The military is making more 'requests' that any statements regarding the alien be sent through them for so-called security review before being released. They're actually demanding the right to censor what we say."

"Let them know we appreciate their concerns, share their desire to protect, et cetera, et cetera, et cetera," Camacho said. "But we will not allow them to tell us what we can say."

"I'll express that in diplomatic terms," Raymound said. "Speaking of statements regarding the alien, that's the primary reason I needed to talk to you. We're getting a lot of pressure to make a public statement about the girl. Why was she shot? Was she with the alien and Lieutenant Owen? That sort of thing."

Camacho pinched the bridge of her nose as she thought. "The girl was with them, and insists that she acted as a decoy on her own initiative. You can report that. You can also report the girl claims to have been rescued from an abusive situation by Genji and Owen, and that she wanted them to bring her back to Earth. I'll send you a copy of the interview Costanza did with her. See what else we can say from that."

"If she was with the alien and Owen, people will want to see and hear her for themselves," Raymound said. "And, even though she's a minor, legally we can't prevent her from making public statements if she wants to and is medically cleared for that kind of exertion. There would have to be some compelling, overriding consideration for refusing to let her do that."

"I can't honestly say there is such a consideration," Camacho said. "Having Krysta make statements is going to complicate Council actions regarding Genji and Owen, but we can't stop her."

"Can you give me a heads-up on what she'll say?"

Camacho breathed a small laugh. "That girl idolizes Genji and Owen. Assume Krysta will tell the world they are good people who only want to do good things." She paused as a tone pulsed. "I have another call coming in."

"That's all right," Raymound said. "We've covered what I needed."

His image vanished, replaced by that of Ranveer Nahdi, one of her fellow special representatives. "Cerise!" he said in greeting. "Have you got time to talk about an alien?"

"What else did she do?" Camacho asked, looking out a window at the other cars keeping pace with hers.

"It's not that. You know we've got investigators talking to people on Mars, right? There's something unusual happening there."

"Unusual?"

"When we talk to Earth Guard, it's always the blue and silver wall," Nahdi said. "Not open refusal to talk or cooperate, but nobody knows anything. That's not happening this time. We've got some Earth Guard officers talking to our investigators."

"Really?" Cerise Camacho sat up straighter, surprised. "What are they telling us?"

"Maybe where Genji came from, at least in the immediate sense. Seems there was a report sent from the Earth Guard cruiser *Vigilant* that they'd encountered an inexplicable piece of wreckage from an unidentified source, and taken a survivor off that wreckage." Nahdi made a brief, humorless smile. "That report disappeared from Earth Guard databases. All reference to a survivor vanished as well."

"What about the wreckage?"

"I managed to trace that. Picked up by engineers, and scrapped using routine procedures."

"Scrapped?" Camacho gritted her teeth. "Routine procedures? How many people have substituted routine procedures for *thinking*? So it's a dead end?"

"Not entirely," Nahdi said. "Two things. The wreckage also had a dead person on it. Male, approximate age estimated around thirty. His DNA had no hits."

"No hits?" Camacho stared at her friend. "How could anyone get into space, or even be born, without having their DNA on file?"

"Good question. Totally human DNA, by the way, but no record of this guy anywhere. Naturally, the engineers followed routine procedures for unclaimed bodies and cremated the remains, so all we have left of that is the DNA sample from the body." He paused. "Second thing. I talked to Rear Admiral Raven Tecumseh a little while back. Remember her? She said something interesting that I only recently think I figured out. I'd asked about why Lieutenant Owen would have been put alone on that sabotaged courier ship, and Tecumseh said maybe Owen wasn't alone."

Camacho twisted a puzzled look at Nahdi. "No one else

was reported missing or dead. Why would . . . ? Wait. *Vigilant* was Owen's ship."

"Which," Nahdi said, "appears to have picked up a survivor off that wreckage, a survivor who subsequently disappeared."

"Genji. She was on *Vigilant*, she was transferred to that courier ship as well. The sabotage was designed to eliminate *her*."

"With Owen as cover for the so-called accident."

"But why Owen?" Camacho asked.

Nahdi sighed. "Does the name *Sentinel* ring a bell? About ten years ago, a new Earth Guard cruiser, on its first patrol, suffered multiple catastrophic failures. Over a hundred Earth Guard personnel died, including the captain. That captain was Lieutenant Owen's father."

"You're saying it's some sort of vendetta?"

"Not exactly." Nahdi shook his head, tapping something on his desk. "Earth Guard charged Owen's father with being at fault. The court-martial collapsed when an independent investigation found beyond reasonable doubt that the failures were due to design decisions dictated by Earth Guard. But Earth Guard never accepted the investigation results, and unofficially still blames Owen's father for what happened."

"Wait," Camacho said. "We let them just shut it down? There was no follow-up, no accountability?"

"Nope." Nahdi tapped whatever was on his desk again. "While the Council was arguing over what color the curtains should be in conference rooms, Earth Guard was allowed to brush the whole thing under the rug."

"But," Camacho said, nodding as the pieces came together, "Lieutenant Owen might have somehow drawn renewed attention to it, might have caused some of those things, and the people who made those decisions, to be exposed."

"Maybe," Nahdi said. "It gives us a motive. The Earth Guard officers on Mars talking to our investigators identified the connection to his father as a likely reason why Owen was on that sabotaged ship. I bounced the idea off of Admiral Tecumseh, and she said that was plausible from what she knew." He leaned forward, elbows on his desk. "I'm going to be making a formal request to reopen the investigation into the loss of the *Sentinel*. A hundred lives were lost. We owe it to them, to their families, to find out what really happened and why. To find out who was actually responsible and hold them accountable."

"I'll back you on that," Camacho said. "Have you asked Earth Guard for an official reply on the survivor thing?"

"Of course." Nahdi gave her another grim smile. "They have no records of any survivor, which is certainly true, I think, if all records were destroyed. I did ask for an official explanation of how Earth Guard has been able to confidently assert that Genji has alien DNA among her human DNA if Earth Guard has never had Genji in its possession. The reply was they'd look into that and get back to me if they found anything."

"Meaning they'll try to avoid ever answering you." Camacho sighed. "Is there any other news from Mars?"

"Political ferment still fermenting," Nahdi said. "The Forty-Eight-Hour Martial Law stirred up a lot of political activism. That and the increasingly famous speech on the Martian Commons by our favorite alien. Speaking of whom, the negotiations with the Tramontine have completely stalled. Our negotiators are saying they are trying to get across things to the Tramontine that the aliens just can't seem to grasp, and the Tramontine appear to be trying to explain some of their concepts that we can't figure out. We still don't understand enough of each other's language. Officially, the negotiators are confident they will work through it. Unofficially, nine out of every ten negotiators are pleading with us to find Genji and get her back on Mars. They think she'd break the deadlock in about five minutes."

Ranveer Nahdi gazed at something to the side of his desk.

"The negotiators are unanimous in agreeing that Genji appears to be fluent in the Tramontine language, but also in agreement that when they told the aliens they were surprised at Genji showing up when she did, the Tramontine reply seems to have been 'so were we.' The Tramontine insist they had no knowledge of her existence prior to her appearing on Mars. Everything we think we learn about her just leads to a lot more questions. Such as," Nahdi added in frustration, "the question of whether there's a third party unknown to either us or the Tramontine who is trying to either ensure the success of First Contact, or, if the military is right, trying to set the stage for sabotaging First Contact."

"Or if the Tramontine are lying about not knowing anything about Genji. But what would be the point of that?" Camacho shook her head in aggravation. "Where in hell did Genji come from? How does she know what she knows? If those bureaucratic idiots in Earth Guard and the salvage engineers had taken a few seconds to think, they'd have realized how important it was to preserve and study that wreckage, and then we might have some clues to work with. Didn't anyone study it at all?"

"The investigation of the wreckage," Nahdi said, "was done by an officer named Lieutenant Owen."

"Why doesn't that surprise me? Another reason why someone could have wanted to silence him permanently."

"Genji may be the only one who could answer our questions," Nahdi said. "And maybe Owen as well. The Earth Guard officers on Mars told us those two did not seem to have any secrets between them. Very close relationship. So did the officers who were sticking to the official line, who told us there was evidence of physical perversion on Owen's part."

"Physical perversion?"

"Kissing," Nahdi said, his smile this time genuinely amused. "A human kissing an alien! It must have been horrible to watch."

"I guess. She looks fundamentally human in the videos I've seen," Camacho said. "I haven't heard anyone claim otherwise. Except for the eyes and the skin, you'd never know from external signs."

"Cerise, you know how humans are. Keying on minor physical differences has caused immense problems in the past and still does. Throw in alien DNA and you've got a very combustible mix in some people's minds." He paused. "Is that part of why Genji is here? To make us confront that issue and, hopefully, realize we should have grown past it by now?"

"Are you saying that you believe that third party hypothesis?"

"I'm saying I don't know," Nahdi emphasized. "How do we judge Genji when we don't know where she came from or why? We have her statements that she's here to protect the Earth and its people, but that still leaves the why question. Who wakes up in the morning and says, 'I need to protect the Earth and its people'?"

Cerise Camacho smiled at him. "Why did you go to work for the Earth Cooperation Council, Ranveer?"

He paused, a rueful smile forming. "All right. I guess that I, and you, did exactly that at one point. What else do we have to judge her on, though? What evidence exists?"

"We have what she did on Mars," Camacho said. "And at Wallops." She waved toward the southeast. "Genji got her hands on a mag rifle during their escape. Firing using manual aiming from a moving vehicle, she knocked down several drones with direct hits."

"She's a sharpshooter. What about it?"

"Not one person was hit by a shot," Camacho said. "People would have been much easier targets than drones. If she'd aimed at any, she would have hit them. Meaning Genji didn't try to shoot any people. And the security personnel she engaged in hand-to-hand combat were all taken out with disabling blows. No lethal blows. Faced with overwhelming force attempting to kill her and the man she's emotionally involved with, Genji did not respond in kind. I think that's pretty powerful evidence."

"That is compelling," Nahdi agreed. "Did you speak to the military about that? What was their interpretation of it?"

Camacho waved an irritated hand. "Part of a devious, long-term plan to make us complacent before she strikes. They interpret everything in ways that fit their existing conclusions. Too many of them are *afraid* of Genji. And you know what we were taught about fear."

Nahdi nodded. "When fear enters, thinking departs so silently you don't even realize it's gone. We need to— Hmm. Incoming message, high priority." He read, another smile forming, this one enigmatic. "It's a complaint to the Security Committee regarding the interference of Special Representative Cerise Camacho in defense matters. They're insisting that you be removed from any defense-related inquiries."

Camacho laughed. "That will certainly please the members of the Committee. I've been telling them that parts of the defense apparatus appear to have forgotten who is working for who. It's so nice of General Molstad to provide me with proof of my argument."

"You personally told him to cancel the shoot-on-sight orders, didn't you? The message complains about that, as well."

"I did." Cerise Camacho shook her head, her humor vanishing. "But I don't believe for one minute that will end the threat to Genji or to Owen. Assuming they escaped the Eastern Shore, and I think they somehow have, any guesses where they might be headed?"

Nahdi considered the question. "They came to Earth for a reason, and it's probable that reason has to do with Genji's self-proclaimed goal of protecting the Earth and its people. Or, if the military is right, undermining us. There are a lot of possible goals for them, but maybe the reason is pretty simple. They have a chance of hiding on Earth. Once Genji was known to be on Mars, the colony was too small for her to hide in. The lunar colonies are even worse for someone trying to hide, except for the Free Zone, but at best that would have been an even smaller cage for them."

"They were originally headed for Tanegashima," Camacho noted. "Within easy range of the Japanese islands, and every other place in the Far East with many people, many cities, and lots of transportation options. Do you think they might just be in survival mode at the moment? Trying to avoid being captured or killed?"

"And maybe looking for opportunities along the way to further her mission, whatever it is," Nahdi said. "Which doesn't narrow things down at all. I do think they're going to keep moving until they're well away from this area. You know, we could give them an objective, a place to head for."

"How?"

"Offer them protection if they surrender to us."

"We don't have authority to do that," Camacho said. "Something like that would require the approval of the Security Committee at least, and maybe the full Earth Cooperation Council." She paused. "Should we be looking into that? Sounding people out?"

"The members of the Council will want to know what's in it for Earth, what's in it for them," Nahdi said. "What can Genji and Owen offer us? Certainly, we can say the negotiators on Mars consider Genji to be critical to their job. But is that enough? My own sense is that, because Genji did so much to get First Contact going well, it's going to be a while yet before the Council develops a sense of urgency over the current stalemate."

"Everywhere Genji and Owen go, we find problems surfacing," Cerise Camacho said. "Problems that were already there but which we didn't know about, or had ignored, or decided were too difficult to take on."

"That sounds like an argument for letting them run free."

"I suppose it does." Camacho shook her head. "But that means leaving them exposed to danger from every individual in every security and police organization and every vigilante wanting to save the Earth from the aliens or make a name for themselves."

"Do we have any alternative at this time?" Nahdi asked. "Until we convince the Council, or at least the Committee, of the need to act, our ability to help Genji and Owen is extremely limited." He paused. "I just spoke of helping them. Is that a bad mindset to adopt?"

"We still want them in our custody, right?" Camacho said.

"Yes. And just because reopening the investigation into the *Sentinel* will help Owen is no reason *not* to do it. It's simply right, regardless."

"Let's get the ball rolling on this, Ranveer. The issues are clear enough that members of the Council might finally come together on something important."

"I agree, Cerise." Nahdi smiled. "If that truly happens, we will owe a large debt to our alien friend Genji. Perhaps she'll live long enough for us to thank her."

4

THEY'D FOUND A MULTILANE highway, and along that highway the usual businesses catering to those using it. Including a low-end but homey-looking restaurant using human waitstaff not to display status but because for smaller businesses, humans could be cheaper than lease arrangements for bots. Owen was also concerned because bots could receive wanted person alerts, so it was just as well to avoid them if possible in case Owen's information had been sent out along those channels.

Owen picked a booth in a corner, away from other patrons. Selene had her bucket hat crammed down on her head and was keeping her face lowered, her hands beneath the table.

"Your friend okay?" the waitress asked as she brought water.

"Allergies," Owen said.

"Oh, yeah. They can be bad this time of year. What do you want?"

Owen ordered the chicken strips and fries, which were a safe bet anywhere. "Iced tea for both of us. How are you doing?" he asked Selene as the waitress moved off.

"Okay," she grumbled in a low voice still slightly hoarse from her earlier allergy attack.

"Did they know llamas would be a problem?" Owen asked cautiously.

"No." She didn't look up, but even though her voice sounded grumpy, Selene didn't seem as angry as she had been. "Unexpected side effect, just like my skin. The Tramontine themselves don't have any problems with llamas. Just alloys."

"Sorry."

"Stop apologizing for things you didn't cause!" Selene

paused as the waitress returned with two glasses of tea, then took a quick drink. "Augh. It's really sweet."

"I forgot we're in the South now," Kayl said. "Sorry I didn't specify unsweet. That is my fault."

"Yes, this time it is." She raised her head just enough to look at him from under the edge of the hat, her eyes still reddened from the allergy attack. "I'll be okay as long as we don't run into any more herds of llamas."

The waitress returned with generic chicken tenders and decent-looking fries, also depositing a small container on the table. "If you need 'em," she said.

Owen took a look, passing the container to Selene. "Antihistamines. Are these safe for you?"

She studied the container. "No. But it was still nice of her."

The door slid open, letting in a pair of police officers who waved at the waitress with the ease of long familiarity. "Two coffees. The usual," the male officer said.

They walked to the counter, waiting, but Owen saw the female officer looking his way. "Hey, you guys from that college?"

Why was she asking that? Their borrowed clothing. The only way to avoid attracting more attention was to act typical. Owen looked over at the officer. "Us? Yeah."

"How long you been out here?"

Why was she asking *that*? "We've been hiking. Several days."

The female police officer shook her head. "I hope you're not planning on going back that way today."

"Why not?"

The male officer bent a not-unsympathetic look toward Owen. "That area is being sealed off. Every way in and out."

"Why?" another customer asked.

"They're not saying," the officer replied.

The waitress gave a derisive snort. "It's about Wallops, isn't it? She's out there, and they lost her."

"Maybe it is," the female officer said. "Maybe it isn't. I'm just letting these guys know they can't get back there today or probably tomorrow."

"Oh, hell," the waitress said with a laugh. "You know as well as I do that sealing off places like that is a lot easier said than done. Some fool looks at a map and says 'seal it off.' But folks have been smuggling things along that coast as long as folks have lived there."

"She ought to be easier to spot, though," another customer chimed in. "I mean, an alien. How could she hide?"

"They say she looks human," the waitress said, her sympathies clear. "I don't know why they're chasing her. Or trying to kill her."

"Shoot-to-kill orders have been canceled," the male officer said. "I mean, officially."

"That doesn't mean we can't defend ourselves," the female officer said. "If she's as dangerous as they say."

"What's she done?" the waitress demanded.

"Gracie, that's not our call to make," the male officer said. "If we find them, we have to take them in."

"Them? That Earth Guard guy still with her?"

"Yeah. I'd sure like to know what he's thinking."

"Seems maybe somebody could ask," the waitress said.

"How many did that alien kill at Wallops?" the first customer asked. "I heard every morgue in the region was full up because of her."

The male officer shook his head. "The official reporting says no deaths. The only life-threatening injury was to that teenage girl."

"It figures they wouldn't admit it!"

"Earl," the waitress said, "why would they cover up her killing people if they wanted us to be afraid of her?"

Earl hesitated. "Because they don't want us to panic! Because they don't want us to know how bad they've handled this whole thing!"

The female officer also shook her head. "Earl, if morgues

had been filled up, I would've heard. That hasn't happened."

Earl waved away her words. "Yeah. Sure. You're going to give me the official line. Keep your job safe."

"Don't accuse me of lying, Earl," the officer warned, her voice getting harsher.

"Everybody calm down," the male officer said. "We're going to help find that alien, and if we do, we'll take her in. Or take her down if we have to. But let me give everyone some friendly words of warning. If you think you've spotted that alien, don't try to take her yourself. She made it past everything at Wallops. Just call it in and let the military handle it. And, assuming they don't nail her soon on the other side of the river, anybody who has business outside this county ought to get it done before they expand the security lockdown trying to catch her. Thanks for the coffee, Gracie."

Owen turned his head back toward Selene as the officers left, thinking about their words.

"We can't afford to keep walking," Selene murmured. "Too slow."

"We haven't found any cars free for use yet," Owen said. "We'll have to head down this road and hope we come across one pretty soon. Or keep walking west until we reach a place that might have a rail stop."

He ate faster, feeling the same urgency that Selene did.

The waitress came by just as Selene was reaching for some fries, her hand exposed to the light, the glossy skin easy to spot.

"Y'all need refills on that tea?" She paused, her eyes on Selene's hand before it was yanked back under the table. "You okay, hon?" she asked, her voice pitched much lower.

"I'm fine," Selene said, not raising her head.

"You tell me honest, now. Are you out to hurt anybody?"

Selene looked up, meeting the waitress's gaze with her own. "No."

The waitress dug in a pocket, sliding a car fob onto the table where it was concealed by one of the plates. "I just misplaced my car keys. Red two-door. To the left as you leave. Take it a couple hours' drive wherever you're heading, then send it back. Okay?"

"Okay," Kayl said. "Thanks."

"Most folks here are good people," Gracie said, "but they worry about how things seem to be drifting. It sounds like you want to fix that."

"Yes," Selene said. "If I can."

"Big job."

"I'm finding people to help me with it," Selene said, smiling.

The waitress grinned and walked off.

"Where are we going with our new car?" Selene asked him.

Owen paused. "If we really want to throw off our pursuers, there's a risky option that might do it."

"What option is that?"

"Fort Walker."

FORT WALKER HAD GONE through a variety of roles and more than one name since being first established. For the last couple of decades, it had been a joint base providing training for mutual defense forces as well as the local military. Sprawling over a considerable amount of real estate, its perimeter was defended primarily by automated sentries and sensors. The fact that a significant public highway ran through the middle of the base rendered security particularly difficult.

As such, ways through the automated watchdogs had been widely shared among trainees for almost as long as they'd been in place. Kayl had explained to Genji that sneaking out to bars during training was considered an unofficial part of whatever training someone was officially undergoing.

"Living with all that peacetime negligence must have been

nice," Genji told him. She hadn't wanted to rain on his parade of memories, but sometimes it was hard to deal with the 2140 reality of slackness that had helped lead to the horrible events of the 2160s and 2170s. Her mood hadn't been improved by watching advertisements for topless bars outside the fort. Topless bars in 2140. Never mind the Tramontine. Sometimes men seemed to qualify as an alien species.

Automated kiosks outside the base offered civilian clothing around the clock for anyone seeking a quick change of garb, which gave Genji a means to replace her UV Aversive hat and other clothes. She spent a moment looking at the hat after the kiosk delivered it, thinking about Krysta and how odd it was that the thought of her possibly dying had in some ways been as emotionally wrenching as thinking about the death of the entire planet. Rear Admiral Tecumseh had been right that mourning billions was too immense for anyone to grasp, but it was all too easy to feel the pain of the loss of a single life.

Getting onto Fort Walker had been as simple as spotting small groups of people coming out of the woods and locating the trails they'd taken through gaps in perimeter security. A publicly available map of the fort (which had almost launched her into another lecture to Kayl about incredibly lax security) led them to a warehouse. Genji had no trouble hacking a lock so they could gain access, after which finding an Earth Guard uniform in her size was also easy.

"We can pass for authorized personnel now," Kayl said as he finished putting on his own Earth Guard uniform.

"As long as no one gets too close to us," Genji said. The uniform left her face and head exposed, revealing her eyes and her facial skin. "We have to avoid any surveillance cameras. Aren't there any authorized head coverings?"

"Earth Guard is a space service," Kayl said. "So, no. Unless you're in a spacesuit."

"Let me see if I can get into the fort security system through the panel in this warehouse." Genji didn't have any trouble breaking through the protective measures designed for a low-threat environment and forty years older than what she had trained on. "Okay. We're in. Cameras. Here. Coverage. Where do we need to go next?"

"One of these buildings," Kayl said, pointing to the online map they were using. "Operations offices. They won't be occupied at night."

"All right." She studied the unfamiliar layout of the system. "This one, then. I can shift the focus of some of the outside cameras so we have a narrow path to the building that won't be covered. There are more cameras inside the building. Disable. Disable. Disable. Security bot patrolling the inside. Disable. Reactivate in three hours. In the morning, no one will know we temporarily shut things down unless they examine the system logs."

With no time to waste, they went back out into the darkness, heading for the operations building that Kayl had identified. Scattered groups of people in uniform or civilian clothing could be seen walking about, some of them talking loudly or even singing. Genji didn't need that scene interpreted for her. It had been the same in the 2170s, personnel returning from liberty, buzzed or drunk. The only difference between now and that period in the future was the military members in the 2140s didn't have the frantic intensity to their celebrations that those in the 2170s did, because in the 2140s, they weren't worried about dying soon in some part of the Universal War.

They tried to avoid getting too close to any of the revelers, sticking to the unlighted paths, Kayl positioning himself between Genji and the nearest groups.

"Hey, 'Lid, 'sup?" someone shouted, their head turned toward Kayl.

Kayl raised one arm and waved a wordless response to a small group about one hundred meters away.

"That Ori? Way to go, man!"

Kayl waved a second time, generating a gust of laughter.

Luckily, the other group continued on without trying to get closer or engage in conversation.

Since Genji had disabled the locks on the building, entry was simply a matter of walking up to a side door and opening it, the security camera gazing vacantly off to one side where she had aimed it.

Inside, Kayl led the way again, consulting a building directory. "The first thing we need is new official IDs."

The ID office systems were easily broken into, letting Genji create new IDs for first Kayl and then herself, using false names. "We are now, officially, lieutenants in good standing with Earth Guard," she said. "Or at least our fake names are."

After that, the office of the operations director proved to have links to every subsystem Genji needed. She worked quickly, feeling the press of time. "There's a flight scheduled for early morning to Fort Eisenhower. A routine passenger suborbital. How's that sound?" she asked.

"It sounds far away but not far enough," Kayl said. "Is there anything headed off this continent?"

"Not for three days. There's a suborbital scheduled for the West Coast, but it doesn't leave until early afternoon."

"That's way too long to risk hanging around here. I guess we're going to Fort Eisenhower."

Genji changed the names of the officers designated as pilot and co-pilot to the false names matching her and Kayl's new IDs, remembering to send notices to the original flight crew that they'd been reassigned and wouldn't have to show up for this flight. "How's this look? Any problems you can see?"

Kayl studied it before nodding. "It looks good. Are we listed in the system for access to the suit lockers?"

"Umm . . . yes."

"Then let's go."

After shutting down the systems she'd activated and checking the time, Genji followed Kayl out the same side door. "The security systems for this building will reactivate and reset in another hour. The flight leaves in two hours. Can we check in this early?"

"We should be able to," Kayl said. "Once we get you into a suit, your helmet will help conceal your face and eyes."

"How do we explain me being fully suited with helmet on before the flight?" Genji asked.

He grinned. "Like any good sailor, you'll be sleeping while waiting for the flight."

Getting into the building containing the suit lockers required Kayl trying to block security camera views of Genji without being obvious about it. Their new IDs let them into the building without any hindrance, though, and then into the locker area. There wasn't anyone else there so early.

Genji pulled out a suit, eyeing it. "It looks okay."

"It is," Kayl said, sounding angry. "On the ships, we have to make do with older suits, but the installations on the surface of the planet get the newest production models!"

"It's still old," Genji said. She pulled on the suit over the stolen Earth Guard uniform, sighing with relief as it adjusted to her body. She hefted the helmet just as the sound of voices warned of others coming. Sealing the helmet, Genji took a seat against a wall, leaning back, head down, like someone dozing.

"Morning," someone said to Kayl, the word sounding half-yawned.

"Morning," he replied in the same manner.

"You got the lift to Ike?" the woman asked.

"Yeah," Kayl said.

"At least you're going somewhere. I'm going nowhere fast today, just doing bounces up high for the new trainees and then back down here."

"Sucks," Kayl sympathized.

"You new here?"

"Nah," Kayl said. "Stationed at Ike. Been on leave, volunteered to fly this hop to get home."

"Smart. No wonder you're here early. Hey, Ren," the woman said to someone else. "See her?"

That must be a reference to her, Genji thought, trying not to tense, to still seem relaxed in sleep. She almost looked up before she stopped herself.

"That," the woman continued, "is a true sailor. If you've got five minutes, try to sleep. Learn from your elders."

"Why does she have her helmet on?" someone who must be Ren asked.

"Shut off the external mics and it blocks a lot of noise. Makes it easier to grab some rest." She and her companion, Ren, engaged in quiet conversation for several minutes before heading out.

Genji raised her head to see Kayl watching them go. "Nervous?" she asked him.

"Yup," he said.

"Me, too. You're not showing it, though."

"Thanks." He paused. "I don't like not being truthful with them."

"I don't blame you. Maybe someday we'll be able to convince them we're all on the same side."

He nodded. "I hope so. We've got another half hour before we can head out."

"Guess I'd better start studying." Genji called up one of the guides in the suit's memory, projecting it on the face screen of her helmet, learning the controls and procedures for the lifter they'd use on this suborbital hop.

A few other pilots wandered through, offering no or minimal conversation, before Kayl stood up, walked over, and nudged her with his foot as if waking her. "Time to go."

Genji stood up like someone waking from a nap, following Kayl out of the building and onto the field where several lifters waited.

One of the lifters already had a line of trainees waiting to board it, getting their first experiences in zero g and exposure to space.

Kayl headed for the lifter at the end of the line, where a few others were already lined up, none of them in suits, a bot waiting to check them aboard. Passengers on a routine hop. What would they say if they knew who their pilots really were?

The bot readily accepted their new IDs, letting them board immediately. On the flight deck, Genji took the co-pilot position and started running through the preflight checks.

"We're good on this side," Kayl said.

"Good over here," she said, trying to fight down the tension building in her as they got closer to liftoff. The nearer they were to actually making this happen, the rougher it was to stay calm.

It took considerable self-control to sit quietly while the passengers slowly boarded and strapped in. Genji watched the progress of boarding on her monitors while Kayl handled the routine communications.

The last five minutes before liftoff were almost agonizing.

"Clear to lift on time," the approval finally came.

Kayl let the lifter launch on automatic, watching their progress as the lifter leapt skyward. A sudden sunrise washed over the lifter as it rose to greet the dawn in the east. The sky had barely shifted to blue before they climbed high enough for it to darken again at the edge of space, the lifter following a ballistic trajectory that formed an immense arc up and then back down toward the still-darkness-enshrouded center of the continent.

"My sister once asked me why I liked being in Earth Guard so much," Kayl said. "I told her it was for times like this." He glanced her way. "Are you okay?"

"Just a little tense," Genji said. "When a lifter is at the top of its flight path, it's at maximum vulnerability. We always had to sweat out these seconds, wondering if someone was going to take shots at us."

He fell silent, perhaps once again feeling guilty that his peacetime experience had been so different from what she would experience in the Universal War.

"Sorry," Genji said. "I didn't mean to step on your moment."

"No problem," Kayl said. "I'd rather know what you're really feeling than for you to fake something."

The lifter crested the top of the parabola and began angling down, its path a smooth arc. The propulsion lit off again, slowing the velocity of the lifter.

On her monitors, Genji watched the Earth getting closer again. It still felt strange to see an Earth lacking in the recent craters she'd become used to as a result of the worst bombardments of the Universal War. It still felt strange at some moments to see the Earth at all, after watching it be totally destroyed. June 12, 2180. She never had nightmares about it. It didn't trouble her dreams. But awake, the memories haunted her, especially at moments like this.

What if she couldn't change enough to prevent that from happening?

IT WAS WAY TOO early to be getting work calls. Cerise Camacho took a drink of coffee before accepting the incoming call. "What's up, Jamie?"

Investigative Specialist Costanza made a face. "Maybe nothing. But you told me to pass on anything that might link to the alien. You know about the DNA skeeters, don't you?"

"Remind me," Camacho said.

"Tiny bots that pick up anything shed by humans that could offer DNA samples. Skin flakes, little drops of moisture from a sneeze, whatever," Costanza explained. "Top secret in part because they're randomly collecting DNA in places where there isn't any open warrant for that."

"Uh-huh," Camacho said. "Not real-time, last I heard. Has that changed?"

"No," Costanza said. "They still have to finish their flight pattern and then dock before any samples they've collected are run through a DNA sampler for possible IDs. Early today, a

DNA skeeter at Fort Eisenhower brought in a skin flake that might be a hit on Lieutenant Kayl Owen's genome."

"Eisenhower?"

"That's an Earth Guard base in Kansas," Costanza said. "The hit has been tagged as likely erroneous due to DNA transfer because there's no way Owen could have gotten to there from the East Coast this fast. It's a lot more likely someone who encountered Owen, maybe at Wallops, maybe on the lunar shuttle they came in on, carried that skin flake with them to Eisenhower."

"How reliable are the latest DNA skeeters?" Camacho asked.

He shrugged. "DNA skeeters at Miranda spaceport on the Moon tipped everyone off that Owen probably boarded that lunar shuttle. Once you allow for the fact that the time lag between picking up a sample and getting it analyzed could be anywhere from five minutes to hours, they're reliable enough. And there's no telling how long that sample might have been drifting around before it was picked up. Of course, DNA skeeters aren't everywhere. There aren't enough of them, and whenever the general public learns about them, the outcry is probably going to be huge. Being able to say they were only deployed in certain high-risk locations will help contain the outrage."

"So," Camacho said, "false alarm. Let me know if we hear anything else."

LANDING AT FORT EISENHOWER had been almost ridiculously easy, coming down on autopilot and merging with the debarking passengers. The room holding the suit lockers was almost deserted here since they'd jumped back in time by entering a new time zone and it was still predawn in Kansas.

Getting out of the suit unobserved and out of the building was still nerve-racking, knowing how Selene's face and eyes were unobscured by any head covering.

Outside, they found themselves on the edge of a large vehicle lot already dotted with cars. "Here's our ride," Kayl said.

"There are a lot of cameras watching the vehicle lot," Genji pointed out.

"With no way to cover your head and face, they'll spot you quickly," Kayl said. "Especially with the sun coming up. I'll go in alone, get a car, and meet you here with it."

She didn't like them being separated by even that small a distance, unable to help each other, but she knew Kayl was right. "Okay. Give me your pack so you won't look odd. Be careful."

"Always am," he said.

Genji leaned against the side of the entrance to the lot, staying in the shadow of the building, watching Kayl walk nonchalantly toward a nondescript government car.

A horn honked in warning.

Turning, Genji saw a large bus approaching, loaded with passengers in Earth Guard uniforms. She backed away from the entrance, trying to stay in shadow, hoping that Kayl would be able to quickly get into the car he was aiming for.

But as the bus entered the lot, almost immediately stopping to let out passengers, Genji saw Kayl turning away from the car with a shake of his head. Their IDs hadn't allowed him into it. It must be a security vehicle, or one reserved for VIPs.

A crowd of people from the bus headed for the building, past Kayl, who was walking in a purposeful but not attention-drawing fast way toward another car.

"Owen?" a woman's voice called.

Kayl had almost reached a car, not reacting to the calling of his name.

Genji tensed herself, trying to plan a way to get them both out of this no matter what happened.

"That's Owen!" the woman officer called out again, this time to the Earth Guard personnel around her. "That's the guy they're looking for!"

At least a dozen officers and enlisted started running toward Kayl, the rest of the crowd following within a few seconds.

They were all between her and Kayl.

Kayl turned enough for Selene to see, making a gesture that clearly conveyed a message to flee, before he turned and ran away from where she waited.

Genji hesitated, unwilling to do what she'd always told Kayl to do, prioritizing the mission over either of them. As she did so, security officers came running out of the building to intercept Kayl.

It was hopeless.

Mentally cursing, Genji moved away, looking for a place where she could hide and plan her next move.

5

OWEN SAT IN THE high-security cell, acutely aware of the developing bruises on his body inflicted during his capture even though he hadn't fought back. He suspected he would have been beaten up worse if some of the Earth Guard officers present hadn't intervened.

At least they hadn't taken his uniform and put him in prison garb. Probably because they didn't plan on wasting any time transferring him to someplace much more secure than this cell in the small prison that was part of the fort.

The panel on one wall used to keep watch on the entire inside of the cell flared to life, showing an admiral seated at a desk.

Admiral Besson himself. Owen felt himself smiling at the compliment he was being paid. The top officer in Earth Guard was personally interrogating him.

"Attention on deck!" someone outside the cell shouted.

Owen, not feeling particularly obedient at the moment, stayed sitting instead of coming to attention.

"Attention on deck!" the command came again.

"Come in here and make me," Owen said, smiling a bit again. If this was it, if his story ended here, he wasn't going to crawl for the last moments of it.

Owen imagined his father, if he'd survived the loss of the *Sentinel*, being given this same treatment by those seeking to blame Cathal Owen for the disaster. Hopefully his father would approve of his actions now.

After a couple more seconds spent waiting to see if Owen would comply, Admiral Besson leaned forward in a threatening manner. "Is there something funny?" Besson demanded angrily.

"No, sir," Owen said, deciding to react moment by moment.

"Where is the alien?"

"What alien?" Owen asked, looking puzzled.

"Don't play games with me!" Besson shouted. "Where is it?"

Owen shook his head. "I don't know where *she* is, Admiral. We split up. Good luck finding out where she went while I came here."

"You're claiming you came to this base to draw our attention here?"

"Why do you think I let myself be captured so easily?" Owen said.

"Tell me where you last saw the alien," Besson ordered. "Don't lie! Your life is riding on this, Owen!"

"Why?" Owen said, trying to throw the admiral off his own line of questioning. Those outside the cell were listening, too, doubtless hoping to witness an historic confession. Instead, maybe he could give them something to think about. "What have I done?"

"Desertion!"

"That's not a death penalty offense, sir. Except in time of war. Are we at war?"

Besson looked as if he might explode at any moment. "You do think this is funny, don't you? Betraying the human species is *funny* to you."

Owen shook his head. "I'm not betraying anything. I want to live up to my oath to protect people. But the people who ordered me killed on that courier ship, they betrayed everything. The people trying to kill Lieutenant Genji, they are betraying everything. Because they're scared."

"Shut up until I tell you to speak, Lieutenant!"

"How frightened, how pathetic, do you have to be to order the death of an Earth Guard officer like me just because you needed a fall guy, Admiral?"

For a few seconds, Besson appeared to be on the edge of a

stroke. "You're going to be transferred to a place where you'll talk. And then, you'll get to see your alien whore die."

The panel blanked.

Owen looked at the guards outside his cell. "Are you guys comfortable with what you're doing?"

Instead of an answer, the access panel slammed shut, leaving him alone except for the electronic eyes watching his every movement.

He had a feeling he wouldn't be here long.

It took less than half an hour to prove him right.

THE DOOR TO HIS cell unlocked with a series of heavy clicks that told of how secure this cell was.

Owen stood up, hoping that Selene had taken advantage of the attention on him to already get far away from here.

Two guards in full riot-control gear entered the cell, one carrying arm restraints. Owen saw at least four more guards waiting outside. Every guard was armed with a stun rifle.

If he were Selene, trained and experienced in close combat, he might have a chance. But he was an Earth Guard officer with only regular self-defense training. Resisting would only earn him more bruises.

Owen yielded to one of the guards yanking his arms painfully behind him as the second clamped on the arm restraints, locking and tightening them beyond what was needed to hold him.

A shove sent Owen toward the open cell door.

Once outside the cell, the two who'd entered paused to close the cell door. Those two then led the way along an otherwise deserted corridor, the other four falling in behind Owen.

If they'd found Selene, killed her, they'd be boasting of that, wouldn't they? Owen tried not to let his fear for Selene show. The only protection he could offer her was pretending not to know anything, and keeping attention focused on him while she hopefully put a lot of distance between herself and this place.

They passed sealed cell doors giving no hint as to who their occupants might be. Some of the doors were ajar, though, probably to allow cleaning crews into unoccupied cells.

Halfway down the corridor, one of the guards in the lead raised one hand to the side of their head in the manner of someone trying to hear a call better. "What's that about the security cameras? Hello?"

Owen heard a thump behind him, turning just enough to see that Selene had leapt out of a cell and into the middle of the four trailing guards, already slamming one against the nearest wall.

Not taking time to think, he threw himself forward at the two leading guards, ramming into one of them with a shoulder and lashing out with a kick at the second.

The guard he'd rammed cursed and swung his weapon at Owen's head. He jumped backward, into the second leading guard, who was trying to regain her balance and also bringing her weapon up. They hit the opposite wall together, that guard's head rebounding from the wall. As she fell, dazed, the first guard reversed his weapon to aim at Owen. Unable to think of anything else to do, Owen hurled himself at the guard, off-balance, as much falling as lunging toward the guard's legs.

The guard leapt aside, yelling, trying to line up a shot, while Owen hit the far wall painfully.

He twisted to look toward the guard just as Selene struck.

As the guard collapsed to the floor, Selene turned and hit the dazed female guard who was trying to get back on her feet.

Grabbing one of the stunners, Selene hauled Owen up and spun him about. He heard and felt the muzzle of the stunner hit his arm restraints, then the discharge of the weapon.

The restraints fell away.

"Electronic locks are stupid," Selene said. "Are you okay?"

"So far," Owen gasped, bringing his arms forward and flexing them. "You shouldn't have—"

"We can argue later! Come on!"

Selene shoved a stunner into Owen's hands, tugging him along in a run down the corridor.

"They'll have seen what happened," Owen said, his mind and body still playing catch-up with events. "Maybe heard over comms—"

"No, they didn't," Selene said. "The entire security system is down, as are the communications repeaters in the building. The cell block access door is around the corner."

Coming to the end of the corridor and turning the corner, they confronted two guards and a supervisor clustered around a control panel, trying to reactivate the system.

Owen managed to stun one of the startled guards while two quick shots from Selene's weapon dropped the other two.

He hit the door control, the barrier swinging open.

On the other side were six more guards in the postures of people waiting and wondering if they needed to do something.

Three of the guards fell stunned from their shots before Selene waded into the remaining three, striking mercilessly.

Owen stunned one of those guards as she bounced off the nearest wall.

The other two were down, Selene grabbing a second stun rifle from one of them.

At the end of this short corridor, desk workers and a couple more guards were bent over panels at the main entry, everybody engrossed in trying to get the system working again. Selene dropped four of them with stunner hits while Owen got two more, the last he stunned almost getting a call out to warn others before the guard fell.

Selene leaned over the desk to grab the uniform of the last conscious desk worker. "We don't want to hurt anyone. I'm here to help people. You're being lied to. Sorry about this."

Stepping back, she fired a stun shot into the last worker, who collapsed face down on the desk.

Another turn, down a hallway lined with offices, both Owen and Selene firing their stun rifles at people in the doorways or walking down the corridor. Selene tossed aside her second rifle as it expended its last charge.

At the end of the hallway, two guards were talking and just beginning to turn to look toward the source of a warning shout.

Owen paused to aim and fire a stun shot at long range for the weapon, staggering one of the guards. The second hit the alarm as Selene got close enough to stun him with a shot.

They went out the last door together, into blindingly bright sunlight and oppressive heat.

An armored transport was idling at the entrance to the building, the driver standing by the open door talking to a couple more guards, all of them in the act of looking toward the sound of the alarm.

Owen stunned the driver, grabbing her ID and key fob, as Selene took out the two startled guards.

He jumped into the driver's seat while Selene leapt into the back and hit the control to shut the door.

With the alarm blaring behind them, and people beginning to run on all sides, Owen didn't try to sneak out of the parking lot. He accelerated the heavy car all out toward the gate that was swinging closed, hitting it and forcing it open enough to get through. Still accelerating, Owen took off down the main road between buildings.

A siren began shrieking, alerting the entire base, as Owen spun through a turn and into a crowded parking lot. Entering commands into the car's autopilot, he called back to Selene. "Get ready to bail out!"

Swerving between aisles of cars, Owen swung the car into another turn. "Now!"

He rolled out onto the hard surface, slamming quickly into the back of the nearest car. Staggering to his feet as Selene stood up nearby, Owen limped to the nearest uncommitted car, using the ID of the armored vehicle driver they'd knocked out to commandeer it.

As he sat down inside the car and slammed the door, two warbirds shot past overhead, pursuing the abandoned armored car as it raced along the roads toward the main gate.

"A ground vehicle isn't going to get us off this base," Selene said as she slid into the passenger seat.

"It'll get us to something that can fly," Owen said, starting the car toward one of the spaceport pads. "Selene, how many times have you told me that the mission has to be the first priority, that we couldn't allow our feelings to get in the way of that? You shouldn't have—"

She rounded on him, angry. "I did it because I realized that there wouldn't be any point in saving an Earth without you in it! Because you caused me to fall in love with you and messed up my mind! If you're smart, your next words will be 'Thank you, Selene,' and then you won't say anything else!"

He spared a glance from the road to look at her. "Thank you, Selene."

"You're welcome!" Selene gazed out the window for a moment. "What's the plan? How do we get our hands on a bird?"

"By asking," Owen said, speeding up like someone who'd just received orders to be somewhere. "See that flight line up ahead? They're prepping all the birds."

"For search and pursuit of us?" Selene said.

"You can be sure of that. And calling in pilots for those birds," Owen said. "We're both in Earth Guard uniforms. Do you still have your fake ID from Walker?"

She grinned. "I do."

He screeched the car to a halt in the nearest parking spot to the flight line, he and Selene jumping out and running toward the waiting aircraft. "Which one is ready to go?" Owen called to the ground crews.

"Number three!" someone called back, gesturing. "Flight orders are already loaded!"

Owen tried to keep between Selene and anyone else as they dashed to the third bird in the line.

He climbed into the pilot seat as Selene pulled herself into the co-pilot position. "She's ready to lift," Owen said, putting on the helmet waiting for the pilot. "What are the flight orders?"

"Perimeter sweep," Selene said, putting on her own helmet as she scanned the bird's flight system.

Owen lifted the bird fast in keeping with the alert situation, swinging it about and heading along the ordered flight track toward one edge of the base in the general direction the chase of the armored car was heading.

The command frequency came to life. "All units, this base is on lockdown. All personnel stay inside buildings and work areas unless participating in security operations. All vehicles stay off the roads unless part of security operations."

"No shoot-on-sight orders?" Selene asked, looking out at the base below as the bird zipped toward the perimeter.

"They don't know you're here," Owen said. "The moment we take this bird past the perimeter, they'll key on us. Any ideas?"

"Tell them we're in pursuit?"

"Of what?"

"Unidentified aerial phenomenon?"

He glanced at her. "We're going to announce we're chasing a UAP?"

"Do you have any better ideas?" Selene asked. "They're all worked up about aliens, right? And trying to figure out how you got here?"

"And how I escaped. You are a genius."

"I know."

The perimeter fence was coming into view ahead. Owen swung the bird to fly along it, slowing his speed.

"All units, Owen is not in the stolen vehicle. The search will be concentrated along the route it took. It is critical that Owen be captured alive. Report any unusual sightings."

"There's our cue," Owen said. He keyed his own transmitter. "We're seeing something weird out here. Beyond the fence and heading outward. Nothing showing on any sensors, but we're getting intermittent visuals. Request permission to pursue."

"Visuals, Alpha Three? What kind of visuals?"

"Flashes of light about six meters off the ground. Rapid course changes. It's moving fast. We're going to lose it!"

"Pursue it, Alpha Three! All units, watch for unexplained flashes of light."

Owen gunned the bird's engine, heading out across the perimeter fence and arrowing over the landscape. "Roger. Conducting pursuit."

"We are sending additional assets to assist in your search, Alpha Three. Keep on it!"

Selene had been checking area maps as he flew. "There's a train station about twenty kilometers ahead. According to the schedules . . . there'll be a high-speed train leaving in half an hour, heading west. Do you think we can do a touch and go with this bird near that station without anyone noticing?"

"Get me a satellite view of the area around the station," Owen said. "Any buildings with flat roofs?"

"Half a dozen," Selene said.

"Okay. Our UAP will start jinking around, we'll 'follow,' and at some point, we'll touch on one of those roofs." He yanked the bird to one side as if following the UAP. "This is Alpha Three, our target is slowing and maneuvering erratically. We're trying to close on it."

"Be careful, Alpha Three!"

Selene had been listening to another communications channel. "There are reports of you being seen all over the fort. They're chasing those down. No one seems to have figured out—"

"Alpha Three, what's your ID?"

Selene sighed and passed her fake ID to Owen. He scanned it in. "Here you go."

"Who assigned you to Alpha Three?"

"I was told every available pilot, and when I got there, I was told Alpha Three," Owen said.

"Understood. Continue pursuit. All units, all units, the presence of the alien on the base is confirmed. Shoot on sight. Repeat. Shoot on sight."

Owen, concentrating on yanking the bird through tight maneuvers over the buildings near the train station, called to Selene. "Set the autopilot to keep acting like it's pursuing the UAP over this area and then back toward the base. Have it land at the fort at the same spot we took off from."

"Got it. Give me one minute."

Another call, in a different voice. "All units, this is Colonel Baceda. Cancel the shoot-on-sight order. Repeat. Cancel the shoot-on-sight order. The alien is to be taken alive."

Selene paused in her work. "That's nice to hear."

"We've got aerospace fighters inbound to assist us," Owen warned.

"Got it," Selene repeated. "Okay. Done."

Yet another transmission, a woman speaking. "All units, this is base commander General Pravat. The shoot-to-kill order remains in effect. Take no chances. The alien has already killed a dozen personnel on this base. Shoot to kill."

"Liar," Selene growled.

"Pravat is worried that she's going to be blamed for losing us," Owen said. "That building. I won't touch the roof with the bird. We'll go to a slow near-hover a meter above the roof for two seconds before the autopilot kicks in."

"Three Alpha, request search status."

"It's bouncing all over the place," Owen called back. "We're trying to get close enough to image it."

"You have support on the way, estimated arrival one minute."

"Got it." Owen angled down toward the flat roof he'd chosen. "Let's go."

Yanking off her helmet, Selene jumped down as the bird slid over the roof. Owen discarded his helmet as well, dropping to join her just before the bird slid past the edge. Selene grabbed his arm to steady him, uncomfortably close to a fall, as the bird accelerated away under the autopilot's direction.

"Get off the roof," Owen urged Selene.

They ran to the edge where the fire escape was, dropping down to the first landing before huddling against the side of the building as two aerospace fighters roared past overhead.

Hastening down the fire escape ladders, trying to avoid being seen from inside the building as they passed windows, they reached the alley along this side. Selene had hung on to both of their packs through everything, now finally tossing his to Owen. Hoping no one happened to look down the alley, Owen pulled off his uniform and hastily put on the civilian clothes that would hopefully blend in here. Selene did the same, shifting into her UV Aversive outfit to hide her face, hands, and other skin.

They both paused to get their breathing to a normal pace before walking out of the alley.

No one noticed. Everyone on the street was looking up, where the aerospace fighters were angling in wide turns around the bird heading with jerky course changes off to the south.

The train station, part of the high-speed rail line network built in the 2080s and 2090s, bore its age with quiet dignity. "Trains always feel kind of old-fashioned, don't they?" Owen commented as they walked to the ticket kiosk.

"Everything in 2140 is old-fashioned," Selene said. "They took your fake IDs? I've still got the ones from our packs."

"How about anonymous cash cards?" Owen asked.

"Two left. Hopefully there's enough on them."

"How does Las Vegas sound?"

"Far enough away," Selene said.

They made the train with four minutes to spare, sitting and listening to the passengers around them gossiping about the unusual activity in the air and strange rumors coming out of Fort Eisenhower.

CERISE CAMACHO GAVE A worried glance at her phone. A top-priority call from fellow Special Representative Ranveer Nahdi couldn't be good news. "What's up?"

Nahdi shook his head. "Did Investigator Costanza tell you about the apparent false hit on Owen in Kansas?"

"Yes. Was it a real hit?"

"They had him in custody on Fort Eisenhower."

"What? Where is Owen now?" Camacho said.

"Good question," Nahdi said. "They lost him. From what I've been able to find out, Genji showed up, broke him out, and they somehow got away from the fort. The best guess at this point is that they may have stolen a bird and used it to fly a good distance away before abandoning it. There's a chance they got on a train at a nearby station, but so far they haven't been spotted yet."

"How in hell did they get to Kansas in the first place?"

"That remains to be determined," Nahdi said. "Needless to say, the searches and security lockdowns along the Chesapeake Bay are all being shut down. Here's the important fallout from our perspective. We weren't notified when Owen was captured. Earth Guard still hasn't provided the Council with any official report."

Camacho shook her head angrily. "Did someone at Eisenhower not realize how important Owen is?"

"Oh, someone did. I was able to confirm that Earth Guard headquarters used a link to interrogate Owen."

"They weren't going to tell us," Camacho said. "That's going to light a fire under the Council."

"Not just that," Nahdi said. "The fort commander ordered shoot on sight for Genji, even after the fort security chief tried to change it to a capture order. Some of the senior commanders are outright defying orders from civilian authority."

"They won't admit to it, though," Camacho said, still angry. "They'll claim an oversight or a misunderstanding or some other explanation. We can nail that base commander, but if we're going to fix these problems, hold the others to account, we have to catch them unquestionably defying Council orders."

"Agreed." Nahdi frowned. "Genji is the key, isn't she?"

"I'm afraid so."

GENJI AND KAYL HAD left their train at the next large station instead of continuing on with their original tickets. Other false IDs got them on a different train heading north, before changing trains again at another station to go west.

They splurged on a private room on the third train. It was small, but with enough space for them to sit together, looking out at the landscape as it blurred past.

"Long day," Kayl said.

"I was scared," Genji admitted. "For you."

"Thanks."

"What, no more lectures about the mission being our priority?" she asked.

"That is your lecture," he said. "Which I have been on the receiving end of more than once."

"Okay. I admit I'm guilty," Genji said, leaning against him. "But I assume you're grateful for that."

"Very grateful," Kayl said.

"Do you want to talk about it? What happened while they had you?"

"It wasn't much," he said, looking out the window. "A pretty short round of questioning from Admiral Besson, then letting me sweat until they were ready to move me."

"Who's Admiral Besson?" Genji said.

"Earth Guard chief of operations," Kayl said. "The top commander."

"What's he like? Any redeeming qualities?"

"No," Kayl said. She could feel his body tensing. "I'm pretty sure he was one of those who tried to pin blame on my father for the *Sentinel* disaster. I made it clear what I thought of him."

"Good for you." Genji sighed. "Can you believe that fort commander? Claiming that I'd killed a dozen people while breaking you free? I wonder how she's explaining that lie to everyone who heard it."

"That's easy," Kayl said. "She'll just claim someone gave her that information, while being unable to recall exactly who it was."

She pulled back a little to look at him. "You're saying that like it happens all the time."

Kayl spread his hands, looking unhappy. "There's a saying among junior officers in Earth Guard that you're more likely to be punished for telling the truth than you are for telling a lie, especially if it's a lie your bosses want to hear."

"That's messed up, Kayl. You know how messed up that is, right?"

"Sure, I do." He shrugged, that old, hapless shrug she'd seen when first getting to know him. "I didn't play along. It didn't go very well."

Kayl looked relieved when his phone chirped and offered a distraction. "News item, maybe something about Eisenhower." He looked. "Huh. There's going to be a genetics conference in LA in a week. Talking about the 'challenges and opportunities created by contact with the Tramontine.' I wonder why I got two hits on that story? Oh, Malani is going to attend that."

"Malani?" Genji leaned in close to look. "Your sister?"

"Yes. Dr. Malani Owen, head of—" Kayl blinked before reading again. "Head of the Genetics Opportunities Research

Office at Solomons Genetics? Mal was just a junior researcher at Solomons the last I knew."

"If she's anything like her brother, maybe she got promoted on merit," Genji said, smiling. "Let me see." She studied the story, clicking through links. "Huh. The conference seems to be approaching the questions without any anti-alien hysteria. That's good. But the talks are all theoretical because they don't have any DNA from the Tramontine or from . . . me." She paused, a thought rising to the surface.

"That's good, isn't it?" Kayl asked. "That they don't have your genome? That's what Dorcas wanted to steal."

"Yeah, but . . ." Genji organized her thoughts, entering some new searches. "Legal representative. Genome. Yes! Those are already a thing. Kayl, I could make Malani the legal representative, the guardian, of my DNA. I could give her a sample. She could protect it from misuse, and let people know I don't have any weird weaponized DNA, and maybe see if my genetics could help someone."

"How do we do that?" Kayl asked.

"We'd have to figure out how to meet Malani while she's in LA," Genji said. "Can we get there?"

"Easily. Getting there without being tracked, though, might be a little harder. Let me check something." Kayl took his phone back, running through searches. "Yeah, we can do that. Leave this train here, take this hiking trail through the mountains to this resort town, pick up an available car there, and take the roads into LA. That should throw off anyone trying to figure out where we are, and get us there with a few days to spare."

"Kayl, we need to do this," Genji said. "I need to get my genome out there under controlled conditions. That's the only way to reassure people that I'm not a monster."

"All right," he said, nodding. "They'll be watching Mal, though. We'll have to get past whoever is keeping an eye on her in case we tried to contact her."

"But you're okay with us trying?"

"Sure." He smiled at her. "You said we need to do it. Have you ever lied to me?"

She hesitated. "Honestly? Yes."

Kayl shook his head. "Not really."

"Okay, not directly. But by omission."

Another shrug, this time more relaxed. "We both brought a lot of baggage to this relationship. Will you ever lie to me again, even by omission?"

"No," Genji said.

Fifty-five minutes later, the high-speed train slowed to a stop and they joined the passengers debarking into the early evening.

They were able to acquire supplies for the three days Kayl estimated it would take to hike to the town they were aiming for, but it was too late to start out that night. He got them a room at a small place that used a human check-in and seemed unlikely to provide current occupancy reports. "Let's get some dinner and crash," Kayl suggested.

Delivery seemed too risky compared to using an anonymous cash card for pickup, so they chose a busy place near their room. Genji, in her full UV Aversive outfit to avoid anyone seeing her face or hands, couldn't help noticing that she'd become the center of attention as soon as she walked in. Kayl noticed, too. Getting their orders, they headed out.

"Hey! Off with that hat!"

Genji glanced back, seeing an angry woman standing up, her hostility clearly focused on Genji herself.

Deciding to ignore the provocation, she kept walking without saying a word. But the woman darted forward, shouting. "There are monsters among us! Nobody gets to hide themselves! Take that off!"

Kayl held out a restraining hand, speaking in a firm voice. "She has a right to wear whatever she wants."

"Not here she doesn't! If she doesn't have anything to hide, why is she hiding herself?"

Genji, sensing the mood in the room, stopped and looked back as well. "I don't have to justify my choices to you."

"Yes, you do!" The angry woman lunged forward, one hand reaching for Genji's hat.

Prepared for such a move, Genji countered with a parry that sent the woman sprawling.

She scrambled to her feet and lunged again.

This time Genji caught her arm, twisted it, spun the woman around, and held her. "Does someone want to intervene before I have to hurt her?"

6

A MAN IN A police uniform stood up. "Spencie! Knock it off!"

Genji shoved the woman away, waiting to see what would happen.

"I mean it, Spencie!" the officer warned. "One more step toward that woman and you'll be talking to the judge tomorrow."

"What's she hiding?" the angry woman demanded.

"What exactly are you scared of?" Genji asked.

The simple question seemed to baffle the room.

"I'm sorry," the officer said to Genji. "People are on edge these days, what with the aliens and all. One of them's on Earth, you know."

Genji was searching for anything to say when Kayl spoke up.

"Isn't it amazing?" he said, drawing surprised looks. "I mean, I understand being worried. But, isn't this amazing? You guys look up at the stars, right? We're looking at infinity when we do that, at hundreds and thousands and millions of years in the past. Have any of you been up in space? Isn't it awesome?"

Kayl paused, while Genji watched him with growing surprise.

"It makes you think how amazing it is," Kayl said, "that in that infinity, we're here, able to look up at it, and try to understand it. And now, out of every human that has ever lived, we're here when someone from another star visits. For the first time ever, we're getting to talk to someone really different, and hear what they feel when they look at the stars. Isn't that the hugest thing you can imagine?"

After a brief moment of silence, another woman spoke up. "But why are they here?"

"Haven't you been told?" Kayl asked. "They know on Mars. The Tramontine, the aliens, are here to learn things. They're curious, and want to know about other people. Have you heard what that big ship is? It's so big because it's a town. They built a ship so big it could carry a whole town's worth of their people, and animals, and plants, and go to visit other stars. Can you imagine? Knowing your children, and their children, are going to see and learn things no one else ever has, without leaving home, because home is coming along with you?"

"They know this on Mars?" a third person asked. "Why aren't we being told?"

Kayl shook his head. "I don't understand why more people aren't being told. I really don't. But I do know what I told you. It's true. You've seen the news from Mars, haven't you? You've seen that alien they're all warning you about. Does she look like a monster? Who has she hurt? Can they tell you that? All she did on Mars was push back against martial law. She defended the freedom of the colonists. Is that bad?"

"I saw an interview with that girl," another woman said. "The one that alien rescued on the Moon. She couldn't say enough about how nice that Lieutenant Genji was. Why did it take an alien to save a human girl from that man? He was the monster, if you ask me."

"I don't want to take any more of your time," Kayl said. "I just wanted to answer your questions. Thanks for listening."

Genji could feel how the mood in the room had shifted, no longer hostile and suspicious as she walked out with Kayl. "Where the hell did that come from?" she asked him as they walked back to their room. "Who have you been hiding in there, Lieutenant Owen?"

"Just me, Lieutenant Genji," Kayl said. "I don't know. I've just been thinking, and suddenly I wanted to say some of the things I've been thinking."

"You defused the situation in there beautifully," Genji said. "I bow before your skill. We'll have to add Master of Speech to your Master of Flight title."

"Don't," Kayl said, laughing. "Please."

THEY LEFT AS DAWN was breaking, trudging to where the hiking trail began, hefting extra packs with the supplies for their walk. Apparently most hikers left a little later, so their path was unencumbered by others.

It was the sort of thing Genji had rarely been able to enjoy, walking without worrying about how other people would see and react to her, simply delighting in the air and the land and the trees, listening to the birds. Even though her memory tried to flash another vision of it all being destroyed in 2180, she was able to suppress that horror and take pleasure in what was here in 2140.

That first day she spent not saying much of anything to Kayl, just absorbing the life of the world about her. It gave her a luxury she'd only had a few times in her life, hours and hours in which she didn't have to think, didn't have to plan, didn't have to worry about how the full humans around her saw her and would react to her, but could just walk and let the world wash over her.

That night, wrapped in a lightweight two-person sleeping bag, she held Kayl and let other memories run through her. Memories of the war, of friends who had died fighting in it, of the things she had seen, the things she had done. Facing all that, and wondering.

"Are you okay?" Kayl whispered to her. "You feel pretty tense."

"I'm okay," Genji said. "Just . . . dealing with things."

The sky was overcast the next day, threatening a storm, and they encountered more hikers along the path. Genji let her thoughts roam through memories she'd tried to block, remembering her mother, remembering those last moments before the shock wave from the destruction of the Earth hit her ship. Kayl surely noticed how moody she was, but he didn't intrude on her thoughts. "Thanks," she said when they had stopped for the night and were warming their meals.

"For what?" Kayl asked.

"Giving me space, and time. There are things I never had a chance to work through."

"I've kind of been doing the same thing," Kayl admitted. "This is the kind of hike I hoped to do with my father someday."

"My mother wasn't a hiker," Genji said. "But she would have planned out this whole thing with exactly where to stop and exactly when and where the best views were and everything."

"And then she would have read to you from Marcus Aurelius?" Kayl said, grinning.

"Or other great thinkers," Genji said. She paused as another memory came to the fore. "One time, after a very bad day in middle school, I asked her why I was here. Why was I alive and here when no one seemed to want me to be here? I expected my mother to quote Marcus Aurelius. But, instead, she quoted Abraham Lincoln. Do you know him? Saying 'Broken by it I, too, may be; bow to it I never will.' And my mother told me, as long as I never gave up, as long as I never bowed to it even if it broke me, there must be a reason I was here, and I would learn it someday."

"To save the Earth," Kayl said.

"Yeah. Who would've thought?" Genji said.

She slept much better that night, and the third day dawned clear and bright.

She hiked along beside Kayl, realizing she had never been happier. Wondering how long that could last.

"What's on your mind?" Genji asked Kayl.

"Are we talking today?" Kayl asked her, smiling.

"We are talking today," Genji said. "You seem a little

moody, so I thought I'd ask. You don't have to share if you don't want to."

Kayl shrugged. "I was thinking about how much you changed my life. And that got me thinking about what my life was like originally, I mean, before you came back in time. How was my life going to play out after February 2140 without Lieutenant Selene Genji showing up in it? It's a little depressing to think about."

"You wouldn't have been on the run," Genji pointed out. "People wouldn't have been trying to kill you or capture you."

"No," Kayl said, looking down at the ground as they walked. "I would've served another six months on the *Vigilant*, unhappy and being worked to death, then I would've been transferred to some dead-end job, maybe on Mars, and after a couple more years I would have failed to promote and been kicked out of Earth Guard. And then . . . I don't know. Would I have tried to get a job in space, maybe with a private outfit? Maybe even with Dorcas Funds, working for that guy? Or would I have been so embittered by my failure that I turned my back on space and Earth Guard forever?"

"You're not the sort to give up," Genji said, trying to think of words to help Kayl feel better.

"I was getting there," he said, shaking his head. "Giving up was starting to look like common sense. I'd died on that hill too many times. The careerists and self-dealers in Earth Guard would have won in that original history of mine. By 2180 I would have probably been a bitter older man working a job he hated."

"I think you would have found ways to turn it around," Genji said. "The Kayl Owen I met in 2140 impressed me, and not a lot of guys have done that."

He smiled for a moment. "So you told me that you and I were impossible."

"We were. It'd never work, Kayl," she teased him. "Can you imagine the two of us in a relationship?"

"It would be pretty exciting and wonderful, I think," Kayl said, smiling again. "I wonder . . ."

"What?"

He shrugged. "Just . . . would I have ended up with someone else? Who would she have been? What would she have been like?"

"You're already pining for an alternate history with another woman?" Genji asked, hearing the slight edge in her voice despite her effort to keep the comment light.

"No! Not at all. Just wondering. Don't you ever wonder what your life might have been like if Earth hadn't been destroyed and you hadn't ended up back in 2140?"

"Not much," Genji said. "It would've been short and angry and mostly alone. I probably would have died in another battle within a couple of years, fighting against people who hated the very idea of me existing. And I would have been alone, because there wasn't any Kayl Owen in 2180." That had certainly dragged the conversation into a dark place. She should try to lighten it up again. "Maybe that girl on your ship would've finally asked you out."

"Sabita?" Kayl laughed. "She never acted interested in me that way."

"Jeyssi thought she might be. How about Jeyssi? Would you have made another try at her when you got to Mars?"

"Selene, are you going to try to ship me with every woman I've known?" He shook his head again, staring at the ground. "Whoever that other person might have been, it couldn't have been like this, with you. Maybe I lived out that life until 2180 knowing that something wasn't right. Maybe that woman and I would've gotten divorced because I was still looking for someone who wasn't there. I'm thinking whoever I'd become by 2180 wouldn't have been happy, would have looked back on his life with a lot of regrets. And then I would've died along with everyone else on Earth. If I hadn't died earlier in some part of the Universal War."

"You're sounding depressed," Genji said.

"No, I'm happy," Kayl protested. "Because that didn't happen. I mean, *won't* happen. One more change to the past, or rather the future, made by Lieutenant Selene Genji."

"Yeah," she said. "Thanks to me you've nearly been murdered six times."

"I thought it was five times."

"*Six* times counting what Earth Guard would have done to you after you were caught, and now you're hiding from every security service known to humanity while wondering when you're going to be killed. And while a good portion of the human species thinks you're a really sick pervert for hooking up with an alien girl."

"As long as I'm with you," he said, smiling at her. "You forgot to say that thanks to you I got to taste taratarabis."

"That's right!" Genji said, grinning. "In that other life you probably never had any taratarabis and never learned how great alien rabbit tastes. Okay, I'll take credit for making your life better that way."

As they continued on along the shade-dappled path, she couldn't stop thinking about what Kayl had said. Before she'd had any intention of trying to change things, the moment she and the wreckage of her ship had appeared in 2140, she had thrown Kayl's life onto a new path, a different one than he'd originally had in the history Genji knew. How many other lives had she impacted in small and large ways simply by existing in 2140?

And how had those lives impacted her own?

"Hey, Lieutenant Owen."

"Yes, Lieutenant Genji?"

"I'm glad we're fighting on the same hill. Sometimes," Genji added, "I think maybe we won't die on that hill. That, together, we'll hold the hill and throw back everyone trying to knock us off it. And somehow we'll save the Earth."

He smiled at her. "It's now officially our hill? Not my hill?"

"Yeah, it's officially our hill. Kararii fessandri etheria. My words are truth."

They walked on a little ways more, birds calling out in the trees above them, while Genji thought about many things. Thought about whether while trying to change history she should remain bound by her own history. Or whether she could manage to change the legacies of her own past. Whether she should change the vector her life had been on for too long. How she'd felt when Kayl was captured, wondering if she would ever see him again.

Wondering what the hell she was waiting for if not this.

"Hey, Lieutenant Owen," Genji finally said, trying not to let her nervousness sound in her voice.

"What now, Lieutenant Genji?" he asked.

"Do you still want to get married?"

He came to a sudden halt, staring at her. "Where did that come from?"

"It came from a happy place, which is something I have thanks to you," Genji said.

"I promised never to bring that up again."

"And you didn't," she said. "I did. Now answer the question. Do you still want to get married?"

"Hell, yes."

"Then ask me again."

Kayl swallowed nervously, his eyes wide. "Will you? Marry me?"

"Yes. Let's do that. I mean, as long as we've got the same hill and everything." Genji smiled at him. "Wow. You look like I could tap you and you'd fall apart into a thousand pieces. Hello? Are you okay?"

"Yeah," Kayl said. He stepped toward her, his arms going about her.

"The past does not rule," Genji murmured as she held him. "The future is mine. That's a Tramontine saying. Aren't you going to say anything else?"

"I'm afraid to," Kayl said. "I'm afraid this isn't real and if I say too much I'll wake up. How can we make this happen? We'd need to use our real names on the marriage license."

She leaned back a bit, shaking her head. "There's a bigger obstacle than that, Kayl. I'm not legally human yet."

"What?"

"The legal determinations declaring that alloys are 'persons' in terms of rights and responsibilities and everything else won't get decided until the late 2160s," Genji said. "And even then, they weren't fully accepted in some places, or accepted at all in other places. For two people to get married, they both have to be human. Legally, it hasn't yet been established anywhere that I'm human. If we tried to get married, you can be sure someone would bring that up."

"That can't be right," Kayl said.

"It's not right, but that's the way it is," Genji said. "So, legally, it will probably be a while before we can do it. But we've committed to each other, right? We've decided to share our lives in every way. I can live with that for now. Because at the moment there's no way you and I can march into a courtroom and ask for a legal ruling on whether or not I'm a person."

He looked unhappy, but nodded. "We'll live with that. For now. But I want the world to know you're just as much a person as anyone else." His frown faded into a look of wonder as Kayl gazed at her. "You really want to marry me?"

Genji smiled. "Whenever we can. But before we do that, we have a planet to save. Okay, Lieutenant Owen?"

"Sure, Lieutenant Genji." He grinned. "We're probably the only couple in existence whose pet names for each other start with 'lieutenant.'"

"Do you want me to call you something else?" Genji asked.

"No. I love it when you call me that. It makes me want to . . ." He looked away as if embarrassed. "It makes me want to do with you what I want to do when we stop for the night."

"Why wait for tonight?" Genji looked around before pointing. "It looks like there's somewhere that way where we couldn't be seen from the trail."

"Are you serious?"

Was she? "Maybe."

He eyed her for a moment, then grabbed her hand. "Come on, then!"

CLOSE TO AN HOUR later, Genji walked back onto the path, pausing to stretch slowly. "I am going to have to tell you I want to marry you more often. That was *epic*. I hope you're not planning a repeat tonight, though. I don't think my body could handle it."

"I'm actually glad to hear you say that," Kayl replied as he walked onto the path. "I was afraid you'd want that, and I don't think my body could handle it, either."

Genji linked her arm with his as they continued their hike toward the nearest town. "I owe you a better explanation of why I raised the issue of marriage after sort of losing it the first time you asked me. But getting there required me to confront something inside me. I've been doing that for the last couple of days."

He waited, saying nothing, the soil underfoot crunching softly as they walked.

"Ever since my mother was murdered," Genji said, her eyes fixed far ahead of them, "I've been seeking a personal Ragnarok. I knew I was going to die, probably sooner rather than later. Alloys were, will be, top-priority targets for the Spear of Humanity. A lot of us had already died. I resolved that when I died, it would be on my terms, and it would mean something. I joined the Unified Fleet, I chose close combat, and I got very good at it. And I fought, charging in, killing Spears, trying to ensure the death that awaited me would accomplish something. I nearly died at least twice from my wounds, but as soon as I recovered, I went right back into the fight."

Kayl's feet faltered in their steady pace, his eyes on her filled with concern. "You never told me about all that. You got that badly wounded? You don't have any scars."

"By the 2170s, scar tissue was easy to remove," Genji said. "Anyway, I didn't succeed in achieving my own personal apocalypse. Not before Earth was destroyed. And then here I was in 2140, and I saw a chance to really make my death count. Because I knew right from the start that changing the past meant possibly erasing me. That's why I could accept that, because I never expected to live long anyway. But the oblivion of never having existed at all proved a lot harder to accept than I'd thought. And I didn't admit to even myself, let alone you, that my aim of a meaningful death was still driving me."

"Like on Mars," Kayl said. "When you nearly died on the surface."

"Yes," Genji admitted. "And later when I suggested that crazy plan to escape from the Earth Guard ships around Mars. And even when I insisted on going aboard the *Lifeguard* to save that ship despite knowing I might not survive. I wasn't consciously pursuing that meaningful death anymore, but it was still there."

"And now?" Kayl asked.

"Then we got to the Moon, and I was able to help Abraham Pradeesh. I don't know if you understood how much that affected me, Kayl. And we were able to help Krysta. And then there's you." She fixed a demanding look on him. "Staying with me, risking your life for me and alongside me, refusing to do the smart thing and walk away from an alloy. How many times did I ask you what was wrong with you?"

"I lost count," Kayl admitted.

Genji took a deep breath, looking down at the path, seeing the grass and weeds stubbornly pushing up through the dirt, refusing to accept the reality that they'd be trampled. "I finally faced myself, finally looked deep inside, finally questioned what my fate should be and would be. Finally asked myself whether I should continue thinking of my life as something certain to end soon. Asked myself whether it was something that might last, and what I should do with it if it did last."

She turned her head to look at Kayl, who was watching her with a sad, worried expression. "I finally got to the bottom of that well inside me, finally pushed aside everything I didn't want to admit even to myself. And you know what I saw when I did that?"

"I couldn't guess," Kayl said.

"I saw you." Genji smiled at his reaction. "At that point, I realized I wanted to be with you, us fighting off every challenge together, us sharing every moment for as long as it could last. And that's why I brought up marriage."

Kayl nodded to her, trying a small smile, but his eyes still looked concerned. "You've told me before that everything was resolved inside of you."

"And I meant it every time," Genji said. "I'm not promising there's not still some serious issues hidden from me. But I've done my best to try to find all of them."

Kayl nodded, a smile flickering on his lips for a moment. "I guess I never told you how I was feeling before you showed up aboard that piece of wreckage out of nowhere."

"No, not really."

He looked down, pensive, watching his feet move. "I wasn't seeking death. Not even close. But if, the day before you showed up, someone had asked me why I was living, what the point of my life was, I wouldn't have been able to tell you. I hadn't totally given up. I was still going to go through the motions. But I couldn't have told you why."

"Aunt Hokulani told me you were looking for a new hill to die on," Genji said.

"I guess I was, even though I didn't want to admit I'd never redeem my father's reputation. But what would I do if I admitted that? What goal would replace that? I had no idea."

"And then the goddess of chaos, in the form of me, showed up to shower you with her gifts," Genji said.

"And I found reasons again," Kayl said, nodding. This time his smile stayed in place as he looked at her.

"That's funny, isn't it?" Genji said. "A woman seeking a death with purpose, and a man who no longer knew why he was alive. When those two negatives came together, we ended up with a huge positive. Eventually."

"Yeah." Kayl looked at her again, his smile vanished. "Selene, I've never pushed you for details on what you experienced, will experience, in the Universal War. But every once in a while you reveal something, and then I wonder how much else there is. I mean, you'd never told me that the Spear of Humanity regarded alloys like you as a primary target. You'd never told me you were so badly wounded you almost died. Twice."

"How am I supposed to tell you such things?" Genji asked. "Do you want the details? I've got a lot of very vivid memories, but I don't like calling them up. Do you really want to know?" She pointed to herself. "My right boob. Your favorite. Should I describe how it got ripped up and had to undergo regeneration reconstruction? Should I talk about how I killed that Spear whose shot tore up my chest? And then how I killed the female Spear who was taunting me about it because she thought I was so badly wounded I was helpless?"

Kayl flinched and looked away.

"I'm not trying to make it hard, Kayl," Genji said. "It is hard. There's no other way for it to be. Do you want me to share things like that?"

"If I'm honest," Kayl said, "no. Unless you need to share them. If that's what you need, then I will listen."

"That is exactly the answer I needed," Genji said. "And that is part of why you are the partner I need. And that is why I asked if you still wanted to get married. Did you like how I did that? Brought it back around to the topic of marriage?"

Kayl managed a half smile in response. "Your relationship skills are dazzling."

"My relationship skills? I have relationship skills? When did that happen?" She couldn't stop laughing for more than a minute, and eventually Kayl joined in.

WHEN OWEN AWOKE THE next morning, he was still uncertain whether or not he was dreaming all of this. But they were in the room they'd found in the resort town at the other end of the trail, and Selene was in his arms.

They hadn't found any trace of increased security here. Apparently they had completely thrown off those pursuing them. "These are our last fake IDs," Selene noted when they found an available car with a full charge of power. "I found another cash card in my pack, but even with that we haven't got cash to burn anymore."

"We'll have enough for at least a few days once we reach LA," Owen said. "Ready, Lieutenant Genji?"

She gestured forward as if giving a command. "Proceed as directed, Lieutenant Owen."

"Let's see how far we get today before we decide where to stop."

The scenery was pleasant, the car handled driving along the winding, up-and-down mountain road, and Selene was beside him, still smiling at him whenever he looked at her. They were still up in the mountains, not yet wending down onto one of the routes leading into LA. "I had an idea last night," Owen said. "If Malani can be appointed by you as the guardian of your genome, could she also represent you in other legal matters?"

"Such as what?" Selene asked.

"Such as that getting you declared legally a person thing."

She stared at him, startled. "That doesn't happen until the 2160s . . . But it could happen earlier, couldn't it? Because I'm in 2140."

"That's what I was thinking," Owen said. "Attitudes haven't hardened. Yes, you're an alloy, but to most people, you're a human-appearing person who has some alien DNA. Maybe we can get you legally declared a person long before it originally happened, and maybe it wouldn't arouse as much opposition as that caused, or will cause, in the future you lived."

Selene had to take a moment to absorb that idea. "Let's do that. Even if Malani can't do it, or doesn't want to, maybe Aunt Hokulani can do it."

"All right, then."

She leaned against him. He held her, watching the road, hoping he wouldn't wake from this dream.

They'd seen a few other cars, usually maintaining the same distance ahead and behind since the autopilots tended to use the same speeds. But in midmorning, as their vehicle followed a winding road through a heavily forested area, another car came into sight behind them, overtaking them quickly. Owen watched it, wondering if it was an unmarked security vehicle. But why would a single car be sent after them?

"Problem?" Selene asked, following his gaze. "They're moving fast."

"They're driving on manual," Owen said. "I guess they think it's safe to race because there are so few cars on this road." The car reached them and swerved around their vehicle, heading for the next turn at high speed. "I guess they weren't after us."

The car vanished around the turn up ahead.

A few moments later, they heard the whump of something heavy hitting something else heavy.

As their car came around the curve, Owen saw the other vehicle had bounced off a massive tree. The front and one side of the car was wrecked, flames flickering inside, one door open and a body sprawled partway out.

He hit the manual override on their car, accelerating and

then braking hard to a halt about three meters from the wrecked vehicle. Selene leapt out from her side as Owen followed.

"Get him!" Selene called, pointing to the person halfway out of the car and making disjointed efforts to pull himself clear. "There's someone else inside!"

Owen grabbed the injured person, seeing that it was a teenage boy and pulling him away from the car. "My leg!" the boy sobbed. "My dad!"

Propping the boy against the same tree that had destroyed their vehicle, Owen turned to help Selene.

She had already dived into the car despite the flames, her UV Aversive clothing offering only partial protection. As Owen watched, Selene pulled a large man clear of the car. Just as the man's feet cleared the wrecked vehicle, the car's power supply went up, turning the car into a blowtorch. Selene staggered backward several more steps, dragging the limp man clear, before lowering him to the ground and dropping to her knees.

"Is he dead?" the boy cried.

Owen knew the feeling behind those words. Knew how it had felt when his family had received word of Cathal Owen's death. He knelt beside the man, using his first aid training. "He's breathing. Pulse seems okay." Peeling back the man's eyelids, Owen checked his pupils. "I think it's a concussion, but not one that'll kill him quickly. If we can get responders here fast, he should be okay. Do you have your phone?"

"Yeah." The boy hauled it out, gazing at it frantically. "It's finding a link."

Selene, wincing, was pulling off her UV Aversive hat, jacket, and gloves, her skin glowing in the light of the sun.

"You're the alien," the boy said, his voice reflecting a different kind of shock.

Selene looked at him. "Most of me is human. And parts of that got burned. Kayl, does the first aid kit in the car have any burn spray?"

"It should." Owen ran to get it and bring it back, applying the spray to Selene's hands and lower arms.

"Ahhhh," she sighed in relief. "He's got some burns, too. Take care of him."

Owen bent over the man, applying the spray to burned areas of the skin. "Are you sure I got all of yours?"

"I'll let you know if anything else hurts really bad."

"You're the alien," the boy repeated, staring at her. "Dad said . . . Dad said you were here to hurt us."

Selene shook her head. "Lucky for your dad, he was wrong. I just want to save a lot of lives."

"He's . . . he's got a stunner on him. He said if we saw you, we should make sure we . . . we took you out. Are you hurt bad?"

"I've been hurt worse," Selene said, getting up and wincing some more.

"I couldn't move," the boy said, looking like he was barely holding back tears. "But you went right in there. It was on fire and you went right in there."

Selene gave him a brief smile. "That's what you do when someone needs help, right? I'm glad we were here. How's your phone link coming?"

"It's— Yes. Yes! Hello! Yes, we have an emergency. Our car wrecked and my dad is hurt. A concussion, maybe. And I think my leg is broken. We need help. No, we're not alone. Thanks." The boy looked at Selene and Owen. "They're scrambling a responder bird."

Selene turned to Owen. "We've done what we can. We should get out of here."

"I agree," Owen said. "Let me check the boy's father again and—"

"ID confirmation?" the boy was saying. "Okay. I'm Frederick Hoster. Frederick David Hoster. My dad is David Hoster."

Owen saw Selene jerk, her eyes widening in shock. She

turned toward where the boy sat, her gaze fixed on him, her expression rigid, her hands twitching as if preparing to attack a dangerous foe. "It's him."

"Selene?"

"I recognize him now. Younger, but it's him." Her hands stiffened as if preparing to strike at an enemy.

As she took a step toward the boy, Owen grabbed her arm. "Selene? What are you—?"

She threw off his grasp with a quick motion, taking another step toward the boy, her breathing ragged.

"*Selene*," Owen said again, not touching her this time, but putting all the urgency he could into his voice. "What's happening? What's wrong? What are you doing?"

Selene's leg jerked, as if she was going to take another step, but was fighting herself against the impulse.

Her expression as she gazed at the boy had shifted to loathing and anger.

The boy hadn't noticed, bent over his phone as he talked to the emergency responder line.

"Selene, please tell me what's wrong!" Owen said, wondering if he should try to physically restrain her again, knowing that if he did, he might end up knocked out on the ground given her strange behavior.

She abruptly turned away from the boy, taking deep breaths, actually shaking with some emotion that twisted her face. "I can't," she whispered in an agonized voice.

"Can't what?" Owen asked.

"Kill him," she said, her words barely able to be heard even from this close.

7

THEY'RE GOING TO BE here soon," the boy called out, oblivious to the drama occurring near him.

"Selene, what the hell?" Owen whispered, his own voice fierce now. "What are you talking about?"

"Just get us out of here," she whispered, her voice shaking. "Get us out of here before I . . ."

Owen turned to look at the boy. "We have to leave. You understand."

"Yeah," the boy called back. "I know. They're looking for you. I thought . . . My dad said you were evil. Her especially. He was wrong. He'd be dead if not for you. If not for her pulling him out through the fire. I'm going to tell him. I'm going to tell everybody."

"Okay," Owen said. "Just give us a little head start out of here, all right? Before you tell the responders exactly who helped you?"

"A full day," the boy said. "Is that long enough? Then I'll tell everybody."

"That's long enough." Owen tried to lead Selene back to their car, but she resisted, her hands twitching again. "Should I push, or would that be dangerous for me?" he murmured to her.

She jerked as if coming out of a daze, walking with rough movements to the car, getting in, sitting rigidly as the door closed.

Not wanting to waste a moment, Owen jumped into the driver's seat and activated the autopilot again, the car gliding forward, his last view of the boy and his father in the rearview quickly obscured by trees as the road turned, the pale smoke from the burning vehicle still rising into the sky.

They traveled in silence for a couple of minutes before Selene spoke. "Monster."

"Who?" Owen asked in what he hoped was a calm voice.

"Him."

"That boy?"

"Will grow into a man whose words will help inspire and grow the Spear of Humanity," she said, each word sounding as if it had been forced out. "So many deaths . . . because of him . . ."

"He's just a boy," Owen objected.

"A boy who will grow into a monster!" Selene yelled, her face filled with fury. "I could have stopped him! I could have killed him before he made a single speech, wrote a single word, gained a single follower! And I couldn't! What the hell is wrong with me? Why couldn't I kill him?"

How to answer that? Owen wondered, shocked by her words. "Are you sure that's him?"

"Yes! He couldn't be anyone else! Turn us around, Kayl! Take us back there!"

"No."

She faced him, her eyes blazing with anger. "Don't make me hurt you! Take us back there!"

"Do you think you'd be able to kill him this time?" Owen asked, keeping his voice calm with great difficulty.

"I . . . !" Selene buried her face in her hands. "No. I . . . can't. I've failed."

Neither of them said anything for several minutes, the car purring along at the maximum safe speed, Selene keeping her face hidden in her hands, the pillar of smoke behind them diminishing in size. Owen spotted a dot in the sky that was probably the emergency responder bird. "The responders are there," he said, knowing she would understand that meant their window to do anything else had closed.

Selene's shoulders shook. "I want to hurt you. I want to hurt myself," she said in a low voice. "I'm so . . . so angry. I could've stopped him."

"You couldn't kill a teenage boy for the crimes he hadn't yet committed," Owen said.

"So many deaths . . ." Selene whispered.

"I don't get something, though," Owen added. "Just before we left, he told me his father had been wrong in saying you were evil. He said he was going to tell everyone."

"He's going to tell everyone how awful I am," Selene said, bent over, her voice still muffled behind the hands covering her face. "How awful all aliens are."

"He seemed really grateful that you'd pulled his father out of the car."

"He's a monster. He won't care. Why was I so weak? Why couldn't I . . . ?"

"Selene," Owen said, "you will never convince me that you were wrong to not kill a boy for something he hadn't done yet."

"Shut up." The words came out harsh, like a warning. "Earth is going to be destroyed in 2180. Because I was weak. Everything else we've done was useless."

"Selene—"

"Shut up!"

She didn't say anything else, and he was smart enough not to, either.

The car kept moving through the rest of the day, down from the mountains along a winding road, a storm marching past to their left, dark clouds and sheets of rain visible, the sun dipping toward the horizon. Just before nightfall, the car pulled into a recharge facility and swapped out its power packs, asking if it should keep going or find a hotel for them. Kayl tapped the keep going command without speaking.

Selene had lowered her hands, but kept her face averted from him, staring out her window into the growing darkness.

The day before this had been the happiest of his life. Selene agreeing they should marry, finally opening up about some of the things that had driven her, both of them sharing things they'd still withheld from the other. There hadn't seemed to be any barriers left between them.

But now there was a wall again. A wall of ice between his side of the car and the side where Selene sat, unmoving, saying nothing. Was she hurt? Angry? What else could he have done, though? Assist her in killing a teenage boy for what he would or might someday do?

Maybe, after all, Selene had been right soon after they met, when she said it could never work, that he knew too little about her. Maybe that day of joy had been a bonfire of delusion, both of them pretending they could be happy together. She had said surgery in the 2170s could remove all scars, but that had only meant the physical scars. The scars inside were still there.

What else could he have done?

That was the worst part, in some ways, knowing that he wouldn't have been able to act otherwise. That there hadn't been any other choice he could have accepted. If Selene couldn't live with that . . . maybe forever had always been an illusion. Maybe even tomorrow was too much to hope for.

Or, maybe, this was where he was demanded to step up. Selene was obviously in pain, obviously torn. She hadn't killed the boy. If she had, he'd be facing a whole different set of far worse misgivings now, wondering who Selene really was. But Selene had stopped herself. What was it she was feeling now? *You're not just in this relationship for the good times, the happy times, are you?* Owen asked himself. Did Selene's inability to ask for help right now mean he had a bigger obligation to provide it? This wasn't a long-term thing yet, not a pattern. It was several hours of pain for both of them, but mostly, he thought, for Selene. If he walked away because of this, he'd be making a mockery of his own expressed desire to stay with her through the worst as well as the best.

But this was some kind of misery. It felt as if the universe had decided to balance the extreme happiness of the day before by showing him how tough life with Selene could be. Showing him . . . or testing him.

Owen didn't know the answer. So he resolved to keep doing his best, and see what happened. Because he did know that Selene Genji deserved his best, especially when she was feeling her worst.

He had the car pull over about midnight to a drive-through vending stop. His appetite had vanished somewhere in the mountains, so Owen only got some coffee. Selene refused to order anything, so he got her some tea and set it in the cupholder nearest her. She ignored it.

As dawn turned the sky behind them to a pale bar of growing light, the stars dimming, the car entered the eastern suburbs of Greater LA.

Owen gazed out at the glowing lights, his vision blurry with fatigue. He'd only napped sporadically. "We need to stop to rest."

Selene didn't say anything.

"I'm going to stop us so we can rest," Owen said.

Still nothing.

He picked a mid-scale hotel. Not a cheap one the police would search first, nor a high-end one that might ask questions, but a comfortable, safe place with fully automated check-in. Their last set of fake IDs was accepted without any hesitation, the last anonymous cash card covered the room for the day and the next night, and the hotel directed the car to a parking spot near the room.

Owen got out of the car, waiting.

After nearly a minute, Selene got out, too, standing facing away from him.

Grabbing their backpacks, Owen led the way to their room. It wasn't bad, generic as hotel rooms went, which meant comfortable enough.

Selene lay down on one side of the bed, facing away, saying nothing.

Sighing, Owen lay down on the other side, looking up at the ceiling. "Privacy," he ordered the hotel digital assistants.

He woke up in the afternoon. Selene hadn't moved, still on her side facing away from him. Even though he wasn't particularly hungry, he knew they couldn't keep on without food. "I'm going to order something. What do you want? Selene, please talk to me."

Nothing.

"Are you punishing me or yourself?"

Nothing.

Tempted to order something he knew she didn't particularly like, Owen instead got some of their favorites, along with sencha green tea. When it arrived, he set it on the table near her. "Selene, please."

She sat up on the bed. With shocking suddenness, Selene grabbed her pillow, stuffed her face in it, and screamed as if her lungs were being scalded by acid, the pillow unable to completely muffle the sound.

"Emergency?" the hotel assistant inquired, jarred out of privacy mode by the sound of distress.

"No emergency," Owen said, watching Selene anxiously.

"No emergency," Selene gasped, raising her face from the pillow.

"Confirm no emergency?"

"No emergency," Selene repeated.

"No emergency," Owen added. "Resume privacy." He watched Selene, slumped on the bed. "Can I tell you how scared I am right now?"

She shook her head in despair. "Failed. Everything for nothing. I could have . . ."

"Killed a boy? How many times have you said that you need to save lives to save the Earth?"

"Not that life," Selene said.

"I don't think I'll ever believe you were wrong not to kill him."

"That's because you don't know how much pain and death he'll cause," Selene said, her voice dull. "You'll see. It's inevitable now. Because I failed."

He had no idea what to say.

His phone beeped with a news alert. Since Owen had set it to be alert for any items on the "alien," he checked it.

A news conference. A familiar-looking boy standing in front, speaking. Nerving himself for a blast of hate, Owen turned up the volume on a private setting.

Owen watched and listened, seeing a powerful but still budding charisma in the words, the gestures, and the eyes of Frederick David Hoster. When he reached adulthood, he'd be mesmerizing.

Maybe Selene had been right.

But, as he listened to Hoster, Owen felt his jaw drop.

"Selene? Listen to this."

She looked over, seeing the face of Frederick David Hoster. "No."

"It's important."

"No! There's nothing he can say that I want to hear!"

Owen nodded slowly, thinking through his words. "Selene, do you trust me?" She didn't answer. "I think you need to hear this. I think it's very important that you hear this."

"Fine!" Her expression was as angry as her tone of voice as Selene turned up the volume.

"—judge people by what they do?" Hoster was saying. "Shouldn't *we* judge these aliens the same way? Shouldn't *we* look at what they do? I saw one of them, the one we're being told to fear, crawl through *flames* to save my father's life! She . . . I'm calling her *she*, not 'the alien,' because that was a *person* who saved my father. *She* got hurt saving him. I'll *never* be able to pay *her* back. And I think we should all give *her* a chance. I think she's *human* in all the ways that count."

Selene's expression had shifted through skepticism to amazement to disbelief. "That's . . . that's . . . What's he doing?"

"He saw you save his father's life," Owen said.

"But . . . but . . . he's . . ."

"You collided with his life, Selene. You changed his vector."

"That's impossible." She looked at him, totally baffled. "Someone like that . . . It's impossible."

"The earlier you change a vector," Owen said, "the larger the impact on the course of something. In the history you knew, we weren't there when that car wrecked. Hoster grew up angry, remembering his father's words about the Tramontine, probably filled with guilt because he couldn't move while his father burned to death in that car, probably blaming the aliens for everything wrong in his life. In the history you just made, he knows an alien saved his father's life. Maybe, in this history, he won't be a force behind the growth of the Spear of Humanity. Maybe, because you risk yourself to help others without thinking about who they are, and because you couldn't kill a boy, maybe something big just tipped in a different direction than it originally did."

"Is that possible?" Selene stared at the image, listening. "He's really . . . He's saying aliens are human, too, Kayl. He is saying that. Do you know what he was going to say about alloys in the 2160s? Inhuman monsters who needed to be exterminated. That's what he said about *me*. What did we do?"

"Sometimes," Owen said, "the things we do by accident seem to have as much impact as what we're trying to do."

"What if I'd—" Selene buried her face in her hands again for a moment. "What if— Some of the Spears who killed my mother had his tracts on them. Preaching hate. Despite that, my mother wouldn't have wanted me to kill him. I know that. But after she was murdered, I just wanted to kill Spears. And when I saw him, that face . . ." She shuddered. "If you hadn't stopped me . . ."

"Selene," Owen said. "I didn't stop you. You stopped yourself. You know full well that if you'd been determined to get to that boy, I would have ended up dazed on the ground while you . . . broke his neck, or however someone gets killed using bare hands."

"Breaking the neck is kind of a crude way of doing it," Selene said.

"I wouldn't know," Owen said, "since I've never seen you kill anyone with your bare hands."

"Hopefully you never will." She looked down at her hands. "Kayl? Do you remember what I was like when you interrogated me aboard the *Vigilant* the first time?"

"Yes," Owen said. "You thought it was an interrogation of a prisoner of war, and I thought it was just a witness statement of a survivor."

Selene met his eyes with her own gaze. "That Lieutenant Selene Genji would have killed that boy. It would have been hard for her, but she would have done it."

He stared back at her, startled and unsettled by her words. "I don't think you were that hard-core back then."

"You don't? Until you convinced me of the possibility it was 2140, I was planning on how to break out of the sickbay and kill as many of your crew as possible before I got taken down," Selene said. "You never realized that, did you? We were from different times. Literally. My time had taught me some very hard lessons. Kayl, I told you once that I thought my mother had sent me to you. Now I know it. Because I couldn't kill that boy. Not anymore. She knew you could help me reconnect with her, with who I was trying to be before my mother was murdered. And she was right."

Owen blinked, trying to absorb what Selene had told him. "That is definitely the nicest thing you ever said to me."

"You're making it about you again?" she asked. Then she smiled for just a moment to take any sting from the words. "How do I thank you for helping me once more reconnect with the person my mother wanted me to be?"

He shrugged, uncomfortable with such an appraisal of himself. "I don't know. Maybe you could marry me?"

"Didn't I already agree to that?"

"I was seriously wondering if that had changed," Owen said.

She nodded ruefully. "I can understand why. Are you sure you still want to spend forever with me?"

"Just tell me whether that long silent treatment was because you were mad at me."

Selene shook her head. "I was mad at myself. For my weakness. I wanted to punish myself. I found myself wondering if you'd walk away, because I deserved that kind of punishment for failing my battle comrades who would die in the future as a result of my weakness. But . . . yes . . . I guess I was also mad at you for being someone who'd influenced me that way. Who'd helped me regain some things, so I couldn't kill that boy."

"I take it you're not mad at me for that anymore," Owen said.

"And you sound resentful, as you should," Selene said. "I'm sorry. Can you forgive me?"

"Of course I can," Owen said. "If you'd stayed mad day after day, refusing to speak with me, that would have been different. But I don't think Selene Genji is that sort of person. I do think I've learned that much about her."

Selene looked at him, her expression somber. "I'm still learning who she is."

"We can do that together. You were trying to make me leave you?" Owen asked. "To punish yourself?"

"Yes."

He nodded. "All right. That means you think having me around is a good thing?"

She looked at him, a smile forming. "Yes."

"In that case, spending forever together would be good," Owen said. "Or maybe longer."

"Hopefully we've still got at least until June twelfth, 2180. But if we manage to succeed in our mission, forever with you is sounding better all the time," Selene said. "I can't believe . . . I am so hungry. What did you get us to eat? Spam fried rice and Spam musubi? Seriously?"

"I couldn't find any place with taratarabis on the menu," Owen said.

"You'd think you could find alien rabbit on the menu somewhere in LA," Selene said.

"You're telling jokes," Owen said, surprised to realize how much tension had filled him until its absence let him know it had gone. "I'm glad you're back."

"Me, too." Selene leaned in and held him so tightly it hurt. "Me, too."

THEY HAD TWO DAYS until Malani was due in LA for the genetics conference, barely enough money to cover that time, and no idea how to get more money. "What about Admiral Tecumseh?" Selene asked.

"Rear Admiral Tecumseh?" Owen shook his head. "They must be watching her home. We'd never make it to her."

Selene held out a phone. "This is one of the burner phones Tecumseh gave us. Yes, I held on to it through everything."

Owen gazed at the phone in surprise. "I love you."

"Of course you do." Selene offered him the phone. "Text or call?"

"Text is safer if there's any chance of the call being monitored." Owen paused to think before drafting a short text.

In town. Any chance meet up?

"Let's wait a couple of hours for a reply," Owen said. "Are you looking up something?"

Selene paused in her input to the room entertainment panel. "Do you remember that one woman saying something about watching an interview with Krysta? I'm trying to see if I can call that up."

The interview was hard to watch. Krysta, still in a hospital bed, still attached to various monitors, looking weak. Text alongside the image explained that she'd taken four injuries, three from bullets and one from an energy bolt.

"Stupid kid," Selene said, blinking back tears as she watched. "Why did she do that?"

"She seems to think a whole lot of that Lieutenant Genji," Owen said.

"And that Lieutenant Owen." As the short interview ended, Selene paused. "Wait. There's another link. Kayl, it's your aunt Hokulani."

"What?" Owen watched and listened in growing amazement.

"She has asked if she can stay with me once she's healthy enough," Aunt Hokulani was saying. "And they say it's okay if I do that. And Kayl, he's my nephew, told her to come to me if she needed help. So I'm going to do that. He obviously cares about this girl Krysta. And so does Lieutenant Genji, who I have said before is a very good person. You heard Krysta say that, too, didn't you? So, in a couple of weeks, I will put her up for the time being, so Kayl and Selene Genji will know Krysta is okay."

They sat watching for a moment after the brief interview ended. "I love Aunt Hokulani," Selene finally said.

Hours went by without any reply to the text. "What are our options?" Selene asked. "Just lay low until the conference, figure out how to meet Malani, and then . . . ?"

"It's hard to plan when we know so little of what's going on and have to stay undercover." Owen had been trying to think through possibilities. "There's someone who could tell us what's going on inside Earth Guard, and maybe why Rear Admiral Tecumseh isn't answering me. He's down in San Diego, though. I'll have to see if we can get there and back with the money we have left."

"About that," Selene said, holding up a cash card. "I checked the pockets in my uniform and found a card that I must have picked up on Dorcas's ship."

"Really? How much is on it?"

"Enough for several days more if we don't spend lavishly and get a room at one of those by-the-week temp worker places. Who's this person in San Diego? Another ex-girlfriend?"

"We have yet to meet any ex-girlfriend of mine," Owen said. "It's Edourd Guyon, the ex–juvenile delinquent Martian colonist. I haven't talked to him in at least a couple of years, but he's still in Earth Guard. He should be able to tell us what's going on from an insider perspective."

"And he's reliable?" Selene asked. "He won't turn on us?"

"Not if he's the Edourd Guyon I knew."

"People do change, Kayl. But if he's our best option, it's worth a try. Your old acquaintances on Mars certainly helped us. And if we get spotted around San Diego, and they start seriously looking for us around there, that's all to the good, because we'll be heading back up here to LA."

GENJI SAT WATCHING THE endless city roll past the windows of the train. When she would take this trip in the 2160s with her mother, she had played a game of trying to tell where Los Angeles ended and San Diego began. It was impossible to tell by then, the two megalopolises having grown north and south until the northward and the southern marches of suburbs and town centers and industry and everything else had collided and merged. Maps provided dividing lines that were no longer visible to the eye.

It was already like that in 2140, Genji saw. She wondered when growth had slowed, when the stagnation of the 2140s melded into the decline of the 2150s, until growing disruptions in the 2160s led to the Universal War.

What would it be like to be able to see what was here, and not see what was to come?

"Do I want to know?" Kayl asked her. He'd read her mood, and assumed she was thinking of places devastated by the war.

"Nothing happened to this area until June twelfth, 2180," Genji said. "It was well defended by the time anyone tried strikes against it."

"That's good to know," Kayl said. "I guess."

"Yeah. Same outcome in the end, if we don't manage to change things enough."

From the train station, they were able to hop a fairly short ride to where Ed Guyon's address was listed. Genji insisted they get tickets heading back north using their last set of false IDs before they left the station, though. "Just in case," she said. "Because it has been years since you talked to him."

From what Kayl had told her about Edourd, Genji wasn't surprised when they reached the address and it turned out to be for a high-rise near a beach.

Kayl brought out a spare phone and punched in the number, waiting. "Hey, Ed. It's Duke." A pause. "Yeah." Another pause. "I thought I'd drop by. Is that okay by you? Good. Okay."

Ending the call, he turned to Genji. "He sounded happy to hear from me."

"But?" she prompted.

"No but," Kayl said. "He sounded like Ed. And he said he'll turn off his security systems, including the door."

"Okay." Genji walked with Kayl, trying not to let her worries prejudice her against Kayl's old friend.

As they approached Ed's apartment, the door remained silent, appearing to confirm that the security was off.

Kayl rapped out a pattern on the door. "I think you'll like Ed," he said as they waited.

"I hope so," Genji said.

A moment later the door opened to reveal a man with a wide smile and the narrow, tall body of someone raised on Mars. "Long time, Duke! Come on in!"

Genji followed Kayl, trying not to read anything into the lack of a greeting for her.

"This is Selene," Kayl said as the door closed behind them.

"Hey!" Ed said with another smile, accompanied by a small wave at her but only a glance in her direction.

"Hey," Genji said, waving back in the same fashion. Normally this was when she'd pull off her UV Aversive hat, but she decided to wait to relax until she got a better feel for things here.

As Kayl and Ed exchanged the greetings of old friends who hadn't seen each other in years, Genji looked about the apartment. The furnishings clearly reflected Ed's love for large bodies of water, as did the many pictures on the wall, portraying static or moving images of water sports. There weren't any pictures at all of Mars, though. Ed didn't seem to want to be reminded of his youth.

There was one image of a younger Kayl Owen along with a younger Edourd, both of them on a beach along with a couple of young women. "Who's this?" Genji asked Kayl with a smile.

He looked, and laughed. "The blonde was with Ed, and the one with bright green hair was a friend of hers. I think that's the only time I met her, right, Ed?"

Edourd once again glanced quickly toward Genji, then away. "Yeah. I think so."

"Ed kept trying to set me up," Kayl said.

"Lucky for me, he failed," Genji said, watching the reflection of Ed in the protective coating of a nearby picture. Not aware he was being watched, Ed displayed an instant of discomfort.

Was she reading too much into this? Into Ed not trying to talk to her at all despite Kayl's attempts to bring her into the conversation? She had a lot of experience with being shunned in social situations, though, and this was feeling too much like that. Ed didn't have to like her, but was there more to it than social discomfort?

"Ed, can you tell us anything about what's going on inside Earth Guard?" Kayl asked.

"Inside Earth Guard?" Ed made a dismissive gesture. "Same old."

"What about Selene and me, specifically?"

"I'm not working that," Ed said, sounding apologetic. "It's being held in tight channels. You understand."

Kayl glanced at Genji, letting her see that he was puzzled by Ed's lack of information. "What about attitudes, then? How are people thinking and talking about Selene? Is there any more talk about what really happened aboard the *Lifeguard*?"

Ed hesitated. "I haven't heard much."

Genji decided to try a specific question. "How about the modifications to the power regulation system on the *Lifeguard*? Is there any discussion of that?"

"I haven't heard anything," Ed said, keeping his attention on Kayl.

"Nothing?" Kayl asked, startled. "What about Commander Montoya? What's happened to her?"

"Montoya?" Ed shrugged. "I might've heard something. I need to think. Why are you asking about her?"

"We're worried," Kayl said. "She took a big risk letting us off the ship again after Selene saved it from blowing up."

"So she helped you?"

"She kept her promise after her ship and crew were saved."

"Really?" Ed looked away for a moment. "Have you talked to anyone else? In Earth Guard?"

Kayl hesitated, giving Genji another look. She shook her head slightly, bothered by Ed's attitude and lack of information.

"No," Kayl said. "Why do you ask?"

"Somebody helped you on Mars," Ed pointed out.

"No, not really," Kayl said.

"Oh, come on," Ed said with a laugh. "You must have met some people. I mean, that bit on the Moon! How'd you do that? I know some of the Earth Guard people up there. Who'd you run into?"

Kayl shook his head. Genji could see he was growing uneasy with Ed's questions. "Nobody, really," he said.

Deciding to test her suspicions, Genji walked past Ed as she pretended to be engrossed in the pictures, deliberately moving within less than arm's length from him.

As she did so, he flinched backward.

Oh, hell. This had gone from uncomfortable to worrisome.

Genji caught Kayl's eye, jogging her head slightly toward the kitchen, hoping he would get the hint.

Kayl nodded back almost imperceptibly. "Hey, Ed, what've you got to drink?" Kayl headed for the kitchen without waiting for a reply, Ed hastily following.

As soon as they were out of sight, Genji moved to the nearest home control panel, calling up the security systems. Finding the override for the antiquated system took her only three quick tries.

She wasn't surprised, but was saddened for Kayl's sake, to see that the security systems were still on. They had been set to passive mode so they would record information but not act in ways that would alert anyone to the activity.

Genji erased all the saved data and video, including the most recent, and deactivated all the security systems. She turned to pretend to be examining a nearby picture as Kayl and Ed came back out of the kitchen holding soft drinks.

"Did you want anything, Selene?" Kayl said, acting as if that had just occurred to him.

"Some water," she said, her eyes meeting his with a warning message in them.

"I'm a lousy host!" Ed announced. "Let me get some!" He turned and went back into the kitchen quickly.

Kayl jerked his thumb toward the kitchen, a question on his face.

Genji shook her head. Pointing her own thumb at the door,

she nodded her head that way as well, warning him they should leave.

Kayl nodded, glancing toward the kitchen, clearly wondering what was taking Ed so long.

Ed finally came out, smiling, with a paper cup of water that he sat on an end table rather than handing it to Genji. "Sorry! Where were we, Kayl?"

Kayl smiled regretfully. "We just stopped by to say hi, Ed. We need to go."

"What? No, no! You need a place to stay, right? You'll be okay here."

"We have to go," Kayl said.

"I might be able to help you," Ed said. "You were asking about people. How about Hector Thanh?"

"Hector Thanh?" Kayl repeated as if the name were only vaguely familiar.

"Yeah, on Mars. Didn't he help you out?"

"Hector Thanh," Kayl said again, as if dredging through his memory. "I trained with him, didn't I? He's on Mars?"

"Yeah," Ed said. "He's been talking about helping you. What did he do?"

"I thought you hadn't heard anything relating to Selene or me," Kayl said.

"No details, I meant."

"Okay," Kayl said. "Hey, we have to go."

"But . . . look, I didn't want to worry you," Ed said. "Earth Guard was tipped off that the local police are going to be DNA checking everyone on the streets tonight. You should stay here."

"They can't be checking everyone's DNA outside of a transportation node," Kayl said. "DNA street dragnets were outlawed in 2134."

"Well, yeah," Ed said. "But not for, you know." He made a jerky motion toward Genji.

"You mean for *her*?" Kayl said.

"Yeah."

"How come you haven't talked to her, Ed?"

"What are you implying?"

Kayl looked around him. "That was an awful long time to get a glass of water. And why'd you use a disposable cup instead of an actual glass?"

"It was handy."

"Why don't you want us to leave, Ed? You notified the police about us when you were in the kitchen just now, didn't you?"

8

ED LOOKED SHOCKED. "WHY would you think that? Unless you're being controlled somehow. You listened to her, didn't you? Gave her a chance to get into your brain. Kayl, our orders were clear. Don't let her talk. Don't let her touch you."

"I never received orders not to talk to her or touch her," Kayl said, his voice rough with anger. "What's supposed to be so dangerous about touching her?"

"Alien tech!" Ed shouted. "We don't know what it could do. A touch could inject us with something. The chain of command knows more than any of us. That's why we got those orders, and why we follow those orders. I know what happens when people don't listen to authority! Instead, you're listening to an alien. What'd she tell you about me?"

"You didn't shut off your security systems," Genji said.

"How did you—?" Ed fixed his gaze on Kayl again. "Everything is being recorded. Just tell me you need help, and together we can hold off . . . that until the police get here."

"Ed," Kayl said, "I do need help, but that's because of people who are scared of Selene. She isn't any danger to me or anyone else. She wants to protect the Earth. She wants to protect everyone on Earth."

"You protect people by following orders, Kayl! By doing what you're told!"

"Like you did growing up on Mars?" Kayl demanded.

"I was a young idiot on Mars! Fighting against the rules and procedures that kept us all safe and alive. I grew up and learned better." Ed shook his head. "I learned to trust authority. You should, too."

"Even after Earth Guard tried to kill me?"

"Who told you that?"

"Nobody told me, Ed," Kayl said. "After three tries to murder me in quick succession, I kind of figured it out for myself!"

"You can't be serious," Edourd said. "Earth Guard is trying to help you."

"That's not how Admiral Besson came across when he interrogated me," Kayl said. "Ed, *you* are being used, not me."

"You're blind, Kayl. Either that, or you're a traitor to the species. Alarm, alarm, alarm!" Ed called, pausing and looking about him when nothing happened.

"I already shut off the systems," Genji said.

"Ed, why the hell?" Kayl demanded. "You're the last person I'd expect to—" He stopped, gazing at Edourd. "You alerted the authorities on Mars that we were there, didn't you? Your cousin told you Duke was there, and you passed that on to the security forces who were trying to kill both her and *me*."

"My cousin is a young idiot," Ed said, dropping all pretense. "Like I used to be. He's still fighting the system. He thinks that nonsense on the Martian Commons was inspiring instead of dangerous. Kayl, you took an oath to protect people and help people. It's about time you remembered that oath instead of being manipulated by an alien agent out to turn us into slaves!"

"The Tramontine aren't a threat," Kayl said.

"Because that alien agent told you so?"

"I've met the Tramontine. I've been on their ship. Doesn't that make me more qualified to judge them than you?"

"The people in charge make those decisions, not you! Especially when you're not thinking straight. That thing doesn't belong on our planet and you can't see that because it's controlling you! Free yourself!"

"The team sent to our apartment on Mars targeted both of us," Kayl said. "Every attack has targeted both Selene and me. We were friends. Doesn't that bother you? That your actions might have resulted in my death?"

"*If* that happened," Ed said heatedly, "it would have been your fault for associating with an enemy of humanity."

Genji had taken advantage of Ed switching his attention back and forth to move closer to him. Now she nodded to Kayl.

Kayl made a swift motion with his hand on the side away from Genji, drawing Ed's gaze.

Genji moved in fast, her first blow hitting as Ed began to turn back toward her. As he fell onto the couch, she struck again, ensuring he was unconscious.

She and Kayl exited fast before slowing to a sedate pace that wouldn't attract attention as they reached the street again.

"I guess you and your buddy Ed never talked politics," Genji said as they walked, trying to look like a pair of lovers out for a stroll.

"We did," Kayl said, sounding wounded. "Sometimes. He never expressed those kind of sentiments, though he did seem to be increasingly bothered by the things he did growing up on Mars. It's like he's gone the full arc from juvenile delinquent to authoritarian."

"People do change," Genji said.

"Did you have to hit him a second time? He looked like he was out after the first blow."

"It was the only way to be sure," Genji said, feeling only the tiniest bit guilty. She clasped his arm, leaning her head against him as a police vehicle zipped past, followed by a second and then a third.

"I didn't mind that you hit him twice," Kayl added. "I was just worried that you weren't at your best."

Genji laughed, drawing brief looks from a pair of police officers on the opposite side of the street racing in the direction they'd come from. "You were worried about me because I couldn't take out a bad guy in one hit?"

They reached a car waiting for riders. "Let's go back to your place!" Genji said. "I can't wait to get there!"

That earned her some brief eye rolls and head shakes from another pair of police heading past at a fast clip.

They settled into the car, Kayl entering an address a couple of blocks from the train station. "We'll walk to catch the next train north from there. We should be able to leave while they're still trying to figure out whether Ed really saw us."

"He might be a little hard to wake up," Genji said. "None of those police are likely to connect our happy, amorous couple with the dangerous alien and her servant that they're looking for."

"That was just camouflage?" Kayl asked, looking disappointed in a way that showed he wasn't serious. "We're not going back to my place?"

"Sorry, sailor, not tonight. Maybe you'll get lucky some other time." Genji sat back, breathing in and out slowly as the car wove through the dense downtown traffic, turning her head to look at the bright colors of the signs and the bright colors of the clothing on the people they were going past. "Sorry about your friend. I mean, the guy who used to be your friend."

Kayl sighed heavily. "How does someone go from being Edourd to being . . . Edourd? I've known a couple of people like that, who went from wild early years to becoming sort of puritans, or who were straitlaced as teens but went wild as adults. But I've never understood why deciding your past was a mistake meant swinging all the way in the other direction. Do you mind telling me how you realized so quickly what he was up to?"

Genji shrugged, still watching the colorful signs go by. "I've had a lot of experience being around people who don't want to be in the same room with me. There are tells. My main worry is not lumping people who are just feeling awkward around me in with the ones who think I'm an affront to nature."

"I was thinking it was strange he couldn't tell us anything, but then when he started trying to pump me for information on who had helped us, it went from strange to suspicious."

"That was a good job covering for Hector," Genji said.

He stayed silent for a moment. "How can anyone look at you, talk to you, and not think you're a person?"

"I don't know, Kayl. I am an alloy."

"People today don't know anything about alloys, except what they know about you."

"So, it's back on me again?" Genji said, not sure whether or not she was joking.

"That's not what I meant," Kayl said.

"I know." The car swung in beside the curb and stopped. "Let's get on a train before the security forces down here realize we really might be here."

THEY HAD GOTTEN PRETTY good at hiding in LA, hoping the burner phone would provide a message response from Admiral Tecumseh, and waiting for the genetics conference to start while scoping out the security features of the conference. The conference center had proven to be crawling with not only security equipment but also far too many security officers, in response to anonymous threats for studying alien DNA from people who hadn't read the description of the conference well enough to realize there wasn't any actual alien DNA to study.

Fortunately, the hotel where Dr. Malani Owen was staying hadn't been nearly as hard to get into undetected.

Concealed in the darkness of the hotel room, Genji heard the door lock click. Malani Owen appeared in the doorway, yawning, a cup of coffee in one hand. She stepped inside, letting the door swing closed behind her. "Lights," she said.

Nothing happened, because Genji had disabled the voice circuits in the room.

"Great," Malani grumbled, her hand fumbling for the manual light switch. The room lights came on, showing her brother sitting in one of the chairs.

"Hi, Mal," Kayl said.

Malani frantically bobbled her coffee, trying not to spill any. "Dammit, Kayl! You almost made me scald myself!"

"I've missed you, too, sis."

She set down the coffee, looking as if she wasn't sure whether to hug or hit her brother. "What are—?" The question died as Malani realized there was someone leaning against the wall behind her brother, watching her.

Genji nodded to her, smiling to hide her own nervousness.

"This is Lieutenant Selene Genji," Kayl said.

"Um, hi," Malani said. "It's nice to finally be able to meet my brother's . . . alien . . . woman . . . friend."

"It's nice to meet you, Dr. Owen," Genji said. "Kayl has told me a lot about you."

"He has?" Malani aimed a suspicious glance at Kayl. "Call me Malani, please. Or Mal. That's what we . . . in the family . . . um . . . What are . . . ?"

"We're not married, yet," Kayl hastened to assure her.

"Yet?"

"We're engaged," Kayl said.

"Does Mom know?"

"No."

"You haven't told Mom you're engaged?" Malani rolled her eyes in despair. "I'm pretty sure she wants to know about that."

"It's very hard to get through to Mom," Kayl said. "We'd be giving our location away."

"Always ready with an excuse, aren't you, Kayl?" Malani looked at Genji. "I guess we really are going to be sisters. What should I call you?"

"Selene, please."

"Are you okay?" Malani asked. "Did I say something wrong?"

"No," Genji hastened to assure her. "It's just that . . . sisters has been a difficult thing for me. Very difficult. Kayl can tell you about that someday. But now I have my Tramontine name, because they also called me Sister, and you just called me that, too . . . I'm sorry. It's hard to believe that's a happy thing now." Genji smiled at her. "And I am very happy to be sharing my life with your brother."

Malani smiled in return. "I'm happy for you, and for Kayl, even though sharing my life with him has sometimes been a pain."

"I love you, too, Mal," Kayl said.

"Selene, Kayl, it's not that I'm not happy to see you," Malani added, "but the building security system will have already reported your presence and— Why are you shaking your head, Selene?"

Genji shrugged. "It was pretty easy to hack. The building doesn't know we're here."

"Easy? The hotel staff told me they just upgraded the security system."

"It's antiquated," Genji said. "From my perspective, anyway."

"Oh. Right." Malani sat down at the desk. "Please take a seat, Selene. My brother is an oaf or he would have given you that chair."

Genji shook her head as she sat on the bed. "I told him to go ahead since I was a little nervous and wanted to stand. Your brother is pretty amazing. I hope you realize that."

"You really must be in love with him." Malani took a drink of her coffee, and then winced. "I'm sorry! Do you want me to get you any coffee, Selene?"

"No, thank you. Alloys and coffee don't mix."

"Oh, yeah. Aunt Hokulani told me that." She paused. "I'm sorry about your mother."

"Thank you. Although, it's sort of weird," Genji said. "My mother, the girl who will someday be my mother, who will be murdered when I'm seventeen, is alive right now. And . . . it's possible I'll never be born to her."

Malani eyed her. "How could that work? You have to be born to be."

"Possibly not," Genji said. "Because of all the changes Kayl and I have made to the history I knew. It's sort of complicated."

"I'll bet. It sounds like something more involved with physics than biology."

"Yes," Genji said. "Basically, the Tramontine think I have to exist now because I'm causing things to happen, and that is independent of whether or not I exist in the future. In fact, the universe may actually prefer I exist now but don't get born in the future because that would complicate things a whole lot more."

"Uh-huh," Malani said. "I'll assume that makes sense to the Tramontine. If you're not born in the future, how do you time travel back to now?"

"If I'm not born in the future," Genji said, "I don't have to time travel back to now. I'm here. No paradoxes to trouble the universe."

"Except the never being born thing."

"Yeah, except for that." Genji held out her arm. "Go ahead."

"Umm . . . what?" Malani said.

"You want to know how my skin feels. Go ahead."

"Are you sure?" Malani reached out, touching cautiously, then more firmly. "Like Aunt Hokulani said, it feels like typical skin. Is the glossiness purely cosmetic?"

"No," Genji said. "My skin is more resistant to radiation than that of full humans."

"Really? And your eyes? No problems there?"

"No," Genji said. "Not so far."

"I had someone ask me how you did eye makeup, and I was like, I have no idea," Malani said.

Genji smiled. "I don't usually attempt eye makeup. Like I told Kayl, makeup made for full human skin doesn't adhere well to my skin."

"Thanks," Malani said, looking a bit awkward. "I imagine you get tired of answering questions like that."

"I do," Genji said. "But it's okay."

"How are you, Mal?" Kayl asked.

"I'm fine," Malani said. "Except I've got government agents and countless other people watching me constantly and listening in on my calls. Do you have any idea what my life has been like the last several months?"

"I'm sorry," Genji said. "That's my fault."

"You don't have a brother, do you?" Malani asked. "It's always their fault. I understand why you haven't been able to see Mom yet, Kayl. But Mom really wants to see you again, and she really wants to meet you, Selene. What's the matter?"

Genji shrugged uncomfortably. "I've gotten Kayl into a lot of trouble. People trying to kill us. That sort of thing. I'm going to need to apologize to your mother."

"Selene, Kayl has always been getting into trouble. He attracts trouble. I think Mom, and me for that matter, are both glad to know someone else is responsible for getting him out of trouble now."

"How does Mom feel about Selene, Mal?" Kayl asked, looking worried.

"Oh, gee," Malani said. "Let's see. A woman who's taken it upon herself to try to save the entire world. A woman who has apparently saved your life . . . How many times is it now?"

"Five times," Kayl said.

"Six," Genji said.

"Six times," Malani repeated. "Strong, smart, capable enough to run rings around Earth Guard and a bunch of other people, and, yes, part alien, but everybody's got something, right? Nobody's perfect."

Genji smiled. "Kayl has done so much of that, you know. Without him, I couldn't have done any of this."

"He is my brother," Malani said, "so he's not totally without redeeming value. Why'd you come to see me? Given the risks, I'm assuming this isn't just to introduce me to my future sister."

"Two reasons," Genji said, knowing that Kayl would let her take the lead on this. "The first reason is about my genome."

"Your Tramontine heritage, you mean?" Malani asked.

"Heritage?" Genji questioned in reply. "I didn't inherit those genes. They were placed in me."

"Okay. Are you unhappy about that?"

Genji made a vague gesture. "It's what I am."

"It's *who* you are."

"I know you have good intentions," Genji said, "but please don't tell me how I should talk about myself."

Malani winced. "I deserved that."

"That's all right. Kayl used the term 'pure human' once and I nearly took his head off."

"'Pure human' is bad?"

"Yes," Genji said. "It's the term favored by the Spear of Humanity. It makes a value judgment. Full human is a much better way of saying it, because it's just a physical description. Dr. Owen, I need someone involved in genetic engineering and research who I can trust."

"Do you need me to contact someone?" Malani asked.

"She's talking about you, Mal," Kayl said.

"Me?" Malani looked at Genji. "What has he told you about me?"

"The truth," Genji said. "Besides which, you are Kayl's sister, and the daughter of his father, and the niece of Aunt Hokulani. I don't know much about your mother yet, but I'm sure she fits right in there."

Malani shook her head. "Selene, I'm honored that you trust me, but you do realize that just because people are related doesn't mean they're the same, right?"

Genji nodded, her expression serious. "I am very aware that sisters can be very different from others in their family. As I said, I do not want to talk about that. Dr. Owen, you know I have a unique genetic profile."

"That's putting it mildly," Malani said.

"I want to make sure that genetic profile is used properly and responsibly. It might help people. Having it analyzed might also reduce some of the public concern about me. But I know how many problems might arise, how many difficulties might be involved, how many temptations might exist. That's why I want you to be the authorized guardian of my genome."

Malani's mouth hung open for a moment before she closed it. "I assume you realize how huge a thing that is? Every genetics researcher, every lab, would move mountains for that."

"I can't trust them," Genji said. "I can trust you, can't I?"

"Yes," Malani said. "Myself, and the lab where I work, which is ethically run, and will not ever pressure me to unlawfully exploit or misuse your DNA. I can promise you that."

"What do I need to do?" Genji said.

"You're really serious? Right now?"

"We shouldn't hang around too long," Kayl said.

"Umm . . . yeah. Yes, I can handle it. There are contracts and releases and agreements, which I should have on my personal work pad here, and I'll need a couple of DNA samples, but I always carry some samplers because you never know, and . . ." Malani paused, looking dazed. "Excuse me. This is huge. I already said that, didn't I?"

"It's not easy to render Mal speechless," Kayl said, grinning.

"Shut up, Kayl. Umm . . . I should have everything. Wait. Compensation. You'll want some custom arrangement, I'm sure."

"No," Genji said, shaking her head. "Whatever is standard, as long as it's fair."

"In my lab, it is fair," Malani said. "We've got a five-star rating from the ethics council. Wait. You said standard? Selene, you could ask for enough money to buy the Moon and someone would try to raise it."

"That's not why I'm here," Genji said.

"Okay. I mean, even under a standard compensation arrangement you might end up with a whole lot of money. Just not enough to buy the Moon."

"I don't really like the Moon," Genji said. "I don't want any barriers to the right and necessary things being done with my DNA. I think that is part of the reason I'm here."

Malani stared at her. "You also mean why you're here in 2140, don't you? That this is somehow tied in to what you're trying to do?"

"It might be," Genji said. "I have to try. I don't know everything that is going to happen, how many changes my being in 2140 is causing and will cause. I just have to hope the changes are at least mostly for the better. So I can save the world. So Kayl and I can save the world. And, before you ask, Kayl is fine with all this."

"If you're not married yet, Kayl doesn't have a voice in it unless you want him to have one."

"I understand that. So does Kayl. I have the final and only say in this. But out of respect for our relationship, I did speak to him about it. We share our lives."

"Life sharing. All right, then." Malani ran through her menus. "I've got all the standard forms. We'll use those. Standard compensation on research discoveries stemming from your DNA and practical treatments and everything else? You're sure about that? Kayl, if you have a voice in this, are you sure about that?"

"It's what our father would have wanted," Kayl said.

"That's one thing I would never argue with you about," Malani said. "Selene, I'm so honored. I really am. Did I say that already? Kayl, you know our father would've loved this girl, right?"

"I like to think so," Kayl said, smiling.

"As the eldest, I can assure you he would have."

"I knew you'd bring that eldest thing up at some point," Kayl said.

"Because it's true." Malani shook her head at him. "Does Selene know about your hill thing?"

"Our hill to die on?" Genji asked. "Yes. My mission. Our mission. We've got the same hill."

"You're kidding." Malani laughed. "It looks like you found the perfect partner, Kayl. You know, when Aunt Hokulani first told us about you two, she said Selene wanted to keep your relationship at arm's length."

"That's how I felt at that time," Genji said. "Speaking of Aunt Hokulani . . . you don't mind if I call her that, do you?"

"Of course not."

"We saw an interview where Aunt Hokulani said she was going to take in Krysta."

Malani looked away from the forms she'd been studying to nod to Genji. "Yes. She got a call from, believe it or not, a representative of the Earth Cooperation Council's Security Committee, saying my brother here had wanted Krysta to go to Aunt Hokulani, and would she be interested in doing that?"

Kayl sat up. "The Earth Cooperation Council got involved in that? Why?"

"Good question. I don't know the answer. It was some woman named . . . umm . . . Camacho."

"The Earth Cooperation Council?" Genji questioned. "They're . . . active?"

Malani laughed. "I'm not surprised that you're surprised, because I am, too. It seems like the ECC has mostly avoided doing things lately because doing something was too hard. Is that one of the things you were going to try to change to save the Earth?"

"I hadn't aimed that high," Genji said. "How could I possibly have that much influence?"

"Is she serious?" Malani asked Kayl. "Selene, everybody who isn't afraid of you is hoping to meet you."

Genji shook her head, smiling. "I'm sure that's not true. I'm an alloy."

"Yeah, people know that. They also know you saved that kid's dad in the mountains, and you raised hell in Kansas. What happened there, anyway? There are reports you took out half the fort without killing anyone."

"Kayl helped," Genji said. "They took him prisoner, and I wanted him free, and so we did that. Without killing anyone."

"Kayl helped?" Malani laughed again. "Anyway, back to Aunt Hokulani and your girl Krysta."

"She's not actually our girl," Kayl said.

"You might have some trouble convincing Krysta of that," Malani said, still looking amused. "Aunt Hokulani has had some long talks with her. Krysta's therapists have encouraged that, because of Aunt Hokulani's connection to you two. In one of those talks, Krysta tearfully asked if Aunt Hokulani thought Lieutenant Genji and Lieutenant Owen would ever consider adopting her."

"Adopting her?" Kayl said, looking stunned at the idea.

Genji didn't blame him for being shocked. She felt the same. "Where did Krysta get that idea? We never talked to her about that."

This time Malani nodded. "Krysta told Aunt Hokulani it was a fantasy she'd come up with. Like, her dream. I've got to admit, little brother, you really impressed that girl."

"But," Genji said, feeling helpless, "how could we . . . ?"

"Krysta knows it's a fantasy," Malani repeated.

"She risked her life for us. We didn't ask her to. We told her not to! But she did."

"That doesn't necessarily place that kind of obligation on you," Malani said.

"We couldn't do that, anyway," Kayl said. "For the same reason we can't get married, right, Selene?"

"Yeah," Genji said, giving a sad nod.

"Why can't you get married?" Malani asked. "Don't worry about Mom objecting. That won't happen."

"It's because of the second reason why we wanted to talk to

you," Kayl said. "We don't know if you can help with this, or if you'd want to get involved in it."

"Tell me what it is," Malani said impatiently.

"I'm not yet legally a person," Genji said. "My genome is not one hundred percent human, and the personhood of someone like that hasn't been established by any court decisions. In the 2160s, after alloys will be born, there will be a lot of lawsuits, seeking to establish whether alloys could be prevented from boarding public transport or could be denied service in restaurants. That sort of thing."

Malani stared at her, momentarily shocked into silence. "Excuse me? Whether you could ride a train? That was, I mean, will be an issue?"

"Malani," Genji said, "if you're not human, what are you? Alloys had not been legally established to be human. Some people will argue they aren't."

"So, what, they tried, I mean, will try, to argue you're animals or something?"

"Yes. Pretty much."

"That's . . ." Malani blinked as if fighting back tears. "You had to deal with that? You'll be born in, what, 2158, right? So, you're this little girl, and some people are arguing you're not human, you're some kind of animal? I am so sorry, Selene. I am so sorry you had to endure that."

Genji managed a reassuring smile. "As I told Kayl, you're not the ones who hurt me. You don't have to apologize."

"I'm going to anyway." Malani ran one hand through her hair, clearly distressed.

"But, if you want to, if you can, you could help with that. Can we authorize you to start a lawsuit on my behalf?" Genji said. "Asking that I be declared legally human? Start this now, get it resolved long before the 2160s, so any alloys born will have their status clear from the start? And so Kayl and I can legally marry?"

Malani stared at her. "You want me . . . Yes. If I can. Will I have legal standing? I don't know. I'd have to talk to some lawyers. And I'll probably need a statement from you authorizing me to act on your behalf in that. But . . . yes. Absolutely. I can try. No one deserves to be considered less than fully human."

"Thank you," Genji said.

"Of course, if they decide that, then you could also . . ." Malani paused, thinking. "Krysta. The adoption thing. Would you two consider that? I mean, if you legally could?"

"Why would we need to decide that now?" Kayl asked.

"Because it would make the personhood lawsuit also about Krysta!" Malani said. "Not just about you two being able to marry. I've got to tell you, that girl, and her clear adoration of the two of you for rescuing her, after no official authority anywhere even knew she needed help, has been playing really well with people. At this conference I've had so many people walk up to me and tell me if I ever have the chance, to let you, Kayl, and you, Selene, know how grateful they are for you guys helping that girl. Oh, I'm telling you that now. Anyway, if you go in asking for a legal ruling that Selene is human also on the basis of wanting to be able to adopt that girl, an awful lot of people are going to be backing you."

Genji tried to control her breathing as she thought through Malani's words. "That would mean Kayl and I would be committing to adopt Krysta. We couldn't go through that and then deny her adoption."

"Yeah," Malani said. "There is that. I have no idea how you two feel about that, whether you're ready to be a mother to a teenage girl, Selene. That's tough enough even with a teenage girl who hasn't experienced the trauma that Krysta has."

"A mother?" Genji felt that strange sensation inside her again. "I never . . ."

"This is a really delicate subject," Kayl said to Malani.

"I'm sorry. Forget I said anything."

"No," Genji said, looking at Kayl. "What do you think?"

"What do I think?" Kayl asked her. "Aren't you the one who matters here?"

"I don't know." Genji sighed, looking at Malani now. "It was never . . . I was never going to be a mother."

"Oh," Malani said, appearing distraught. "Yeah. You're genetically engineered, so—"

"No," Genji said. "It's not that. I'm not infertile, as far as I know. I've been told I should be cross-fertile with full humans. With Kayl. But I never . . . Malani, no first-generation alloy had children. None of us planned to ever have children. It was partly what we'd endured growing up, aliens on our own world, and partly fear of what might happen to our children, whether the second generation would have unforeseen problems due to the genetic mixing. We didn't even know if we'd develop serious problems, though that hasn't happened yet. Having a child would mean experimenting. I was never going to do that."

She shifted her gaze to Kayl. "But then I got hurled forty years into the past and met this guy. And things got complicated."

"Selene," Kayl said, "I've accepted that. It's not something you expect, and not something you'll necessarily ever want. You've been honest with me about that."

"But maybe now I want *our* child, Kayl! Someday. I don't know anymore! And now there's Krysta. How do you feel about her, Kayl?"

"She's a sweet kid," Kayl said. "I hadn't thought about long-term, but . . . she's still our responsibility, isn't she?"

"Only if you want that," Malani said.

"I . . ." Genji shook her head helplessly. "I really liked having her. And she risked her life for us! But we're still probably going to die sooner rather than later, even if I don't cease to exist, which could still happen, and probably I'm not even going to be born now even if I am here, and how can someone who hasn't been born be a mother? I . . ."

"Selene," Kayl said, smiling, "you want to say yes, don't you?"

"Yeah. I do."

"Then go ahead."

"You're really okay with it?" Genji asked.

"I'm frankly terrified at the idea," Kayl said. "But, as my favorite part-alien person once said, you can't save the Earth unless you're willing to save one individual."

Genji looked back at Malani. "Yes. We'll try to adopt Krysta. Make it part of the legal battle to establish that I am legally human. Kayl, if Krysta becomes our daughter, you'll be in charge of reining in her coffee intake."

"Why me?" Kayl demanded.

"Because I can't drink coffee, so I can't judge when she has had too much!"

"Oh," Kayl said. "That's so unfair of you to use an argument I can't refute."

Genji smiled. "I play to win, Lieutenant Owen."

"And I love you for it, Lieutenant Genji."

Malani made a disgusted noise. "I hope you two aren't always like this. What's with the lieutenant stuff?"

"Pet names," Kayl said.

"That is so weird. Is that an Earth Guard thing?"

"Not to my knowledge. It's our thing."

"I'm glad you found each other," Malani said. "Umm . . . which reminds me of the topic of children. I know you're not actively interested at this time, Selene, but, since I'm going to have your genome, I can run it against Kayl's. There'll be some unknowns because of the alien DNA, but I can try to see if I can spot any potential problems if you two did decide you wanted to have some of your own. If you want me to."

Genji lowered her gaze to the floor, then looked over at Kayl, who was clearly trying not to project any feelings that might pressure her. "I would like to know, Malani. In case I ever know what I want."

"I'll keep that side of the research private," Malani said.

"Thank you. Let's get this done."

Malani indicated a series of open screens. "Paperwork time. I know you probably want to leave as soon as possible, but this will take a little while. Kayl, you'll need to witness it all, so try to pay attention."

"I love you, too, Mal. Oh, you understand you have to keep this quiet until you get back home. We can't tip off people that we're in this area."

Malani hesitated. "Right. I should've thought of that. They were looking for you down in San Diego, weren't they? It would have made such a splash to announce it on the last day of the conference, but I don't want you two to end up in more danger because of it." She looked at him. "Kayl, we haven't always gotten on perfectly together, but I really am worried for you."

Kayl smiled reassuringly at her. "I've got Selene with me. That makes me pretty safe."

"I'm a threat magnet, Kayl," Genji said. "Being with me is the opposite of pretty safe."

"I still feel safer around you."

Genji smiled at him. "I feel safer around you, too."

Malani shook her head. "You two are going to be very hard to live with. Can we get going on this paperwork?"

IT TOOK NEARLY TWO hours. Two tedious hours of what seemed like highly repetitive forms that needed to be signed and certified and witnessed.

Genji checked the time when the last item was finally done. "We should be going. My hacks to the hotel security system will reset in about forty-five minutes."

Kayl nodded, standing up and stretching. "It really was great to see you again, Mal."

"It's nice to see you," Malani said. "Hey, it just occurred to me, you two are on the run. Do you need anything?"

Kayl hesitated. "No. Not really."

"Kayl," Genji said, the single word carrying a lot of meaning. He was obviously reluctant to bring up their need, but this opportunity might be their only chance.

He gave her an unhappy look. "All right. Mal, the truth is, we need to pay for everything using anonymous cash cards, and we're about tapped out."

"You're out of money?" Malani nodded. "Sure. I can see where that would be a problem. How much do you need?"

"Mal, I don't want to—"

"How much do you need?" Mal repeated, looking at Selene this time.

"What can you spare?" Selene asked.

"A fair amount. I can get some regular cash cards in the lobby and bring them back up here. Can you hold on for a few minutes while I do that?"

"Yes. Thank you so much."

Malani grinned. "I'll make Kayl pay me back."

After Malani rushed out, Selene looked at Kayl. "Sorry," she said. "But we needed to tell her we needed money."

"It's a bit awkward," Kayl mumbled, looking at the floor. "For the rest of my life I'm going to be hearing Malani talk about how she bailed us out."

"There are worse things, Kayl. At least she'll be talking to you."

Kayl flinched, recognizing that she was referencing her own sisters.

Malani returned within ten minutes, handing four cash cards to Selene. "There you go. Now, get out of here, and stay safe, and please try to keep Kayl from getting hurt. He's my favorite brother."

"I'm your only brother," Kayl said. "Thanks, Mal."

"Thanks," Selene echoed, nearly leaping back a moment later when Malani enveloped her in a quick goodbye hug. She still hadn't gotten used to full humans being so willing to touch an alloy.

They still had a half hour before the security systems reset when Selene led the way out of Malani's room, the cameras monitoring the corridor seeing nothing as they displayed old footage on the monitors and to the AI watching for unusual events.

THE NEXT MORNING, AS Malani took the elevator down to the lobby, she encountered two other doctors she'd met the day before.

"Did you know there was a break-in last night?" one of them asked Malani.

"A break-in?" Malani asked.

"That's what they're saying. There are security officers all over the place. Somebody said they're checking everything before people can leave."

Security officers. Checking everything. Malani was abruptly aware of the DNA samples nestled in a small bag she carried, as well as the completed forms on her work pad, all of which would betray the fact that Kayl and Selene had been here last night.

9

DID SHE DARE TRUST these two? Malani thought. They'd both been among those who had expressed interest and sympathy in Selene. Had that been an act, though? Every crime and spy thriller she'd ever read or watched or listened to came back to her with memories of plots in which supposed friends turned out to be double-crossers and double-agents and double-dealers.

She had less than half a minute before the elevator reached the lobby.

"Could you guys help me?" Malani held up her work pad, reaching into her pocket for the holder with the DNA samples inside. "I want to make sure this stuff gets past the security people. Will you take it through for me? Say it's yours?"

The two doctors exchanged startled glances. "Does this have to do with Genji?" one asked in a low voice.

"Yes."

That doctor reached for the pad, the other grabbing the DNA pack.

The elevator door opened on a lobby with a line of grumbling people waiting to get past screeners before they could leave the building. As soon as Malani and the others stepped out of the elevator, two security officers watching them gestured all three into the line.

Malani did her best to look aggravated rather than worried as the line moved forward, acutely aware of all the eyes on her. She didn't dare look at the two doctors who had taken her pad and samples. All she could do was worry about what they might do when they reached the screeners.

Finally at the checkpoint, Malani produced her ID in response to a demand.

"Dr. Owen?" one of the officers said, gesturing to others nearby. Malani suddenly found herself the center of a group eyeing her as if they expected an alien to burst out of her chest at any moment. "Your phone, please. All electronics."

"Excuse me?" Malani said, not having to fake outrage. "By what right are you taking my phone?"

"We have a warrant," an officer said, quickly displaying a screen of text. "All electronics. You're not hiding anything, are you?"

"Of course not!" Fuming, Malani turned over her phone.

"Password or biometrics?" the officer with her phone asked.

"Password," Malani said.

"What is it?"

Malani shook her head. "I know that, warrant or not, I do not have to divulge a password unless I am charged with an offense. Figure it out yourself."

After an uncomfortable few seconds, another officer looked her over. "No work pad?"

"I travel light," Malani said. "I'm mostly just observing this conference. What business is it of yours?"

"Has she got anything else on her?"

"No," an officer at a monitor reported. "No other electronics or equipment."

"Have you heard from your brother?" the first officer asked Malani.

"My brother?" It was funny how easy it was to make nervousness look like outrage. "That's what this is about?"

"Have you heard from him?"

There were voice stress monitors that would key on apparent lies, Malani knew. Did the security officers have some of those trained on her? If so, her gift of sarcasm might finally serve a useful purpose. "Oh, sure. He was in my room last night. So was Genji! Didn't you see them in the lobby?"

"This isn't funny," one of the officers said. "If you are contacted, it's in everyone's best interests if you let appropriate authorities know. For the safety of everyone."

"You have a funny way of making people feel safe," Malani snapped. "My phone, please?"

"You'll have to request its return through proper channels," another officer said.

Once again, Malani didn't have to fake being upset as she stomped away from the screeners.

Later in the day, before the conference ended, the two doctors who'd helped her discreetly passed back her work pad and DNA samples. Malani promptly used the conference business office to securely mail all of that back to her office.

The records of conversations with her mother and Aunt Hokulani on the phone were supposedly so well encrypted that no one could view them without authorization. Nothing else on the phone should involve Kayl or Selene except for the contact information for Kayl, and that was probably no longer any good. But the phone also held all her travel information and tickets, requiring her to hastily buy a disposable phone and download all of that again.

She wasn't surprised at the airport that evening when the disposable phone was also confiscated and she was once more scanned for other electronic devices. While waiting to once more download the same tickets on yet another disposable phone purchased after passing through security, Malani vowed to ensure that Kayl never forgot what she'd gone through for him.

And worried about whether or not he and Selene were safe.

THEY HAD FOUND THE right people to convert their new cash cards to anonymous cash cards, and then the right people to provide some new false IDs and burner phones. The ease of doing that once again disturbed Owen. He was beginning to suspect that the world hidden from the official databases was at least as large as that visible to and included in the official picture of the world, its people, and the economies in various places.

Even though they had a day left on their week at the temp worker apartments, Owen and Selene changed to another such place in another neighborhood. They had barely arrived, and started discussing their next steps, when one of the burner phones buzzed.

"It's the phone from Admiral Tecumseh," Owen said, scooping it up.

Still in town?

Yes, Kayl typed in reply.

U R being tracked. DNA hits. Guard knows O here.

"DNA hits?" Owen said. "How are they getting DNA hits?"

"But just on you," Selene said, reading. "Not from a blood sampler, then."

"Skin flakes?" Owen asked.

"That might be it," Selene said. "Whenever possible, I wear the UV Aversive stuff to hide my appearance. Jacket, gloves, hat, neck covering. All of that would also keep me from shedding and leaving behind skin flakes wherever we go. Let me check something." She searched rapidly before nodding to Owen. "A big fuss this morning at Malani's hotel. Security screening everyone. They found out we were there."

"But not in time to nail us," Owen said. He typed a single word into the burner phone. **How?**

Secret program. Don't know details.

As Owen was trying to decide what to type next, another text came in.

Talking to possible allies. Wait for word. Lay low.

"Possible allies?" Selene said. "Who?"

"Hopefully not another helper like Thomas Dorcas," Owen said.

"Do we trust her?" Selene asked.

"I think we should," Owen said, feeling the weight of his decision. "What else can we do?"

"Head somewhere else." But the moment after she'd said that, Selene shook her head. "But they're tracking us somehow using DNA hits, probably focusing on transportation hubs and places we might show up, like Malani's hotel."

"Which is how we threw them off by our hike and then travel by private car," Owen said. "Maybe that's how they knew we were on that lunar shuttle, too."

Selene sighed. "It looks like Tecumseh's advice to lie low is our best option. They can't spot us if we aren't moving around. But I am going to get very nervous if we don't hear from her again within another day or so."

MALANI ARRIVED AT WORK the next day. She'd gotten in last night, but decided not to inform the lab then. Not until she had her work pad and the DNA samples back.

Her first stop was her office, where a package waited on the desk.

Malani opened it, fearing that it might have been intercepted and the contents removed, but her work pad was inside, as were the DNA samplers. She checked everything, confirming the completed forms were still loaded, and the DNA samples were in good condition.

"Anything happen at the conference?" one of her co-workers getting coffee asked.

"Oh, yeah," Malani said. "I have to report to the bosses first."

Malani took the elevator to the top floor. "I need to see the heads of the lab," Malani told the senior executive assistant.

"They've just begun the morning meeting," the executive assistant said. "I can get you an appointment later today at—"

"Now," Malani said. "Right now. It's very important. They need to know this."

The executive assistant raised both eyebrows. "What does this pertain to?"

"I can't tell you. I'm sorry."

"All right, Doctor. It's your neck, not mine."

The doctors who made up the lab's leadership were seated in comfortable chairs forming a rough circle in the center of the large meeting room. They all looked over at Malani as she walked in. "Is something wrong, Dr. Owen?" Dr. Jerez asked. "Did something major happen at that conference that we haven't heard about?"

Malani held up the DNA sampler she was cradling. "Something very important happened. She gave us a sample. And full rights to use it on her behalf."

"She? A sample?"

"Selene Genji. I met with her. She gave me DNA samples and made all the agreements for us to work with it. Full authority to represent her in all matters pertaining to her genome."

"Oh. My. God," Dr. Nasser said, her face working with shock. "We just became the most important genetics research lab in the world."

"How much did she ask for?" Dr. Warren asked. "I'm sure we'll pay it, we'll be able to raise it, but how much? That could impact a lot of our spending decisions."

"Standard compensation," Malani said.

"Standard compensation? How did you get her to agree to that?"

"She insisted on it. She wouldn't take more," Malani said. "I explained she could ask for a lot more, but Lieutenant Genji refused anything except standard compensation."

"These agreements needed a witness," Dr. Jerez said. "Did you have a witness?"

"Yes," Malani said. "My brother."

Dr. Nasser was jolted out of her stunned state. "Where did this happen? And when? Last night?"

"As you'll see from the dates on the agreements," Malani said, "it was not last night. I agreed not to tell anyone until today so as not to provide any information on where my brother and Genji were until they had time to go somewhere else."

Malani waited a bit nervously as the lab heads exchanged looks, wondering if she'd be chewed out for withholding the information until now.

Finally, Dr. Nasser nodded. "We can't fault you for agreeing to that. Not under current circumstances."

"What do we need to do?" Dr. Spengler asked. "Legal. Have them review the agreements and make sure Dr. Owen got everything. If you followed the checklists, Dr. Owen, that should have ensured there are no problems, but we need to be certain. We'll need to call a press conference once that is done and have a statement ready for release. And prepare an announcement for the employees of the lab. Is there anything else?"

"How many samples do you have?" Dr. Warren asked.

"Two," Malani said.

"Excellent. Now, who is assigned guardianship of the genome? This lab? Or you, specifically?"

"Me, specifically," Malani said. "Selene . . . excuse me, Lieutenant Genji insisted on that. She wouldn't have signed otherwise."

"That's understandable," Dr. Nasser said, looking a bit worried. "Not standard, but not unheard of. You're not planning on leaving this lab, are you?"

"No, Doctor," Malani said as the other partners in the lab laughed in a way that held a nervous tinge to it.

Dr. Jerez nodded. "I think that brings up one more item. Dr. Owen, why did Genji select our lab?"

"Selene said because she trusted me. Really, honestly, she selected me, not the lab. But I assured her this lab would not violate her trust in any way."

"Selene? You are on a first-name basis with her?"

"Yes," Malani said. "I mean, she and my brother . . . they're close. Sharing lives, is how she described it." It didn't seem the right time and place to announce her brother's engagement to Selene.

Dr. Jerez looked around the room. "We have this opportunity because of Dr. Owen being here. Is everyone in agreement that we'd like Dr. Owen to stay at this lab?"

"You don't have to spell it out," Dr. Nasser said. "I nominate Dr. Owen to become a full partner in the lab, effective immediately."

"Seconded," Dr. Jerez said.

"Any objections?" Dr. Warren asked. "Then it's done. Congratulations, Dr. Owen. Welcome to the top floor team. Your extra stock options will take effect immediately, which should be really important once we make our announcement."

Malani stood staring at them.

"Dr. Owen?"

"I... I..." Less than a year ago she'd been a junior researcher in a tiny office doing boring, repetitive work. She heard Genji's voice in her mind. *I don't know everything that is going to happen, how many changes my being in 2140 is causing and will cause. I just have to hope the changes are at least mostly for the better.*

"Dr. Owen, sit down. Somebody get her some water. Do you think we should call the in-office medical service?"

That triggered something that wrenched Malani's mind out of its daze. "Medical. I need to tell you this. Kayl, my brother, told me that when Selene . . . Lieutenant Genji, was first rescued, Kayl's ship's doctor took a DNA sample from her as part of the emergency medical treatment."

"That's routine procedure for emergency medical care," Dr. Nasser said. "They destroyed it immediately afterwards as required, correct?"

"Kayl said he didn't know. Right after that, he got orders saying everyone was supposed to pretend that Genji didn't exist. He doesn't know whether Earth Guard destroyed that DNA sample."

Dr. Nasser frowned in thought. "Earth Guard might claim they have no record of Genji existing. Or they might claim the law doesn't apply to Genji because she's not pure human."

"Full human," Malani interjected quickly. "Lieutenant Genji says 'pure human' is a term used by people trying to claim she's not human at all, that she's contaminating the human species."

"Oh! I will avoid it in the future, then," Dr. Nasser said. "We couldn't do anything about this before, but now that we're legally representatives for Genji's DNA, we can demand that Earth Guard provide proof that sample was destroyed."

"And if they refuse to do so?" Dr. Warren asked.

Dr. Jerez smiled. "Cry havoc and let slip the lawyers. Can you imagine how many of them would eagerly volunteer to be part of that historic legal action?" He winked at Malani.

Malani's mind had started working again. "Unleash society's immune system. I should inform you that Selene Genji and my brother asked me to initiate some legal action on their behalf. It's related to her genome."

"What is it?" Dr. Spengler asked.

"Selene Genji wants a legal determination that she is a person."

THE LAWYER MALANI WAS speaking to at the Civil Liberties Union took close to a minute to get an answer out after Malani had explained what she wanted to do.

"Legal determinations that the alien, Selene Genji, is a person? That's . . . Wow."

"I'll be able to give you an analysis of her genome," Malani said. "That should assist you, shouldn't it?"

"You have her genome?"

"She's appointed me the legal guardian of it."

"Excellent! And this girl Krysta is fine with this? She wants to be adopted by them?"

"That's what she told my aunt."

The lawyer sat back, his eyes looking dazed. "This would be so precedent setting. It'd go all the way to the World Court. And it's so important! We've got security people telling us who is and who isn't human! That's wrong! We need this determination, we need it established that one hundred percent human DNA is not required to be legally treated as if you're human, with all the rights and responsibilities and protections under the law. What about the aliens on that ship at Mars? The same questions apply to them. I'm going to call a meeting, and we'll talk about this, but I can guarantee you we want this case. You have a request from Selene Genji to file for this determination? Great. We'll need a deposition from Krysta as well, saying she wants this to happen. As soon as we get this formally rolling, we'll send someone to get a statement from her. It'd be a good idea if you gave Krysta a heads-up so she can be thinking what she wants to say."

Malani's next call was to the group labeled "family." "Hi, Mom. Hi, Aunt Hokulani."

"How was LA?" Leilani Owen asked.

"It was LA. Mom, I'm sorry I couldn't tell you before this, but Kayl asked me to keep quiet for a few days."

"Kayl? You talked to Kayl?"

"Yes," Malani said, "and Selene Genji. They're both fine. They were when I left them, anyway."

Hokulani's eyes lit up. "You finally met her? Come on, now. Admit it. She's right for Kayl."

"I admit it," Malani said. "Selene will make me a great sister, if she and Kayl manage to live that long."

"Sister?" her mother asked. "Do you have some news for me?"

"They're engaged, Mom. Kayl was really sorry he couldn't tell you himself. And Selene is really worried you won't like her."

"Is she treating Kayl right?"

"Oh, yeah. They are disgustingly in love."

"I was worried about her at first, but it's pretty obvious by now that is one exceptional woman Kayl has found," Malani's mother said. "Why does she think I wouldn't like her?"

"Oh, you know, her partly alien DNA, threats on Kayl's life because of her, running from the law because of her, being from the future, stuff like that."

"Nobody's perfect."

"That's what I said! Oh, we discussed her worries about a second generation of alloys, so you no longer need hide that from me, Aunt Hokulani."

"I had an obligation," Aunt Hokulani said. "You see why now, right?"

"I see why," Malani admitted. "It's a deeply personal thing for her."

"Kayl understands why she doesn't want children, doesn't he?"

"He does, but now she might. She no longer knows for sure."

Leilani laughed. "I knew exactly what I was going to do with my life and exactly what kind of man I wanted to find to share it. And then Cathal Owen showed up, and all my plans changed. You'll see someday, Malani. You meet that person and life goes to places you never imagined."

"Life going to places I never imagined has already happened over the last several months," Malani said. "Did I mention I was made a full partner in the lab this morning? Oh, and I'm going to court to get Selene declared human so she and Kayl can marry and they can adopt Krysta. Is everybody good with that?"

IT CAME AS AN immense relief when the burner phone given to them by Rear Admiral Tecumseh buzzed to alert Owen to another message.

Still okay?

Yes, Owen typed back.

Someone wants to meet you. Rep for ECC SC.

"ECC SC?" Selene asked, moving close to read.

"Earth Cooperation Council," Owen said. "Security Committee. It has to mean Security Committee."

"The Security Committee." Selene's voice had gone flat.

"Why did you say it like that? The Security Committee is supposed to oversee all ECC common defense forces, such as Earth Guard."

"Supposed to," Selene repeated. "Are they doing that in 2140?"

"They've pretty much let Earth Guard run itself for a long time."

"So," Selene said, "they're not doing anything."

"What is it you need to tell me about this?" Owen asked.

She paused, her eyes filled with memories that clearly brought her no happiness. "What I know of the Security Committee is that through the 2140s and 2150s, right up to 2169, they held meetings sometimes, but didn't make decisions."

"What happened in 2169?"

She gazed at him. "Karachi. Remember?"

Owen looked at the message, thinking. "But if they want to talk to you, maybe they're going to start doing their job again. Maybe all of the junk around you being in 2140 is jump-starting the Security Committee."

Selene took a while to reply. "That would be big, if that's what's happening. I guess the only way to find out if it's true is to talk to this person. Can we trust whoever it is?"

"Admiral Tecumseh thinks so."

"Yeah, she also thought we could trust Thomas Dorcas."

Owen grimaced. "Can we afford not to meet with whoever this is?"

Selene sat back, frowning. "You should understand that, to me, the Earth Cooperation Council and everything to do with it are symbols of failure. That's what I grew up with. I remember the news reports when the Council finally, formally dissolved after not meeting for decades. Nobody really cared, because they didn't realize that with the ECC gone, an important symbol had disappeared. Something that *might* have made a difference was gone, and nobody understood that until too late. I remember the outrage when the Security Committee, which had been still meeting, didn't react to Karachi. From the perspective of someone who lived through the 2160s and 2170s, it's hard to believe that whoever we meet with will actually do anything. Or that we can trust them."

Owen thought through her words before trying to come up with an answer. "Is that something we can change?" he finally asked.

"Me? Lieutenant Selene Genji? Change the Earth Cooperation Council and the Security Committee?"

"We have to save the Earth," Owen said. "That's the mission."

"That's the mission," she agreed. "Why do you think this person wants to meet with us? What's their agenda?"

"Someone already talked to Aunt Hokulani about Krysta. What was the name Malani told us?"

Selene paused. "Camacho."

Owen typed a reply on the burner phone. **Name?**

The answer came less than a minute later. **Camacho.**

"I guess we have to give it a shot," Selene said. "And hope it's not a trap. Because if it is, we probably won't make it out."

"We can't keep hiding," Owen said.

"Not if we want to accomplish anything," she agreed.

Okay, Owen typed. **When? Where?**

THERE HADN'T BEEN ANY obvious signs of danger when they approached the restaurant, but neither of them expected an ambush to be easy to spot.

Falstaff's was set back from the street, the entrance discreetly screened by trees and bushes. This was the sort of place Owen had heard of but never visited, where people with important business met to talk, negotiate, and agree to deals without worrying about being overheard or spied on. Inside, human waitstaff guided Owen and Selene to a back table in a corner, pointing out the controls that would raise or lower a privacy screen around the table.

Their drink order of coffee and green tea arrived quickly, the waitstaff discreetly engaging in little conversation.

If anyone had taken notice of Selene's full UV Aversive clothing, they gave no sign of it.

At precisely the moment when they had agreed to meet, a woman entered the restaurant on her own. Owen studied her, thinking that she had the look of someone who knew how to stay in the background while making important things happen. Her clothes, her movements, all seemed carefully calibrated to avoid drawing attention.

She stopped at their booth. "Unless I'm mistaken, you're the two I'm here to meet."

"You have the advantage of us there," Owen said.

"Can introductions wait until we have privacy?"

"Sure." Owen waited until she had sat down opposite him and Selene before activating the privacy controls, a shield rising from the floor to block sound and any view of the table.

"I am Cerise Camacho, Special Representative of the Security Committee of the Earth Cooperation Council," she said. "You are Lieutenant Genji and Lieutenant Owen?"

"Yes," Selene said.

"It's nice to meet you both in person. I've been working your cases."

"We understand that you've been involved with Krysta," Selene said.

"I have been able to assist the girl, yes," Camacho said. She smiled. "It's been a pleasure to help her. She thinks the world of you two."

"What do you think of us?" Owen asked.

Camacho eyed him before replying. "I think you two are the most effective troublemakers I've ever heard of. One of the meanings of 'trouble' is public disturbance, and you've certainly caused that. Another, older meaning is to stir up things. Things which, if I'm candid, have perhaps been allowed to go astray, and things which have slumbered rather than doing what they were supposed to do."

She looked at Selene. "And, you in particular, Lieutenant Genji, are the strangest puzzle I've ever encountered. Where did you come from, and how?"

"I'd rather not say," Selene replied. But she also removed her hat and gloves and sunglasses, fully exposing her eyes, face, and hands. "Isn't why I'm here more important?"

"Is there a third party?" Camacho said. "We need to know."

"A third party?" Selene asked.

"Do you represent, are you an agent of, someone who is neither humans in this solar system or the Tramontine aliens? Is there a third entity out there that sent you here to carry out a mission?"

"No," Selene said without hesitating. "Earth is my home, the planet of my birth. My heart is human."

"Who are you working for, then?"

"Everyone," Selene said. "I am trying to save everyone."

Camacho sat back, obviously perplexed.

"She's telling the truth," Owen said.

"Do you know where Lieutenant Genji came from?"

"Yes, I do."

Cerise Camacho leaned forward again, her eyes fixed on him. "You investigated the wreckage on which Lieutenant Genji was found. Is that correct?"

Owen glanced at Selene before replying. "Yes. That's true."

"Are you willing to tell me anything about that wreckage?"

He paused, thinking. He had written up a report, and he had no idea what had happened to it. Camacho might have seen it. Others in Earth Guard certainly had. "We were unable to identify it. Based on the piece of wreckage, the apparent size of the ship did not match anything we knew of. None of the equipment exteriors could be matched to known equipment. That's about all I was able to determine. I recommended the wreckage be marked for special study, but I was . . . overruled."

"And Lieutenant Genji was aboard it. Along with a dead companion."

So Camacho did know something about the wreckage. Owen nodded, glad that he'd been honest. "Yes."

"You've been on the Tramontine ship, haven't you, Lieutenant Owen?"

"Yes, I have."

"Did anything about that ship remind you of anything about the wreckage?"

Owen imagined that his surprise at the question showed. "I'd never thought about that. No. The wreckage felt like a human ship."

Camacho shook her head. "It's a little worrisome that a large spaceship could have been operating near Earth without anyone knowing. Without any record of its construction. Lieutenant Genji, your actions certainly seem to match your words. But that question of where you came from is of great concern to us. It will be difficult for us to move forward without knowing."

"I came from Earth," Selene said. But then she paused. "That's . . . not strictly true. Earth . . ." She inhaled slowly, looking at Owen, clearly asking his advice.

What should he say? What would this woman do with the knowledge of Selene Genji's origin?

But Camacho's concerns were legitimate. How could they ask her to trust them, if they didn't trust her?

Others had already been told. Lieutenant Jeyssi Arronax on Mars. Rear Admiral Tecumseh here in LA. This felt like another case where that information had to be shared in order to further Selene's mission. Especially if it meant getting something as potentially powerful as the Security Committee on their side.

Owen nodded slowly to Selene, conveying his opinion that she should tell everything.

Selene must have felt the same way. She looked at Camacho. "I saw the Earth die. It ceased to exist just before I came here, so I didn't really, couldn't really, come from the Earth."

Whatever Camacho had been expecting, it wasn't that. "You saw . . . ?" She swallowed, her face reflecting shock at what Selene had said. "You saw the Earth die? The entire planet?"

"The entire planet," Selene said. "Destroyed in the culmination of the Universal War. The shock wave from that destroyed my ship, and sent me here."

Camacho inhaled a shaky breath. "And . . . when will this happen?"

"The twelfth of June, 2180."

"Twenty-one eighty." Camacho nodded, her expression still stunned. "Did the Tramontine—?"

"Humans. Humans will destroy the Earth," Selene said.

"Why?"

"Supposedly because of me. Because of alloys like me. Because of the Tramontine. Trying to 'cleanse' the Earth of alien contamination. Fear of aliens is how the Spear of Humanity gained strength and support. But, really, it was the same old story of fear of the other, and finding scapegoats for everything that had gone wrong."

Cerise Camacho stared at Selene for several seconds without saying anything. "Forty years?" she finally said. "That's all we have left?"

"Unless I can change enough things to prevent it," Selene said.

"To protect the Earth. To save everyone. What you said on Mars. It's literally true."

"Yes," Selene said.

"But why did you come back to 2140?" Camacho asked. "Because this was when First Contact took place?"

Selene shook her head. "I didn't choose to come back to 2140. It was, as far as I know, an accident. Something caused by the immense energy released by the destruction of Earth. I'm not some chosen special person. I didn't get special training for this. I'm just a lieutenant in the Unified Fleet, which may now never exist, trying my best to prevent the ultimate tragedy." She reached over to grasp Owen's hand. "And I was extremely lucky that fate threw me together with Lieutenant Owen. If Earth still has a chance, it's because of him as well as me."

Camacho sat back again, her face reflecting intense thought. "You're trying to change the history you know? You've already been doing that, haven't you? What happened in First Contact when you weren't there?"

"A long period of misunderstanding and miscommunication, growing fears of the Tramontine, intense arguments about what to do. You know some of that."

"I do?"

"The Earth Cooperation Council has already postponed its next meeting, hasn't it?" Selene demanded. "Over intractable disputes about how to respond to the Tramontine, and whether they're a threat?"

"No." Camacho shook her head. "The next meeting of the Council is scheduled for two weeks from now. It's going ahead. There's been no talk of postponement."

Owen saw Selene stare at Camacho in disbelief. "But . . . there won't be any more meetings of the ECC. Not until it formally dissolves."

"There will be a meeting in two weeks," Camacho said. "I've been talking to many of the delegates. They're eager to come up with a consensus on how to respond to the Tramontine, and the majority accept what the negotiators on Mars have told us, that the Tramontine are here on a peaceful mission of exploration and learning."

"But . . . but . . . that doesn't . . ."

Owen shifted his hand to grip Selene's. "Selene, look what you've done by fixing those problems with First Contact. You've made a big change."

She turned her stare to him. "How . . . ?"

Camacho studied Selene. "Archimedes said if he had a long enough lever, he could move the world. Maybe your lever, Lieutenant Genji, has already moved the history of this world."

"It's probably not enough," Selene said. "I need to keep trying."

"Why aren't you doubting her story?" Owen asked.

"Because she's fluent in the Tramontine language but the Tramontine say they never met her before First Contact. Because she came off a piece of wreckage with no known origin. Because she contains alien DNA even though that is flat-out impossible in someone her age. Because she was able to predict exactly when the Tramontine would first communicate with us and exactly what would be in that first message. How many reasons do I need, Lieutenant Owen?"

"Then maybe you know why Earth Guard never even asked her where she came from, and why it has been doing its best to kill her."

"Because some senior officers are scared, Lieutenant Owen," Camacho said. "Just like they were scared that you would cause someone to take a second look at the *Sentinel* disaster. Which we are doing. My colleague has made a formal request that the investigation into the loss of the *Sentinel*, into who or what bears responsibility, be reopened."

It was Owen's turn to be shocked. "Are you serious?"

"On my word, Lieutenant Owen. Though I must add that the investigation is not going to be focused on exonerating or finding fault with any particular person. It's going to be impartial, and follow the evidence where it leads."

"I have no doubt of the outcome if it does that," Owen said, trying not to feel elated.

Selene was giving him a warning look, though. Why?

All right. He'd stay cautious.

"Why did you want to meet with us?" Selene asked. "Just to find out more about me?"

"Partly," Camacho said. "But also, if I could find out where you came from, to make you both an offer."

10

"I HAVEN'T FOUND ANY justification for the push to kill you, Lieutenant Genji," Cerise Camacho continued, "other than the fear some have because of your genome. Some senior officials' focus on killing you by any means possible has served to expose just how weak oversight of the mutual defense forces has been. In that respect, you have done us a great service, at considerable risk to yourself. Here, then, is the offer, coupled with a request.

"Surrender yourselves to representatives of the Security Committee, myself and my colleague, and we will guarantee your safety and protection. In exchange, we will ask that you coordinate future actions with us. Your goal, to protect the Earth and its people, is the same as that of the Earth Cooperation Council. We should help each other, not be fighting each other." Camacho smiled. "Which is, after all, the basis for the Earth Cooperation Council, and why every country is a member."

"What's the request?" Selene asked.

"That you return to Mars to get the First Contact negotiations back on track and ensure human relations with the Tramontine are peaceful and to the benefit of both parties."

Selene glanced at Owen. "I won't go anywhere, let alone Mars, without Lieutenant Owen."

"I'm sorry," Camacho said. "I should have specified. We would of course agree to Lieutenant Owen traveling with you."

"Lieutenant Owen has been charged with crimes," Selene continued. "What about that?"

Camacho swept her hand in a swift cutting motion. "All

charges for any crimes will be dropped. The warrant for his arrest for questioning in the matter of Thomas Dorcas's disappearance has already been canceled."

"It has?" Owen asked.

"There wasn't enough evidence to support it," Camacho said. "Investigators may still wish to speak with you, but they're pursuing so many other leads, it may be a while before they do, if ever."

"Other leads?" Selene asked. Did some of those lead to her?

Cerise Camacho shook her head. "Do you know those murder mysteries where it turns out everybody had a motive for killing the deceased? Thomas Dorcas's disappearance is a real-life version of that. In the wake of him vanishing, more and more details of his actions have come to light as other people fought over control of Dorcas Funds. He's been implicated in at least two disappearances of other people, some very shady business deals, some of which cost others everything they had, and a variety of crimes, including assaults on underage individuals. There are literally dozens of suspects with motives to have killed Dorcas, and no evidence tying any of them to the disappearance. It may never be solved. The only thing linking either of you to Dorcas is a DNA hit possibly putting Lieutenant Owen at Los Angeles Interplanetary in the period when Dorcas possibly boarded a lifter there, but by the time they were examined, the lifter's own records for that period had been automatically wiped and overwritten using Dorcas's own security protocols, so nothing can be proven."

Camacho shrugged. "One of the leading theories at the moment is that Dorcas may have arranged his own disappearance because of fears some of his activities were about to come to light. That would explain why his ship so effectively sabotaged itself soon after it reached Mars, to avoid anyone knowing he hadn't ridden on it from Earth. Regardless, you're no longer being sought in connection with that, Lieutenant Owen."

"But the other crimes he's been charged with," Selene

pressed. "By Earth Guard. They imprisoned him in Kansas. Threatened to make him disappear. Who was that admiral, Lieutenant Owen?"

"Admiral Besson," Owen said.

Camacho nodded, her eyes on Owen. "We are taking a very close look at Admiral Besson, though we do not yet have grounds to move. If you surrender to me, all Earth Guard charges will also be dropped, and your personal safety will be guaranteed by the Council."

"What about our freedom?" Owen asked.

"Your freedom as well," Camacho said. "Will you agree?"

"But what will Lieutenant Owen's status be?" Selene asked. "If all charges are dropped, will he be expected to report back to Earth Guard and be assigned to whatever duties in whatever place they require?"

"I see your concern," Camacho said. "What are your wishes in that regard?"

"That he stay with me," Selene said. "We are a team. I need his assistance if I am to go to Mars and help with First Contact again. The Tramontine already know Lieutenant Owen and respect him. I want to ensure that even if Lieutenant Owen is restored to regular status as an officer in good standing with Earth Guard then he will also be assigned to assist me in my work for as long as I deem necessary."

"Are there any personal reasons for that request?" Camacho asked, looking slightly amused.

"Yes. We are engaged to marry. And Lieutenant Owen has my complete trust when it comes to my interests and my safety. I do not want to be separated from him."

"Engaged?" Camacho smiled again, this time in the manner of someone about to watch a spectacle. "That news would certainly provoke interesting reactions."

"It's going to become public knowledge," Owen said. "Someone is going to see about filing a lawsuit to have Selene declared legally a person so we can marry."

"Although," Selene added, "the implications for me, and for the Tramontine and any other species humanity encounters in the future, will go far beyond that."

"Far, far beyond that," Camacho said, nodding. "That is an issue the Council will probably want to get involved in, because of the implications for relations with the Tramontine. You said this person is only exploring possibly filing a lawsuit, though?"

"We don't know if she'll have legal standing to do it," Owen said.

"Ah," Camacho said. "Your sister? You did meet with her recently, didn't you?"

"Nothing was done to Malani, was it?" Owen asked, hearing the edge in his voice.

"Her phone was confiscated," Camacho said. "I wasn't informed of the matter until too late to intervene. I was able to confirm she safely returned home. You can rest easy on that score. And, it seems, in keeping with the traditions of the Owen family, she managed to outfox the security people who directly asked her if she'd seen you. All right, then, Lieutenant Genji. If you agree to assist the Council, Lieutenant Owen will be assigned to the Council indefinitely, and the Council will in turn assign Owen to you, indefinitely. That is a firm commitment."

"How can you make a promise like that?" Owen asked.

"Because I already have official approval to negotiate your surrender with you. The Security Committee has already voted for that. And, canvassing of the full Council indicates substantial support for it as well. There won't be any problem confirming whatever deal we make because I won't agree to anything the Council would balk at. I am certain that nothing you have requested is outside the boundaries of what the full Council will approve."

"What about the shoot-on-sight orders?" Owen said. "Those are still being given."

For the first time since they'd seen her, Cerise Camacho looked angry. "Shoot-on-sight orders for Lieutenant Genji have already been canceled by order of the Council. That was done immediately after Wallops. We are aware that not everyone involved in the hunt for Lieutenant Genji is committed to following our instructions. General Pravat at Eisenhower has already been relieved of command for failing to follow orders from the Council. But, given the possibility that others will claim justification for trying to kill Lieutenant Genji despite those orders, and because of potential threats from ordinary citizens who also fear Lieutenant Genji, the Council will provide you both with continuous security protection."

"Security protection?" Selene asked.

"Diplomatic security," Camacho said. "The same as protects me and members of the Council."

Owen, watching Selene, saw her eye twitch at the mention of diplomatic security. What did that mean? He'd have to ask her. But he also had another question for Camacho. "How are you going to keep that quiet? It sounds like something people will hear about."

"Everyone will hear about it," Camacho said. "Your surrender to the Council, your agreement to work with the Council, your agreement to go to Mars to assist in First Contact, will be publicly announced. No gray areas. Nothing under the table. You won't be hiding anymore."

"Even the flight to Mars?" Selene asked. "That will be public knowledge?"

"Yes, of course. Everyone will know you're going to help all of humanity with First Contact."

It sounded like everything they could have hoped for. But when Owen glanced at Selene, he saw a guarded look in her eyes. "Do you mind if Lieutenant Genji and I discuss this privately?" Owen asked Camacho.

"Not a problem," Camacho said. "I'll wait at the bar. When

you've decided, you can lower your privacy shield again. But let me assure you before you discuss the matter that the commitments I make to you are binding. I won't, the Council won't, go back on them. We have the same priorities, Lieutenant Genji. Your actions have already shown that. Please let the Council show you by its actions that it supports your efforts."

Selene nodded but didn't say anything. Owen lowered the privacy shield, looking about the restaurant as he did so for any new patrons who looked like undercover security officers. No one like that was visible, though there were privacy shields up around other tables that prevented whoever was there from being seen.

They both sat silently for a moment after the privacy shield raised again.

Selene exhaled slowly before looking at him. "What do you think?"

"It's risky as hell," Owen said. "But can we afford to pass this up?"

"Telling us they were reopening the investigation into the loss of the *Sentinel* might have been intended just to sway you," she warned.

"That's true," Owen said. "But she also ruled out any specific outcome. If telling me that was designed to influence my decision, wouldn't Camacho have at least implied the new investigation would be sure to clear my father?"

Selene paused, thinking. "Yes. She would have done that. But it is still your dream, isn't it? You want it to happen, more than anything."

Owen shook his head at her. "Not more than anything. I have a new hill, remember? I can't be lured down off of it that easily."

That earned him a quick smile from Selene. "You'd never leave me alone on our hill, would you? Camacho might be lying about the offer, though."

"If she wanted to kill us, she could have done that already."

"Yes." Selene shifted her gaze to the table. "Getting the shoot-to-kill orders lifted, and knowing that general has been relieved of command for trying to order it regardless, is good news. But if we buy into this, it will mean anyone wanting to kill us will know where to find us."

"I noticed your eye twitched when she mentioned diplomatic security guarding us," Owen said. "What did that mean?"

"You spotted that? I thought I'd hidden my reaction." Selene sighed. "Lorraine Esperanza will be murdered by one of her diplomatic security guards who is secretly a Spear of Humanity supporter."

Owen nodded slowly. "Lorraine was . . . will be, another alloy?"

"Yes. We'd still have to stay on full guard, including against the people supposedly guarding us."

"I guess I assumed that," Owen said. "I've gotten a bit paranoid in the last few months."

"It's not paranoia if you have good reasons for being afraid," Selene said. "But you're right. We can't afford to pass up this chance. 'They who will not risk, cannot win.'" Selene looked at him again. "No comment on the quote?"

"That's a quote?"

"John Paul Jones. Famous sailor in ancient times. 'They who will not risk, cannot win.' How can you not know that?"

"I'm sorry I'm not up on my ancient sailor quotes," Owen said.

"You're joking about it," Selene said. "But that is exactly where the rot starts! When the wisdom of the past is disregarded and eventually forgotten because 'everything is different now.' Only everything isn't different. *People* aren't really different." She sat back, covering her eyes with one hand. "And I'm snapping at you because I'm worried about agreeing to this, but I know we have to. Kayl, you know why she wants to take us public, right? Why the Council wants us to be public? Why our transport back to Mars will be public?"

Owen nodded slowly, admitting to the worries he had tried to ignore. "Anyone wanting to kill you will know exactly where you are. And anyone wanting me will know where I am. We're going to be high-class, shiny bait."

"On a high-priority, highly important mission," Selene said, lowering her hand to look at him. "If we succeed in it, many more people will believe that I am not a threat even though I'm an alloy. Many people will accept that you did the right thing. Those who fear my very existence, who fear the example you have set, will feel a need to act before we reach Mars. They will have to openly show their hands. That's why the Council wants us out there, so they'll have grounds to act against people like Admiral Besson, who otherwise might keep doing more and more damage, who otherwise will be threats to us as long as they have any power or influence."

He thought about that, feeling a sad inevitability looming ahead of them. "And that's why we need to do it, isn't it? We need to have those people exposed. Both for our personal safety in the long term, and for the mission. Because the people so scared of you are the same people who would enable the Spear of Humanity in the future, or the collapse of Earth Guard, or other problems."

"Yes," Selene said. "The only way for us to hope for safety is to take extraordinary risks. Time travel isn't the only thing that creates paradoxes, is it? Are we in agreement on this?"

"I think so," Owen said. "I don't like it. But everything you've said is true." He smiled slightly. "Kararii fessandri etheria."

"I'm teaching you Tramontine," Selene said, smiling as well. "Kararii fessandri etheria. Kayl, there's a positive element here. People have been focusing on your family, on someone like Malani, because they couldn't find us. Now they'll know where we are. Security forces, police, Earth Guard, soldiers, the press, gossip magazines, everyone. Including potential assassins. That should take some pressure off your mother, your sister, and Aunt Hokulani."

"That's true," Owen said. "And that's a very positive thing, especially with Krysta going to be with Aunt Hokulani once she's recovered enough."

"But," Selene added, leaning forward, her eyes on him intent, "speaking of protecting others, since we're going to be public, since we're going to be bait, I don't want anything like what happened on the Martian Commons. I don't want you once again putting yourself between me and people shooting at us."

Owen cupped one hand to his ear. "What was that? I thought I just heard something that didn't make any sense."

"Stop channeling Aunt Hokulani. I'm serious."

"So am I," Owen said. "I told you before that I'm not strong enough to let you die. You'll just have to accept that I am going to do everything I can to protect you. No matter what."

She looked back at him, her eyes somber. "I don't want to save the world at the cost of losing you."

"Same here," Owen said. "I guess we both have to live, then."

"Yeah." Selene leaned in to kiss him, holding it for a long moment. "Let's get her back, and tell her we accept the offer, and hope we survive no longer being hunted."

Owen lowered the privacy screen. They both stood up as Cerise Camacho returned.

Selene nodded to Owen.

"It's a deal," he said. "We accept your offer."

"We have to trust you," Selene added.

"Thank you," Camacho said.

"When and where?" Owen asked.

"Right now, if you want. I have a car standing by. Do we need to collect any belongings of yours?"

"There's a public locker," Owen said.

"We'll swing by it," Camacho said. She eyed the UV Aversive hat and gloves and sunglasses still on the table. "Do you—?"

"No," Selene said. "I'm tired of hiding what I am."

Camacho smiled and nodded. "Then please follow me."

They walked out, idle glances toward the small group quickly changing to surprise and startled conversations focused on Selene.

Outside, Camacho raised her phone. "Denis? Issue that press release about Genji and Owen immediately. Also send out the official notification to all agencies and commands that Lieutenant Genji and Lieutenant Owen are in the custody of the Council and under the protection of the Council. Yes, they're with me. We're on our way to their rooms."

"Our rooms?" Owen asked, noticing people on the street turning to stare as they caught sight of Selene.

"At the Interplanet," Camacho said. "A diplomatic suite. It's easier to provide security that way."

"Okay." Owen looked at Selene, noticing that even though she wasn't reacting to the stares, her eyes showed unhappiness. "Are you all right?" he asked in a low voice.

"I just have to get used to it again," Selene said. "And so will you. I told you what it would be like to be seen with an alloy."

Owen gazed about them, seeing surprise and wonder, and on a few faces, worry or fear. "I hope they all realize how lucky I am."

She didn't answer as they reached a large vehicle. The rear door swung open, revealing a back seat area large enough to hold a small party.

Inside, they found a man awaiting them. He nodded in greeting as Owen and Selene took seats next to each other. "I am Ranveer Nahdi, Special Representative of the Security Committee. Cerise Camacho is a co-worker of mine," he added as Camacho joined them and the door sealed.

"You know who we are," Owen said.

"Introductions are not necessary," Nahdi said with a slight smile. "You're both either famous or infamous."

"Ranveer," Camacho said, "was responsible for convincing the Council to reopen investigation into the loss of the cruiser *Sentinel*."

"Really?" Owen said warily. "Why did you do that?"

"Because," Nahdi said, "recent events involving you two have raised significant questions regarding the competence of some people in Earth Guard leadership, and whether it was wise and appropriate to let the investigation into the loss of the *Sentinel* lapse without any official findings. Particularly given the loss of one hundred and two Earth Guard personnel in the disaster. Their lost lives demand that we find answers."

"Good," Owen said. "All I ever wanted was justice for my father and the others who died on the *Sentinel*."

"You have no concerns about what might be found?" Nahdi asked.

"No, sir," Owen said. "I do not."

Nahdi smiled again, though in a way that held a strong promise. "Your attitude is not shared among senior officers at Earth Guard, Lieutenant Owen. They are pushing back for all they are worth. But, this time, answers will be found."

The car had pulled out into the street, proceeding through traffic with ease despite its size. Camacho, seated facing back, nodded to her fellow representative. "We have company."

Owen turned to look, seeing a police vehicle following them. "I imagine someone notified them that Selene got in this car."

"Don't worry," Nahdi said. "We have security personnel already waiting at the hotel, and our credentials immunize us, and anyone with us, from arrest by local police."

"Do your credentials stop bullets?" Owen asked.

"If we see that sort of threat, I assure you, we will deal with it."

"We need our backpacks," Selene said.

"Of course." After Owen gave them the location, the car swung onto a new street, the police still following. When it came to a halt at the lockers, Nahdi accepted the locker information from Owen, going out himself to recover their backpacks.

As he was doing so, two police officers emerged from their car and approached. Cerise Camacho got out to meet them. "Is there a problem?"

"We have a report," one of the officers said, "of a fugitive who was seen entering your vehicle."

"You see our license plates? Would you like to see my credentials? This vehicle, and everyone in it, is outside your jurisdiction."

"We understand that, but—" The officer paused, listening to something. "Say again? That's official? Really? Okay, got it." He nodded to Camacho. "I'm sorry for bothering you. That particular alert has been suspended."

His companion pushed forward a half step. "Is Genji really in there?" she asked.

"Yes," Camacho said, standing like a stone guardian.

"Could I—? I mean, do you think she'd let me take a pic with her? My daughter is a big fan."

Camacho turned enough to look back. "Lieutenant Genji? It's up to you."

Selene, appearing worried and confused, got out, Owen right behind her. "What did you want?"

"A picture," the officer said. "Is that okay? Ever since my daughter saw you on Mars, she's followed everything about you."

"Umm . . . all right," Selene said, standing a bit awkwardly as the officer moved beside her and raised her phone with a broad smile.

"Say 'peace,'" Owen prompted Selene.

"Peace," Selene said, her lips automatically forming a smile as she said the word.

"Thanks!" the officer said, grinning. "So glad we're not chasing you anymore! Do you need an escort?" she asked Camacho.

"If it's not any trouble," Camacho said.

"No problem at all!"

Nahdi returned, passing their backpacks to Owen and Selene as they all got back into the car. "It looked like everything resolved well," he commented to Camacho.

Owen saw Selene looking into her pack, her expression troubled. "Are you okay?"

"Just making sure my uniform is all right," she said.

"Your uniform," Camacho said. "The one you wore on Mars? That came from that fleet you spoke of?"

"Yes," Selene said.

"If I may speak as just me, and not in an official capacity, you're doing them proud, Lieutenant Genji. Whoever your comrades were, you're doing them proud."

Selene looked up, smiling slightly. "Thank you."

At the grand entrance to the Interplanet, several men and women were already waiting, all of them dressed similarly and all of them watching everyone else intently. It felt weird to Owen to follow Camacho through the lobby knowing everyone could see Selene, know who she was. Even though the security personnel were on all sides, moving with purpose to shield him and Selene, he still felt exposed, still wanted to move between Selene and anyone who looked remotely dangerous.

"News channels are reporting your arrival here," Nahdi said, checking his phone while they were in the elevator. "And the Council's announcement that you are under our protection. The local police have contacted the Council asking if we want extra people around the hotel in case of crowds. That would probably be wise."

"Yes," Camacho said.

Their "room" proved to be a suite with a separate bedroom,

a dining area, and a nice sitting area. "We don't need all of this," Owen said.

"Sorry," Cerise Camacho said. "This is standard treatment for two lieutenants of considerable importance. Here's my contact information. I need to report in. There'll be guards posted outside this door, and elsewhere around the hotel. Please tell me immediately if you need anything or have any concerns. You're part of our team now."

"Thank you," Owen said. After they had left him and Selene alone in the room, he looked at her. "Selene, are you all right?"

"Are you?" she asked. "With everyone looking at us?"

"That didn't bother you on Mars."

"I was going for shock effect on Mars," Selene said. "You looked a little . . . unhappy while we were walking here."

"I was worried someone might take a shot at you," Owen said. "That's all."

"You're sure?"

"Yes." He smiled. "Kararii fessandri etheria."

That finally got a smile out of her.

NAHDI LOOKED AT CAMACHO as they went back into the car. "I'm assuming you learned the answer to the most important question."

"Yes," Camacho said. "Lieutenant Genji came from the year 2180. That's how she acquired her knowledge, and her alien DNA, and her motivation. You're not surprised?"

"The idea has been tossed around," Nahdi said. "And there's some other evidence that pointed me in that direction. Remember I told you about the remains of a roughly thirty-year-old man on the same wreckage where Genji was found? There were no DNA hits on him, but yesterday I received a detailed report in response to my request for an exhaustive search. There was a possible hit on the man's mother, which the report discounted as erroneous because it identified a ten-year-old girl as the likely mother."

"Not an erroneous result after all," Camacho said, wondering how it would feel to a ten-year-old to be told her thirty-year-old son had died. Was that death inevitable? Or was that an outcome that could change? Genji clearly thought it could be changed. "He'll be born in ten years."

"Why did he die?" Nahdi said. "Did Genji tell you that?"

Camacho nodded. "He died because his and Genji's ship was destroyed by the shock wave created when the Earth was destroyed on the twelfth of June, 2180."

Nahdi stared at her. "That's her motivation? She's trying to prevent that from happening?"

"Yes."

"She's trying to protect the Earth from being destroyed at some date not too far in the future, and the forces tasked with protecting the Earth are trying to stop her," Nahdi added. "Because they never bothered asking her what she was doing or why. All they cared about was that she had partly nonhuman DNA."

"Lieutenant Owen apparently did ask," Camacho said. "Resulting in a decision to silence him. I can understand being concerned that the Tramontine might pose a threat when they first arrived. That's reasonable. But they haven't shown themselves to be a threat by their actions. Genji has repeatedly told people the Tramontine are not a danger, which is what she'd do if she was an agent of theirs, but everything else she's reported about them has proven to be true."

"Genji outright told some of the negotiators on Mars that the danger to Earth would come from humanity itself," Nahdi said. "I find that all too easy to believe. Though I wonder how we could get from a generally peaceful here to a destruction of Earth there in only forty years."

"Genji can tell us some of what led to that," Camacho said. "But the history she knows, the events that led to the destruction of Earth, is already changing because of her. Genji was shocked to hear that the Council will meet again in two weeks. In her history, arguments over how to respond to the Tramontine led to postponements that resulted in the Council never meeting again."

"You're joking! It was that bad? We have to tell the Council what you learned, even though the impact on Genji herself and what she is trying to do could be huge if it becomes widespread knowledge." Nahdi paused. "You know what this means? The Council matters. Whether or not it meets matters. What we're doing matters. Am I alone in wondering in recent years whether any of those things were still true?"

"You know you're not," Camacho said. "Genji told me she *has* to trust us. Which means we're part of the solution."

"To save the Earth. Literally, it seems," Nahdi said. "I'm suddenly feeling a greater burden of responsibility."

"Imagine what Genji is living with. Can you imagine seeing what she saw?"

"Cerise, should we be going ahead with this plan?" he asked. "Without Genji and Owen knowing where it's intended to lead?"

Camacho understood what he meant. "Ranveer, they've figured out exactly what we're doing. I could tell. They know we're doing this publicly in order to draw into the open and precisely identify the people in authority who decided on sight that Genji needed to die, who claim to be motivated by higher principles but are acting on their own fears. Genji and Owen know that they are being dangled as bait, and that the way we're doing this will force those in the shadows to act openly at considerable risk to both of them. And, knowing that, they agreed to it."

"You're sure of that?" Nahdi said.

"Absolutely."

"Make sure they live, Cerise. Do everything you have to do."

"I'll do my best," Camacho said. "But, in the end, it may come down to them again."

11

GENJI WANDERED RESTLESSLY AROUND the suite, feeling uncertain.

Was this the right thing? Had her and Kayl's decision been the best they could make, or driven by despair or uncertainty? Did it really make sense to paint targets on themselves in the hopes of bringing their worst foes out into the open?

Kayl seemed a bit moody as well, even though he was trying to act as if he wasn't.

How much had he been affected by seeing the way people reacted to her? Genji no longer thought Kayl would leave her rather than endure social ostracism, but she still hated the idea of him being subjected to what she had known in the 2160s and 2170s.

A brisk knock provided warning of their head of security, a man who'd asked them to call him Alejandro, looking inside the suite. "We're ordering food. Would you like anything?"

"Yes," Kayl said. "Thanks for asking."

"It's part of the job. What, um, do you eat?"

Genji sighed, knowing that question was aimed primarily at her. "Are there any places nearby that make good French fries?"

Sure," Alejandro replied, surprised. "There's a great place. They make excellent burgers, too."

"How about anything Southwest or Mexican?" Kayl asked. "We've had a lot of fries and chicken and burgers. It's been a while since I had a good sit-down meal."

"There's a Sonoran place nearby. Amazing tamales, pozole, you name it."

"Pozole?" Kayl said. "Yes. If it's not too much trouble."

Pozole? Some fond memories went through Genji's mind. "How spicy is the pozole?"

"Moderate. They can make it really hot."

"Moderate is fine," Genji said. "It's good? I'd like that, too."

"Seriously? Fries, as well? No problem. What do you drink?"

"Tea," Genji said. "Green tea, if possible."

"This is LA. We can get you green tea. Sir?"

"Coffee," Kayl said. "Black."

"Oh, yeah. You're a sailor. We'll send someone to pick it up. Sure you don't want a beer?"

Kayl looked at Genji.

"Is Angel City available?" she asked.

"Sure it is. You're familiar with that?"

"Who isn't? An IPA or a pilsner, please," Genji said.

"Same," Kayl said.

Alejandro grinned. "I never thought the first meal I ordered for an alien would be pozole and beer. I guess people really are the same all over."

After he'd left, Kayl looked at Genji. "What happened to Angel City Brewery?"

"Nothing! I wasn't sure when they'd started up, even though I thought it was way back before 2100." She paused, eyeing him. "No. It wasn't destroyed. Not until June twelfth, 2180. Not everything I ask about was destroyed in the Universal War."

"Are you okay?" he asked for what must have been the hundredth time today.

"Yes, I'm okay!" Genji walked to look out the window at the street below. A small crowd had already gathered, held away from the hotel's entrance by a line of police. Her eyes could pick out the ugly words on the signs carried by some in the crowd. Because she was here, now, sentiments that had originally surfaced later on were already coming out into the open. "I don't know, that's all. This is a new phase. I wish I knew how it would come out, whether we made the right decision."

Kayl nodded, coming to stand with her and look down at the protesters. "I worry about that, too. What is the matter with those people?"

"It happens," Genji said. "Wherever I go. Whenever I go."

"That is about them, not you," Kayl said.

"I know. 'Someone despises me? That is his concern.' Marcus Aurelius was right, but it's not easy to accept that emotionally." Genji raised her gaze to look down the street. "Here come more of them. A lot more. Is this hopeless, Kayl? Hopeless to think I can change the way people react to aliens, to me, in ways that will save the Earth from its fate?"

"Nothing is hopeless," Kayl said. "My father told me that. As someone else said, 'Kindness is invincible if it is sincere.'"

"Seriously?" Genji turned a disbelieving look his way. "You just quoted Marcus Aurelius to me? Have you been reading his works?"

Kayl shrugged. "You like him, and I wanted to share that with you."

"Mom definitely sent me to you." She looked down again as the much larger crowd reached the line of police. "But sometimes . . . What the hell?"

"What's the matter?" Kayl followed her gaze. "What do those signs say?"

"'Welcome to Earth,'" Genji said in disbelief as she read. "'Thank you.' 'We're glad you're here.' 'Protect the Earth.' What. The. Hell? Kayl, how many people have I told that I was born on Earth?"

"Quite a few," Kayl said. "But shouldn't we focus on the sentiments? These people are supporting you."

"How can those be real? It's insane! It's impossible!" Genji said. "I wasn't aware of things when alloys like me were being born, but I saw the old reports. There weren't any signs saying 'Welcome to Earth.' There was massive security and secrecy and death threats. I saw images of my mother being transported in an armored ambulance with police escorts in front and behind and overhead. What is *this*? They know I'm an alloy!"

Kayl touched her hand lightly. "Selene, they probably have no idea what an alloy is, let alone that they're supposed to fear and hate an alloy. But they do know who you are. That's who they're welcoming."

"How could I have changed this?" Genji asked, baffled.

"Maybe by just doing what seemed right."

THE POZOLE AND BEER were tastes from heaven, reminding her of days spent with people who, like her, hadn't been born yet.

After asking her, Kayl had put on the news. Unsurprisingly, it was dominated by her and Kayl and related issues.

"That's Admiral Besson?" Genji asked as coverage of a news conference showed.

"That's him," Kayl said. "Though the last time I saw him he looked a lot angrier."

She laughed, her mood considerably improved by the beer and pozole. "Imagine how he looked after he learned we busted you out of Eisenhower."

"The mutual defense forces cannot guarantee the safety of humans or their homes if our hands are tied behind our backs," Admiral Besson was saying. "I have expressed in the strongest terms my disagreements with the decision of the Earth Cooperation Council to grant amnesty and protection to an alien whose intentions have been demonstrated by acts of sabotage aimed at an Earth Guard cruiser, and at installations on the surface of the Earth itself where only quick and effective action prevented massive loss of life and property."

"Are you referring to Wallops and Eisenhower?" one of the reporters present called.

"Of course."

"No one died at either place, Admiral. The only person badly injured was a young girl shot by the security forces."

"Admiral, what is your response to reports that some members of the Earth Guard cruiser *Lifeguard*'s crew are claiming the alien actually saved their ship?"

"Admiral, do you have any comment on reports that the Council is reopening the investigation into the loss of the cruiser *Sentinel* ten years ago?"

"No more questions!" an Earth Guard captain announced as Admiral Besson quickly left.

Another channel showed an image of the outside of their hotel, disorientingly zoomed in on their window to show Genji herself looking out. "That is weird," Genji said. "I look awful."

"You look gorgeous," Kayl said.

"—pozole and beer," a woman was saying. "A perfect LA meal for our visitor from another world!"

"I was born on Earth!" Genji yelled.

Another channel, this one showing several people sitting around a table. "—wisdom of this action?" one was saying.

"Who do the mutual defense forces work for?" another asked. "Why is there this pushback as if the Council has no right to question their actions?"

Genji activated the controls, flipping through channels.

"—unprecedented danger—"

"—such a cute couple—"

"—perverted, against the laws of nature—"

"—trying to protect the Earth—"

"—who decides—"

"—remarkable legal action—"

She stopped flipping, rapidly backtracking. "Kayl, it's Malani!" He leaned forward, intent.

"—on behalf of Lieutenant Selene Genji, whose genome is partly made up of alien DNA, but who is essentially human in all ways," someone was saying. "We are proud to have the opportunity to represent Dr. Owen, on behalf of Lieutenant Genji, in seeking to establish the legal personhood of Lieutenant Genji and, by extension, the Tramontine aliens in orbit about Mars. Humans cannot aspire to join the community of other intelligent species unless we are willing to acknowledge that these others are our brethren in every way that matters. We wish to emphasize that we want to establish personhood both in terms of rights *and* responsibilities under law."

Genji listened, wondering what would come of this, wondering if the arguments made in the 2160s would appear early. *If they are human, we'll have to treat animals as human. Where do you draw the line? The only real humans are pure humans!* She waited to hear shouted questions along those lines.

But the first question wasn't an objection. "Your lawsuit also cites a desire by Lieutenant Genji and Lieutenant Owen to adopt the girl Krysta who was injured at Wallops. Is that in accordance with Krysta's wishes?"

"Yes, she has asked us to represent her in that. The two specific issues we ask the courts to rule on are the ability of Lieutenant Genji to marry Lieutenant Owen, and the ability of those two to adopt Krysta. We hope the broader issues will also be addressed, namely the question of whether Lieutenant Genji is in all ways a person in the eyes of the law."

"Dr. Owen!" another reporter called out. "Do you believe Lieutenant Genji is human? Will you welcome her into your family?"

"She is human," Malani said. "I will be very happy to have her as a sister someday, once the courts have allowed her and my brother to marry, just like anyone else can."

Kayl reached over to grasp Genji's arm. "That's *my* sister."

"Yeah," Genji said. "I know. Do you think we have a chance?"

The image shifted to one showing Krysta, still in a hospital bed, but sitting up and looking far healthier. "Have you heard about the lawsuit filed by Dr. Owen?"

"Yes," Krysta said, the single word coming out like a squeak.

"Do you want to be adopted by Lieutenant Owen and Lieutenant Genji?"

"Yes! More than anything!"

"Are you in any way worried about Lieutenant Genji? About why she's here and what she wants to do?"

"She told me what she wants to do," Krysta said. "She thought I was sleeping, and she whispered it, but I heard her. She said what she wanted to do."

"What did she say?"

"Lieutenant Genji said she was going to save the entire world, even if she had to do it one person at a time. I hope she doesn't mind that I told you she said that. Because she did whisper it like it was a secret."

Kayl laughed. "Yeah, Selene, I think we have a chance. You said that to Krysta?"

"I thought she was asleep," Genji said, feeling embarrassed.

She heard noise filtering in from outside, and went to the closest window to listen.

The crowd, grown even larger, had begun chanting to drown out catcalls from the much smaller anti-alien protesters.

"Protect! The! Earth! Protect! The! Earth!"

Kayl came up beside her again. "I think we can do it, Selene. I think we can hold our hill, and just maybe save this planet."

"I should've asked for more beers," Genji muttered. "This is all a little hard to accept. Kayl, you're going to think I'm being excessively cautious, but tonight—"

"We should still sleep in shifts with one of us alert and on guard at all times," Kayl said.

She smiled at him. "I love you."

GENJI HAD INSISTED ON taking the midnight to four in the morning guarding/watching shift, refusing to yield to Kayl's objections until he finally agreed.

She still hadn't told him why those hours were hard for her to sleep through, adding guilt to the usual difficulties after midnight.

Sitting in a chair not far from the large bed where Kayl slept, Genji looked about the darkened room. She'd kept the curtains partly open, so the windows showed reflections of the many lights in many colors on the streets of LA even at this time of the night.

After midnight, usually about one in the morning, was when the ghosts came. Memories of comrades who had died alongside her in the war. Memories of fellow alloys who had died, some murdered, some while fighting, some by their own hands when the hate and despair became too terrible to bear any longer. Sometimes, too, memories of Spears she had killed in desperate fighting, their eyes still vivid in her mind. Visions of places destroyed, the craters dotting the ruins of Albuquerque, the eerie emptiness of the Dead Zone on the Moon, looking down from orbit on where Karachi had been. Visions of fields of death where crowds of people had once lived and worked and dreamed.

What right did she have to still be alive?

She'd never been able to talk about this particular thing with Kayl. As sincere as he was, as tough as his time in Earth Guard had been, he had lived such a sheltered life by comparison. Kayl had lost his father when he was even younger than she had been when her mother had been murdered, but trying to equate those losses felt terribly wrong. Genji feared blurting out resentment of Kayl for the life he hadn't been forced to live, couldn't have lived. There was nothing he could do about that except feel resentful of her in turn.

Genji sat in the near dark, the rainbow lights of LA playing on the windows, seeing the Earth die again in her memory. The awful light covering the globe, everything vanishing, coming apart, the terrible energy unleashed reaching out toward her ship.

Why was she still alive? Was it truly because she had this last mission to carry out? To try to make amends for lives lost and a world destroyed? Why her?

She had been totally honest with Kayl about her rethinking of her path in life. She was no longer seeking that meaningful death, not when life meant Kayl, and an Earth that still lived, and chances to save both of those things. But that meant death now held a dread she had denied for years. It would mean her failure, it would mean the loss of life with Kayl, it would mean the end of any dreams of a someday life that wasn't defined by her mission and the hate of those who wanted her dead because they thought she should never have existed.

Mom, I'm scared. This is too big. I'm too small. I know how to die if I have to. But I don't want to. Not anymore. I want to save you, even if you'll never know me. But what if we fail?

We. Genji looked at Kayl again. What had he done to deserve to be saddled with her, with this fate she'd brought along with her? Yet he seemed weirdly happy with it.

Could she ever tell him about the ghosts?

Because Genji was looking that way, because the curtain was partly open, she saw an intense dot of light appear on the window.

Instinct and experience kicked in without any thought as she bolted from the chair, grabbing Kayl's arm, dragging him along as he woke with a startled cry, then, without asking why, tried to get his feet under him and help her, toward the door to the next room, through the door, shoving Kayl and herself to one side, falling in front of the couch against that wall . . .

The sound of glass being shattered by the missile lasted only a fraction of a second before the warhead detonated in the bedroom.

Genji had fallen atop Kayl, shielding his body with hers, feeling the pressure wave wash over her, hearing shrapnel tear through the wall and into objects, a strange, all-too-familiar chorus of destruction.

Something ripped through the sofa and tore a shallow trench across the skin of her lower back, leaving a trail of pain in its wake.

Then the eerie silence, the roar of the explosion and chaos of destruction replaced by quiet magnified by temporarily deadened hearing, seeing light flare around them as the main door burst open and security guards dashed into the room, weapons out.

Lost in reactions to combat, Genji nearly leapt to engage the security guards, her instincts warning against armed people who weren't in the uniforms of friendly forces.

She held herself still, though, trying to calm her mind, feeling a slight, warm trickle across her lower back where blood must be spreading, also a too-familiar sensation.

Kayl shifted under her. She heard him calling her name, the sound fainter than it should have been. "Wait," she called back to him.

And he listened, because for some unfathomable reason, he trusted her, even now, even when something like this had just happened.

A man leaned down to look at her, his face filled with worry. Genji's mind provided a name. Alejandro.

He was shouting her name. "Lieutenant Genji! Are you all right?"

She moved cautiously, feeling the thread of pain across her lower back protest. "Mostly," Genji yelled back, wondering if her voice was too loud.

Kayl sat up, staring at her, eyes wide with not fear for himself, but concern for her.

It felt strange to find comfort in that, in this moment.

SPECIAL REPRESENTATIVE CERISE CAMACHO paced back and forth through the living area, a space now rendered strange by the debris and destruction from the missile, and the firefighting equipment and extra security people and the emergency medical teams who had tended to Genji's injury.

Sitting on the couch ripped by shrapnel, Genji watched Camacho in between reassuring looks toward Kayl. He was still badly rattled. So was she, in a way, but this had been too familiar to her. That made it easier.

"How's your back?" Kayl asked.

"It doesn't hurt," Genji said. "Just a shallow cut, that's all. The wound strip they put on it will accelerate healing. In a couple of days I won't even know it was there."

"What was with covering my body with yours?" he said, upset. "Didn't you tell me again today not to do that sort of thing for you?"

Genji shrugged. "What's your point?"

He sighed, shaking his head.

Camacho came over, bearing the look of someone who wanted to break things but was restraining herself. "The hotel is, rightly, concerned about the safety of the other guests, and of the building itself."

"So was whoever fired that missile," Genji said. "The warhead was big enough to kill anyone in that bedroom, but small enough to limit the damage it did."

"That's—" Camacho choked off her initial response. "Yes. We'd like to move you to a more secure location. It's the VIP Quarters on Vandenberg for visiting dignitaries. Because it's a joint mutual defense and national defense installation, we had to get approval from national authorities," Camacho explained. "They agreed, and volunteered some national forces to provide extra security around the site."

Genji gave a quick glance at Kayl, seeing him looking back in a way that clearly conveyed he was deferring to her on this decision. "That's fine," she said. "Was anyone else hurt here?"

"No," Camacho said. "Except for a twisted ankle among those using the fire stairs to evacuate the hotel after the explosion. They're sending a bird to pick us up and fly us to Vandenberg."

"Any word on whoever fired that missile at us?" Genji asked.

"No. They found the discarded launcher." Cerise Camacho breathed in slowly. "Once again, I wish to express my sincerest regret for what happened. It's a miracle neither of you was badly injured or killed."

Genji shrugged again. "'Chance favors the prepared mind.'"

No one reacted to the quote from an ancient scientist named Pasteur. She was getting used to that. Her mother had taught her a lot of old sayings that people further in the past seemed unfamiliar with. Which was, really, very strange.

Packing up was simple since they hadn't removed much from their backpacks.

As they walked out of the hotel and toward the bird resting in the street, Genji saw two lines of police facing out toward anxious crowds. Everyone seemed to be recording this, some shouting slogans or good wishes and the occasional warning or threat.

One particular question yelled at her caused Genji to turn that way.

"Is it true you were hurt by the attempt on your life?"

She waved at the questioner and everyone else on that side. "It's only a scratch!"

Genji waited for grins at the joke which was far older than her, and common in the 2170s, but no one reacted.

She let herself be escorted to the waiting bird, then inside, sitting beside Kayl. The armored bird only had panels in the back compartment, no windows, and those were being monopolized by the security personnel.

"Have you ever been to Vandenberg?" Kayl asked her, looking about as thrilled with all this as she was.

"No," Genji said.

"It's got beaches, sand dunes, and snakes."

"Yay."

/ / / / /

"THIS IS COLONEL VASQUEZ," Camacho said. "He's in command of the national forces providing extra security for you while you're staying at Vandenberg."

Genji looked over the colonel, spotting a familiar insignia. "You didn't tell me that we'd be guarded by Marines."

Vasquez, trying not to show any reaction, wiped all emotion from his face as Camacho gave Genji an anxious look. "Is that a problem?" Camacho asked.

"The opposite of a problem," Genji said. "I didn't know we'd have the best protection anyone could ask for. I'll have no worries knowing who is standing sentry." Despite not being in uniform, she brought her hand up in a salute to the colonel, Kayl hastily copying the gesture.

Colonel Vasquez smiled as he returned the salute. "I was not aware our reputation was quite that widely known. We heard you were wounded, Lieutenant. Will you require any extra assistance?"

"It's only a scratch," Genji said, wondering if these Marines would get it.

They did, grins breaking out around her. "Only a flesh wound!" several chorused.

Once inside, the others having finally left them alone, Genji looked about her. "Visiting dignitaries have it pretty nice, don't they?"

"I guess," Kayl said, checking out the bedroom. "What was that with the Marines?"

"I'm still alive," Genji said, "because in March 2178, a force of Marines attached to the Unified Fleet fought their way through to my unit and helped us hold off attacks that should have swamped us. Don't say anything bad about them around me."

"Huh." Kayl looked toward the outside. "I've never seen them fight, of course. Except when they're on liberty. As a matter of fact, there sometimes seems to be a real fine line between fighting and liberty when it comes to Marines."

"I will not argue that," Genji said. "But I will be able to sleep knowing they are standing sentry outside. Do you mind taking the watch? I'm pretty exhausted."

"Go ahead," Kayl said. "My nerves are still jumping." He paused. "That fight where the Marines will save your life. Is that something you can tell me about?"

She hesitated, vivid images and memories of sensations and emotions, all very powerful, flashing through her mind. "Maybe someday. It was pretty intense."

"Why are you looking at your hand?"

Genji jerked in surprise, realizing she had been gazing at the hand that had been splashed with blood, knowing whose blood it had been, clamping down any feelings because feelings would distract and slow her, refocusing on the fight, thinking the odds were too bad, they'd never make it out of this . . . "No reason."

She looked up, seeing him watching her. Knowing he could see through the lie.

No more secrets.

"Come on," Genji said. "If you want to listen, I'll tell you about it. It might do me some good. It might also give you nightmares, though."

"Does it give you nightmares?"

"Yeah. Sometimes."

He nodded, somber. "Then I want to share that with you. Maybe take some of it on me so it doesn't weigh as heavily on you."

"I don't think it works like that," Genji said. "But maybe it does. It's worth a try anyway."

OWEN WAS ON WATCH the next morning, sitting in a chair, when Selene woke, blinking up at the ceiling before turning a smile on him. "That's what I like to see when I wake," she said.

He smiled back despite his tiredness. "How are you doing?"

"Okay." She studied him, as if searching for signs of how her stories last night had affected Owen. "How are you doing?"

"A little more burdened, I think, since we're honest with each other. But I understand better now. How's the back?"

Still lying down, she arched her back tentatively. "Not bad. Why are you staring?"

Owen looked away, laughing. "You look very good when you do that."

"Do men ever think of anything else?" Selene got up carefully. "Do you want some sleep now?"

"I could use it, but we should probably eat something first."

"In that case . . ." Selene pulled out her Unified Fleet uniform, running one hand along the medium-blue-with-gold-trim fabric. "I want to do honor to my absent friends."

"Good idea, since I'm apparently a lieutenant in good standing again." Owen brought out his light-blue-with-silver-trim uniform, gazing at it. "Remember the first time you saw me in this? And told me I must be a fraud because Earth Guard had ceased to exist a decade before?"

"I remember that very clearly," Selene said, smoothing her uniform. "And you thought I was insane."

"At least we were both wrong." They walked to the outer door, opening it to find two diplomatic security agents standing alongside two Marines. "Where do we get breakfast?" Owen asked.

"We'll bring it to you, Lieutenant," one of the Marines said.

"I think we'd prefer to eat with everyone else," Owen said. "I miss doing that."

"So do I," Selene said.

That required several minutes of waiting as the colonel was notified and the base commander was notified and Special Representative Camacho was notified and extra Marines and diplomatic security personnel were summoned. Owen shook his head as they waited. "If I'd known it was going to cause this much trouble, I'd have let them bring us breakfast."

Eventually, they headed for the mess hall, surrounded by a small army of protectors. Inside, all those eating, wearing a variety of uniforms, stopped to watch Owen and Selene go through the line, their protectors still maintaining a perimeter around them.

"We can sit wherever we want, right?" Owen asked the Marine captain closest to him.

"Wherever you want," the captain agreed.

Owen led Selene to a table occupied by a couple of Marines, several planetary defense soldiers, and three Earth Guard enlisted. Sitting down, he nodded to them, feeling very awkward. Some of them seemed to want to move to another table, but stopped after looking at the Marines and security guards now surrounding the table. Owen had looked forward to regaining some sense of normalcy, but nothing about this felt normal.

Selene took a bite of her eggs, chewing. "They're rubbery. How do they do that? Every ship I've served on, every surface base, even on Mars, the eggs are rubbery."

"Same here," Owen said.

"It's a special process," one of the Marines said. She eyed Owen before continuing. "I'd heard rations on Mars were a lot better, Lieutenant."

Owen and Selene shook their heads. "They tell you that to get you to accept a transfer there," he said.

One of the Earth Guard personnel, a senior enlisted, nodded to Owen. "You're pretty cool for someone who got a missile dropped on their bed last night, Lieutenant," she said.

"I've had some pretty rough wake-ups on ships," Owen said. "You kind of get used to it."

The sailor grinned. "I never have."

Selene held up a piece of bacon, staring at it. "This is real bacon."

"You like bacon?" one of the soldiers asked.

"Of course I like bacon. Who doesn't like bacon?"

"Where are you from?" the soldier blurted.

Selene eyed him as she chewed on bacon. "I was born within one hundred miles of here," she finally said. "Earth is my home."

"How . . . how is that possible?" another Earth Guard sailor demanded. "Weren't you sent here by the aliens on the ship at Mars?"

"Nope," Selene said. "I can talk to them, but I did that to help the human negotiators on Mars. The Tramontine on the ship orbiting Mars had nothing to do with me being there, or being here."

"But you're an alien," a soldier said.

"Am I?" Selene paused, emotions flitting across her face. "Some people thought a few alien genes added to our genome would benefit humanity. So they tried that with some embryos. They failed to ask humanity how it felt about that. Obviously, they didn't ask me, either."

The Earth Guard senior enlisted shook her head. "You mean you're a human with some alien DNA added, not an alien with human DNA added."

"Yes," Selene said.

"Then why have we been hunting you the way we have? Why have we been told you're an alien?"

Selene looked at Owen.

It was his turn to shake his head. "I brought Lieutenant Genji aboard my ship, the *Vigilant*. I did the initial interview of her. Then orders came that she officially didn't exist, and no one was to talk to her or about her. Unfortunately for me, I'd already talked to her."

The senior enlisted studied Owen for a moment. "I saw that recalled safety report about the ship you were on being sabotaged. Who did it, Lieutenant?"

"I'd really like to know the answer to that myself," Owen said.

"No interrogation, then? Just, she doesn't exist? Were they going to send her somewhere?"

"Yes," Owen said. "On the same ship rigged to kill me." He paused while the Earth Guard sailors exchanged looks. "I decided instead of dying, I'd stay alive and help Lieutenant Genji protect the Earth."

"And that's why the Council ordered you be returned to duty?" The senior enlisted spread her hands. "Makes sense."

It seemed to be going well. For about one more second.

One of the soldiers, a man who had been silent throughout, suddenly picked up a bowl in front of him and hurled it at Selene.

12

OWEN DIDN'T HAVE TIME to react, but Selene did, possibly having noticed him preparing for the move. She grabbed the bowl in midair, catching it short of her face.

Selene held up the bowl, her other hand raised to restrain the guards, who were just starting to react. "Is this yours?" she asked the soldier.

He didn't answer.

"You know," Selene said, "if I was in a bad mood, I would have tossed this back immediately and put a big dent in that thick skull of yours. Lucky for you, I've been eating bacon." She flicked the bowl back toward the soldier so it hit the table, slid, and came to a stop directly in front of him.

Owen was still debating how to respond when the soldier muttered something under his breath.

"Alien bitch."

"Did you say something?" Selene said, her eyes fixed on the soldier. "Is there something you want to say to me?"

The soldier sat, his eyes on the table before him.

"Go ahead, soldier," Selene continued. "Say it loud enough for everyone to hear. Don't you have the guts to do that? Do you only whisper insults when you think no one can hear you? Stand up and say it again."

The soldier sat silent, quiet spreading throughout the mess hall as others became aware of the drama.

"What's the matter, soldier?" Selene asked. Her voice had stayed flat, but was slowly rising in volume. "Are you afraid to say that to my face? Get up, come over here, and say it again. Unless you're the kind of coward who talks big but never wants to get hurt."

The soldier had begun trembling, his eyes big, but didn't otherwise move or speak.

"Come on, big man," Selene said, her voice carrying now. "Why can't you talk now? Are you afraid of me?"

"Selene," Owen muttered to her.

She shook her head without turning to look at him, keeping her eyes fixed on the soldier, slowly coming to her feet. "I've shed blood to defend this world, and to defend worms like you, while you were making entries in databases and crying to your mommy every time you got a paper cut. You think you're better than me? Let's find out. One on one, right now. What's the matter, hero? Come on. Get up. Let's go. I can't wait to kick your cowardly ass."

The mess hall had gone totally silent, everyone looking toward their table. Owen looked around, trying to judge reactions. Most of those watching seemed to be trying to hide their feelings, though.

A major walked up to the table. "Is there anything wrong here?"

"No, Major," Selene said, her voice gone back to normal volume. "This individual and I were having a private discussion. My apologies to everyone else present for disturbing their meal."

The major raised his eyebrows at Selene. "All right, Lieutenant. You might want to moderate your voice a bit more the next time you're having a private discussion." He looked at the object of Selene's wrath, sitting quivering in his seat. "Do you have anything to say?"

"No, sir," the soldier got out.

"By your leave, Major," Selene said. She looked at Owen. "I'm done. Are you?"

"Yeah," he said, having lost what appetite remained to him.

Selene got up with a final disdainful glance at the soldier. "Pissant," she tossed over her shoulder as she left.

Owen walked with Selene out of the mess hall, hearing the roar of conversation starting up the moment they cleared the door. He took sidelong glances at the Marines escorting them, looking for clues to their feelings about what had happened.

Selene herself said nothing, walking along at a steady pace.

When they reached their quarters, two of the Marines ran forward to hold the door for Selene. "Thank you," she said as she walked inside.

Owen fixed the Marine captain leading their military guards with a demanding look. "Out with it, okay?"

The captain shook her head, smiling. In fact, all the Marines were smiling. "Nothing to come out with, Lieutenant. That was a pleasure to observe."

The Marine sergeant nodded. "The lieutenant's eloquent example of correctional counseling was truly inspiring."

"The truth is," the captain said, "we were all hoping he'd get up and face her."

"It wouldn't have lasted very long," Owen said. "We'll try to have less drama at lunch."

"Maybe order in?" the captain suggested.

The diplomatic security guards nodded vigorous agreement to that.

"Just maybe," Owen said.

Inside, he found Selene standing, looking out a window at the base.

"Hi," Owen said.

She looked at him. "Hi. Sorry. But you need to get used to that. I never have, but it's just something you have to expect. Every time you're in public with me."

"It's okay," Owen said.

"No. It's not. It's never okay. Please don't pretend it is."

He paused to think through possible replies before simply nodding. "Yeah. It's been like that all your life?"

"All my life," Selene said, looking out the window again. "When I was little, I'd have to ask my mother what certain words thrown at me meant. Sometimes she didn't want to tell me, and I'd insist."

"I kind of wish you had beaten him into a pulp."

She glanced at him again, smiling slightly. "I didn't want to embarrass you any more than the situation already had."

"Do you think it embarrasses me to be seen with you?" Owen asked, deciding to confront that issue head-on.

"Yes."

"No, it doesn't," Owen said. "I get angry if I hear insults thrown at you, I get worried if there seems to be a threat, I feel . . . happy that I'm being seen alongside you. I never feel embarrassed, except on your behalf, and then I want to show everyone how proud I am that someone like you actually thinks someone like me deserves your love."

Selene looked at him again, smiling fully this time. "You live in your own strange world, don't you?"

"As long as you're there with me, I'm happy."

"Oh, I won't be leaving you, Lieutenant Owen. Not a chance. Somebody has to protect you from after-midnight missile attacks."

BY MIDMORNING, OWEN WAS starting to wonder what the difference would be between prison and being protected in the VIP Quarters. He felt restless, but was unable to go out. Selene was still moody, deservedly so, but didn't want to talk about it.

The entertainment panel was full of breathless news items about the surrender of the alien to the Earth Cooperation Council and the search for the perpetrators of the attack on their hotel. Reports of the breakfast altercation were already making the rounds. An outraged Admiral Besson was demanding to know why national defense forces were intervening in a mutual defense forces situation.

Owen finally put on music, listening to a current hits station, trying to lose himself in the words, the melodies, and the harmonies.

"I didn't know you liked oldies," Selene said.

"These are current hits," Owen said.

"Oh . . . sorry."

Fortunately, the Marines intervened at that point to deliver enough beer to fully stock the refrigerator. "Compliments of the corps," they said.

Immediately after that, Special Representative Cerise Camacho arrived. "I heard there was an incident."

Owen glanced at Selene, who shook her head.

"Nothing to speak of," she said.

"I wanted to update you," Camacho said. "Are you familiar with the fast transport *Yamanaka*? It arrived in Earth orbit yesterday and is currently restocking. Our plans are to lift you both, as well as me and your diplomatic security guards, to the *Yamanaka* tomorrow afternoon. Once we're all aboard, the *Yamanaka* will make a fast transit to Mars. I'm told that, given current orbital positions, that will take roughly four and a half weeks."

She paused. "There will be two Earth Guard cruisers escorting the *Yamanaka*. The *Lifeguard* and the *Diligent*."

"You're going to make it that easy for them?" Owen asked.

Camacho hesitated before replying. "The commanding officers of both ships have been handpicked by Earth Guard's senior officers."

"You are going to make it that easy for them," Owen said, turning it into a statement.

There was a long pause before Camacho spoke again. "If anything happens, if there are any attempts against you, there has to be no doubt who gave the orders. But we do not believe anything will be attempted that we cannot protect you against. No one believes the crews of those ships would follow orders to destroy the *Yamanaka*."

"I'm not sure I'm that confident of even that," Owen said. Selene was staying silent, letting him express their worries. He knew that was one of the ways she displayed her confidence in him, which made him more determined to state his concerns.

Camacho didn't directly argue the point, instead gesturing to herself. "I'm going to be on the *Yamanaka*, along with you."

Owen took a glance toward Selene, who was gazing to one side as she thought. Finally, Selene looked back at him and nodded, her expression that of someone resigned to doing a task they had no desire to do.

"All right," Owen said. "We understand."

"Thank you." Camacho smiled and quickly changed the subject. "Are you two willing to participate in a press availability this afternoon? There's an immense amount of interest in you, and the Council would like you to be able to present yourselves directly to everyone."

Selene actually shuddered slightly before nodding again.

He knew how she felt, having seen the sorts of things being tossed around in news programs and commentaries and opinion pieces and gossip sites. But this wasn't something they could avoid if they wanted to change attitudes. "All right," Owen said again.

Various high-ranking officers from the base stopped by before noon, all dropping broad hints that maybe future visits to the mess hall would be unwise. When lunchtime rolled around, Owen firmly rejected offers to get food from off-base, insisting they should eat what was being offered to everyone else in the mess hall. He was pretty sure Selene wanted to go back and face down everyone while they ate lunch, but she didn't object to eating in their quarters when that food was brought to them.

The arrival of the Council press officials to set up for the media interview was a relief from the tension of waiting.

Juanita Hussein, the head of the Council press contingent, fussed over Owen's and Selene's appearance before the interview went live. "It's better to be honest than clever," she advised them. "Just be yourselves. Do you want us to try to do something about your skin? It's going to look very glossy on the cameras."

"That's because it is," Selene said in a flat voice.

"Umm . . . okay. Sorry. If you'll move over here . . ."

They were seated on the sofa, about an arm's length apart. Owen looked over at Selene, then got up and moved closer. She smiled at him, reaching out one hand. He grasped it as the interview went live, more than a dozen virtual screens appearing before them.

Hussein began with an introduction. "Lieutenant Selene Genji and Lieutenant Kayl Owen, currently serving the Earth Cooperation Council, wish to speak with the people of the world and answer their questions."

Owen marveled at Selene's patience as the same questions came at them. Where are you from? Why are you here? Does Earth feel strange to you? (This after repeating again that she had been born on Earth.)

"You say the aliens want to share with us?" a woman asked, sounding wary. "What is it they want to share?"

"Information," Selene said. "Knowledge. Technology. The Tramontine believe that sharing such things is the highest virtue and among the greatest pleasures."

"What sort of things do they know?"

"Their technology could jump-start the terraforming of Mars," Selene said. "Allow us to do within decades what would otherwise have taken us centuries. And, they didn't come here directly from their home world. The star system we tracked their ship back to was another one they've explored. There is a planet there suitable for human habitation. The Tramontine will gladly share with us everything they learned about that planet. Its climate, its environment, its life-forms, everything. And, with that knowledge, we can build ships, if we want, that can explore that world, and establish human colonies upon its surface."

That surprised the questioners enough that there was a slight pause before the next person spoke. "Don't the aliens, the Tramontine, want that world for themselves?"

"No," Selene said, shaking her head, "they don't. That's not why they explore. They want to find new things. They don't want to own those things, or necessarily use those things. They just want to find new answers which will create new questions whose answers they can seek. That's what motivates the Tramontine. If we want to make use of that world, they would have no objection at all. They would help us with whatever information they can supply."

"In trade for information about us?"

"No," Selene said, looking aggravated for a moment. "The Tramontine don't see it as a trade. They don't try to assign value to certain knowledge. They just want to tell us what they know, and hear what we can tell them."

"That seems strange," a man commented.

"They're aliens!" Selene said. "To them, the ultimate goal in life is to find new answers and new questions. They don't want to know everything, because if they did, they wouldn't have any reason to live or explore or study. They're not human. So many of the worries people have are because we think they're going to act like we would. They don't. They won't. They're *aliens*."

The idea that aliens might actually think and act differently than humans seemed to stun everyone listening. Owen, who had yet to be asked a single question, wondered whether a moment like this might matter a great deal in changing feelings about the Tramontine.

And about Selene herself.

A short time later, he did get a question lobbed at him. "Lieutenant Owen, what do you say to those who consider your relationship with Lieutenant Genji to be perverted and unnatural?"

That took him a moment to work through an answer that wouldn't sound defensive or angry. "I fail to understand their point. Lieutenant Genji is a person. She has some differences from other people, but she's a person. I admired that person, I liked that person, before I came to love her. When I look at her, I don't see the differences. I see her. Before we had any kind of relationship, she risked her life to save me, because that's the kind of person she is. So, I don't understand why anyone would find it odd that I care for such a person and want to spend my life with her."

"But . . . physically . . . she's not human."

"No," Owen said, "that's wrong. Physically, she is human." It was only after he said it that he realized he'd addressed something he hadn't meant to, discussing a private aspect of Selene that he had no right to share with anyone else. It was one thing to say that to a few others, with Selene's approval, in a sailboat. Another thing entirely to say it to the world.

And, embarrassingly, his answer produced an uproar of interest among the questioners.

"Sorry," he whispered to Selene.

"It's okay," she replied, her voice carrying an undertone of tension that belied her words, but a reassuring squeeze of his hand letting him know she didn't fault him for it.

The questioner persisted, though. "Then why do you think some people object to your . . . relationship with her?"

Owen considered possible replies, remembering the advice to just be himself. "It's probably envy," he said. "I mean, how fortunate can I be?"

That earned him some laughs, as well as a half-amused, half-pained look from Selene.

"Can you have children together?" another person asked eagerly.

"Perhaps," Selene said, sounding remarkably cool to Owen's ears as she publicly discussed such a private matter.

"Are you planning on having children?"

"Our priority is protecting the Earth," Selene said. "Beyond that, if we . . . survive our work, that is something we would have to address between us. Certainly, we look forward to having the chance to help raise Krysta, if we're allowed to do that."

"Some people say that you're just using the girl Krysta to get what you want."

"No," Selene said. "Why would we hurt her that way? She's been hurt enough."

"We care about her," Owen added. "We risked our lives on the Moon to help her. We want to keep helping her, if we can."

"Lieutenant Genji, can you tell us why we should trust you? Why we should believe what you are telling us?"

Selene took a moment to reply. "I'm not asking you to trust me," she finally said. "All I am asking is that you give me a chance, and watch what I do, and judge that. Listen to me, to what I'm trying to say, and judge that."

"Has anyone refused to listen to you?"

"Excuse me?" Selene said, her voice rising. "Has anyone refused to listen to me? Do you mean like the Earth Guard leaders who jammed every transmission I tried to make? Do you mean the people who issued the shoot-to-kill orders on me, orders which specifically stated I should not be allowed to speak, that anyone who got me in their sights should shoot immediately, and not give me any chance to say even one word? Do you mean the soldiers on Mars who were ordered to shoot and kill me as I stood speaking on the Martian Commons? Do you mean whoever ordered that I be killed, along with Lieutenant Owen here, before anyone had officially interrogated me? Without benefit of any charges? After issuing orders saying that I didn't exist?"

"Who was responsible for those things?"

"I don't know," Selene said. "Nobody knows. That's pretty scary, isn't it? That someone in an official position can order someone else silenced, someone else killed, and nobody even knows who they are? That's why the Council got involved, you know. They're worried that someone is doing that. You should be worried, too."

"Why?" another person asked. "Why would someone do that?"

Selene looked at the questioner, her hand tightening on Owen's. "Because I'm different. I look different. That's all. That's all it's ever been. All through human history. This person is different. That's the only reason some people need. And they tell everyone else to be afraid. They tell everyone else they should do something, they have to do something, because that person is different.

"I know exactly where that kind of thing can lead. I know how thinking of someone different as less than human can lead to thinking their lives matter less. And then anyone who defends those who are different deserves whatever happens to them. And then they're all a danger, and danger needs to be destroyed, and more and more people need to die to supposedly protect other lives. But it's all a lie. 'If any question why we died, tell them, because our fathers lied.' Kipling said that a long time ago after an awful war. It has happened before. If we do not fight against such things, advocate for the worth of everyone, see the worth of everyone, stop searching for demons to blame our troubles on, it will happen again, on a far wider and more terrible scale than ever before."

When Selene spoke of such things, Owen thought, her entire self took on an aura of terrible certainty, sounding not like someone warning of a possibility, but someone prophesying a future they had seen. Which was literally true. Would enough others see that in her, heed her words, to alter the future to come?

A longer silence followed Selene's statement this time, before an unexpectedly familiar voice spoke. "Lieutenant Genji, this is Frederick Hoster. I wanted to thank you again for saving my father's life."

"I'm glad I did," Selene said. "I'm glad that you're all right, too."

Would anyone else spot the slight catch in her voice as she said that? Was she thinking of the man who'd spewed hatred and helped lead the world to its end, or the boy she'd wanted to kill, or the boy who'd become something else because of her actions? Or all those things, a mix of what once would be and what no longer would be and what had replaced that?

"Do you have some sort of code you live by?" Hoster said. "Something that would let people know what sort of person you want to be?"

Selene nodded. "'If it is not right, don't do it: if it is not true, don't say it.' Marcus Aurelius said that. My mother told me she hoped I would take those words to heart. I have . . . tried to live them."

"You do! You do! Thank you for your answer and again for your heroism saving my father! I've told people they need to judge you by your actions. I hope they do."

"Thank you," Selene said. "I hope they do as well."

Another voice broke in. "What actions would you like to be judged on?"

"My help with First Contact," Selene said. "That, primarily, at this point."

"What about your destruction of a mutual forces aircraft at Wallops?" someone else demanded. "That was one of your actions."

"I was trying to not be killed," Selene said.

"If I may point out," Owen said, "Lieutenant Genji did not destroy that bird. It was destroyed by all of the people and drones and automated defenses shooting at it. Shooting at her and at me."

Owen waited, hoping those listening would take a moment to realize the truth of his statement. "I was driving that bird. Not Lieutenant Genji. I want to emphasize something, since we're talking about actions. Despite shoot-to-kill orders against us, at Wallops and at Fort Eisenhower, and on Mars, we never tried to kill anyone who was trying to kill us. We used the minimum possible force, even when missiles were fired at us by Earth Guard warships. That's because we always knew we were on the same side as those shooting at us, and we kept hoping they'd realize the same thing."

"Lieutenant Owen, you've brought up Earth Guard. You were charged with quite a few crimes before the Council intervened. You assisted Lieutenant Genji in sabotaging a cruiser—"

"We did not sabotage that cruiser," Owen interrupted. "Talk to the crew. They'll tell you the truth. Lieutenant Genji saved that ship, and the lives of every Earth Guard officer and sailor aboard it. Ask Commander Montoya, the former commanding officer of that ship. She'll tell you that."

"We've been denied access to Commander Montoya for security reasons."

"I wonder why?" Owen said. "Why won't those in charge of Earth Guard let you talk to Commander Montoya? What was the rest of your question?"

"Is there anything you would like to say to everyone in Earth Guard, Lieutenant Owen?"

Owen nodded. "I'd like to tell them that I never violated my oath, and I never took any action that would endanger any of them, or sought to harm any of them. They are all, still, my comrades. I never stopped seeing them as comrades."

"What about those in Earth Guard who believe that you betrayed them?"

"I did not," Owen said, keeping his tone even. "I was betrayed by whoever in Earth Guard ordered my death. Whoever that was could also order the death of anyone else who was inconvenient or in the way or whose death might suit their purposes. My attempts to survive, to find out who was behind those actions, were aimed at protecting my comrades in Earth Guard."

"But what about those who disagree with your actions?"

Was the question being repeated to provoke him? Owen bit back his initial response, finally speaking again in a calm voice. "I was not, and am not, under any obligation to let myself be killed because they think I should have handled things differently. The next time they're in a ship sabotaged to fill the air with carbon monoxide and make a destructive entry into atmosphere, they are more than welcome to ride that ship all the way to hell."

"Lieutenant Owen, your father was involved in the loss of the cruiser *Sentinel* ten years ago. How do you feel about the investigation into that disaster being reopened?"

"I welcome it," Owen said. "I have no doubt the new investigation, like the independent investigation soon after the disaster, will find my father blameless. Hopefully it will identify those truly at fault, if there are such individuals."

"Retired Rear Admiral Raven Tecumseh has charged that Earth Guard's current leaders are self-serving careerists who put themselves ahead of Earth Guard's mission. Do you agree with her?"

Owen paused to think through his words before speaking. "I would not presume to contradict Rear Admiral Tecumseh. I think most of the people serving in Earth Guard are dedicated to the mission and do their best every day. I think they deserve leaders who are equally dedicated."

And so it went, many questions variations on those that had come before, until Juanita Hussein finally called a halt.

"That went pretty well," Hussein said cheerfully.

Dinner was a surprise delivery of various kinds of pizza, courtesy of the diplomatic security guards. One of the guards, Angielyke, paused to gush about how well the interview earlier in the day had gone. "I'm going to be accompanying you to Mars, providing security aboard the *Yamanaka*. It's such an honor!"

"Pizza and beer," Owen said as they sat down, the entertainment panel set to nature scenes and music. "Not bad for our last dinner on Earth."

"Did you really just call it that?" Selene demanded.

/////

MORNING CAME, GENJI YAWNING as the light grew outside, brightening the world beyond their windows. Sleeping in shifts, one of them always on watch, was wearying. But Kayl hadn't protested.

Breakfast delivered from the mess hall included a lot of bacon. "Let us know if you want more bacon, Lieutenant!"

Apparently she'd impressed somebody when she dressed down that jerk yesterday.

Cerise Camacho showed up soon after breakfast. "We're not leaving from the spaceport here at Vandenberg. We're going to be lifted into orbit from LA Interplanetary so there can be maximum public coverage of the event. We'll leave for LAI at 1500."

"Maximum public coverage. That's going to be very different from previous orbital lifts we've done together," Kayl remarked to Genji.

"At least we have plenty of time to paint targets on our backs before we leave," she replied.

"We have some more visitors for you," Camacho said, acting as if she hadn't heard Genji's last remark. "In a couple of hours."

"Fine," Genji said. "It's not like we have much packing to do. Is this going to be another set of interviews?"

"No," Camacho said.

"Mystery guests," Kayl muttered.

"Maybe Admiral Besson is coming to apologize to you," Genji suggested.

"Yeah, I'm sure that's it."

Roughly two hours later, Camacho knocked on their door again. "Your visitors are here. They know they can only stay about an hour. We're having the lunch you requested delivered for you." Camacho went out the door, leaving it open.

A moment later, a familiar woman came rushing through it. "Kayl!"

"Aunt Hokulani?" Kayl jumped to his feet and laughed as Aunt Hokulani hugged him.

"I'm not alone! Selene! How nice to see you again!"

"Hi . . . Aunt Hokulani." It felt strange to call her that to her face. Genji, feeling awkward already, watched as two more women entered the room, one of whom she also recognized. "Hello, Malani." Who was the other woman? Could that be . . . ?

"Mom!" Kayl said, running to meet her. "I'm so sorry I haven't been able to get to you."

"You've been busy. I understand," his mother said. Her gaze rested on Genji, who tried not to look as nervous as she felt.

This was never supposed to happen. Not in her life. She was never supposed to get engaged, never supposed to meet the mother of her future husband. Such a life was for others, not for an alloy like her.

Unaware of the turmoil inside Genji, Kayl turned to smile at her. "Mom, this is Lieutenant Selene Genji. Selene, this is Leilani, my mother."

Genji smiled and extended her hand. "I'm so glad to—" Her words were cut off as Leilani brushed aside her hand and enveloped Genji in a tight hug.

"I understand you're already my daughter in every way that matters," Leilani said as she stepped back. "Thank you for looking after Kayl."

Genji laughed with relief. "I was ready to apologize for getting him into so much trouble, so much danger."

"I admit to being concerned about that," Kayl's mother said. "But I understand that you've saved his life a few times."

"Six times," Kayl said.

"Seven times, now," Genji said. "Not that I'm counting. I'm so happy to meet you, Leilani."

"Please call me Mother if you wish," Leilani said. "I cannot replace who you lost, but I promise to love you as a daughter."

"Thank you," Genji said, wondering why it was suddenly so hard to speak. "And, uh, thank you, Malani, for getting that lawsuit going."

"It was the least I could do," Malani said, taking a seat and looking around. "This is how Earth Guard treats lieutenants, huh?"

"Not normally," Kayl said. "Are you okay at work? Not getting any pushback for getting involved with all this?"

"Pushback?" Malani laughed. "The lab made me a full partner. My life is good, little brother."

"We've got coffee or tea," Genji said. "I guess you're all coffee drinkers, though."

"We won't discriminate against a tea drinker," Aunt Hokulani said, sitting down next to Leilani. "You made me look bad, you know, Selene. I told these two there wasn't going to be any personal relationship between you and Kayl because you told me the mission was top priority, and anyway, you were an alloy. Next thing I know, we're getting questions from reporters about you two making out in public on Mars!"

Genji laughed, covering her face with her hands in embarrassment. "I was sort of drunk. I mean, not really drunk. I was given a mild sedative as part of treatment for a power rifle burn, and that interacted with my alloy metabolism just as if I'd chugged half a bottle of whiskey. But Kayl was fine. He could have stopped me from kissing him!"

"I didn't want to stop you," Kayl said, grinning.

"We were in uniform!" Genji looked at Aunt Hokulani. "You were right that I was underestimating Kayl. He completely respected the limits I set. He didn't push on them. If he had, I never would have yielded. But when someone respects your limits, respects your needs and your priorities, listens to your advice and your ideas, it's hard not to like them, maybe a lot more than you thought you could like them."

Leilani smiled. "Kayl is like his father that way."

"Tell us about the proposal of marriage!" Aunt Hokulani said. "I hope it was romantic."

Kayl glanced at Genji. "I don't know how romantic it was.

I proposed aboard that stolen Martian lifter soon after we reached the Tramontine ship."

Genji smiled at him. "And I got very angry with Kayl, refused to give him an answer, and told him he shouldn't have asked. Later that day he accidentally brought it up again, and I yelled at him and told him it was impossible and could never happen and I would never give him an answer. And then Kayl promised to never bring it up again."

Leilani nodded. "I guess you changed your mind, though."

"Eventually," Genji said. "When I realized that I finally knew my answer. Kayl kept his promise, though. He never brought it up again until I did. He always keeps his promises. Except that one time on Mars when he wouldn't let me sacrifice myself to ensure he escaped."

"I'll admit to that one," Kayl said.

"You should have seen him," Genji said, smiling wider as she looked at Kayl. "Standing in the air lock of the lifter, firing his rifle at the soldiers trying to kill me, ignoring their return fire aimed at him, not retreating a centimeter until I got close enough for him to grab me and pull me into the lifter. I was so close to dying. And then lifting off while they tried to shoot us down, and getting us through the Earth Guard ships trying to kill us with amazing ship-driving. I should have realized then that I wanted to have this guy beside me forever." She glanced at the others, who were watching her with stunned expressions. "Did Kayl never tell you about that?"

Aunt Hokulani sighed. "Just like his father, eh, Leilani?"

"Just like his father," Kayl's mother agreed, looking upset.

"I'm sorry," Genji said. "I didn't mean to worry you."

"We already knew people were trying to kill both of you," Aunt Hokulani said. "But, yeah, the details can be a little scary."

"You don't seem rattled by talking about things like that, though," Malani said.

"I had a lot of experience in the Unified Fleet," Genji said. "During the Universal War."

"What exactly did you do in your fleet, Selene?" Leilani asked.

Genji glanced at Kayl as she answered. "My secondary specialty was targeting. My primary specialty was close combat."

"Close combat?"

"I killed people," Genji said. "A lot of people. I was trained specifically to take out Spear of Humanity shock troops, but I could handle anyone else who got in the way." She saw the others trying not to react to her frank admission. "That's what I wanted to do, because they'd murdered my mother, and they'd killed a lot of alloys like me. But that didn't bring me satisfaction, and it didn't win the war. Since arriving here, in 2140, I've tried not to kill. But I am good at it. You deserve to know that."

"She had to fight in some terrible wars," Kayl said, sounding anxious to further explain. "Entire cities were being destroyed. The world sort of goes crazy."

"It will unless we manage to change enough things," Genji said. "Unless we can keep changing things. To prevent that from happening. To maybe prevent the Universal War as well as the death of the Earth. But I'll probably always see the ghosts of what was to be, even though hopefully places like Albuquerque will never be destroyed."

"Albuquerque?" Aunt Hokulani said, startled.

"Your place should be outside the zone of destruction," Genji said. "If it happens. Hopefully it won't. You weren't planning on moving closer to the center of the city, were you?"

"Not now, I'm not! This is before the Earth is destroyed?" Aunt Hokulani said. "Yeah, let's hope that doesn't happen. You'd let me know if I should move, right?"

"Yes," Genji said. "I would. If I can save the Earth from its fate, none of you should be hurt. As far as I know."

"Malani told us you weren't as worried about never being born because of the changes," Leilani said. "That must have been terrifying."

"It was. It is," Genji admitted. "It's still possible that could happen. But the Tramontine were pretty certain if that was going to happen, it would have already happened. I'll probably never be born, but I'm here."

"That still doesn't make sense," Malani said.

"Me being here doesn't make sense," Genji said. "I mean, I was born in 2158. How can I be in 2140? But I am."

"We saw the interview yesterday," Kayl's mother said. "I thought you both came across very well. All of my co-workers and friends did, too. They were all asking me what I thought of you, Selene. Whether or not I was worried about Kayl marrying you. I told them, look at her, listen to her. The only thing I worry about is people trying to hurt them."

She paused. "I saw a video of you on Mars, Selene, taking down all those soldiers. They slowed it down a lot so they could analyze your moves, and they said you could've killed every one of those soldiers, easy. But instead you, um . . ."

"Disarmed and disabled," Genji said.

"Yes! People notice that kind of thing. They're trying to kill her, but she's holding back. She's not killing. Like you said in that interview yesterday. Things like that are why more and more people believe what you said on the Martian Commons, Selene, that you're here to protect people and protect the Earth."

Genji nodded. "'Whatever anyone does or says, I must be a good man.' 'Man' in the sense of 'human,' of course."

"Is that an alien saying?" Malani asked.

"No. Marcus Aurelius." Genji smiled, her memory shaded by sorrow. "I've told Kayl my mother used to read to me a lot. One of the things she read to me was Marcus Aurelius's *Meditations*. Yes, my mother read philosophy texts to her little girl for bedtime! And then we'd talk about what he or some other philosopher had said." She blinked, trying to fight off tears. "I miss Mom so much. I wanted to avenge her even though I knew she wouldn't have wanted that. But I know she'd be happy with what I'm doing now. And I'm sure she'd be happy with Kayl, too."

Genji looked at Kayl. "I believe that my mother sent me to Kayl because she knew I needed him, and because he needed me, and she knew together we could save the world." She smiled at Kayl again. "That's our hill, to save the world."

"But you're not planning on dying on that hill, right?" Aunt Hokulani said.

"No," Genji said. "We're going to hold that hill against everything that gets thrown at us. Right, Lieutenant Owen?"

"Right, Lieutenant Genji." He smiled at her, his hand tightening on hers slightly. "We are one."

"We are one," Genji said.

Malani shook her head. "I told you they were hard to be around," she told Aunt Hokulani and Leilani. "Who calls someone 'lieutenant' as a term of affection?"

"Your father used to call me 'the admiral,'" Leilani said.

"That girl Krysta always calls them 'lieutenant,'" Aunt Hokulani added.

"And I am once again the only sane person in the room," Malani said. "Are you guys safe now? I mean, aside from that missile attack? You've got all those guards outside, and you're working for the Earth Cooperation Council. The worst is over, isn't it?"

Kayl looked at Genji, his question easy to see. She nodded to him. These people deserved to know what was really going on.

13

"MALANI, MOM, AUNT HOKULANI," Kayl said, "the truth is, it's probably not over. All of this publicity, letting everyone know we're going to Mars on the *Yamanaka*, is designed to draw out the people who've been working behind the scenes to kill us."

"You're bait?" Malani demanded.

"Yes," Kayl said. "I mean, they haven't come out and bluntly told us, but Selene and I both know that's what's going on."

"Why did you agree to this?" Leilani asked, looking stricken.

"Because if those people aren't exposed, we'll never be safe," Kayl said. "Selene and I talked about it. We have to take this risk."

"It's part of the mission," Genji said. "You can blame me for this. The people after us are the same people who will, in the future, continue to undermine Earth Guard and other institutions, who will feed the fear of aliens and contribute to the growth of the Spear of Humanity. If we expose them, rob them of their power, they won't be able to do the damage they will otherwise. And new people, who want to reform and fix problems, will hopefully come in. People who won't fear other people just because they're different. We have to try, even though it might be very dangerous."

"You deserve to know that," Kayl said. "And despite what Selene says, I'm not doing this because she urged it on me. It's because we both see the need for it. To save the Earth."

"To prevent what will happen on June twelfth, 2180," Genji said.

The three women looked at them unhappily for some time before Leilani nodded. "Like your father," she said. "Kayl, he would be doing the same thing, and I would be as worried as I am now."

"He won't be alone," Genji said. "Not as long as I'm alive. It's all right if you hate me because of this."

"How could we hate you?" Aunt Hokulani said. "You're trying to save the entire world. At considerable risk to yourself."

"Kayl made his own decision," Leilani said. "Didn't you? I never told you something, from my last conversation with your father. He was in orbit, about to take the *Sentinel* out on its first patrol. We talked for a long time. He told me he had a lot of concerns about the ship. I asked him why he was doing it. And he told me someone had to. Who should he ask to run that risk in his place? When he might be able to make a difference, to save people who might die if someone else was in command? I tell myself, the nearly one hundred sailors who lived after that disaster probably owe their lives to your father, who must have died trying to save the other hundred."

"Mom," Malani said in a choked voice, tears in her eyes.

"And now," Leilani continued, "it's you facing that choice, and also knowing it's something you must do. It's not easy. Please try to come back. But know that I understand. This comes from both sides of the family, the understanding that sometimes fate calls on you, and you must either answer or turn away. It's not in us to turn away. The Earth has called you, has sent us Selene to show us what to do, and I know you must do what is asked of you. Selene, I do not hate you, because your every action places you at greater risk than Kayl, and because you are doing this for everyone. Never doubt that I want you *both* back."

"Thank you, Mom," Kayl said, his voice a whisper.

"Thank you," Genji said. She looked at the floor, unable to meet the gazes of the others.

A knock on the door provided a welcome distraction. "I'll get it," Genji said, jumping up before Kayl could react.

At the door, a couple of extra diplomatic security guards were waiting with carryout. "The lunch you asked for," Alejandro said.

"Oh. Lunch," Genji said.

"Special Representative Camacho told us to get enough for five," Alejandro assured her.

"Thank you." That disaster had been averted, at least. Genji waited as the agents brought in the food, thanking them again as they left, before turning to the Owen family. "I'm sorry, but I didn't know you were coming, so I asked for a special meal for Kayl and me. It's sort of special to us, anyway."

"What is it?" Kayl asked, checking the containers. "Spam musubi? And Spam fried rice?"

"Yes," Genji said, wondering what Leilani and Aunt Hokulani would think.

"This is your special meal?" Aunt Hokulani asked. "What do you think, Leilani?"

Kayl's mother tasted the Spam fried rice. "That's not bad. Not as good as my own, of course. But not bad."

"The musubi is good, too," Aunt Hokulani said. "Why are you apologizing, Selene? Anytime you and Kayl serve brunch, I want to be invited."

"This is really your special meal?" Malani asked. "Are you going to serve this at your wedding?"

"That's an idea," Genji said, relieved that something had distracted everyone from the last topic.

"Unless we can get taratarabis," Kayl said.

"Oh, yeah," Genji said. "That has to be on the menu."

"What is tara—?" Malani asked.

"Taratarabis. Alien rabbit," Genji said. "It is so good."

"Amazing," Kayl agreed.

"What, is it green?" Aunt Hokulani asked.

"No," Genji said, "it's a carbon-based, oxygen-breathing

life-form, like the Tramontine, like us. The meat is sort of a pale red before it's cooked."

"Oh, of course it would be," Malani said. "It's nice to bond with my future sister over biochemistry and Spam."

"And beer," Kayl added, opening the refrigerator.

The visit whose prolonging she'd been dreading turned out to be too short, Genji thought as she and Kayl said their goodbyes. "It really was wonderful to see you."

"You'll get sick of us at times," Aunt Hokulani said. "Family is like that."

"You two be careful," Malani said, looking worried.

"Watch out for ninjas," Leilani said, hugging Kayl.

"Any ninjas will have to get through me before they reach Kayl," Genji said.

"Then I won't have to worry about ninjas," Kayl's mother said, also hugging Genji. "I will see you both again."

And then they were gone, and Cerise Camacho was reminding Genji and Kayl that they'd be leaving in an hour.

Genji thought she'd already been through the most emotionally difficult part of the day. But she discovered at Los Angeles Interplanetary Spaceport that this day had another surprise in store for her.

THEY HAD AN IMPRESSIVE escort on the way to the spaceport, police and mutual defense forces in vehicles stationed on the ground along the route, warbirds and police birds in the air around them, a couple of security agents riding in the armored bird with them. One of them was happy Angielyke. The other was supposed to be a friendly man named Pyotor, but at the last minute, Alejandro had pulled rank to ride on their bird while Pyotor was sent to one of the escort birds. "We scramble schedules and assignments at the last minute sometimes," Alejandro explained. "It messes with anyone trying to exploit patterns."

Watching all the firepower surrounding them, protecting them, Genji couldn't help thinking that only a few days ago, this same array of force would have been making every effort to catch Kayl and kill her. Thinking about how last time they'd come to this spaceport, they had been in a vehicle controlled by Thomas Dorcas.

She didn't really regret killing Dorcas, though it had been by accident when he was threatening her. And he had intended killing her. Genji wondered about Dorcas's assistant, though, the man who was going to do the dirty work but had found himself too slow when trying to kill an alloy trained in close combat. She'd never known his name, just the variety of false IDs he had carried. No one had mentioned him since. He had disappeared, too, like at least one of his victims, but remained nameless and unknown.

Who else had he killed in the history Genji had known, before she had ended up back in 2140 to change that history? It seemed likely there would have been others. How many had her self-defense actions saved?

And now, here she was, going back to Mars. The first time, she and Kayl had been wary of Dorcas, but unsure if he would try anything. This time, Genji didn't doubt the sincerity of Cerise Camacho, but remembering a friend who would die thirty-four years from now, she didn't feel the same way about the diplomatic security guards. And she especially didn't trust the two Earth Guard cruisers that would be escorting the *Yamanaka*.

Please, if the worst happens, let Kayl live. I can handle it if I die and that helps Earth along a path to avoiding its destruction on the twelfth of June, 2180. I've already found more happiness than I thought my entire life could ever hold. Please let Kayl live. She didn't know who or what she was making that plea to. Maybe just to the universe that seemed too vast and impersonal to care about the fate of a couple of humans on a tiny speck of a world in an insignificant galaxy. But it didn't hurt to ask, just in case there was something or someone who might hear her.

Their bird grounded on the field not far from an official lifter. There were many, many security vehicles and personnel on the field, some of them holding back a substantial crowd come to see her and Kayl off to Mars. That felt so weird, like a mirror universe version of what had "greeted" them at Wallops. Genji read the signs being projected or just held up, seeing many calling out to her in support or welcome. That felt even weirder. The much fewer signs calling for her to leave and "go back where she came from" almost felt reassuring in their familiarity.

Kayl was looking toward the signs as well. "No matter how many times you say you were born here, some people keep thinking you're from someplace else."

"I'll always be an alien on my home world," Genji said.

"Maybe not always," he said.

"I stopped hoping for that a long time ago," she said.

Cerise Camacho approached them. "There's a small local delegation that wanted to give you some going-away gifts. Is that all right?"

"Sure," Genji said, nodding and thinking she might as well accept the strangeness of all this.

The group escorted up to them included a couple of officials who presented official welcomes and goodbyes, followed by a serious-looking teenage boy who presented Genji and Kayl with a basket of local snacks.

Last, a girl who appeared to be in her young teens carrying a bouquet of flowers was escorted up to them. "For you," she said, gazing excitedly at Genji.

"Thank you," Genji said, bending slightly to take the offered flowers, thinking the girl looked oddly familiar.

She looked in the girl's eyes.

Ohmigod.

"Selene?" Kayl asked, his voice urgent. "Are you all right?"

She realized that she was still bent over a little, looking into the girl's eyes, seeing someone she'd never dreamt she would ever see again. "Yes," Genji got out. "Thank you," she said to the girl, who had seemed a little disconcerted by Genji's first reaction but now smiled again.

"It's such an honor to meet you! I worked really hard to get picked for this! 'Luck is the good fortune you determine for yourself'!"

"'Good fortune,'" Genji said, finishing the quote, "'consists in good inclinations of the soul, good impulses, good actions.'"

The girl laughed. "You quoted Marcus Aurelius in that interview, so I started reading him, and he's amazing!"

"Yes, he is," Genji said, gazing at the girl. "'Fit yourself for the matters which have fallen to your lot, and love these people among whom destiny has cast you—but your love must be genuine.'"

"I am never going to forget this!" the girl said as she was led back to join the others.

"Neither will I," Genji said. She realized she had extended her arm partway, trying to reach out to her before the girl left.

"What just happened?" Kayl whispered to her.

"I'll tell you in the lifter," Genji managed to say. "Can we get on the lifter?"

She didn't really see anything around her while Kayl walked with her as if they were just walking together rather than him guiding her. Up the boarding ramp, the bright sunlight giving way to the softer lights inside the lifter, then the main passenger compartment, rows of seats, Kayl leading them both to the two seats designated for them.

They were, for the moment, the only two inside this compartment. "What was it?" Kayl asked again. "Did you know that girl?"

She inhaled deeply, trying to stop the memories flooding her mind. "That was my mother."

He stared back at her, stunned. "Are . . . are you sure?" Kayl finally got out.

"Yes. Absolutely certain. I looked in her eyes and I knew.

Didn't you hear us quoting Marcus Aurelius to each other?" Genji leaned her head back, breathing too quickly, trying to get it under control. "It was her, Kayl. The woman who is supposed to give birth to me in 2158. The woman who loved me more than anything, who protected me, and taught me, and . . . and . . . died because of me."

Genji stopped herself with an effort. "She didn't know me," Genji whispered to Kayl. "She'll never know me."

"Selene . . ."

"But that doesn't matter," Genji said, hearing the unsteadiness in her voice. "She'll probably never give birth to me. Not anymore. But she's still my mother. Fate did bring us together again, and I will always love her with all my heart."

Kayl held Genji's hand, looking lost for words.

Genji tightened her grip on his hand. "She won't die in 2175, Kayl. I'll make sure of that. We'll keep changing things, and my mother won't be murdered in 2175. Even though I'll never get to hold her again, she'll be alive. That's worth it, right?"

He didn't answer for a moment. "I can't imagine what you're feeling right now, Selene. But, what you said, making sure she lives. That's . . . well, she gave you life. And now you're going to be giving her life. Making sure she doesn't die when she was fated to."

Genji found herself able to look at him again. "Yes. I'm going to give her life. Thanks for putting it that way. I can finally balance those scales."

He nodded to her, eyes serious and concerned.

A thought came to her. "Kayl, do you think I could ever . . . ? Ever tell her?"

"Tell her?"

"Yes," Genji said. "Someday. A long time from now. I would've been born in eighteen years. And then I was seventeen years old when she was murdered in 2175. Maybe . . . maybe in the early 2170s? Do you think I could do that?"

"Maybe," Kayl said cautiously. "By then she'd be old enough to handle that kind of news, and we'd know whether or not you were born in 2158 after all."

"I'm not expecting that, Kayl. I don't think the universe would be happy with me meeting myself after I'm born."

"That would be very strange," he agreed. "Unless the daughter born to her in 2158 isn't you. Like, if she's full human instead of . . ." Seeing the look on her face, Kayl let his words trail off.

"Let's not talk about me being replaced when it comes to my mother," Genji said, hearing the sharp edge in her voice. "Okay?"

"Okay," Kayl hastily agreed. "Anyway, hopefully you and I will still be around in 2175, and the Universal War won't be going on all around us."

"Hopefully," Genji said, her emotions finally calming, joy shining through the turmoil. "I got to see her again. I never thought I could . . . But at least you got to see her, too, and . . ." A strange thought struck her. "Kayl, she met you."

"Umm, yeah?"

"I met your mother today. And you just met my mother."

Kayl's jaw actually dropped for a moment. "That's . . . I don't know what that is."

"My mother got to meet my future husband," Genji said. "I never imagined that would be possible. Is it funny or strange or sad or . . . what?"

"Weird? I mean, you told me your mother is twelve years old right now?"

"Yeah," Genji said. "Weird. Did you like her?"

"What?" Kayl seemed baffled by the question.

"My mother. Did you like her?"

"Uh . . . I guess. She seemed like a nice kid. I didn't really get to talk to her," Kayl said. "But she seemed nice."

"Yes." Genji suddenly realized she still had the flowers in her other hand. "The flowers my mother gave me," she murmured. "We need to save these. Forever."

"We will," Kayl said, looking about. "Representative Camacho? Is there time to send these flowers to be preserved? We'd like them to be permanently preserved . . . in, um, memory of this day."

"Certainly," Camacho said. "We'll get it done, and then send them on to Mars on a later ship. All right?" She extended a hand for the flowers.

Genji found herself clutching the flowers, not wanting to let them loose, knowing her mother had held them. With a tremendous effort, she managed to pass the flowers to Camacho, almost failing in her attempt to let go at the end.

They were alone again for a moment, other people just beginning to enter the compartment and take their seats.

"What happened to your home?" Kayl asked. "After your mom died? Didn't you have anything to remember her by?"

"After they murdered her, they burned it down," Genji said, trying to keep her voice calm, trying not to remember how it had felt that awful day. "Using a lot of accelerant. There was nothing left but ashes, cracked stones, and twisted metal after the Spears' fire had 'cleansed' the site of my mother's death."

His eyes took on that look they did when she finally let something painful out, that look of hurting and wishing for something that could heal hers. "I'm so sorry."

"That morning I was called from my classroom at school," Genji said. "The police officers took me there, showed me there was nothing left. I couldn't blame the police. The two officers watching my mother's home had been killed defending it. I've never been able to remember whether I thanked the police, whether I expressed sorrow for their loss. That still bothers me. I hope I did. Two other families lost people that day."

She paused, the memories somehow not as raw as they had been. "I looked at the burnt remains of my home, and I told them not to bother contacting social services to find me a place to stay, to instead take me to the nearest Unified Fleet recruiting office. I walked in, and told them I was, as of that morning, an orphan, and I wanted to join. They took me. By then you could join if you were seventeen. They needed people that badly. I didn't want to be placed with some family that would pity me, or be worried about having an alloy in their home. I didn't want to go back to my high school, or any school, and face that again. I wanted to belong to something that would let me strike back."

"I would have done the same," Kayl said.

"I think you would have," Genji said, meeting his gaze with her own. "But, as I told you, from that morning on I lost much interest in living. What mattered was making my death count. I learned to fight, and I fought, and I gained battlefield promotions, but I didn't manage to die."

"You told me you were an officer because you tested well," Kayl said, looking a bit betrayed.

"That was true," Genji said. "But only partly true. I wasn't ready to talk about the battlefields and what happened on them. I wasn't ready for you to see all of me."

"Are you now?"

"I hope so, Kayl. I am trying to tell you these things, but it can be very hard to bring them to the surface."

"Yeah. Tell me what I can do."

"You're doing it," Genji said, squeezing his hand again. She felt tears of joy starting. "Mom's alive. She's really alive. This time I'll make sure she doesn't die."

"It wasn't your fault," Kayl said.

"Yes, it—" Genji stopped her angry reply in mid-word. "It wouldn't have happened if not for me," she continued in a calmer voice. "If I hadn't been her daughter. Now, I will ensure it doesn't happen at all."

He just nodded in reply, smart enough not to try contradicting her again.

Because it was a truth she'd been forced to live with ever since that day.

Her last memory of her mother, seeing her off that morning in 2175, quick goodbyes and see you tonight and be safe today and eye roll yes Mom of course I will. Then smoking ashes. But now another memory laid over that, of a young girl with flowers and a happy smile, her life stretching before her. *You quoted Marcus Aurelius in that interview, so I started reading him, and he's amazing!* Her mother, who had read Aurelius to her as a little girl, had now been inspired to read Aurelius by her. What had the Tramontine called that? A circle. Cause and effect bound together through time. Just as she and her mother were.

Genji smiled, remembering that moment she had once again looked into her mother's eyes. She was still smiling when the lifter rose into the sky, heading for orbit.

THEIR COMPARTMENT ON THE Yamanaka was pretty large by spaceship standards. Nothing like the ridiculously and ostentatiously large rooms onboard Tom Dorcas's luxury yacht, but still a surprise to Genji and Kayl, both used to the cramped quarters normal for a warship. At almost five meters wide by nearly three meters deep, the room had two bunks against one bulkhead, a sofa on the opposite side, and a chair with a table/desk between them. The bulkheads, rather than being utilitarian white or gray, were a soft shade of green. Panels set into three of the walls provided views and information.

Kayl looked over the bunks. "It's going to be challenging to fit two of us into one of those."

Genji glanced his way. "It'll be fun trying. But since when do we need bunks for that in zero g? This ship isn't going to accelerate all the way, is it?" They were in zero gravity right now, of course, since the *Yamanaka* was in orbit. Genji turned back to the panel she was floating in front of, activating window mode, seeing a view of Earth from near orbit just as if she were looking out a window at the scene.

"What are you thinking?" Kayl asked as he moved up beside her, sounding concerned. He seemed startled when she turned a smile his way.

"I was thinking of your family," she said. "For a moment there, I wasn't seeing my memories of watching Earth be destroyed. Pretty cool, huh?" Genji turned her gaze back to the view. "There was a different part of the world in view when the Sigma bomb detonated. That probably helps, since I didn't see some of these particular places, and all of the people in those places, disintegrate and explode. Now you're the gloomy one. Why?"

He shrugged. "I guess I've been wondering where I would be on June twelfth, 2180. Whether I saw it coming. What I would have been doing."

"If it's any consolation, Kayl, there's a really good chance you would have died before then," Genji said. "I mean, you're in Earth Guard. You might have been lost in some of the earlier fighting. And you would have joined the Unified Fleet, wouldn't you? We lost a lot of people."

"I'm not sure 'consolation' is the right word," Kayl said. "I'll be sixty-five years old in 2175, when you joined the Unified Fleet. If I was still around, it doesn't seem likely I still would've been fighting."

"You're *still* thinking in peacetime terms," Genji said. "The Universal War didn't allow the luxury of retiring people who were needed. Some of the people I met in the fleet were seventy and even older. Trying to do their part, using their skills and experience. Because they were badly needed."

"That is actually a little comforting," Kayl said, reaching to put his arm about her as they gazed side by side at the Earth. "Thinking that I would've gone down fighting, trying to prevent what happened."

She put her arm about him as well. "That sounds like it is what will happen. I mean, if we fail. If we succeed . . . what happens then, Kayl?"

"Happily ever after?"

"Happily ever after isn't how the stories of alloys end," Genji said.

"Says who?" he asked.

She didn't answer for a while, gazing at the living world their ship was orbiting. "I don't know. Every other alloy died. Maybe I can rewrite that kind of fate for me along with history. It's scary to imagine it might happen, though."

"It's scary to imagine spending a long, happy life with me?"

"Yes," Genji said. "I never dreamed those dreams. This is unknown territory for me. I mean, if we get there. If we even live to reach Mars. When you've spent your whole life never belonging, when everyone left you, when all that was left to you was fighting against people who hated your very existence . . . Like I said, I didn't have those dreams everyone is supposed to have. Now I don't know what to do. Survive? Yes. Keep fighting? Yes. Save the Earth? Yes." She turned toward him. "Save you? Yes. Be happy? I don't know."

"I hope someday you know the answer to that is also yes," Kayl said, turning to face her. "Not because of me, but because you deserve it. Because you deserve those dreams." He smiled. "You've been opening up to me; I should share a secret with you, a dream fantasy I had when I was a young boy."

"A boy's fantasy? Is this something I really want to hear?"

"I think so." Kayl looked embarrassed as he talked. "I'd imagine being a dashing Earth Guard officer, and encountering a mysterious ship, which would turn out to be carrying a beautiful alien princess. She'd need my help to fight off enemies pursuing her, and then because of my unique abilities, she'd ask me to help her defeat her enemies, and then of course she'd fall in love with me, and then happily ever after as the greatest space hero of all time with my hot alien princess."

Genji couldn't prevent herself from laughing. "Fate sure threw you a surprise, didn't it?" she said. "Instead of a beautiful alien princess, you ended up with an okay-looking part-alien lieutenant."

He grinned. "Fate understood things better than I did as a boy. All it takes to be a princess is to get born into the right family. Making lieutenant, especially coming up through the ranks, especially including battlefield promotions, takes a lot of work. A real alien princess would very likely not be physically identical to a human girl in ways that were very important to a boy, or be in any way interested in a human boy. Whereas a part alien could have just enough differences to be able to save my life a few times, and would want to save me. And, as for beautiful, you've got that. Especially when you smile and it feels like watching the sun come out after thirty days of rain."

She laughed again, embarrassed herself this time. "I really have driven you crazy, haven't I?"

"In a good way," Kayl said.

It was a moment Genji wished wouldn't ever end, but after only a few seconds, the good moment faded as reality intruded on it. The view on the panel showed something moving between their ship and the Earth. An Earth Guard cruiser, gliding into position nearby. One of their escorts, supposedly protection, but actually a source of danger.

"Which Lieutenant Owen do you think the crews of those ships are expecting to encounter?" Genji asked. "The screwup your senior officers tried to paint you as to protect themselves, or the guy who has outthought and outmaneuvered them at every step?"

"Hopefully the first," Kayl said. "It's better to be underestimated in a case like this, isn't it?"

"It certainly is," Genji said. "You're thinking like a combat officer."

"I've had a good mentor," Kayl said, his eyes on the Earth Guard cruiser. "Do you think I should try to contact anyone aboard *Lifeguard*?"

"Are you thinking of anyone in particular?"

"Chief Kaminski. Do you remember her?"

Genji nodded. "Female chief. An engineer. A good one, you said?"

"Yes. And the sort of professional who won't follow orders blindly." Kayl made a face. "But she's unlikely to be told anything about any plans against us, and drawing attention to the fact Kaminski might be well-disposed toward me, toward us, might not be a smart move. What do you think?"

"I think you've already answered your own question," Genji said. "If Chief Kaminski hears anything in advance, she might tell us. But if it's known you've reached out to her, she won't be told anything in advance."

A knock sounded at the door. Kayl shoved off from the wall to answer it, Genji keeping her gaze on the "window" even though her face was partly turned toward the door. As the *Yamanaka* orbited the Earth, different portions of the planet were coming into view. Areas that brought up memories of that horrible light blossoming, spreading, consuming everyone and everything it could reach.

Genji heard Cerise Camacho talking to Kayl.

"We'll break orbit in six hours," Camacho said. "There will always be two diplomatic security agents posted outside your room, and as you've probably noticed, the two Earth Guard cruisers are taking up their positions near us."

"Thank you," Kayl said. "Yes, we saw."

"Is . . . is Lieutenant Genji all right?"

"Yes."

"I'm sorry, but she looks very . . ."

"She's looking at something in her memory that no person should ever have to see," Kayl said. "Lieutenant Genji is seeing again what will happen on June twelfth, 2180."

A long silence followed, with Genji refusing to turn around, keeping her eyes on the turning Earth, reassuring herself that it was there, and promising herself once again that it would be there even after June 12, 2180.

"I hope," Camacho said, "that you two are aware that you're no longer alone in your efforts. No matter what happens to us on this ship, others will continue trying to avert that fate for Earth. Thanks to Lieutenant Genji, they know where business as usual would lead."

"That's good to know," Kayl said.

The door closed and Kayl came back beside Genji, waiting silently until she took a deep breath and turned to him. "No matter what Camacho said, this is still on us. *We* have to win."

"I know, and we will," he said.

She knew why he'd brought up that happily ever after thing, because he was very worried as well, and trying to hope his way past his fears for what might happen before they reached Mars. That was how Kayl dealt with his fears, she'd come to realize, by imagining the happiness beyond them, and he was trying to help her in the same way, giving her an ever after to hope for.

Maybe Kayl was right, and there could be a life for them together after this trip was done. But, as she looked at the globe of the Earth passing beneath her, Genji couldn't shake a foreboding that she might never see such a thing again, that this would mark the last time she would be on a ship breaking orbit about Earth to head into space.

All right, then. If it came to that, it wouldn't be because she hadn't fought her hardest. And even though she was no longer seeking death, if it came for her, she'd make sure those last moments counted.

14

"WHAT ARE YOU LISTENING to?" With three hours until the ship broke orbit, they were finding ways to kill the time, which for Genji had meant calling up memories to try to deal with them, and for Kayl had meant going through music files. She didn't know nearly enough about his tastes in music, Genji realized.

Kayl gave an almost guilty start of surprise. "An old song."

"To me, all songs in 2140 are old songs," Genji said.

"This is a lot older than that." He tapped a command, making the sound fill the room, a man singing to a bouncy tune about meeting someone again on the other side of a sea and a shore.

Kayl muted the sound again. "It's really old, but it was one of my father's favorite songs. Being in space again, it helped me think of him, and how he enjoyed listening to this."

"Any idea why he liked it?" Genji asked.

He hesitated the way he did when discussing something very personal. "Dad thought the song wasn't meant to be literal, like the real sea and a real shore. He thought it was a metaphor, about someone whose love had died, and crossed the sea that old legends say divided our world from the afterlife, and she was waiting past that shore that is the world of the afterlife. And someday he'd cross that sea as well, and meet her again."

Genji considered the idea, trying to get a better glimpse of this side of Kayl Owen. "Is there something in particular about the song that led him to think it was a metaphor?"

"Yeah," Kayl said, relaxing as he explained it. "It talks about this place being on the other side of a star, and being as close as the Moon. That doesn't sound like it's talking about a place that exists in our world, does it?"

"I guess not." She paused, wondering whether to explore the idea more. There were so many things she still didn't know about Kayl. "Do you believe in that?"

"What, you mean the song?"

"No," Genji said. "I mean, an afterlife. That part of us lives on, that we can reunite with our loved ones in some place . . . on the other side of the sea."

"I think so," Kayl said. "I've had a few odd experiences that make me wonder whether there might be something to that. I admit that I *want* to believe that I'll see my father again someday. And that everything doesn't end when our bodies give out. How about you?"

Genji shrugged. "I don't know. If there were ghosts, I think I'd be haunted by a lot more of them."

"Aren't you?" Kayl asked. "In the hours after midnight?"

She paused, glad that she had confessed to Kayl about that. "I suppose I am. I think those are just my own memories, though."

"Some people think those who have gone live on as long as they're remembered."

"Then I definitely have a lot of ghosts," Genji said.

"You've said you believe your mom led you to me," Kayl said.

She hesitated, thinking through that. "I do. So, I guess that means I do believe she can still influence my life. Maybe it's just my memory of her, but it does feel like that. I'll give you that one. What about the big picture? Are you into the whole religious thing? Any particular belief system?" She felt nervous asking, even as close as they were now.

He shrugged. "Not formally, I guess. Spiritual, I think the term is. Believing there's something, but not believing in any particular rituals or systems. Just trying to do what's right." Kayl gave her a cautious look. "How about you?"

Genji shook her head, old hurts surfacing again. "No. I sort of checked out of the whole idea of organized religions when all of those religious leaders gathered—will gather, in 2165, I think it was—to debate whether alloys, including me, had souls."

"What?"

She'd managed to surprise, and upset, Kayl again. "They debated whether we had souls. Yeah, can you believe that? Like, how would they know? What gave them the right to argue about that, or think they could somehow determine whether or not someone like me was a soulless monster because I've got some alien DNA mixed into my genome?"

"What did . . . ? What did they . . . ?" Kayl couldn't seem to get the words out.

"They didn't," Genji said, hearing the pain of the past come into her voice. "They did something almost worse, deciding that was up to each religion and priest, minister, whatever, to decide for themselves whether alloys had souls. How cool is that, to know every one of those people gets to decide for themselves whether *I* have a soul?"

He gazed at her, unhappy. "I'm sorry. I'm saying that again because I don't know what else to say. There are really good people involved with religion who truly want to help others. Not everyone, unfortunately. But I can understand why you'd be unwilling to pay attention to any of them when they thought they had the right to decide something like that about you."

"Kayl, I have no problem with people who believe and use that as motivation to be good and help others. I admire people like that. What I have problems with are the ones who want to be in charge, in control, and make rules for other people, and judge other people. Is that so unreasonable of me?"

"Not at all," Kayl said.

"Maybe in this new history we're making," Genji said, "we can convince all those great religious minds that the all-powerful creator they believe in is powerful enough to put souls in anything the creator feels like putting a soul in. Including the Tramontine, and including me. But if somebody insists I have to believe a certain way, that's not going to happen. Show me a miracle and I might change my mind."

Kayl hesitated. "Do you want me to be honest?"

"When have I ever wanted anything else from you?"

He gestured to the panel on one bulkhead, which showed an outside view, infinite stars shining against infinite space. "It's 2140."

"Yes," Genji said. "I accepted that a while back."

"How did you get here from 2180?"

"You know what happened," Genji said. "Earth was destroyed. The shock wave was so powerful it not only destroyed my ship but bent time and space so that the piece of wreckage I was on got hurled into the past."

"Only that piece of wreckage," Kayl said. "With you, if you'll pardon the term, miraculously still alive, thrown forty years into the past, and given a chance to try to prevent Earth from being destroyed."

She stared at him. "That was just chance, Kayl."

"Maybe," Kayl said. "Haven't you told me you were given this opportunity for a reason?"

"Yes, but that doesn't mean . . ." Genji paused to think. "I guess I can understand why some people would see it that way. But that's impossible to prove."

He nodded. "Absolutely impossible to prove, or disprove. Which is why the idea that Something or Someone sent you back here to give Earth and humanity another chance is purely a question of faith. A miracle, if you will, for those seeing it that way."

Genji frowned, thinking. "I guess," she said again. "Do you believe that?"

Kayl pondered the question. "Maybe," he finally said. "Though it seems presumptuous to claim some divine force wants us to do this. It's enough for me to know it's the right thing, trying to save the Earth and everyone on it. But, if we're talking miracles . . . Selene, your coming into my life really feels like a miracle to me."

She laughed. "I'm a miracle? A gift to you from the divine? Maybe instead you're being punished."

"That's also a possibility," he said, smiling. "But why would I be sent an angel to punish me?"

"Hey, angels are pretty bad actors, you know. I did study some of that stuff." Genji looked at the view of space. "I admit it would be so cool to see my mother again, but I just did. On Earth. Alive."

"Most people don't get that kind of chance," Kayl said.

She looked at him, letting her smile fade to show she understood what he was feeling. "Yeah. Like with your father. Who knows, maybe you will see him again on the other side of that sea. But not soon, I hope."

"Me, too," Kayl said. "Not soon. What do the Tramontine think? Do they have religion as humans understand it?"

Genji twisted her face as she tried to come up with the right words. "Sort of, not really. It's different. It's not really organized. And it's a very different perspective. Like . . . what do humans think heaven is?"

"That's always been really vaguely defined," Kayl said. "What would be a perfect afterlife?"

"The Tramontine think they know," Genji said, pointing to the image of the stars outside the ship. "They're a species that finds its greatest joy in discovering new things and new questions, and they are living in a universe that has an apparently infinite supply of both questions and answers. Ask the average Tramontine what heaven is and they'll probably tell you they are living in it."

"This is heaven to them?" Kayl said. "With disease and anger and all the troubles and pain that exists?"

"How do you appreciate good things if there are no bad

things?" Genji said. "This isn't universal among them, but most Tramontine seem to believe those bad things are here to allow them to know how great the good things are. Like, how good it feels to not be in pain? If you don't experience pain, you have no idea how great it is not to have it. I think that's the general philosophy, but, like I said, it's not universal among the Tramontine, and it's not detailed."

Kayl nodded, frowning as he thought about her words. "You're saying the Tramontine religion is like human philosophy?"

"No," Genji said. "Not even that organized. Philosophy has schools of thought, right? The Tramontine divide things to be known into categories, sort of like humans do with different branches of science, but one of the Tramontine categories is things with no answers that can be tested or proven. Which is what humans call religious beliefs. That's why the Tramontine don't have detailed rituals or rules for religious things, because by definition, to them, those kinds of things can't be tested or proven, so it's all opinion or belief, so arguing over details seems meaningless. If someone wants to do something in particular, fine for them, as long as it doesn't coerce or hurt anyone else. That last is almost like a taboo with them, something that is strongly prohibited. I've wondered whether in the past the Tramontine experienced the equivalent of human religious wars and responded by establishing rules to prevent anyone from trying to do that again. When I asked about it, in the 2170s, they wouldn't discuss that, so I think maybe it did happen at one time."

"But if the Tramontine, a lot of them anyway, think this is heaven, what do they think happens when one of them dies?"

Genji couldn't help a laugh that caused Kayl to look surprised. "They don't know. That's an unanswerable question in this life. Lots of theories, lots of ideas, no certainty. So how do the Tramontine react to a death? With celebration. Because the Tramontine who died is learning the answer to the unanswerable question. It's sort of seen as the ultimate gift, though it's considered improper to try to, um, claim that 'gift' before your time. The universe will give you the answer when it is ready."

"They celebrate deaths?" Kayl said, looking once again baffled.

"They also regret losing someone," Genji said, "but it's more like the regret of seeing someone off on a voyage so long you'll never see them again. Sort of like that 'beyond the sea' thing your father talked about. Sad in that sense, but happy in the sense of what they're going to learn and experience on the other side. Even if that is nothing, they still learn the answer. Again, Kayl, this is just generalized. Talk to one Tramontine and they might spin different ideas. But one thing that is true of all of them is that you won't find any rules saying exactly what you have to believe or to do, and no churches or other special places among the Tramontine to worship the infinite, because to them the universe itself is the infinite cathedral to the infinite." She paused. "I didn't make up that last infinite thing. Another alloy said that. But I think she was right."

"Huh." Kayl looked out at the stars again. "I guess that beats being arrogant enough to think you can decide whether or not someone has a soul. What about you being here in 2140, Selene? How did the Tramontine interpret that?"

She shook her head. "They see it as something to do with physics. Exciting, because of the questions it poses. Also, very worrisome, because of what I told them would be happening among humans. They were worried it would be their fault for showing up. No talk of miracles."

"Humans are going to want to talk to them about religion," Kayl said. "Try to convert them to specific religions."

"Good luck with that," Genji said. "I saw it being tried in the 2170s." She hesitated as a thought struck. "That was used against the Tramontine, the argument that their rejection of human religions meant they didn't believe in anything, and were unholy or something like that. We need to try to change that perception to the idea that they have their own beliefs, which are not incompatible with human ideas of right and wrong."

"I'll add that to the to-do list," Kayl said.

"I hate to think how long that list is," Genji said with a sigh. "What should we do first?"

"I know what I want to do right now," Kayl said.

"What's that?" She looked at him, saw his smile, and knew what it was. "Are you serious? Talking about religion got you turned on?"

"Listening to you think got me turned on," Kayl said.

Genji stared at him for a moment, a smile forming. "You might have me believing in miracles yet, because I thought it would be impossible to find a guy who would say that to me and mean it. But here you are. I know what I want to do right now, too."

"Should we use a tie-down since we're in zero g?"

"Oh, hell no. I love it when we end up on the ceiling."

Later, as they drifted in the center of the room, their bodies still entwined, Kayl murmured in her ear, "Why are you smiling?"

"How can you tell I'm smiling?"

"The side of your face feels different."

"Does it?" Genji asked. "I thought I usually smiled after."

"Yes, but, I don't know. This smile feels a little different."

"I guess it is. I'm thinking."

"Should I be worried?" Kayl whispered in her ear.

"Not this time." Genji held him, organizing the scattered thoughts that had been running through her mind. "I was thinking that maybe the Tramontine are right. That this universe could be heaven, for humans, too. If only humans didn't keep screwing it up."

He didn't answer for a moment. "That would be scary, wouldn't it? If whatever rules the universe had given us life and everything, and it was totally up to us whether we turned that into heaven or hell. The ultimate free choice for humanity, with whatever comes at the end being whatever we'd earned. Not in some afterlife, but right here."

"It doesn't have to be scary," Genji said, realizing that her answer to that had changed over the last few months. "Earth doesn't have to die. That's what we're trying to achieve. Beyond that, we can earn a happy ending, can't we?"

"You believe that now?" Kayl asked, sounding both surprised and happy himself.

"I think it's worth working for," Genji said. "I'm going to keep trying."

"We're both going to keep trying."

"Yeah. Together." She held him tighter, their bodies slowly rotating so the view of the stars came into her line of sight. It was the same universe, wasn't it? But it felt different. Had the universe changed, or had she?

THE BRIEF IDYLL ENDED as they often did, with the outside world intruding. In this case, that meant a meeting with Cerise Camacho in a private room.

The *Yamanaka* had broken orbit precisely on schedule, the Earth Guard cruisers *Lifeguard* and *Diligent* exactly matching her movement. With the *Yamanaka* still accelerating onto its trajectory toward Mars, there was enough sensation of gravity that they could sit in the chairs around the table without strapping in.

Cerise Camacho hesitated, as if unsure how to begin. "I hope you don't mind, but we wanted to pump you for all the information you can provide. We wouldn't want that critical information to be lost if anything should happen."

"Just in case anything happens?" Kayl asked, making his unhappiness clear.

"Just in case," Camacho repeated. "Don't think for one

moment that anyone is happy with this situation. But you agreed to it. And I am sharing the risk with you both."

"Not quite sharing it," Genji said. "I do appreciate the gesture, but Kayl and I are the ducks sitting in a barrel."

"Excuse me?"

"Ducks sitting in a barrel," Genji repeated.

"Do you mean sitting ducks?" Camacho asked.

"I mean ducks sitting in a barrel! So they can't fly away and they're easy targets! Why does no one in 2140 understand such a simple phrase?"

"I see," Camacho said. "Uh . . . anyway, may I record this discussion? Audio and video. So members of the Security Committee can view it."

"That's all right," Genji said, feeling her stomach tighten a bit. She wasn't used to having audiences like that.

"Begin recording," Camacho said. "Are you willing to tell us more about the future you know of, that you experienced, Lieutenant Genji? You've alluded to institutional collapses leading into what you call the Universal War."

"Everyone called it that," Genji said. "They will call it that, anyway."

"We need any specifics you can provide," Camacho said. "Exact events you know of that show how things failed, the whys and the reasons institutions collapsed. What can you tell us? The more exact examples, the better we can work to prevent those things from happening."

Genji sighed, shaking her head. "I wish I knew a lot of specifics. I don't. A lot of it happened before I was born, and when I was little. Later, I thought it was boring. I was a kid, and the often-painful drama of being an alloy occupied a lot of my time. I didn't pay much attention to things that were going wrong until after Karachi. And by then everything was too far gone."

"Karachi?"

"Karachi will be totally destroyed in 2169," Genji said, seeing the shock appear in Camacho's eyes. "About all I know as far as the 'reasons' is something about fanatical religious nationalism. That and the persons responsible will take refuge in the Free Zone on the Moon. Your Security Committee I guess was still meeting occasionally, but deadlocked on what to do about Karachi and finally formally dissolved without ordering any actions by mutual defense forces, so a coalition of national forces went to the Moon, demanded the perpetrators be turned over, and when the Free Zone said no, the national forces turned it into the Dead Zone. After that, things just kept getting worse."

Cerise Camacho sat silently for a long time before blinking and uttering a small gasp. "How . . . ?"

"I can't tell you exactly how it came to that," Genji said, feeling angry with herself. "I wasn't born, or I wasn't paying attention. Mostly I know what my mother told me about those things."

"But . . . what . . ." Camacho paused to gather her thoughts. "Earth Guard. What were they doing when Karachi was destroyed?"

"Earth Guard had been dwindling and fragmenting for decades," Genji said. "What was left of Earth Guard at that point, as it was explained to me, no longer had any legitimacy because it was part of the Earth Cooperation Council, which no longer existed, and was under the authority of the Security Committee, which had just ceased to exist. After Karachi, the remaining ships sought homes with various national forces, until the Unified Fleet was formed in 2171 and picked up some of those Earth Guard remnants as well as contributions from national forces wanting to oppose the rising power of the Spear of Humanity as well as aggressive actions by other nations. That was right after the Sanctions War in 2170 really divided the world into armed camps, with countries tearing up a lot of international agreements and treaties."

Camacho lowered her head, holding it with both hands. "Why is this harder to hear than the destruction of the Earth?"

"The destruction of Earth is too big," Kayl said. "I've had the same reaction. Thinking of the Earth being destroyed is horrible, but so immense a tragedy that it's hard to grasp. But hearing about specific things from Selene, like Karachi, or the dissolution of Earth Guard, or Albuquerque, hits harder because it's easier to get your head around."

"Albuquerque?" Camacho shook her head as if in denial. "It will also be destroyed? How many cities . . . ?"

"Do you want me to list every one I can recall?" Genji said. "It happens all over the world between 2169 and 2180. Strike, retaliation, counter-strike, counter-retaliation. Istanbul, Salt Lake City, Cádiz, Quantico, Hanoi, Saint Petersburg, Shanghai, Nairobi. Some of the lunar colonies. Should I go on?"

"No." Camacho took a deep breath. "Can you tell me general causes?"

"Fear of the alien grafted on failing institutions," Genji said. "As things got worse, aliens were good scapegoats. Collapsing economies? Secret alien plots and alien technology destabilizing everything. A pandemic? Obviously created by aliens. Political corruption? The aliens did it. Mom told me nothing seemed to work anymore. The voices calling for hate and divisiveness were very loud, with a lot of money behind them. People were too busy fighting over whose fault it was, and whether to murder every alien, part alien, and anyone who'd ever met or talked to an alien, to cooperate long enough to fix things. Blowing up cities? People would cooperate to do that. Fix stuff? That was too hard. That's what my mother said. I think she was right."

"People hated the aliens, the Tramontine, that much?"

"It was rooted in the problems with First Contact," Genji explained. "It took a long time for basic concepts to be mutually understood, and the whole time certain people were feeding fear of what the Tramontine wanted, what they intended. By the time it was clearly established that the Tramontine were friendly, the fear had been deeply planted. It seemed to subside for a while, but I'm sure that's because it was hidden deep, not because it had gone away."

"You know details about that," Camacho pointed out. "Exactly when the first message would be sent by the Tramontine. What would be in it. Information like that."

"I had a big personal interest," Genji said. "I did some research papers on it in school, because it was also a safe topic for me. Some people would freak out if an alloy commented on decisions full humans had made, things they'd done, but anything pertaining to First Contact or the Tramontine was safe for an alloy to talk about."

"Safe?" Camacho said, looking shocked again.

Genji shrugged to hide old hurts. "Alloys couldn't be seen as criticizing full humans. Alloys couldn't be seen as acting like we were better than full humans. Most people preferred if alloys weren't seen at all. Even our allies weren't entirely comfortable with us. Creating alloys was a stupid idea because no one laid the groundwork for our acceptance. Every one of us paid the price for that. So I couldn't do a school paper about, say, Karachi, because if I did, I'd be commenting on the actions and decisions of full humans, and even though Earth was my home, I didn't really belong here, you know, so I had no right to do that."

She realized that Kayl was also staring at her in sympathy and sorrow. It made her feel uncomfortable rather than comforted. "Not everyone was like that. But enough were. A smart alloy kept her head down and watched what she said. Until I joined the Unified Fleet after my mother was murdered. Then I stood tall. I didn't have anything left to lose at that point."

"It almost sounds," Cerise Camacho said, speaking carefully, "as if you're arguing your own creation was a mistake."

Genji sighed. "It was. Maybe not in the abstract, in the 'let's see what we can learn and help humanity' sense, but in real terms, it generated fear and resentment and all kinds of other problems because the people who approved the alloy program seem to have thought everyone would just naturally think this was a great thing. I think every alloy would have agreed with me. But all you've got is me, because the others haven't been born yet, and they all died."

"Let me be sure I understand something," Camacho said. "Are you suggesting that alloys should never be created?"

"Not if it's done the way it will be," Genji said.

"That would mean you will never be born."

"I realized that a long time ago." She looked at Kayl.

Kayl nodded, his expression grim. "From the first, Selene realized her actions would probably lead to her never being born. She was nonetheless determined to do whatever was necessary to save the Earth from its fate."

"At the cost of your own existence?" Camacho said to Genji. "Why? Given what you're saying about how you and the other alloys were treated, why pay such a price for people and a planet that treated you that way?"

Genji smiled slightly. "Maybe I'm trying to prove all of them were wrong when they said I didn't belong here, when they said I should never have been created." *And maybe so I'll finally be sure of that answer as well*, she thought, but she didn't say that out loud.

"But . . . Lieutenant Genji . . . none of them will ever know that."

"I'll know it," she said. "Make no mistake, the possibility of being erased terrifies me. But I won't let that stop me."

Camacho took a while before replying. "I am going to recommend that we look at the results of the genetic analysis being done by the lab you selected, and consider the possibility of something like the alloy program that produced you, but only if what you called the proper groundwork is first done so that none of those born as a result will be subjected to what you were." She paused. "What about the male alloys? Was there any difference in how they were treated?"

"There weren't any male alloys," Genji said. "None of the males were viable. Every alloy successfully born will be female. And, no, no one knew why. We were told it seemed highly likely that any successful offspring of ours would also be female, but no one ever tested that."

"Are you . . . ?" Camacho let the question trail off, but it was obvious what she was reluctant to ask.

"I don't know," Genji said. "Kayl and I haven't decided." She knew he would defer to her decision, but she wanted others to see him as having a say. Because what he wanted did matter, even though it wouldn't decide her.

"That's one specific thing," Camacho said, leaning back and running a hand through her hair. "We'll cancel or change the alloy program."

Will this be the moment? Genji wondered. The moment when someone with power and influence decided that the alloy program should not be, or should be done much differently? Because that decision, targeted precisely on the circumstances of her birth, would be an arrow aimed at her existence.

She felt that now-familiar queasiness, as if a hole had opened inside her that would spread until it consumed her and nothing remained of who she had once been, just a might-have-been that never was. Waiting to see if it grew, waiting to see if she would feel that, or if she would simply be gone in an instant, not even able to realize she had ceased to ever be.

Kayl was watching her, his expression composed, but his eyes worried. He could tell she was holding something inside.

He knew so much of her now. Because unlike so many, he listened to her, he asked her, he . . . observed her.

Kayl was an observer, Genji realized with a shock. The Tramontine had talked about that. Because she had observed the destruction of the Earth, it was something that had been, an outcome she had to change even though it hadn't happened yet. Kayl had observed her, knew her as close to exactly as she was better than anyone ever had except her own mother. Was he helping to hold her to reality? Was her outcome, her existence, not just linked to the universe's need to have a cause for the events she was triggering, but also linked to someone else knowing her so well, observing her do those things? She'd have to ask the Tramontine about that. They'd be thrilled to have that new question to consider.

Oblivious to Genji's internal turmoil, Camacho was still talking. "And we're dealing with First Contact, which you have already had a huge impact on. I can safely say that the fear you tell me developed because of the drawn-out process of learning what the Tramontine wanted isn't working the same way. Because you enabled us to quickly determine the Tramontines' peaceful intent, and purpose, most people seem more intrigued than fearful. Even more than that, the initial response has been extremely positive to what you said in that interview, that the Tramontine could help us terraform Mars quickly and tell us everything about a planet orbiting another star that humanity could colonize."

"Good," Genji said.

"One thing you haven't mentioned, though, is what will happen to the Tramontine," Camacho said. "That shock wave from the destruction of the Earth would even imperil the human colonies on Mars, you said. What about the Tramontine and their ship?"

Genji sighed. "Hopefully they were far enough away. The Tramontine had left the solar system in 2178, over a decade earlier than they'd planned, because of the Universal War. Aside from increasing attempts to target them by the Spear of Humanity, the Tramontine hoped that their leaving would defuse some of the hate. Instead, the Spear used claims they'd driven out the aliens as a recruitment tool, and at the same time warned their followers that not all of the aliens had left, that some were secretly still trying to manipulate humanity. Giving the Spear what they claimed to want just encouraged the Spear to demand more."

Camacho nodded. "Fear of the aliens motivated them and their followers. Admitting they'd driven off the aliens would rob them of support. So they could never admit victory, could they?"

"No," Selene said. "Even if there hadn't been alloys like me, the Spear of Humanity would still have seen alien threats behind every rock and every tree."

"At least we know what didn't work," Camacho said. "Or, rather, what won't work. But none of that helps us understand why so many institutions failed in the 2150s and 2160s," she lamented. "You don't remember anything from college history courses?"

Genji favored her with a brief, humorless smile. "From the age of seventeen on, I was fighting in the Universal War."

"Oh." Cerise Camacho seemed lost for words for a moment. "I should have realized that. I keep trying to fit your experiences into the world I know, even though it was very different."

"I've done the same thing," Kayl said. "I think I can help with answering your question, because of what I've learned during the time when Selene and I were being hunted. She showed me a lot of stuff I could have seen before, but didn't. I think those things show a big reason why major institutions are going to develop worse and worse problems."

"Tell me," Camacho said, looking skeptical but ready to listen.

"There's a huge problem the Earth Cooperation Council isn't even aware of," Kayl said. "That every major institution isn't aware of. We've got automated data collection for everything we think is important. Economic activity, people, travel, crime, you name it. Our databases give us detailed information accurate out to twenty decimal places."

He paused, shaking his head. "And it's all wrong."

15

CAMACHO SAT BACK, HER gaze dubious. "Why is it all wrong?"

"Because, as I have discovered in recent months, while governments and other organizations were figuring out various means to automatically collect all of that data, everyone with a different agenda was figuring out means to avoid having their data seen by the automatic collectors. Do you know how easy it is to get false identity documents and travel without your actual movements being known? Do you know how much economic activity is carried out using anonymous cash cards that don't allow tracing of purchases or who made them?"

Camacho tapped the desk, her eyes on Kayl. "There are supposed to be algorithms in the code to allow for error, allow for the possible use of false IDs and the small percentage of purchases that wouldn't appear in the data collection."

"It's not small," Kayl said. "It's a whole other economy that's operating beneath the radar of official data collection. Not just a black market. An entire other economy, used by a tremendous number of people. People who aren't being tracked when they travel, or make purchases, or do things. Poor people, rich people, everyone. It's right out in front of our noses, and we don't see it, because the automated systems can't see it, because it was designed to avoid the gaze of those systems, and we trust those systems to tell us everything."

"Give me another specific example," Camacho said.

"Selene and I found out how easy it is to get past DNA samplers at travel nodes."

"Easy?"

"Very easy," Genji said. "There are loopholes in the ways the systems work, and people have found those loopholes. They use them. That's how Krysta could be sold as a child bride, and be hauled around for more than three years without any official source noticing anything was wrong. That's how Kayl and I could board that shuttle on the Moon without being detected even though every passenger was supposedly having DNA samples taken before boarding."

"What happened to Krysta is a terrible thing, I admit, and one which was missed. Do you think what you're talking about is that big a problem?" Cerise Camacho asked. "How many people know how to fool the DNA samplers?"

"It's apparently widely known," Kayl said. "Krysta isn't exactly a master criminal. Neither was Ivan, who was instructing her. They knew. Krysta said it was common knowledge among the petty thugs Ivan ran with. And what about rich people? You lost Thomas Dorcas, right? How could he disappear, given everything that should have tracked when and where he was going?"

Genji didn't comment, not wanting to drop any hint that she knew a lot more about Dorcas's disappearance than authorities had guessed. Or, if they had guessed, had decided to overlook.

"That's a reasonable question," Camacho said.

"And you talked about all that had been discovered since his disappearance," Kayl continued. "Secret deals and other things. How much money, how many people, did those things involve? How many cases of someone as wealthy as Thomas Dorcas engaging in actions you don't know about does it take before you're talking about a significant chunk of economic activity that is hidden from the people making decisions about governing and economies and everything else?"

Camacho nodded, her eyes hooded in thought. "That could be a significant factor."

Kayl leaned forward. "I know how much Earth Guard

depends on projections based on existing data. If the data is wrong, the projections are wrong, and the actions taken will be wrong. Extrapolate that across every program and every action taken by governments today. They think they know exactly what is required because they're using exact, precise numbers and other data. But those numbers and that data are incomplete at best and therefore riddled with errors. You want to know how everything could fall apart? That's how. And, as things get worse, corrective actions based on more bad data will instead create more problems. We have the illusion of a digital crystal ball guiding us. But it's all an illusion that could lead us off a cliff."

Camacho's expression had shifted to worry. "Like a worldwide Potemkin village."

"A what village?"

"Potemkin," Camacho explained. "There was a government official named Potemkin who constructed fake villages for his ruler to tour so they'd think everything was great. You're saying we've inadvertently done that same thing, created a digital picture of the world that only shows us what we're allowed to see. Why haven't our data collection analyses spotted the errors?"

Kayl shook his head. "What happens to data that doesn't fit projections? It gets thrown out. Obviously erroneous. I've dealt with bureaucrats in Earth Guard. If the data is assumed to be right, if the data can't be questioned, then the fault has to be with whoever is trying to carry out the actions ordered as a result of the data. They have to try harder. We need to redouble the same efforts that failed last time. The fault has to lie with the individuals, or the funding, not with the program or the data."

Cerise Camacho looked to one side, the fingers of one hand tapping on the surface of the table. "You're not the first to warn of this. About six months ago I looked over a paper co-authored by a number of mid-level officials warning that there were signs of serious problems with our data collection which were impacting the effectiveness of our actions. They used an old phrase, 'garbage in, garbage out,' to emphasize how serious the problems were. Needless to say, those in charge of their organizations did not endorse the paper. The senior officials argued that there were no fundamental problems with data collection that could not be solved with simple tweaks to the analysis programming."

She sighed. "Automating the data collection process was the cheapest and easiest way to collect everything we thought we needed. Changing that, using more humans to collect and check the data itself, will cost significantly more money. And require changes in the way institutions make their decisions."

"I'd think," Kayl said, "that they should be concerned about wasting the money they're already spending."

"I know where this leads," Genji said. "I think Kayl is right. It fits with the way my mother described things going badly, and what I remember of events. Anyone worried about spending a little more should think about how much it will cost them when their economies crash in slow motion, how much it will cost to replace cities that have been turned into fields of craters, and to build the military forces to defend their remaining cities, and to strike back. That really is the choice they face. Leave their institutions on the vectors they're currently following, and watch it all fall apart bit by bit over the next couple of decades, or change what they're doing and how they do it."

Camacho sat staring at the table, her expression grim. "You've just told them, Lieutenant Genji. But I will do my best. Are there any other measures that might help? You spoke about voices calling for division, fomenting hatred of others. I don't know what we can do about that. Our laws don't allow us to shut down speech just because it's awful."

"You can encourage other voices," Genji said. "Voices that are going to help, not hurt."

"Do you know of any such voices?"

Genji considered the question for a long moment. "Please stop recording."

"Stop recording," Camacho said.

"I do know of one such voice," Genji said. "I have already done something that should ensure that voice is much more widely heard than it was in the history I know." Even though this wasn't being recorded, how much should she tell Camacho about Abraham Pradeesh? "A new company is going to be announced soon. It will have patents on a lot of technological improvements derived from Tramontine technology. It would be a mistake for obstacles to be thrown up against that company and its owner. He can do a great deal of good if his voice is allowed to be heard."

Camacho gazed at Genji, plainly worried. "Just how disruptive will this technology be? How dangerous?"

"What he has won't be dangerous. It's not weapons-related. Disruptive? I don't think so. It's improvements to existing human technology. Making that technology significantly better."

"Significantly better," Camacho said, nodding. "Such as enabling a short-range lifter to make the journey from Mars orbit to the Moon with reaction mass to spare?"

"Maybe," Genji said. "I heard that did happen."

"Everyone knows who was aboard that lifter, Lieutenant Genji. There will be those who argue such technology should be controlled and distributed by responsible authorities," Camacho said, spacing her words for emphasis.

Genji let out a derisive snort. "I happen to know in general how that worked out. In my history, the responsible authorities made sure their already rich and powerful friends got control of that tech, which allowed them to become even more rich and powerful, tilting economies even further out of balance. If you want to try to repeat that, I can't stop you."

Camacho grimaced. "That isn't something I can decide."

"You can decide what you recommend, and you can decide

what you do," Genji said. "Even if that is only allowing that new company to get its feet under it by not asking awkward questions about where their innovations came from. I can tell you one of the members of that company is a skilled engineer in her own right who will invent some useful devices."

"Is that why you went to the Moon?" Camacho asked.

"No," Genji said. "It was . . ."

"Serendipitous," Kayl said.

"He went to college," Genji said. "That's one of the reasons I keep him around."

Camacho smiled for a moment. "All right. I will carefully consider your advice on that matter. Is there anything else that should be recorded?"

Genji nodded. "One more thing."

"Begin recording."

"While being hunted," Genji said, "I tried to take actions that I thought would help change the fate of Earth. One of those things was First Contact. But not everything happened as I'd hoped. Even though the changes I caused helped First Contact, they triggered other events that I didn't want or foresee. The Forty-Eight-Hour Martial Law, for example. That never happened in my history."

"It didn't?" Camacho asked, startled.

"No. Me being here decades before I should has sometimes caused things to happen regardless of whether I wanted them," Genji said. "Even if I did nothing."

"Such as her impact on my life," Kayl said. "The moment the piece of wreckage with Lieutenant Genji on it appeared near my Earth Guard ship, the vector of my life changed dramatically. There's no telling how many other lives have been changed just by Lieutenant Genji being in this time. And wider trends, like the anti-alloy sentiments she had to grow up with, have appeared twenty years early because she's in 2140. But she says they don't seem to be the same. Not as widespread or as deeply rooted."

"I don't understand it at all," Genji said. "I'm an alloy. My eyes, my skin, mark me as different. Every alloy experienced . . . difficult lives. Full humans did not . . . embrace me. Except for my mother. But here, they do. I don't understand."

"Obviously," Kayl said, "some people still want to kill her, just because she has some alien DNA in her genome. That's all they think they need to know. I think Lieutenant Genji may be able to change that kind of narrative around alloys, because of what she's done. That's what I hope, anyway. But given how Tramontine knowledge and technology can help humanity, any measures that lessen our distrust of the alien would be well-advised. In my opinion."

Cerise Camacho nodded. "In other words, this isn't a controlled process. Every intended action has unintended results, just you being here has caused unintended changes, and we can't know where any of that might lead. Thank you. You've given us a great deal to think about. Stop recording. We've got a few weeks before we get to Mars. If you think of anything else, any specifics, that might help us guide Earth away from the fate you saw, away from the Universal War, please let me know."

"Four and a half weeks to Mars?" Kayl asked.

"Yes. Earth and Mars are not at their closest in their respective orbits, so the distance is longer." Camacho paused. "Lieutenant Owen, given your experience with Earth Guard, when do you think something would be most likely to happen?"

Genji saw Kayl thinking through the question. "I would guess, if something is planned, it would be sometime between the first and second weeks of our transit," he finally said.

"Why then?"

"If they badly want to prevent us from reaching Mars," Kayl explained, "they'll want to make their try early enough that if it fails, they can activate and carry out backup plans. They want us far enough from Earth that any response or reaction in defense of us would be delayed, including messages back and forth, but not so close to Mars that we could reach it before they could hit us again."

Camacho frowned. "Why do you think they badly want to prevent our reaching Mars? What would be the motivation at this point?"

Kayl looked at Genji. "They're afraid of Lieutenant Genji. I think it simply comes down to that. She's part alien, but you'll have noticed that Earth Guard communications always referred to her simply as an alien. They're afraid she might be part of some huge plan to betray humanity to the aliens, a plan she'd be well positioned to carry out when she reaches Mars. But I believe they are also afraid that if she *doesn't* launch this nefarious plan as soon as she reaches Mars, Lieutenant Genji will become more popular and be seen as safer by more people, which, to those who are afraid of her, will also be part of her plan to eventually betray humanity."

Camacho considered his words. "You believe that they are that afraid of her?"

"I talked with Admiral Besson when I was briefly in custody at Fort Eisenhower," Kayl said. "He was absolutely certain she was a threat."

"He threatened you, too," Genji added.

"Yes," Kayl admitted. "I was going to disappear. Besson wanted Lieutenant Genji dead. I do think they want me alive at this point, for a show trial, the sort of thing they wanted to do to my father. What do we know about the commanding officers of the two cruisers with us?"

"I know their names," Camacho said. "Captain Yan on the *Lifeguard*, and Captain Issakhanian on the *Diligent*. And I know that Admiral Besson personally selected both of those officers for their commands, and personally assigned those two ships to escort duty."

Kayl shook his head. "Doesn't that worry you?"

"Of course it does," Camacho said. "It does send a strong

signal that Admiral Besson is going to try something. But if he does, the link to him will be impossible to deny. He will have anything that happens pinned on him, not whoever is the most convenient subordinate. Rear Admiral Tecumseh has been adamant that until Besson and his closest allies are removed, there is no realistic chance of instituting real reforms inside Earth Guard."

Genji saw Kayl grimace, his eyes on the table, before he finally turned his head to look at her.

"I can't argue with that."

She nodded to him. "That's why I had to be the bait. With you, they might have played the long game, sure they could trip you up or get their hands on you. But Besson and people like him are too afraid of me to give me any extra time. They think I have to be silenced as quickly as possible. I am trying to understand why someone in Admiral Besson's position would act, knowing responsibility would be pinned on him."

Kayl shook his head, looking angry. "Because Admiral Besson, and those close to him, have never had to accept responsibility for their mistakes. They always shifted the blame. And now they're in powerful positions and, I would guess, unable to even conceive that they can't do whatever they want. When's the last time the Security Committee or the Earth Cooperation Council as a whole overruled Earth Guard's military leadership on any issue?"

"Before our actions regarding you two?" Camacho asked. "It's been a long time. That's our fault, taking the easy path of giving the military leadership as much rein as they wanted instead of accepting our responsibility to provide guidance and oversight. We, and you two in particular, are living with the unintended consequences of that. Lieutenant Genji, you spoke of unexpected events triggered by your mere presence in this time. If the leaders of Earth Guard openly defy Council and Committee authority, that will be such an event. And the consequences of that may be very far-reaching."

/ / / / /

SOMETIMES THEIR ROOM ON the Yamanaka felt like a refuge, and other times like a prison. It never felt really safe, though. Not to Genji, and Kayl didn't try to argue against her advice and instincts. Which reminded her again of one of the reasons she had liked him so soon after meeting him.

"We still sleep in shifts?" Kayl asked.

"Yes," Genji said. "But, since we have guards who may be looking in, there's something else we need to do to mislead any attacker. We've got that chair facing the door, and that couch against the bulkhead opposite where the bunks are."

"We'll be in zero g most of the way, so whoever is on guard won't need a chair or a couch," Kayl pointed out.

"No, we won't. Listen to your lead tactical officer. That's still me." Genji pointed to the chair. "Whenever one of us is on watch while the other sleeps, if someone opens that door, comes in that door, I want them to see the one on watch in that chair. Strapped in if we're in zero g."

"You want them to see us there?" Kayl asked. "Meaning we won't actually be there any other time?"

"Right. The one on watch will be by the couch. Anyone who comes in will target that chair and then the bunks. The one on watch can hit them from the side before they realize the situation isn't what the attacker planned for."

He looked about, nodding. "Okay. Simple enough. You think there's a threat aboard this ship?"

"I'm sure of it," Genji said. "I'm convinced the primary attack is going to be an inside job, using people already aboard this ship. Those two Earth Guard cruisers are distractions, places for our attackers to flee once they've done the job, and backup if the primary attempt fails."

Kayl frowned, moving to one of the panels and bringing up an image of one of the cruisers pacing the *Yamanaka*. "Why didn't you tell Cerise Camacho that?"

Genji shook her head. "If I told Camacho, who would she immediately tell?"

"The diplomatic security guards, who you don't trust."

"You got it on the first try," Genji said.

He gazed unhappily at the image of the Earth Guard ship for a few moments longer before nodding again. "All right."

"If you have objections, I want to hear them."

Kayl spread his hands. "I'm not happy with it, but I'm willing to accept your lead on this, because you've kept us alive so far. Are there any of the diplomatic security agents you're particularly suspicious of?"

"All of them," Genji said.

"Alejandro, Pyotor, and Angielyke all seem like they are well-disposed toward us," Kayl pointed out.

"Maybe," Genji said. "There are always two agents guarding our door, but which two agents shifts every time they turn over. What do we have to worry about?" She was treating him like a member of her assault team, walking him through threats and countermeasures, but he didn't take offense. Kayl was smart enough to know when he needed to learn more about the whys behind something. Another reason she'd almost immediately taken a liking to him.

He took a moment to reply. "If there are two agents that are a threat, they'll wait until they happen to both be on guard at the same time."

"Right," Genji said. "And, since matchups of two particular agents will happen every few days given the number we have available to guard us, a time when they're both on guard, and we'll be unprepared, and reaction time by everyone else will be longer."

"Ship's night," Kayl said. "Which is why we're still going to be on guard every night. All the guards have are stunners, though, not lethal weapons."

"All they're supposed to have are stunners," Genji said. "If

Earth Guard is behind this, coordinating it, and this is an Earth Guard ship . . ."

"Getting other weapons aboard would be easy to arrange," Kayl finished for her, making a face. "I still think we've got at least a week before they try anything. Not that I'm suggesting we relax until then."

KAYL HAD SUGGESTED THEY eat at least a few meals with the others on the ship in the dining area. One of the larger compartments on the *Yamanaka*, it had several tables that could together hold more than thirty people at once.

Expecting a repeat of what had happened at Vandenberg, Genji reluctantly agreed, because Kayl was right that she couldn't keep isolating herself. However, Alejandro had insisted that they alert the diplomatic security detail in advance so he could ensure two extra agents accompanied them to the dining facility while the regular guard shift kept watch on their room.

All eyes went to them as they entered the *Yamanaka*'s dining area. Kayl could have blended in if he were alone since he was once again wearing his Earth Guard uniform all the time, but Genji stood out not just for her skin and eyes, but also because she had decided to wear her Unified Fleet uniform from now on. She couldn't explain even to herself exactly why, but it felt important to her to do so. Amid the sea of light-blue-with-silver-trim Earth Guard uniforms, her medium-blue-with-gold-trim uniform was impossible to miss.

Still under acceleration, they could get food served more or less normally, and eat and drink it more or less normally. Genji followed Kayl to an otherwise empty table, where they began eating, Genji feeling the gazes of those at other tables boring into her back.

Three officers approached their table with laden trays. A commander set down his tray, followed by two lieutenants. Kayl nodded in silent greeting to the others.

After a few bites, the commander looked at Kayl and Genji. "I'm Commander Dejesus, executive officer. This is Lieutenant Cloud, engineering, and Lieutenant Nijmeh, auxiliary systems."

Kayl nodded again. "I'm Lieutenant Owen and this is Lieutenant Genji," he said, just as if the others didn't already know that.

"Welcome aboard *Yamanaka*," Dejesus said. "Lieutenant Owen, I understand you've been declared in good standing and ready for duty." It was hard to tell from his voice how the commander felt about that.

"Yes, sir," Kayl said.

"Who are you reporting to?"

"Special Representative Camacho, sir."

"How's that working for you?" The commander's tone was still professional, neither hostile nor friendly.

Kayl gestured slightly. "So far it's mainly been debriefings."

"What are your long-term plans?"

"I'm still trying to figure out where this vector leads, sir."

Commander Dejesus smiled slightly before turning his gaze to Genji, his eyes looking over her uniform before focusing on her rank insignia. "You're a lieutenant?"

"Yes, sir," Genji said, keeping her voice neutral.

"Where have you served?"

"I'm not at liberty to say, sir."

"Hmm. What kind of jobs have you held?"

Genji took a drink of tea before answering, giving her time to decide to lay it out in detail. "Assistant targeting officer. Lead tactical officer. Assault team leader. Assault section member. Mag rifle sniper."

The reply led to a prolonged moment of silence.

"Most of that is not Earth Guard work," the commander finally said.

"No, sir," Genji said.

"Have you done any service on ships?"

"A lot of my service was with ship-based assault boarding

teams," Genji said. "And assisting with targeting during engagements. I don't have much experience with other ship operations, except for assault boat driving."

"Engagements? Where was this?" Lieutenant Nijmeh asked, looking puzzled, his voice holding more than a hint of skepticism in it.

"I can't say," Genji said.

"You've stated that you have combat experience," Commander Dejesus said.

"That is correct, sir," Genji said.

"Where and how?"

"I am not at liberty to say, sir." No one looked happy at her reply. She didn't blame them.

"You kicked some butt on Mars," Lieutenant Cloud observed.

"Only what I had to," Genji said, still trying to judge the mood of these officers.

"There's a story going around that someone threw a knife at you at Vandenberg and you caught it in midair."

Genji smiled for a moment. "It was a ceramic bowl, not a knife."

Commander Dejesus had been watching her, clearly thinking. Now he spoke again. "You've said you were born on Earth."

"Yes, sir, that is correct."

"And that's where your loyalties lie?"

"Yes, sir. My loyalty is to the world of my birth, and my fellow humans."

"You consider yourself human?" Lieutenant Cloud asked, her tone not challenging, but curious.

"Yes," Genji said, wondering if this conversation was about to head off the rails. "Not fully human, because of the genetic engineering. But nonetheless human."

"Why did you let them do that to you?" Lieutenant Nijmeh asked.

Genji shook her head. "I was born like this. Nobody asked my opinion."

Commander Dejesus gazed at her. "There are obviously things going on that most people don't know about. Why were we warned about you, Lieutenant Genji?"

She held up one hand so the shiny skin on the hand and arm glowed under the light. "I'm different." Genji watched their expressions, still expecting the worry and aversion she had experienced growing up more than twenty years in the future, and still startled to see instead observation and speculation on the parts of Dejesus and Cloud, at least. Kayl kept telling her it was because people in 2140 didn't know they were supposed to be repulsed by the sight of an alloy. As hard as it was for her to believe that, maybe he was right.

"There must have been some other reason," the commander said.

"When Lieutenant Genji was brought aboard *Vigilant*," Kayl said, "she was initially treated as an ordinary survivor. As soon as her genome was analyzed, and some alien DNA identified in there, the ship's doctor put on an isolation suit, she was quarantined, and the crew was told she didn't exist. I was the only one who'd interviewed her, spoken to her, prior to that. Nothing else was known about Lieutenant Genji by the chain of command except the alien DNA that is part of her genome. The next thing that happened was her being placed on a sabotaged courier ship designed to kill her and then destroy itself."

"Lieutenant Owen was aboard, too," Genji pointed out. "Because he'd spoken to me."

Commander Dejesus looked down, unhappy. "I have talked to officers who were in the command center on Mars while you were there assisting in First Contact. Most of them regard you well, Lieutenant Genji. And obviously the Earth Cooperation Council has been convinced of your good intentions. However, it's no secret how the senior levels of

Earth Guard think of you. And the answers you've given me just now are . . . baffling. It's as if you come from a totally different world."

Genji nodded slowly. "In some ways that is true, sir. A world where a lot of things had gone wrong. But, I repeat, I am from Earth, and I wish only to protect Earth and its people."

"I wish we'd all be more fully informed so we could judge you and your actions in full context."

"I do not disagree, sir." She was liking this less and less. How could she get these officers to listen to her, to trust her, if her answers had to remain vague and unsatisfying?

Kayl spoke up again. "The Earth Cooperation Council has been fully informed about Lieutenant Genji's experiences."

"Were you also aware of all that before you made common cause with her?" the commander asked.

"Yes, sir."

"I'd like to be as well before I decide. Why do you think Earth Guard's senior officers disagree with you?"

"And with the Earth Cooperation Council?" Kayl asked. "Because they refuse to look past their own fears or learn anything that would contradict their own preconceptions. That's not my opinion, sir. I was personally interrogated by Admiral Besson when I was briefly held at Fort Eisenhower. I was asked no questions about Lieutenant Genji's goals, or motives, or plans. I was only asked where she was. The admiral plainly stated that his goal was to see her dead. I assume you saw the earlier shoot-to-kill orders regarding Lieutenant Genji. I've been told those orders specified that she was to be killed immediately, and not given any chance to speak."

Commander Dejesus nodded. "Not in those precise words, but, yes, the alien was not to be questioned or given an opportunity to speak if we had a chance to kill her. I assumed that was because those issuing the orders already knew what they needed to know."

"They don't know anything," Genji said, her eyes on her food. "They don't want to know anything. They want to lead Earth Guard, even if that means leading it straight into the sun. Just as long as they're in charge."

"That's a rather serious accusation," Commander Dejesus said, his feelings once again hard to read.

"It's not an accusation," Genji said, meeting his gaze. Something inside her wasn't willing to keep hiding this. She was tired of dancing around the subject of how she knew things, where she was from, what she had done. The members of the Earth Cooperation Council knew. That made it only a matter of time before the news was leaked and everyone knew. "I *know* where they will lead Earth Guard. I have seen the consequences. You wondered why I didn't serve in Earth Guard. It's because in the time I came from, Earth Guard had ceased to exist. And those of us left had to fight to try to fix the messes left behind. Fight the wars that Earth Guard should have prevented. I am wearing the uniform of the Unified Fleet that will be created to fight those wars." She paused. "A lot of us died, but we failed. I've been given another chance to make things right, and I'm not going to fail this time."

The three officers stared at her with various degrees of disbelief and shock.

"How old are you, Lieutenant Genji?" the commander finally said.

"Twenty-two standard years, sir."

"Then you were born in 2118."

"No, sir, I was not."

Dejesus kept his eyes on her. "When did Earth Guard supposedly cease to exist?"

"Twenty-one sixty-nine." Genji met his gaze, refusing to look away. "I was eleven."

This time the silence lasted longer.

"That's . . . that's impossible," Lieutenant Nijmeh finally said.

Lieutenant Cloud spoke in a cautious voice, her eyes full of awe. "The chief engineer on the *Lifeguard* is an old friend of mine. He told me the equipment modifications you printed out seemed to be a generation ahead of existing technology."

Genji nodded. "That's roughly accurate. Not the latest, but considerably in advance of what you have now."

"Would he give me a look at those modifications?" Commander Dejesus asked Lieutenant Cloud.

"He can't. He was ordered to remove them, replace them with standard equipment, and deliver the modified equipment to a special courier ship. He hasn't heard anything since then." She paused. "He was also ordered not to talk about those modifications to anyone, or what Lieutenant Genji had actually done aboard the ship."

"Be careful about repeating things," Commander Dejesus cautioned her.

"Everyone knows about it, sir," Lieutenant Cloud said. "Permission to ask Lieutenant Genji a technical question?"

"Not a good idea," Dejesus said. "Not yet."

"Can I give her a tour of engineering and see if she has any recommendations?"

Genji replied before Commander Dejesus could. "I'm sorry, but I'm not familiar with a lot of these old systems."

"*Old* systems?" Lieutenant Nijmeh asked. "You call these old systems?"

"They're antiques," Genji said. Kayl was watching her, his eyes worried, but he wasn't trying to shut her down. She wasn't sure how much further she'd take this. But after so much silence, it was nice to just say what she wanted to say. "The technology the Tramontine are willing to share with us will bring some dramatic improvements."

"Lieutenant Genji," Commander Dejesus said, "is what you've told us known to the Earth Cooperation Council? You proved what you've said to their satisfaction?"

"Yes, sir."

"Why haven't you told Earth Guard's leaders the same things?"

"Because they keep trying to kill me before I can say anything," Genji said. "Because they refuse to listen to something they don't want to hear. Because they're afraid I'm going to upset their careers built on climbing a ladder made of predictable peacetime requirements. Because they're afraid of me."

"At the moment," Commander Dejesus said, "I'm afraid of you, too."

"Sir," Genji said, "you have nothing to fear from me. I am trying to prevent mistakes that were made. I look different, but I am on your side. We have the same goals, to protect the Earth and protect its people."

"Why are you going to Mars?"

"For exactly the reasons publicly stated, to assist in First Contact negotiations. To ensure the best outcome for humanity. I am *not* an agent of the Tramontine."

"You've been aboard their ship," Dejesus pointed out.

"Yes, sir, I did take refuge aboard the Tramontine ship, as did Lieutenant Owen, in order to avoid being killed by Earth Guard."

Lieutenant Nijmeh shook his head. "Earth Guard wasn't trying to kill you."

"Yes, it was," Lieutenant Cloud said. "It's no secret that missiles were fired."

"If you're talking about the faked video—"

"It's not faked!"

"Enough of that," Commander Dejesus said. "That matter is classified. Not everyone at this table is cleared for it."

"Of course," Genji said. "By the way, pocket disrupters."

"Excuse me?"

"Pocket disrupters," Genji repeated. "Those are some of the defensive weapons employed by the Tramontine. Those are what made those missiles fired at Lieutenant Owen and me in Mars orbit disappear. It's sort of funny that I know more than anyone in Earth Guard about the classified matter that can't be discussed in front of me."

"Except me," Kayl said.

"Except you," Genji conceded.

"Defensive weapons," Commander Dejesus said. "What prevents them from being used for offensive purposes?"

"They're too short-ranged," Genji said. "Great for engaging weapons near your ship. Not useful for attacking anyone else. As I have told any number of people, the Tramontine ship has no offensive weaponry." She leaned forward toward the three officers from the *Yamanaka*. "None of the wars I fought involved the Tramontine. They were all human versus human. The mistakes made will be ours. The consequences will be borne by us. And by your children. Remember that when you decide who to believe, and what to do."

"Why should we believe you?" Lieutenant Nijmeh demanded. "You're not even human."

"Yes, she is," Kayl said, his voice suddenly gone hard.

Genji nodded to him before turning her attention back to Nijmeh. "'Men are born for the sake of each other.' If you won't listen to me, maybe you'll listen to Marcus Aurelius. I am human in my heart."

"Are there going to be a lot of people like you?" Commander Dejesus asked, his eyes studying her again.

Genji shook her head. "There were never very many like me. The others are all dead. I'm the last." The silence that followed her statement felt like a physical thing spreading through the compartment. She realized that nearby tables, those within earshot, had ceased whatever they were doing to listen.

"Lieutenant Genji, I will have to inform the captain of what you've told me," Commander Dejesus said.

"I assumed that would be the case," Genji said. For better or worse, the genie was out of the bottle. She would soon, finally, learn how larger groups of people responded to knowing who she really was.

16

ONCE INSIDE THEIR ROOM again, the door closed on the two diplomatic security agents standing guard, Genji turned to Kayl. "Go ahead."

He held up both hands in a gesture of denial. "I don't have anything to say. I was surprised you told them the truth, and I wondered how far you'd take it. But it's always been ultimately your decision on how much you tell anyone."

"I'm tired, Kayl," Genji said. "I probably shouldn't have spilled my guts to them, but I'm tired of not telling people the truth and expecting them to believe me. I'm tired of them doubting me because my experiences can't fit into 2140."

"Sniper?"

"I must have mentioned that to you before this."

"No," Kayl said. "Though I could've guessed from the way you took down those drones at Wallops. For what it's worth, they weren't believing you. I could see it. Not until you dropped the truth on them."

She sighed, looking toward the nearest panel, currently centered on one of the Earth Guard cruisers, endless stars framing the human warship. Their time spent hiding and being hunted hadn't been fun, but she wasn't looking forward to it becoming common knowledge that part-alien Lieutenant Genji had come from the future. A future that was full of pain and death. "What's your impression of that commander?"

"He seemed open-minded," Kayl said. "At least willing to listen. I think it's very likely before he goes to talk to his captain, he looks up Cerise Camacho to ask her about what you said." He made a face. "It's odd, given how high-profile you are, that the captain hasn't already asked you to visit his cabin for a face-to-face meeting. That worries me."

"You don't know anything about him?"

Kayl shook his head. "What I know is that command of a ship like the *Yamanaka* is not a high-prestige step on the way to higher rank. It's where a captain goes when they're on their last tour before retirement with no real chance of further promotion. Not like command of a warship, which is a stepping stone to promotion. What does that tell me about what Captain Maldonado will do if push comes to shove? Maybe he'll think he has nothing to lose and should follow orders from the Council. Maybe he'll see a last opportunity to get in the promotion pipeline again by making the admirals happy. It could go either way."

Genji sighed again, this time heavily in aggravation. "I hate waiting for the hammer to fall. You'd think I'd have gotten used to it by now. Waiting for an attack to go in, or waiting to get hit by an attack. I've done that enough times. But it never gets better."

"I don't have experiences like that, but I'm not enjoying it, either." Kayl shrugged. "And now we have another hammer to wait for, how the crew reacts as they hear where you came from."

"It shouldn't change how they react to you," Genji said.

"I'm not worried about how they react to *me*."

INEVITABLY, THE ATTITUDES OF the crew of the Yamanaka changed as word raced around the ship. Whenever Genji left their room, she had already found herself being regarded with either open or sidelong stares. Those had always been a constant in her life, except when she had hidden herself under UV Aversive clothing. Before, those looks from this crew had been sometimes hostile, sometimes interested, always curious. But now those stares had taken on aspects of skepticism, or awe, or dread, or wonder, or mixes of any or all of those things.

She had once pretended that she had gotten used to the looks an alloy received, when all she had done was learn how to act as if they didn't bother her. These looks were different, posing new problems.

She and Kayl persisted in visiting the dining compartment for each meal, making it obvious they could be approached. Unfortunately, that produced another unexpected result.

"No," Genji said again. As a disappointed sailor moved away, she stood up, raising her voice. "Now hear this! I know nothing about the scores or winners of any sports ball games played decades before I was born! Or winners of races or elections or lotteries! I would tell you if I knew. I don't! And I especially don't know whether the sequel to the movie *Young Vampyre Baroness* is going to be any good! I didn't watch old movies that often! Thank you!"

As Genji sat down, a wave of low laughter and applause followed her words. "I have to joke about this," she grumbled to Kayl. "Otherwise I'll scream."

"I haven't ever heard you scream," Kayl said, "have I? Oh, wait, in the hotel. After the thing with Hoster. But that was muffled by your pillow."

"You don't want to hear me scream without it being muffled. When I was little, my mother nicknamed me Banshee." To her own surprise, Genji realized the memory was making her smile.

Kayl noticed. "It's unusual to see you smile when you talk about your mom."

"I guess how I feel about that has changed," Genji said. "Ever since, um, LA Interplanetary."

"Right," Kayl said. "Hi, Jeanine," he added as Lieutenant Cloud sat down with her meal. "Is anything wrong?"

Lieutenant Cloud had been joining them whenever she could, often bringing along other crew members. But this time she was alone, and to Genji's eyes, appeared worried.

"I don't know if anything is wrong," Cloud said. "There's

just this feeling whenever I talk to someone on either the *Lifeguard* or the *Diligent*. Like even though they don't know what's coming, they're hyped up. You know that feeling?"

Kayl nodded. "Like waiting for a hammer to fall."

"But there isn't any threat out here," Lieutenant Cloud complained.

"Maybe there is," Genji said.

Cloud gazed at her for a moment before looking down at the table. *Yamanaka* had ceased accelerating days ago, so everyone was in zero g, but, as on every other ship, everyone strapped themselves to a seat at a table to eat. That normalcy was so common that no one took notice of it. "I don't know how you're reading our crew," she told Genji, "but they're getting used to you. It made a big difference when they learned about the . . . where you're from. And that there's only one of you. Nobody doubts that. I don't know why. But you're wearing a uniform like ours, and you talk like us. I mean, like a sailor and someone in the military, you know? You feel right even if you look different. Does that make sense? There are people who still don't trust you. They might never trust you. But you talk to everyone like you are one of us. And you respect everyone when you talk to them. People notice that. More and more our crew is thinking you're what you say you are, and that you do want to help."

Lieutenant Cloud shook her head. "What you say sometimes, things about the wars to come, it's frightening. But you also say we can make a difference. It's not inevitable."

"I don't think it is," Genji said. "Not if we work at it."

"Everyone in Earth Guard joined because we thought it was important," Cloud said. "An important job that needed doing. But you understand how hard that gets. Day after day, month after month, working your butt off, and nobody seems to care. Everyone starts wondering whether what they're doing matters."

"I know that feeling all too well," Kayl said.

"It just wears you down, right?" Lieutenant Cloud said. "I don't think a lot of the senior officers understand how important a gift Lieutenant Genji can be to Earth Guard."

"A gift?" Genji asked, surprised.

"Because you're telling us how important this is! How important we are, and how important our jobs are! Earth Guard ceases to exist, you said, and then wars start. If we save Earth Guard, keep it from going away, we can make a huge difference, maybe keep those wars from happening. Isn't that right?"

"I think so," Genji said. "I mean, I don't know exactly. There's no way to know. But that would be a critical thing, I think."

"You're right," Kayl said to Lieutenant Cloud. "Selene is someone the brass could point at to tell everyone down on the deck plates how critical our work is. But they seem to be afraid to give her that kind of influence."

Cloud bit her lip. "We're not supposed to talk about internal Earth Guard matters to Lieutenant Genji, but I can talk to you about them, Lieutenant Owen. I've been talking occasionally to a guy I know on *Diligent*. He kept mentioning 'the alien' and I finally said, don't you mean Lieutenant Genji? And he said they are prohibited from using that name aboard his ship, and the same is apparently true of *Lifeguard*. They're only allowed to call her 'the alien.'"

Genji felt her jaw tighten in anger.

"That's unacceptable," Kayl said. "It's directly contrary to what the Security Committee ordered, isn't it? I'm going to talk to Special Representative Camacho about that."

"Kayl," Genji said, "I've spent my life living with that sort of thing."

"Selene, this is now, and I think it would be a mistake to let this stand. There's a difference between acknowledging that you're part alien, and dehumanizing you." He waited for Genji to reply, and when she didn't, Kayl spoke again. "Do you object to my talking to Camacho about this? I won't if you don't want me to. But I think I should."

She didn't want to fight this old battle again, but . . . "I should be the one who talks to her."

"No, you can't," Kayl said, "because Lieutenant Cloud told me about it. It's one of those internal Earth Guard things, right? No one told you about it."

Genji nodded, keeping her expression serious. "You're right. I didn't hear a word. Go ahead."

Kayl paused again. "Hey, I've got another idea."

"Should I be worried?" Genji asked.

"I don't think so. Lieutenant Cloud told us that the crew of this ship is getting used to you. They're seeing you, listening to you, realizing that, hey, she's a person, not a scary alien. What if you toured the cruisers? Along with me and Camacho and some other people. Let the crews of those ships see that you're a person, that you're Lieutenant Genji, and not the cardboard alien they're being told to think of you as."

The idea made sense, even if she didn't like it. "Kayl, it's probably a good idea, but . . . it puts me on display. I'm . . . uncomfortable with being paraded around so those sailors can see I don't have three heads and long claws."

"Oh." He nodded, looking regretful. "I should have thought of that, how it would feel to you."

"Are you sure?" Lieutenant Cloud asked. "Please reconsider. I think it might help a lot."

"Jeanine," Kayl said, "her life as an alloy has been rough."

"I should be used to being on display, though," Genji said. Even though she dreaded the thought, it probably would be smart to try. Better than just waiting around for someone to attempt to kill her. "Jeanine knows these crews. So do you. I should listen to your advice. Kayl, go ahead and propose that idea to Camacho as well."

"Are you sure?"

She shrugged. "It won't be fun, but if it helps reduce prejudice and suspicion, I'll try. I can't quit now."

AFTER THAT TOUGH DECISION, the outcome was particularly dispiriting. "Camacho is trying to set up the tours of the cruisers, but the commanding officers of *Diligent* and *Lifeguard* keep putting it off," Kayl reported a couple of days later. "Seems there are special training activities and drills that supposedly have to be worked around. We should have expected them to find reasons they couldn't let you on their ships, I guess."

Genji closed her eyes, trying to block off the old anger and frustration. She'd been dealing with this sort of thing as far back as she could remember, and her mother had probably dealt with it when Genji was a baby. "Kayl, you estimated if they were going to make a move, it would be sometime before the end of the second week of this transit."

"That's right," Kayl said, sounding worried. "And tomorrow will mark the end of the second week since we broke Earth orbit."

"The hammer is going to fall pretty soon," Genji said. "If worse comes to worst, Kayl, remember your promise. The mission is the hill we will die on. Not me. Regardless of what happens to me, you have to live to continue the mission."

He didn't answer. She opened her eyes to look at him, hanging in the middle of the room, his eyes fixed on her. "Kayl."

"I heard you," he said.

"Are you going to do as I ask? I am asking. I have no right to demand it of you. Not anymore. Please, Kayl. I don't want the Earth to die on June twelfth, 2180."

"I'll remember my promise," Kayl muttered, his gaze going to the panel showing the outside starscape. "I will do what seems best to ensure our mission succeeds."

She could push him harder, but he didn't seem in the mood to be pushed. And her heart wasn't really in it, Genji realized.

"Do you have any idea how badly you have messed me up, Lieutenant Owen?"

His gaze went back to her. "I've been messed up, too, Lieutenant Genji."

"Why do I feel stronger and weaker at the same time?" she demanded. "You did that."

"Same here," Kayl said. "We are one."

Genji nodded to him, smiling despite the turmoil inside her. "We are one."

THE NIGHT PASSED WITHOUT incident, giving way to another day of delays by the two cruiser captains and an increasingly aggravated Cerise Camacho.

Commander Dejesus finally agreed to let Genji tour the engineering spaces. She and Kayl, escorted by an eager Lieutenant Cloud, walked among the equipment and talked to the engineering personnel. She couldn't answer most of their questions, but did recall some items that generated a lot of enthusiasm. As Genji talked to the sailors, she could feel the truth in what Cloud had said. To these members of the crew, Genji was no longer an alien monster. Whether they liked her or remained suspicious of her, they saw her as a person.

But they still hadn't met Captain Maldonado, which was odd. The commanding officer of the *Yamanaka* should have at least asked them to his cabin by now to welcome aboard such high-profile guests. Lieutenant Cloud had a positive opinion of Maldonado, but that was no guarantee of how the captain would react if something went down.

At midafternoon on the ship's day, a message arrived for Kayl. Genji stood back as he viewed it on one of the panels in their room.

"I'm remembering your father again today," Kayl's mother, Leilani, said. "As I am sure you are. He would be proud of you, Kayl. If you haven't seen, the World Court at the urging of the Earth Cooperation Council has taken up the lawsuit Malani filed on your behalf. Normally it would have taken years to get that through all the lower courts, but everyone knows it would end up at the World Court eventually, and many people think we need to clarify the legal status of aliens, and part aliens, as soon as possible. My love and my prayers are with you and Selene."

"Why today?" Genji asked him.

Kayl looked toward the stars as he answered. "It's the anniversary of my father's death, and of the *Sentinel* disaster."

"That's today?" It seemed a worrisome omen. "Why didn't you tell me?"

"I . . ." He looked down. "Since leaving home, I've never been able to share it. So I'm used to keeping it inside."

"But not anymore," Genji said. "Because we share our lives, the good and the bad, and the memories of those we love."

Kayl nodded, looking at her. "Yes. It's kind of hard to get used to."

"Tell me about it."

"That's good news about the lawsuit, though, right?"

"I guess." Genji tried to shake the foreboding darkening her mood. "Kayl, I'm going to stay in my uniform all night."

"Okay." He watched her, worried. "I will, too. Is there anything you know is wrong, or just a premonition?"

"Just a feeling, I guess."

Her sense of the hammer being close to falling grew throughout the rest of the day. It was very likely because Kayl had predicted something would happen today at the latest, Genji thought. But she couldn't shake the feeling by telling herself that.

Normally she tried to get in a few hours' sleep before awakening to watch for danger about midnight. But tonight she couldn't rest, starting at the slightest noise. As Kayl went to his bunk to sleep, she knew she was too irritable and too jumpy.

The lights in the passageway sprang to life.

Peering from behind the unconscious second assassin, Genji saw the first assassin's body floating limp, blood spreading from multiple bullet wounds, drifting out to form a mist near the body. As the body turned, she saw his face.

Pyotor. The super friendly and supportive security guard.

Assured there weren't any other killers nearby, Genji twisted the unconscious person she held to see her face.

Angielyke. Happy, admiring, helpful Angielyke.

People came flying down the passageway, led by Agent Alejandro. "What happened?"

Genji disentangled herself from the unconscious Angielyke. She was breathing a bit quicker, but otherwise felt more relaxed now that the first blow had finally come. "These two just tried to kill us."

"Impossible." Alejandro stared at the bodies of Angielyke and Pyotor in disbelief.

"Pyotor came in first, targeting me. You'll find some bullets wedged in the chair in our room. Then Angielyke shot from the door, but all she hit was Pyotor." Genji pointed to Pyotor's body. "Every bullet in him came from her weapon. Which is a mag pistol, not a stunner."

Alejandro grabbed Angielyke, pulling her up as she regained consciousness. "Why?" he demanded.

She shook her head, her face creased with pain, her broken arm still bent at an odd angle. "Why? Are you blind? Look at it. We have to stop them now."

"It?" Alejandro shouted. "You mean the lieutenant? The woman you swore to protect?"

"Woman? Abomination! It must die!"

Alejandro raised his stunner and shot Angielyke in the face at very close range, ensuring that she'd be out for a while and also wake with a headache that would make a migraine feel mild.

Cerise Camacho had arrived just in time to witness

Angielyke's words and Alejandro's action. Commander Dejesus had also shown up. Camacho turned to him. "Does the ship have a place we can confine this person?"

"The brig," Dejesus said. "She also needs that arm seen to."

"I suppose," Camacho said.

Alejandro searched Angielyke, holding out his discoveries. Aside from the stunner she was supposed to be carrying, she also had two more loaded magazines for her mag pistol, and two fully charged capacitor replacements. Another agent searching Pyotor's body found similar armaments.

The ship's doctor had arrived, calling out orders with brisk efficiency and directing medical bots to clean up the drifting blood and bag Pyotor's body.

Genji watched, saying nothing, feeling the old, old sense of being an outsider, the one whose presence had led to conflict. She almost twitched in nervous reaction when Kayl touched her shoulder.

"Are you okay?" he murmured.

"Yeah," she said, knowing her tone of voice clearly conveyed that she wasn't.

Alejandro, having detailed agents to stay with Angielyke until she was locked in the brig, faced Genji. "My apologies for failing in my duties, Lieutenant Genji. I have no excuse to offer." His voice cracked on the last word, showing the depth of his anguish.

Genji took a deep breath, determined not to make things worse. "They fooled a lot of people," she said. "It's not your fault."

"It's my job to ensure your safety," Alejandro insisted.

"Attention on deck!" someone called.

Genji looked to see that Captain Maldonado had arrived and was being briefed by Commander Dejesus. Maldonado nodded with a furious frown, moving past Dejesus and pulling himself up to face Camacho, Kayl, and Genji.

"We must talk," he said in a rough voice, the sweep of his

hand including Genji, Kayl, and Camacho. Captain Maldonado gestured toward the door of their room, entering first and then waiting for the others. He shut the door, his gaze fixed on Genji before shifting to Camacho.

"I have served Earth Guard faithfully," Maldonado said, his expression that of someone about to jump off a cliff. "I have always done my duty. That is why I am now informing you of what is about to happen."

Captain Maldonado waved toward the outside of the ship. "I received a coded word that opened the file of a set of orders previously sent to the ship. Those orders require me to assist boarding parties from the *Lifeguard* and the *Diligent* in ensuring your death, Lieutenant Genji, and your capture, Lieutenant Owen. The orders specifically state they override the earlier orders regarding your status which we were given by the Security Committee."

"No one in Earth Guard has authority to override orders from the Security Committee," Camacho said angrily.

"I am aware of that," Captain Maldonado said, his voice filled with barely suppressed stress. "I will not obey illegal orders, Special Representative Camacho. But my ability to protect these two is extremely limited. My ship can't outrun or outmaneuver those cruisers. I can't fight them, either, since *Yamanaka* lacks anything other than close-in defensive weapons.

"Captain Yan and Captain Issakhanian have informed me they are carrying out these orders, and to expect the arrival of their boarding parties to 'assist' me. Those boarding parties should reach this ship in approximately ten minutes. My crew will attempt to hinder them from reaching this room, but we can't stop them without employing lethal force. Even if I thought my crew would fire on other Earth Guard personnel, we don't have the hand weapons to do that."

Camacho lowered her head, her eyes closed, her expression tight with tension. "We have nine surviving diplomatic security guards. They all have stunners. I'll send off an immediate request for orders from the Council itself to cancel those orders from Earth Guard."

"Nine guards won't be enough," Captain Maldonado said. "And my crew won't be able to stop the boarding parties from getting to this room, very likely before we can receive those new orders. Moreover, you need to realize what my receipt of that code-word transmission means. Someone else aboard this ship is working against you, someone who knew almost as soon as it happened that the assassination attempt had failed, that someone possibly including another one of the diplomatic security agents."

Camacho took a precious moment to compose herself. "What do you suggest we do, Captain? I'm confident we'll receive those new orders from the Council, but it will take time."

"I can offer no suggestions except delay, and my ability to do that is extremely limited."

Genji nodded, feeling herself enter that calm state her mind called forth in emergencies. "We need to buy ourselves more time than Captain Maldonado and his crew can provide."

Maldonado turned a sharp gaze on her. "Do you have any ideas of how to do that, Lieutenant?"

"Yes, sir, I do."

GENJI WATCHED CAMACHO LEAVE the room, the door still open as she issued orders to Alejandro. "There are boarding parties from both Earth Guard cruisers heading for this ship. Divide your guards into two groups. You're going to take up blocking positions near where the boarding groups will enter. Come on."

"Shouldn't we leave some guards here?" Alejandro protested.

"No. We need to delay the boarding parties as long as possible. Move!"

Genji turned to Captain Maldonado as the security agents kicked themselves off to fly down the passageway. "Thank you, sir."

"I'm doing my duty, Lieutenant," Maldonado said. He touched a communications panel. "Bridge, this is the captain. Sound general quarters. This is not a drill."

A second later the urgent blare of the general quarters alarm filled the air, followed by a babel of voices and the sounds of sailors racing to their general quarters stations.

Maldonado pointed to Commander Dejesus, then indicated Kayl and Genji. "Get them to the boat dock as quickly as possible. Try not to be seen. Give them access to and operating codes for the gig. Then maintain a lookout and warn them if any of the personnel from *Lifeguard* or *Diligent* are approaching the dock."

Dejesus took only a moment to absorb his orders before saluting. "Yes, sir. To the dock, access to the gig, maintain lookout for them. Are they prisoners, sir?"

"No, they are not! We are protecting them in accordance with our legitimate orders. I will not violate my oath, and I trust you will not do so, either."

"I will not," Dejesus agreed. "Let's go," he told Kayl and Genji.

With the crew at battle stations, all passengers in their quarters, and the security guards off with Camacho, the passageways were deserted as Dejesus led them flying along past sealed doors. When they came to airtight hatches sealed for general quarters, his command override let them through each with only a moment's delay.

The boat dock access also yielded to Dejesus's codes. He pointed to the smallest boat. "I'm sending you the operating codes for this. Got them? Get inside and wait. I'll let you know if I see anyone coming."

"Thank you, sir," Kayl said.

"I am doing my job, Lieutenant," Dejesus said. "Good luck. You know Earth Guard is better than this."

"We both know that," Genji said. "Earth Guard deserves better leaders."

"This day I won't argue that." Dejesus nodded to her before going back out the access to the dock and sealing it behind him.

Genji followed Kayl into the small gig, just big enough to carry a half dozen people at the most. Kayl strapped into the pilot position, she into the co-pilot seat next to him, making sure the gig's hatch sealed after her.

"Ready us for launch," Genji told Kayl.

He glanced at her, taking the unexpected command in stride. "Can you depressurize and open the dock from your seat?"

"Yes," Genji said, calling up the commands. Captain Maldonado would be on the bridge by now. He would see that the dock was opening, the gig prepping to launch. Would Maldonado recognize that this was part of the last available means of delaying the attackers from reaching her and Kayl?

Apparently he did. No challenge came from the bridge.

Kayl, working to bring the gig's systems online, glanced at her. "You didn't want the security guards to know we weren't in our room."

"No, I didn't," Genji said. "The captain was right. Someone aboard knew almost immediately that Pyotor and Angielyke had failed and sent that code-word transmission. But only the captain, Commander Dejesus, and Cerise Camacho know we're at the boat dock. Every minute we can buy might make the difference."

"I didn't think they'd go all out," Kayl said. "Individual assassins, yes. But this?"

"You heard Angielyke. I need to die."

"I hope I never understand people like that." Kayl tapped a command, opening a virtual window showing the view from a ship's camera monitoring the passageway to the boat dock. Commander Dejesus could be seen standing at the other end of the short passageway.

"Listen to this," Kayl added.

Genji heard voices as Kayl linked to one of the communications channels. "—cease this operation immediately," Cerise Camacho said, her tone hard and demanding. "You are in violation of orders from the Security Committee of the Earth Cooperation Council. Captain Yan, Captain Issakhanian, I have notified the Council of your actions. If you wish to avoid serious consequences for yourselves, you will withdraw your boarding parties and cease to threaten either Lieutenant Genji or Lieutenant Owen."

A woman replied. "This is Captain Yan, commanding officer of *Lifeguard*. I have been informed that you have been compromised, Special Representative, and that those orders from the Security Committee were forged. As such, I must obey the orders to take necessary action to ensure the safety of Earth and humanity."

"Captain Yan, you know that is nonsense! I have requested immediate follow-on orders from the Council itself. Any action against Lieutenant Genji is in direct violation of your orders."

"My orders from Earth Guard do not leave me room for discretion on what action to take," Yan insisted.

"Then you had best be prepared to face charges of murder if Lieutenant Genji is killed! Captain Issakhanian?" Camacho demanded. "Will you follow your oath and obey civilian authority?"

"This is Issakhanian," a man replied. "Like Captain Yan, I must obey orders from Earth Guard."

Kayl shook his head angrily. "Admiral Besson chose his storm troopers well. I hope those orders from the Council show up real soon."

"Owen?" Commander Dejesus spoke in an unruffled voice over another circuit. "I am informed that the boarding parties from the cruisers have overcome the diplomatic security guards as well as resistance from the crew of the *Yamanaka* and are reaching your room as we speak. They're inside . . . and mad as hell. There may not be much time to react if some of them come down this passageway to search the boat dock."

"Thank you, sir," Kayl said. "We're ready."

"Are we?" Genji asked.

"Almost. A few more minutes. Final system preps are running now."

A few more minutes. Normally, nothing but an annoyance at worst. Now, perhaps the difference between life and death.

"Owen!" Dejesus called. "There's a search party on the other side of the hatch. They'll be through within a minute. I doubt I'll be able to stop them."

"Lieutenant Owen?" Genji asked, taking another moment to be glad she was in her Unified Fleet uniform and had been wearing it every day. If this ended as badly as it could, she wanted to be wearing that uniform when death came for her.

"Almost . . ."

On the virtual window, Genji saw the hatch at the end of the passageway open and a dozen Earth Guard sailors storm through, all carrying weapons. Only a few of the weapons looked like stunners, the rest clearly mag carbines or pistols. The sight left no room for doubt that the goal of these sailors was to kill her.

The Spear of Humanity, which would one day destroy the world in order to "save" it, might not yet exist, but its spirit was motivating these sailors. Had she been deluding herself that there was any chance of changing the attitudes that would harden and pit human against human?

Commander Dejesus held out his hands, calling orders to the sailors from *Lifeguard* and *Diligent* to stop, but they rushed past him without delaying.

"*Now*, Lieutenant Owen," Genji said.

17

THEY'LL BE AT THE last hatch in thirty seconds and start trying to close the dock," Genji added.

"Now," Kayl agreed. He hit the release command and the gig floated free of the dock. As the search party reached the hatch leading onto the dock, his hands worked the controls, sending the gig pivoting under the push of thrusters and then gliding out of the dock and into open space. "Where am I going?"

"Someplace neither cruiser can shoot at us."

"Got it." The gig, staying close to the hull of the *Yamanaka*, soared into a position where both cruisers were no longer in sight, blocked by the *Yamanaka* itself. "This won't work for long," Kayl cautioned. "I can keep maneuvering so the *Yamanaka*'s hull blocks them from firing at us, until the two cruisers realize they can sync their combat systems, which will allow them to push us into a position where we can't avoid being in line of sight from one of the cruisers. I can't dodge particle beams for long."

"See how long you can make it last," Genji said. She spotted some of the boats from the cruisers latched on to the hull of the *Yamanaka* at air locks like lampreys sticking to a shark. The sight brought back memories of the boarding actions she had been part of against Spear of Humanity ships, and of Spear attacks on her ship. Then, it had been kill or be killed. Now, she had to avoid killing, even though those hunting her intended her death. "Every minute matters."

"And then?"

"I think we should head for *Lifeguard*."

"What?" Kayl gave her a look as if trying to assess her sanity.

"*Lifeguard*'s crew knows we saved their lives. If anyone on those two cruisers is going to balk at following orders to kill me, it'll be them."

"So, to avoid the crews of those cruisers, we're going to board one of the cruisers."

"Right," Genji said. "We'll have a decent chance until the boarding parties return from the *Yamanaka*. We have to hope we can hold out until the new orders get here, because we're out of other places to run."

"Yeah." Kayl nodded. "Have I mentioned that you're crazy?"

"It's been a few days since you last said that."

"I'm crazy, too, I guess. Uh-oh, here comes company."

One of the cruisers had finally caught on to what was happening and was maneuvering to bring the gig within its line of sight. Genji watched Kayl kick the gig onto a new vector, still staying close to the *Yamanaka* as the boat raced to place the larger transport between it and the cruiser.

But the second cruiser was coming into sight now, swinging up to bring its particle beams to bear.

Kayl pivoted the gig using its thrusters, hitting the main propulsion to push it down along the side of the *Yamanaka*. "They can't shoot at us without—"

Alarms pulsed, while Kayl stared for a moment in disbelief. "*Diligent* is taking shots at us when the *Yamanaka* is in the line of fire. Their shots are hitting the *Yamanaka*! New plan," Kayl said, his voice harsh, punching the thrusters hard enough to wrench Genji against her seat harness. "We have to head for the *Lifeguard* now. We can't let them shoot up the *Yamanaka*. Why aren't the crews refusing to do that?"

"Do they even know?" Genji said, her back pressing into the seat as Kayl activated the primary propulsion to hurl the gig on a vector toward the *Lifeguard*. "Can't your commanding officers handle engaging a target by themselves using automated systems?"

"That's possible." Kayl adjusted their vector slightly. "But right now I'm taking this gig down a path directly between the *Lifeguard* and the *Diligent*. If *Diligent* or *Lifeguard* fires at us, their shots will hit the other cruiser. Maybe that'll make them think twice."

"Or at least hurt each other if they shoot anyway," Genji said, watching the situation on the gig's display, glad that she'd been able to learn how to read and operate these old systems. "Both cruisers are maneuvering."

"I see it," Kayl said, using the gig's maneuvering controls to alter their vector again so it remained on an intercept with *Lifeguard*. "They're not synchronizing their movements. Lucky for us. *Lifeguard* is showing some really sloppy maneuvering. I think you're right, Selene. The commanding officers are trying to handle this on their own, keeping their crews out of the loop. This might work if they don't figure out what we're planning to do."

"That was the idea," Genji said. "*Diligent* is lining up to launch missiles."

"Against a gig?" Kayl changed their vector again to keep the boat on track to reach *Lifeguard*. "We're close enough that shouldn't be a problem, unless *Diligent* is comfortable with hitting *Lifeguard* with those missiles."

Working to keep her breathing steady, Genji admitted to herself that she was nervous even though she had a great deal of confidence in Kayl. There wasn't much she could do except keep Kayl informed. Close combat skills weren't of any use in this situation, and her targeting experience wasn't any good on an unarmed gig. She itched to do something, but instead had to sit and watch.

But not for much longer.

"Intercept with *Lifeguard* in forty-five seconds," Kayl said.

"*Diligent* just launched a missile," Genji told him. "Estimated time to impact forty seconds."

"It's going to lose its lock on us," Kayl said. "*Lifeguard* is too close and too big. That missile will shift targets to *Lifeguard*, and then *Diligent* will have to try to manually shift it back, but there's no time for that. What if *Lifeguard* activates her close-in defenses against this gig?"

"I'm hoping they won't think to do that before we're too close for them to engage."

"We're about to find out." *Lifeguard* was looming close now, the gig swerving under Kayl's control to loop under the cruiser.

"The missile isn't following us," Genji reported. "It's locked on *Lifeguard*. Good call, Lieutenant Owen."

"Thank you, Lieutenant Genji. Two more seconds and we'll be inside their defenses and *Lifeguard* won't be able to attack us."

The missile vanished in a burst of light as it self-destructed on orders from *Diligent*.

Kayl swung the gig about once more, braking velocity hard with the primary propulsion. "If they figure out what we're trying to do, they can frustrate our attempt to board. But they're probably assuming we're going to try hiding behind *Lifeguard*. Which means they'll finally be activating their close-in defenses and waiting for us to veer far enough from their hull to be engaged when *Diligent* moves into position to fire on us. They'll also be bringing their own boats back to try to board this gig. There's the hatch on *Lifeguard* that we want. Hang on."

The gig shifted vector again, the structure of the boat vibrating as it took the strain of the sudden changes in momentum.

The hull of *Lifeguard* was right next to the gig, Kayl hitting the magnetic grapnels to seize a hold on the hull and lock the gig against it. "We're matched to the after air lock. Got a good airtight seal. We need to get aboard before they realize what we're doing and send a greeting party."

Genji released her harness and shoved herself to the gig's

hatch, opening it to reveal the air lock of the cruiser's after hatch. She studied the panel for just a moment, rapidly entering the necessary commands to override the lock and open the outer air lock door. "It's lucky all of Earth Guard's gear is so old."

"State of the art," Kayl said, climbing into the air lock with her.

She joined him as the outer hatch closed, atmospheric pressure building. Genji breathed slowly, readying herself, hoping that if any reception committee arrived quickly, they would be close enough to the air lock that she could get in among them before any of them could fire. "Kayl, get out of the way."

"If they're waiting for us—" he began.

"I won't want any obstacles between me and them," Genji finished. "You got us here, love. Let me do what I'm best at."

He moved aside with obvious reluctance.

The inner air lock door swung open.

There was only one sailor waiting.

Genji moved fast, barely able to stop her attack as she recognized the chief, converting her strike into a slam against the nearest bulkhead.

"Chief Kaminski?" Kayl said.

"Yes, sir," Gayle Kaminski replied, her voice and expression all business. "There'll be other people on the way. I figured out what you were doing and got here first. Please answer this quickly. Did you come to this ship with the intent of harming any Earth Guard personnel or this ship?"

"No," Kayl said.

"Absolutely not," Genji said.

"In that case, if you lieutenants will accompany me?"

Kayl must have seen Genji's hesitation. "Chief Kaminski would not betray me this way."

"I would not," Kaminski said. "I'll do it to your face or I won't do it at all."

"All right." Genji shoved off right after Kayl, following Kaminski in a rapid flight down passageways, grabbing handholds to swing around corners and shove off again down the new passageway, until they reached a heavy hatch where an officer waited.

"Inside," he said, waiting until Kayl and Genji had followed Chief Kaminski in before saying anything else. "Seal the hatch, Chief. I want them to have to use command override to get through."

"Yes, sir."

As Chief Kaminski worked the hatch, the officer nodded to Kayl and Genji. "Lieutenant Commander Biyase, chief engineer of *Lifeguard*. We didn't have the opportunity to meet during your last visit to this ship."

"What's the story, Commander Biyase?" Kayl asked.

Before the chief engineer could answer, the ship's general announcing system flared to life. "All personnel. The alien is aboard this ship. Find her! Shoot on sight!"

Biyase glared in the direction of the speaker. "That is the story. I know two things for certain. One is that Lieutenant Genji saved this ship and the lives of everyone on it. The second is that we have orders from the Security Committee to escort her safely to Mars. I will not assist in trying to murder her on the basis of questionable orders from Earth Guard headquarters."

"What can you do?" Kayl asked.

"Not much. Chief Kaminski here guessed that you were coming to this ship in the hopes that the crew would remember your actions and avoid following those illegal orders. Unfortunately, almost all of them are following those orders. The habit of unquestioning obedience is hard to break."

"It's never supposed to be about unquestioning obedience," Kayl said. "We're not supposed to follow illegal orders."

Lieutenant Commander Biyase snorted. "That's what the regulations say. You know as well as I do, Lieutenant Owen, that in practice, unquestioning obedience has been expected. With the great majority of the crew currently following these orders, what can I do? Stall for time. I can hide you here until they figure out you're inside. Then they'll wait until the boarding party returns from the *Yamanaka* so they have all of the personnel and weapons they need."

"I saw a lot of mag carbines and pistols among the boarding party members," Kayl said.

"Yes," Biyase agreed, looking unhappy. "A lot more than an Earth Guard cruiser routinely carries. This was obviously preplanned, though to my knowledge no one knew of it except the captain. Once they decide to force entry into here, I can keep the two hatches into this compartment locked as long as possible. When the hatches are forced open, the Chief and I and a dozen sailors who have agreed to follow my orders in this matter will try to physically block entry. That's it as far as what I can do."

"Hopefully that will be long enough," Genji said. "Special Representative Camacho sent off a request for new orders directly from the Earth Cooperation Council. We just have to last until those orders get here."

Biyase made a face. "No offense, but I would not be comfortable staking my life on the Council acting with any speed. I recognize that you have no other alternative, though. Lieutenant Genji, I have heard it said that you can kill with your bare hands."

"I can," Genji said. "I swear I will not kill anyone on this ship while trying to defend myself. I am not Earth Guard's enemy."

"Thank you, Lieutenant. I needed to know that. Here are the twelve sailors willing to help defend you, and to defend adherence to regulations rather than the whims of superior officers."

Genji looked them over, seeing an assortment of individuals, various ages and exterior characteristics, the two things in common their uniforms and the looks in their eyes of a strange mix of uncertainty and determination. "Thank you," she said. "If Earth Guard ultimately survives, it will be because of people like you."

"Thank you for staying true to your oaths," Kayl added.

"Lieutenant?" one of the older sailors asked. "I've got a friend on the *Yamanaka*. He told me you're from the future."

"That's right," Genji said.

"And it gets pretty bad? Lots of wars?"

"It did," she said. "It doesn't have to. Not if we work to change the things that led to that."

"It seems like a pretty hard job to take on, Lieutenant."

She nodded to him. "Changing the vector of the future won't be easy. But it can be done if enough people bend their efforts toward it. Look at you. How far are you from retirement?"

"Three months," the sailor said.

"And yet here you are, not playing it safe for those last three months, but putting yourself on the line for what's right," Genji said. "With enough people like you, like all of you here, we can do it. We can save countless human lives in the future."

She'd never been great at inspirational talks, but the dozen sailors smiled with renewed confidence.

Confidence wouldn't do much good against mag carbines, but it wouldn't hurt.

"The boarding parties we sent to the *Yamanaka* are on their way back," Lieutenant Commander Biyase said as he checked the panel next to him. "Search parties are going through this ship looking for you. I told the captain that I've sealed the hatches to this compartment, implying that was to keep you out. That ruse won't work for very long."

Biyase issued orders to Chief Kaminski and the other sailors, sending half to the other hatch into the compartment and keeping the others with him.

Genji looked about her. Engineering compartments had a

certain sameness, varying in size and exact equipment, but all similar in being larger than any other compartment on a ship, and crammed with a lot of critical equipment. When designed, enough room was left between equipment to allow access from all sides, but over time, modifications always gradually limited that access as equipment got larger, new equipment was added, and new cables and other connections were run between different places.

Lifeguard's compartment bore an eerie resemblance to the engineering space on board the *Vigilant*. Genji had once been trained to serve in engineering on the *Vigilant* before that aging cruiser was destroyed in late 2175. Two levels, separated by a deck covered by what were still called "drainage plates" with serrated openings in them. They were on the bottom level, several ladders leading up to the top level. The various pieces of equipment, and ducts and cables running between them, formed a maze of passages. Many of those passages would be dead ends, Genji knew. "This is the best place to hide on a cruiser," she said to Kayl, "and it sucks as a place to hide."

"Let's look around in the time we've got," he said, leading the way.

Together, they did a quick survey of both levels, trying to spot the best paths and the best places to conceal themselves. Unfortunately, the compartment had been well-enough designed, with enough accesses, that there wasn't any place where they couldn't be seen.

Kayl paused, breathing a bit heavily from their hasty search. "If we had mag weapons, there are places we could try forting up."

"We don't," Genji said.

"Maybe we can take some from some of the sailors—"

"No!" Genji held up her hands. "Kayl, if I have a weapon in my hand, I will be a threat. If I have a weapon in my hand, no one will hesitate to kill me. If I have a weapon in my hand, I will be in danger of violating my promise to these sailors that I will not harm anyone on this ship."

He looked away, angry. "All right. Then we should switch uniforms so—"

"No!" Genji glared at him to emphasize her rejection of the idea. "Even if you could fit into my uniform, that would make you the target of lethal force, and *I will not permit that*. Are we clear, Lieutenant Owen? This isn't about you dying to protect me. This isn't even about me necessarily surviving. But you have to survive."

He gave her a stubborn look, not saying anything.

Any further debate was halted by a hail from Lieutenant Commander Biyase. "They've figured out you're in here! Captain Yan has ordered me to open the hatches and I have refused. We have a couple of minutes at best before the boarding party is back aboard and reaches us."

"Understood!" Kayl called back. "Let's choose the best spot—" he started to say to Genji.

"Kayl Owen, you promised to do whatever we needed to do!"

He glared back at her, finally nodding. "I will do whatever I need to do."

"They're overriding this hatch!" Chief Kaminski called.

No time left to argue. "Don't die!" Genji ordered Kayl. "Come on."

In zero g, it was easy to pull themselves into a place she'd spotted, high up between two pieces of equipment, a place where no direct light would reveal them. It was perhaps the best place available to try to conceal themselves, leaving room in three directions to escape from the spot when they were seen.

"Coming through here as well!" Lieutenant Commander Biyase called. His tone shifted from warning to commanding as he addressed the sailors forcing entry. "You are following illegal orders! Stop threatening people granted protection by the Security Committee that oversees Earth Guard! Put down your weapons!"

Chief Kaminski could be heard shouting similar orders to those pushing their way into the compartment at the hatch where she was, her words being drowned by shouts from the attackers and whoever was urging them on.

Kayl looked at Genji, fear in his eyes. But not fear for himself. He reached to grasp her hand. "Thank you."

"You're crazy," she whispered, scared for him.

"I know."

More shouts as sailors forced their way inside both hatches, the sounds of scuffles as Biyase, Kaminski, and the sailors with them made futile efforts to stop the invasion of the engineering compartments, commands to the attackers to spread out, find the alien, shoot to kill . . .

Had she really accomplished anything? Because here she was again, right where she'd started in 2140, targeted for death by the same people whose lives she was trying to save. Earth was doomed to die, because she had failed.

It felt strange to realize that the thought of Earth dying hurt less than the thought of Kayl being killed while trying to defend her. The same Kayl Owen she had once, reluctantly, been willing to sacrifice for her mission.

Once, she would have fought these Earth Guard sailors, doing whatever damage she needed to in order to try to further the mission. The Universal War had indoctrinated her in the lessons of "kill or be killed."

Perhaps the only change she'd managed to make was in herself.

Maybe it wasn't hopeless. Maybe Abraham Pradeesh would offer a stronger vision of charity and harmony to counter the fear preached by those who would become the Spear of Humanity. Maybe the new vector the life of Frederick Hoster had been put on would lead him to offer acceptance instead of hate and change a few minds. Maybe the reinvigorated

Security Committee and Earth Cooperation Council would keep acting, trying to correct problems that otherwise would have slumbered until it was too late to fix them.

Those things might still happen. Her surviving long enough to see any of it seemed very unlikely.

She heard the search parties moving through the compartment, calling to each other, caught glimpses of sailors moving past, their light-blue-and-silver uniforms the same as that of Kayl's beside her. Her medium-blue-and-gold uniform would stand out clearly. But she refused to die in civilian clothing or the uniform of another service.

A head came into view as a sailor pulled herself along, her eyes searching as her head turned, her gaze meeting Genji's, her mouth opening to shout—

Genji swung her body, kicking the sailor hard against the equipment on the other side of the narrow passageway. Kayl followed her out of their hiding place as Genji found herself facing another sailor, this one carrying a mag carbine, her hands moving without conscious thought, strike, strike, the sailor flying backward, stunned.

More shouts nearby, the clang of a mag bullet hitting a piece of equipment near her.

Genji hurled herself through a gap between conduits, Kayl right behind her.

Two more sailors, coming down the ladder from above, one eyeing Genji with fear, the other with excitement as he brought up his mag pistol . . .

Kayl smashing his body into the excited sailor, crushing him back against his companion, hitting hard before turning to follow Genji through another gap.

Shouts on all sides, shouts from the level above, the voice of Lieutenant Commander Biyase still demanding this cease now, sounding like someone being restrained and fighting against it.

Odd to feel better in this moment just knowing that someone was trying to help.

Genji and Kayl reached the end of the short passage they were in, coming face-to-face with a group of three sailors, two with mag carbines and one with a stunner, Genji shoving herself into their midst and striking without pause, the three flying back and to the sides from the force of her blows.

More coming from both sides.

She followed Kayl back down this passage, through another narrow gap, a ladder in front of them. He went up first.

Genji shoved herself hard off the deck, flying up the ladder, seeing Kayl reach the top and be hit by someone already up there, seeing Kayl reeling to the side, momentarily helpless.

She came up out of the ladder well moving fast, a kick knocking back the sailor who'd hit Kayl. Genji rebounded off the overhead, into two more sailors, hitting mercilessly, both of them flying backward into at least a half dozen more sailors at the opening to this passage, already leveling mag weapons, already firing.

Genji took a quick look down the ladder, seeing sailors pressing in along its bottom, pointing weapons up.

She was finally penned in, back against a bulkhead, openings between the equipment to either side too small to pass through, the ladder coming up filled with sailors, the overhead too close above her. At least a dozen sailors were converging on her from the front now, blocking the only way out, more coming behind them.

Too many opponents, too few options to move. Her only chance was an attack to try to force her way through the mass of assailants coming at her. Genji's punch sent another sailor end over end down the passageway, but she couldn't move fast enough to avoid some of the shots being fired by those farther back.

Her lower left arm jolted as a bullet went home, breaking one of the bones before exiting out the other side.

Trying to block out the pain, anchoring her right arm on the railing, Genji spun, her legs hitting a sailor trying to climb up the ladder and hurling him back into the group firing at her from below.

Genji tried to position herself to shove off into the main group of attackers, her left arm spewing blood that formed red droplets floating in the air.

There were too many attackers, all firing into a narrow space.

Genji felt the impact of two more bullets, one in her leg, from the feel of it shattering another bone, the other higher up above her hip. The hits killed her momentum, leaving her drifting. As she tried to recover, a stunner shot grazed her side, rendering her right arm numb. She tried to grab a handhold with her injured left arm, pain tearing through it, her fingers falling just short of a grip, brushing against the metal.

As her body slowly spun, a dropped mag carbine floated within reach of her left hand. She could grab it. Fire. Maybe save Kayl even if she was doomed.

No. She knocked the weapon away with a closed fist, making it clear she was not trying to grab it.

Another bullet hit her upper abdomen, clipping a rib, wedging inside her.

Damn. It was over. She waited for more impacts and the end.

Something, someone, pushed himself between her and the attackers.

"Kayl!" Genji cried. "No!"

They were still firing as Kayl shoved himself in front of her. She saw Kayl's body jerk from an impact in his lower torso. He had a firm grip on the rail, though, and held his body stiffly in position.

Another hit on Kayl in his upper arm, blood flying as the bullet exited.

She tried again to reach a handhold with her left arm as she drifted helplessly behind Kayl. Her blood was forming a growing mist of red droplets, filling the air around her.

But the shots aimed at her, at Kayl, had faltered and ceased.

"Get out of the way, Lieutenant!" a woman shouted. "That's an order!"

"Go to hell!" Kayl yelled.

All Genji could see was his back, but she could imagine Kayl's expression. She knew he wouldn't move. Because, despite his denials of it, she knew she was the hill Kayl would literally die on. She had always known that.

"What are you waiting for?" Kayl shouted, his voice ragged with emotion and pain. "Go ahead and kill me! You'll have to if you want to get at her!"

"Don't be a fool!" the woman cried. Genji recognized the voice now. Captain Yan. "Don't sacrifice yourself for the alien!"

"The alien?" Kayl shouted back. "You mean this person behind me? You can see her blood, can't you? Isn't it as red as mine? As red as yours? How much blood is enough?"

"She's a danger!" a man yelled.

Genji, feeling herself weakening from loss of blood, tried vainly to grab on to something again. Her right arm was still numb, hanging useless.

It was funny, in a way. They were trying to get Kayl to move so they could shoot her, kill her from a slight distance, still afraid to get close to her even though she was all but helpless.

"Where's the blood in here from?" Kayl demanded. "She's a danger? Who's bleeding? Who's trying to kill people? It's not her. It's not me. What's your oath? All of you! What's your oath? To protect and help people! So go ahead and kill me and kill her and make a mockery of that oath! Go ahead and kill me even though I wear the same uniform as you! And then wonder who'll be next, who you'll be ordered to kill next, not because of anything they've done but because someone is *afraid*!"

"Kayl, please," Genji managed to gasp. "Let them finish me. Don't die."

"Go ahead!" Kayl shouted again. "Kill me! Because that's the only way you'll get to her! By following orders you know are illegal because you *want* to kill!"

"Fine," someone said.

Genji could just make out a chief raising a mag pistol.

"That's enough!" a man yelled. A young man, an ensign, too foolish to let common sense deter him, moving out ahead of the others, toward Kayl, but turning to face away from him. "That is enough! Who the hell are we? What are we doing? Cease fire!"

"He's right!" a woman shouted, also moving to place herself between Kayl and the others. "Are we Earth Guard? We protect!"

"We protect!" another man cried, shoving ahead to join the others shielding both Kayl and Genji.

"Earth Guard!" a familiar voice added as Chief Kaminski joined the three, her uniform in disarray from earlier struggles.

Captain Yan must have been surprised, but now found her voice again. "Lieutenant Demetrios, Ensign Kavarai, you are under arrest! All of you others, move! Finish off the alien and arrest Lieutenant Owen!"

"These orders are illegal!" Lieutenant Commander Biyase shouted from not far away, where he was being held. "You know what your duty is, and it is not blind obedience to illegal orders!"

"This is one of our own officers! This woman saved our ship and our lives!" Lieutenant Demetrios cried. "Have you all forgotten that? I am Earth Guard, and I will protect!"

More sailors pushed themselves forward, joining the group shielding Kayl and Genji, while the rest hesitated, the weapons in their hands wavering.

Genji, slowly drifting, swung a hand through the mist of her blood to finally grasp a hold and pull herself to one side, her left arm in agony from the effort. She could see Kayl's blood still coming out, forming its own curtain of red droplets that mingled with her own.

Captain Yan pulled herself to the front of the attackers. "You are all under arrest! Mutiny! Disobedience of orders in the face of the enemy! The rest of you, get in there! Now!"

But, faced with directly fighting their own shipmates, the crew hesitated. "Screw this," one of them said, flinging away the mag pistol he'd been carrying.

A piercing whistle from the general announcing system was followed by a firm, grim voice. "This is Commander Sudarmo. We are in receipt of new orders directly from the Earth Cooperation Council. These orders have been authenticated and are without any doubt genuine. Captain Yan has been relieved of command and is to be placed under arrest. Lieutenant Genji and Lieutenant Owen are not to be harmed or restricted in any way. We are to ensure their safety and arrival at Mars. I have been appointed acting commanding officer of *Lifeguard*. Everyone aboard this ship is ordered to cease all actions against Lieutenant Genji and Lieutenant Owen, and provide them any needed assistance. Be advised that the commanding officer of *Diligent* has also been relieved for cause. Protect!"

Captain Yan stared at the overhead, once more stunned into silence.

Lieutenant Demetrios shoved her way to a communications panel. "Ship's doctor to engineering, on the double! We have serious injuries to personnel!"

Lieutenant Commander Biyase, his uniform in disorder, pulled himself to the fore. "Everyone turn in your weapons to me and Chief Kaminski. Do it now!"

"No!" Captain Yan yelled, having finally recovered enough to find her voice. "This is mutiny!"

"Captain, by order of the Earth Cooperation Council, you are under arrest. Ensign Kavarai, Chief Huaman," Lieutenant Commander Biyase ordered, "take Captain Yan to her stateroom. Make sure she remains in there."

Genji, her vision blurring, saw the sailors part for a woman officer carrying emergency medical bags, who sailed through them. Those in front of Kayl also made way for her.

"Ship's doctor," Genji heard her tell Kayl. "You need—"

"Her first," Kayl insisted, his voice torn by stress and pain, finally moving so the doctor could reach Genji. "Take care of her first."

"All right," the doctor said. "At least hold this compress tightly over that wound. You two, help this officer hold these over his injuries." She came past Kayl, worried eyes quickly assessing Genji. "What do I need to know about you? Is your anatomy different?"

"Drugs," Genji gasped, dizzy from loss of blood. Feeling was returning to her right arm, along with increased awareness of pain that had been numbed by adrenaline. "Different effects . . . sometimes. Antibios okay. Ana . . . tomy . . . ahhhh . . . same. Blood . . . same."

"Any allergies?"

"Llamas."

"Excuse me?"

"L . . . llamas," Genji got out a second time.

"Okay. Got it. Kairos, help me here."

Genji felt universal plasma packs being slapped onto her arm, a tourniquet tightening on one leg and her left arm as pressure bandages were applied, other wound packs pressing onto her skin. The pain subsided a little. "Kayl . . . Lieu . . . tenant . . . Owen . . . take care . . . of him."

"He insists we take care of you first," the doctor said, working with brisk efficiency. "As long as he doesn't bleed out, he'll be fine. You are a mess, though."

"Been worse," Genji gasped.

"And lived through it? You'll live through this, too. Kairos, hold her there while I deal with Owen's most serious injuries."

Genji, her breath coming in and out in quick gasps, turned her head enough to see the doctor begin working on Kayl. His eyes were on her.

"Thanks," she managed to say.

"I love you," Kayl said.

"We . . . are one," Genji said.

He forced a smile through his own pain, but she saw a puzzled look come into his eyes as he gazed at her. No, not at her, at her injuries.

Genji managed to move her head enough to look down at her body, where the doctor had cut away portions of her uniform to—

She wasn't wearing her Unified Fleet uniform.

Despite the blood and the damage, even through the fog of her own pain and the impacts of the drugs the doctor had given her, Genji could tell that she was wearing a regular civilian coverall the same medium blue color as her uniform.

How could that have happened? She'd been wearing her Unified Fleet uniform. She knew that.

As the drugs overtook her consciousness, she looked back at Kayl, bewildered, trying to mouth the word "uniform" with the last traces of her awareness.

18

GENJI REALIZED THAT SHE was awake, her eyes open, looking at the white surface of an overhead on a spacecraft. From the corners of her eyes she could see medical tubes and lines and monitors, meaning she was lying in a hospital bed. Most of her body felt numb, which she knew from wartime experience meant she was undergoing accelerated healing of serious injuries.

For a moment, she was back there, in the Universal War, wondering why she couldn't remember anything about the fight with the Spear of Humanity that must have wounded her so badly, wondering which Unified Fleet warship this was.

Something about her Unified Fleet uniform tugged at her mind. Something strange had happened . . .

"Selene?"

She knew that voice.

Genji felt a mental jolt as her memory reset. June 12, 2180. Earth had been destroyed. She was in 2140. The Unified Fleet didn't exist yet.

She managed to turn her head enough to see the bed next to hers, the young man lying in it also festooned with medical devices, though not nearly so many as her. A name came to her, along with relief and joy. "Kayl . . . alive."

He smiled at her. "You're going to be okay."

"How . . . long?"

"The fight was two days ago. They kept you under to maximize healing. You . . . you were really hurt bad."

"Where . . . we?"

"This is the sick bay on the *Yamanaka*."

Genji realized she was smiling. "You . . . okay?"

"I'll be fine. You will, too," he said again, as if also reassuring himself.

That something came back to nag her mind. Something important. "Uni . . . form?"

Kayl blinked, suddenly anxious. "Your Unified Fleet uniform?"

That was it. Something had happened to her uniform. "Yeah."

"It's . . . gone." Kayl licked his lips nervously. "After the fight, I saw you didn't have your uniform on anymore. Just civilian coveralls. Same color. Not your uniform." The longer speech seemed to tire him.

"Gone?" Genji tried to grasp that. Someone had taken her uniform?

"Look." Kayl had an entertainment panel set where he could use it. He moved one hand to enter commands, pivoting the panel so she could see it. "Mars."

Genji knew that image. Herself standing on the Martian Commons, Kayl right beside her, he in his Earth Guard uniform, she in . . .

Medium-blue civilian coveralls.

She had been wearing her Unified Fleet uniform when she did that. She was certain of it. And she'd seen this image many times since then. Always her in uniform.

How could . . . ?

The explanation hit her hard enough to make Genji gasp.

"You okay?" Kayl asked anxiously.

She wasn't able to answer for a moment, shocked by the implications. "Gone?" Genji finally managed to say.

"Gone," Kayl said, looking concerned. "No one else remembers ever seeing it. Just me. Every image that should show it, instead you're in civie coveralls. Same color. Not your uniform. It's . . . gone."

Genji closed her eyes, feeling her breathing coming fast, hearing medical monitors beeping warnings. A medical bot appeared next to her bed. "A doctor will be here soon. Do not worry," the bot advised her.

Gone. Not damaged in the fight whose details were slowly reappearing in her mind. Not removed to treat her wounds. Gone. There was no sign her uniform had ever existed, that she had ever worn it.

Which meant the Unified Fleet would not be formed in 2171. It had never existed. There had been no uniform she could wear. But did that mark success? Or had her efforts to change the future resulted in the failure to form a Unified Fleet that would still be needed?

It was gone. The fleet she would train in, fight in, those she would fight alongside, comrades and shipmates, the ships she would serve on, the battles they would fight, those who would die and those who would be badly wounded, everything, everything she had been part of for five terrible years, the one thing she had felt part of, gone. No one else ever would, ever could, remember those things which would have happened but now would not.

Genji felt tears welling from her eyes. She couldn't move her arms to wipe at them, feeling the tears run down the sides of her face.

"Selene?" Kayl asked, his voice anguished.

Kayl. She felt a small hope. "You . . . remember?"

"Yes. I remember your uniform. No one else does. But I do."

Genji felt herself laughing even though the tears kept coming. Laughing with relief.

Someone else remembered.

She only vaguely noticed two people arriving, checking her medical monitors, adjusting something, a sensation of drowsiness overcoming the sorrow for an awful future that nonetheless would have been her future and now never was to be. Darkness filled her mind, wiping away images of former comrades who now would never know her.

/////

THE NEXT TIME SHE awakened, Genji felt more sensations. Felt the numbness that meant her body was still being forced to heal faster than it would have naturally, as well as the pain in the rest of her because of the accelerated metabolism.

She moved her head, seeing Kayl still in the next bed. He'd been shot twice, she remembered. "Kayl?"

He moved his own head quickly, looking back at her, smiling. "Hi."

"Hi," Genji said. Had the earlier conversation been a delusion, or had it been real? "Uniform?"

His smile faded to a look of anxiousness. "Yes. It's gone, like it never was."

"It . . . never . . . was," Genji said.

Kayl nodded unhappily. "Even me, my memory tells me, no, she never had a uniform. Just civie coveralls. Medium blue. But my mind says no, that's wrong. The uniform was real. It feels like I'm embracing a dream, though, and rejecting what I should know is reality."

"No . . . one . . . else?"

"No," Kayl said. "Maybe the Tramontine?"

That hadn't occurred to her. She'd worn her uniform the entire time aboard the Tramontine ship. Would any of them remember that, or would they also recall only civilian coveralls? "Maybe," Genji said. "You . . . okay?"

"Yeah," Kayl said, smiling again. "You're still stuck with me."

"Remember . . . Kayl. Please . . . remember."

"I won't forget," he said. "I promise, Lieutenant Genji."

Something else finally struck her. "Not . . . lieutenant."

Kayl looked startled. "You mean you? Of course you're a lieutenant."

"No . . . no . . . fleet."

"That doesn't matter, Lieutenant Genji. You are still you

and everything you did still counts, even if it's never going to happen."

She smiled at him, feeling the absurdity of it. "Thanks. Still . . . here!"

"You don't get to disappear," Kayl said, his worried eyes belying his light words. "You have to stay here. You promised."

"I . . . did?"

"You said you'd marry me, and you haven't done that yet."

"Oh . . . right." She couldn't help gasping a single laugh. "Okay."

Kayl looked down, his face working as he thought. "I think it means Earth Guard isn't going to collapse," he finally said, looking at her again. "I think how that fight came out tipped things the right way at last. I think you made something very big, very good, happen."

Hopefully, Genji thought. "We . . . made . . . happen."

He shook his head. "I helped. It couldn't have happened without Lieutenant Selene Genji, who never gave up even after watching the Earth itself be destroyed."

Okay. She'd accept that. She was too tired to argue it, anyway. Genji let herself drift off into what felt more like a natural sleep.

"I'M SORRY I HAVEN'T visited more often," Cerise Camacho said.

"It's okay," Genji said. She'd done the equivalent of nearly two months' healing in a week. Even with her body having extra nutrients pumped into it, and even with other genetically modified aids to healing injected into her, that took a lot out of someone. "I haven't been up to dealing with visitors."

"They tell me you're healing faster than expected," Camacho said. "Except your bones."

"That's normal. For me."

"I wanted to let you know something that I hope will please

you," Camacho said. "Some people have questioned your use of lieutenant as your rank, given that you cannot identify a currently existing or past organization which granted you that rank."

"Unified Fleet," Genji said, to see Camacho's reaction.

"Excuse me? What?"

"Never mind." How many times had she spoken of the Unified Fleet to Camacho? All gone. Never was.

"All right," Camacho said in the manner of someone indulging a hurt friend. "The Security Committee, particularly in the aftermath of your actions aboard the *Lifeguard*, wanted that issue of rank laid to rest. By vote of the Committee, you have been formally granted the rank of lieutenant in Earth Guard, and may cite that in any official or unofficial context."

"Oh." Should she say thank you? Genji glanced at Kayl, who was watching her, waiting to see her reaction.

That reaction was complicated. Her image of Earth Guard, created by her experiences in the wake of its final collapse, was of an institutional failure. Earth Guard had failed to protect Earth, had consumed itself in internal malfunction, and had finally ceased to exist.

That was her perspective from the 2170s. And, here in 2140, that same Earth Guard had tried to kill her any number of times.

This Earth Guard still had a chance to reform, to prevent its collapse, though.

It was the military force Kayl Owen had chosen, and still served in. So had Kayl's father. So were people who had helped her and Kayl, such as Lieutenant Commander Biyase, Chief Kaminski, Captain Maldonado and Commander Dejesus, Lieutenant Jeyssi Arronax and Lieutenant Hector Thanh on Mars, not to mention Captain Yusuke Yesenski and Rear Admiral Raven Tecumseh. Weren't those people worthy of standing alongside the Unified Fleet comrades she would now never have? Wasn't that what should matter to her?

"Thank you," Genji finally said. "Umm, does that mean I am subject to orders from Earth Guard?"

"No," Camacho said with a knowing smile, "it doesn't. Like Lieutenant Owen, Lieutenant Genji is on indefinite assignment to the Security Committee, and takes orders only from the Committee. I know you haven't worn a uniform since arriving in 2140, but I hope you'll feel comfortable in an Earth Guard uniform matching that of Lieutenant Owen."

"Yes," Genji said, choosing her words carefully. "Thank you." Camacho had more than once talked about the Unified Fleet uniform, studied the images of her in it, yet now remembered nothing of what would never be and so had never been. Would this be what it would be like if she herself vanished? No one remembering she had been here, her image gone from every file, only Kayl left, only Kayl remembering, trying to tell others about Lieutenant Selene Genji and what she had done?

She looked at Kayl, seeing in his eyes that he was wondering the same thing, thinking about the hell it would be if only he remembered she had ever been.

Camacho left, leaving them alone with that nightmare.

"I'm sorry," Genji said.

"It won't happen to you," Kayl said.

"I didn't want to get involved with you, Kayl. You remember that. I didn't want to use you for my own happiness, my own purposes, and leave you with nothing but regrets and memories you couldn't trust. You understand now exactly what that could mean."

"You were always honest about that," Kayl said. "I will never regret what we have today, no matter what happens tomorrow."

"I used you, Kayl," Genji insisted. "From almost the first moment we met, I knew you could help me get what I needed. I burdened you with my mission, I put your life in danger, it was all about me. And now we're seeing exactly where that could lead for you."

"Are you claiming you never cared about what happened to me?" Kayl asked calmly.

"No. I meant every word I've ever said about my feelings for you. But when we started out, I didn't have those feelings. You know that."

"I didn't fall in love with you right away," Kayl pointed out. "It wasn't until about half an hour after we finally met face-to-face again on that courier ship that I realized you were the one for me."

"Half an hour?" Genji said, trying not to laugh at the sudden injection of absurdity into the conversation. "It took that long?"

"Yeah. It took a while for me to fully see you as you are. And when I did, I didn't have a chance."

"I guess I enchanted you with my beauty and my charms, huh?"

"That's exactly what happened," Kayl said. "That and your amazing ability to function in a life-threatening crisis and look like you were having a good time as you were doing that. I knew I'd found the beautiful part-alien lieutenant I'd dreamed of."

"You actually remembered that?" Genji did laugh, her emotions still churning. "Kayl, seriously, if I'm no longer here, please remember how much I wanted to stay with you, and please be happy knowing that."

He nodded, smiling, even though she knew he knew the danger to her existence would not stop her from continuing to try to change the fate of the Earth. Because, Genji had come to realize, that was one of the things he loved about her. That made no sense at all, but it was true. "You realize that you lied to me," she said.

"About what?"

"You told me, more than once, that you understood the mission was the hill we were going to die on. Not me. The mission. But there you went, making me the hill. I always knew you didn't mean it when you agreed that I wasn't the hill."

He looked at her for a few moments before replying. "I can have more than one hill."

"At the same time?" Genji demanded. "That's ridiculous. You can only have one hill you are willing to die on at a time."

"Maybe my analysis of the mission," Kayl said, "indicated that saving your life no matter the cost was part of the same hill as saving the Earth."

"I am not part of that hill," Genji insisted.

"Yes, I think you are," Kayl said. "I could not save the Earth unless I saved you. Same hill."

She gave him an exasperated look. "The next time we choose a hill to die on, I will insist on clearly specifying the parameters of that hill."

"First we have to save the Earth from dying," Kayl said.

"Fine. After that. Next time, we are going to be in complete agreement on what the hill is."

"Sure." He smiled again. "We are one."

The motto of a fleet that would never be. But that fleet still lived as long as she did, and as long as Kayl remembered her. "We are one."

GENJI FORCED HERSELF TO watch news reports from Earth, despite the way seeing video of the actions on the *Yamanaka* and the *Lifeguard* made her tense. It felt particularly hard to see images of herself, disabled by her wounds, hanging amid the floating field of her blood.

They kept showing video of Kayl, shielding her from attack, calling on his fellow members of Earth Guard to remember their oaths, to not give in to fear. Watching that made her proud as well as anxious, seeing his blood spilling out, knowing how closely things had been balanced. If Kayl was right, if those moments had tipped Earth Guard's future onto a vector that would see it survive and maybe be reborn, it had been

Kayl's words and example that had provided the necessary push.

Yes, she felt proud. And relieved, knowing he really could carry on the mission if she still vanished from ever existing.

But it felt disorienting every time she saw an image of herself in medium-blue civilian coveralls. What had once been had changed, and no one remembered now except Kayl.

Why did she still exist?

On the other hand, there was considerable satisfaction in watching other news reports. Admiral Besson refusing to relinquish command of Earth Guard, insisting that the Security Committee and the Earth Cooperation Council were betraying Earth and humanity to the aliens, until he was physically removed from his headquarters by Earth Guard security personnel. Admiral Besson currently under arrest and in a cell that was probably a lot nicer than the one he had intended Kayl to occupy.

About half of all currently serving Earth Guard vice admirals and rear admirals had either hastily retired or been forced to retire as the investigations into the loss of the *Sentinel* and into the attack on the *Yamanaka* continued. Rear Admiral Tecumseh had been recalled to active duty, and promoted to vice admiral.

Other senior officers in the mutual defense forces were abruptly leaving active duty, including a General Molstad, who had apparently been involved at Wallops.

And, of course, there was a great deal of reporting and discussion about the revelation that Genji was not simply part alien, but also from the future. To her astonishment, she was described by some as a "super soldier" sent to the past to try to prevent calamitous mistakes around First Contact and prevent future wars. Talk of her being an alien spy or scout had almost vanished, because why would the future need to send a spy into the past? Instead, it was widely assumed she had been sent on purpose, risking her own future existence to try to save the future.

Which was partly true, Genji had to admit. "Why aren't they more afraid of me?" she asked Kayl. "Knowing I'm from the future? Why are they less afraid?"

"Look at this headline." Kayl swung his panel toward her so she could read it. "'The Last of Her Kind, Sent to the Past in a Desperate Attempt to Save Billions of Lives.'"

"That's not . . . entirely accurate," Genji said.

"Okay, you weren't 'sent' by anyone we know of. But you are the last alloy," Kayl said. "And you're not the leading edge of an invasion, you're the sole survivor of a tragedy. And, from the moment you realized you were in 2140, you have been dedicated to trying to save billions of lives. Not an attacker, but a defender. Instead of having alien DNA in your genome to hurt full humans, you are assumed to have that alien DNA added to help you with saving humans. That's why people are less afraid of you. Because it makes sense of your statements that you've come to protect the Earth. You had to come from somewhere, and saying your home was Earth confused people. But not if you're from the future. Then it all fits together. Someone like no one else has ever seen, someone who knows things no one should know before they happen, it all fits. Instead of being an unknown with unknown goals, you make sense."

"Because I came from the future?" Genji said.

"Yes," Kayl said. "And because everything you've done fits that. If you'd tried to tell everyone you were from the future when you first got here, no one would have believed you."

"Except for a certain lieutenant in Earth Guard, who listened to me when no one else would."

"Granted," Kayl said, smiling at her. "But what you've done and said has laid the groundwork for almost everyone to accept it. Surviving every attempt to kill you, making First Contact work well, inspiring resistance to the Forty-Eight-Hour Martial Law on Mars, saving people's lives anytime you could. Have you seen this statement from the Security Committee?" He entered commands to bring up a news item.

Genji saw some serious-looking men and women around a table, one of them speaking in a voice that was soft yet somehow held attention. "We can confirm that Lieutenant Genji has stated she came to this time to attempt to prevent serious mistakes which would lead to immense suffering in the future. The information she has provided so far has served to verify her claims. There is no question that the assistance she has already provided with First Contact has been of immeasurable value to humanity."

"Why," someone off camera asked, "did Earth Guard's leaders attempt to silence her instead of welcoming her?"

Another person around the table answered. "It appears that one of the serious problems today that would lead to future suffering involved some of the leadership of Earth Guard. Those individuals, rather than help reform, sought to prevent Lieutenant Genji from exposing the problems they were causing within Earth Guard. As we are learning from the reopened investigation into the loss of the cruiser *Sentinel* ten years ago, those problems are far more serious than anyone recognized. It is safe to say that by refocusing attention on these matters, and on the refusal of some senior officers to acknowledge civilian authority over them, Lieutenant Genji has already done a great service."

It did fit, even if it wasn't quite accurate. The issue of her differences, her part-alien nature, seemed to have temporarily been merged into her mission and therefore had become not as worrisome. How could those things not matter as much when they had mattered so much all her life? "Why are they not more upset that I'm an alloy?"

"Some people are still talking about it," Kayl pointed out. "But often in terms of how those alloy abilities helped you survive and save lives. Some are even speculating that only an alloy could have survived whatever sent you into the past, which you have to admit may well be true. Would a full human have still been alive when I reached the wreckage of your ship?"

"I guess not." It felt weird. "They should talk more about what you did," Genji said to Kayl. "Give you the credit you deserve."

He shook his head. "This philosopher I've been reading said that if you've done something good, and someone else has benefitted, why should you expect any praise or reward for that? You should be happy with knowing you did right."

She smiled at him. "How could I disagree with you and Marcus Aurelius? Do you really like him?"

"I honestly do," Kayl said. "He's very thought-provoking."

Messages had come in from Earth. Kayl's mother, speaking in a voice choked with emotion, telling him how proud she was of him, and of her "new daughter." That had left Genji blinking away tears for several minutes before she could watch more.

A message came from Kayl's sister as well. "You are both out of your minds," Malani said. "So glad you found each other and managed not to die. I want you to know how happy I am that you're both still alive, and concerning that private matter I was looking into for you, I can't find any problems. Of course, there are a lot of uncertainties because of the alien DNA, but there aren't any red flags that I can see."

"Private matter?" Genji asked Kayl. He was well enough now to have moved back to their room on the *Yamanaka*, but he had insisted on staying with her in sick bay.

"Children," Kayl reminded her.

"Oh."

"That doesn't mean . . . umm . . ."

"I know," Genji said. It would still be up to her.

Her memory flashed an image of the sailors firing at her. Did she want a daughter of hers to face that?

But then there were the authorized interviews with some of the crew of *Lifeguard*, telling the truth at last about how Lieutenant Genji had once saved their ship, and how this time she had promised not to kill and even pushed away a weapon rather than use it to defend herself. Interviews with some of the crew of *Yamanaka*, talking about how "human" Lieutenant Genji really was. Interviews with others on Earth who she'd interacted with, now able to safely come forward and talk about the part alien.

As well as reports about the incorporation of Pradeesh Ship Industries on Earth, accompanied by a flurry of patents for systems with dramatic improvements over current capabilities.

And video of a well-attended mass gathering in which young Frederick Hoster called for more dialogue and less fear of the other using the same rhetorical gifts that in her memory would someday have called for hatred and death. That last left Genji wondering if she was still unconscious from her wounds and was hallucinating all this.

The report that made her, and Kayl, smile the most turned out to be coverage of Krysta arriving in Albuquerque with an impressive police escort, Aunt Hokulani greeting her at the train station as a large group of onlookers applauded. "She cried again," Genji sighed. "A lot."

"You'll have to talk to her about that," Kayl pointed out. "You're going to be her mother, after all, if those legal determinations come through. Selene? Are you okay?"

She realized she'd been staring at him, unable to speak, as that wording hit her. *Her mother.*

What a strange new world this was.

KAYL HELPED GENJI INTO her uniform, easing the sleeve over the light cast still on her left arm and sliding one leg of the uniform over the similar cast on her right leg. The wound packs had been removed where they had been attached, the injuries inflicted almost three weeks before nearly healed now. The bot-assisted physical therapy had been just as unpleasant as she had endured during the Universal War. Taken all together, her body was in remarkably good shape considering all the damage it had taken less than a month earlier, but between forced healing, forced nutrients to compensate for and support the healing, and forced physical therapy, she felt like she'd endured three weeks of targeted torture.

She could mostly move without pain, though the movement of her left arm was still restricted by the cast, and her right leg couldn't take much weight.

Genji looked over at the mirror, seeing herself in the light blue and silver of Earth Guard. "It feels weird."

"Are you okay with it?" Kayl asked.

"Yeah, I guess. It's good to be in uniform again. Maybe someday I'll feel like I belong in Earth Guard the way I did in the Unified Fleet. But for now I'm probably going to pretend to myself that this is a Unified Fleet uniform. Are you okay with that?"

"I'm okay with it," he assured her.

"I saw somebody in a news report," Genji said. "A new ensign they were interviewing. And I recognized the name and then I recognized him. He was going to be a past-retirement-age commander who would be one of my instructors in the Unified Fleet. I don't remember him ever mentioning he'd been in Earth Guard. Strange, huh?"

"I guess you'll see more people like that," Kayl said as he helped her cautiously stand.

"Is it also strange how much it saddens me that the Unified Fleet will probably never exist?"

"No. Not at all."

"I mean," Genji said, "the fact the Unified Fleet existed meant a lot of things had gone wrong. If it never exists, that means, hopefully, those things don't go wrong. But I'm still sad about it."

"You are mostly human," Kayl said, helping to steady her. "We're not exactly the most rational species. Your Tramontine parts are probably asking your human parts why you feel that way."

She gave him a guilty look. "How did you know?"

"I know a little bit about you from close observation over time. How's the leg feel?"

"Wobbly," Genji said, Kayl's words reminding her of one of the questions she had for the Tramontine. "You know all of my secrets, don't you? Remember that time I told you that you didn't know nearly enough about me? You've learned quite a bit about me since then."

"Quite a bit," Kayl agreed.

"And, yet, you're still here."

"Never leaving," he said.

"Is it just because you won't admit you were wrong?" Genji asked, smiling.

"That's it," Kayl said, also smiling. "You got me."

"I'm glad you're stubborn. Are you sure that you're okay?" Genji added. "Everyone seems to focus on me, not you."

"I'm doing fine," Kayl said.

"You look good."

"So do you," Kayl said, smiling again. "Ready to try a few steps?"

She cautiously put weight on her bad leg. "I'm not an invalid. But I will be limping a bit even in Martian gravity, I think."

"The doctor was worried about how slowly your bone was healing," Kayl said, "despite the accelerated knitting treatments. I explained that alloy bones take longer to heal."

"Okay," Genji said. "Did the doctors ask you about anything else?"

"Just about llamas."

"Llamas." She shook her head, aggravated. "What is it about full humans being so fascinated with the llama thing?"

"They wanted to know if the allergy information from the doctor aboard *Lifeguard* was accurate," Kayl explained.

"I guess that's all right," Genji grumbled.

It felt strange to leave their packs, knowing sailors would

take them to the lifter that was waiting to bring them down to the surface. As they reached the door, a warning sounded that propulsion was about to cut off as the *Yamanaka* entered orbit about Mars. Moments later the sensation of gravity ended.

Relieved to not have to put weight on her leg, but having to avoid using her left arm to pull herself along, Genji went out the door with Kayl. Outside, two diplomatic security agents waited. "How are you?" Genji asked.

There were only eight left now. In the wake of the failed attempt by Pyotor and Angielyke, Alejandro had discovered they had ties to a third agent, Bartelli, who had sent the code word that the assassination had failed and activated the attacks by *Lifeguard* and *Diligent*. Bartelli was now in a brig cell alongside that of Angielyke.

Knowing how crushed the remaining security agents were over the treachery within their ranks, Genji had gone out of her way to be respectful of them. It seemed the least she could do, especially after hearing how desperately they had fought to try to keep the boarding parties away from her and Kayl's room on the *Yamanaka*.

The passageways were full of people, most of them sailors happy to have reached Mars and the promise of some time ashore. A few still watched her with worried reserve, but most waved or called greetings. Sometime during the fight for her life, Genji had gone in their minds from being an alien to being one of *their* lieutenants.

Captain Maldonado was waiting with Commander Dejesus to bid farewell to the debarking VIPs.

Genji used her right hand to grip a hold and bring herself to a halt in front of Maldonado before raising that hand up in a salute. "Thank you, sir."

Maldonado returned the salute, his face professionally composed. "I did my duty, Lieutenant Genji. There are signs Earth Guard may place a higher priority on that than it has in the recent past. For that, it seems I must thank you."

"I hope to sail on a ship commanded by you again, Captain," Genji said as she reached to propel herself into the lifter.

"I hope not, Lieutenant Genji," Maldonado said with a serious expression. "You're like a black hole that attracts trouble rather than matter. Please lend the excitement you bring to another commanding officer in the future. Although I suppose our future will still be the past for you."

Genji grinned. "I'll do my best, sir."

Cerise Camacho, waiting at the lifter's hatch, smiled in greeting. "We'll launch fairly soon. There are a lot of people on Mars eager to see you, Lieutenant Genji."

Are any of them armed? Genji thought. But she didn't express that thought out loud. Even she wasn't sure whether or not it would be intended as a joke.

Once aboard the lifter, she saw a lot of seats already taken by the other diplomatic security agents and members of the crew of the *Yamanaka* heading down for liberty. One of the sailors was Lieutenant Cloud, who Genji had heard had suffered a broken wrist trying to keep the boarding parties at bay, and who appeared delighted to see Genji in an Earth Guard uniform. "Hey, battle sister," Genji called to Cloud. "Stay in touch!"

Was it okay for her to say that to a full human she'd known for only a few weeks? Who might be embarrassed to be publicly associated with an alloy? Old doubts born of her experiences resurfaced, only to vanish as Lieutenant Cloud grinned and nodded before holding out her fist in a clear request for a fist bump.

Genji hesitated only a moment before returning the gesture, bumping fists, her skin touching that of Lieutenant Jeanine Cloud, and Cloud not flinching, acting just as if she had made skin contact with another full human.

It was comforting to realize she already had new comrades.

Nonetheless, it irked her to have to let Kayl help fasten her seat harness because of the limited motion of her left arm.

They had been given seats in the first row, where everyone could see her unable to do the task herself.

"Sorry," he murmured, reading her unhappiness at having to be assisted in doing such a simple thing.

What was awaiting them on Mars? Genji felt her nerves prickling, wondering how bad it might be, remembering their last visit when they had literally been chased off the surface by shots being fired at them.

She knew her emotions were bouncing from one extreme to the next, torn between joy that they'd made it here, that her efforts seemed to be accomplishing what they needed to, that she and Kayl were both still alive, and worry about what awaited them on Mars. It would be her first time in public since everything had been revealed about her. How would the full humans on Mars react to the alloy among them? An alloy from the future? Were more assassins waiting to strike when opportunity offered?

Its hatches sealed, the lifter detached from the *Yamanaka* and began the descent toward Mars.

"What does it look like once terraforming is underway?" Kayl asked her.

"Mars?" Genji called up her memories. "Once terraforming is well along, Mars is a lot brighter. The clouds reflect sunlight, while also trapping heat. When I last saw Mars, the process was years from completion, so most of the planet was covered with clouds, and it rained and it rained and it rained. An old colonist told me it didn't feel like Mars anymore because you couldn't see the stars every night. And he said the rain was driving people crazy, water getting in everywhere."

She remembered the small group she'd been hitting the bars with in one of the Martian colonies after the Lowlands War. Her assault team. That gave her memories a different kind of melancholy. Some of them had died later on. What would happen to all of them in the new history being written because of her actions? "There were roughly a million and a half colonists on Mars by then. You told me there are about fifty thousand now, so that will be a huge increase." Another memory, of Earth dying, the shock wave heading outward. "I don't know how many, if any, of the Martian colonists will survive in 2180, though. That shock wave was so tremendously powerful. Even spreading out, it might have still had an awful punch when it reached Mars."

"I'm sorry," Kayl said.

"You didn't do it."

"No, but I asked you to remember it."

"That's okay." Genji looked at the panels showing different scenes of space around them, of the huge Tramontine ship in orbit, and the many human ships also orbiting Mars, and Mars itself. "When we left here, I didn't think we'd ever make it back," she admitted to Kayl. "I had no idea whether or not we could succeed in our mission. Despite what we'd accomplished with First Contact, it still seemed to be so very hard. Impossible."

"'Do not imagine that, if something is hard for you to achieve,'" Kayl said, "'it is therefore impossible.'"

She turned her head to stare at him, her earlier mood suddenly lifted. "Did you just quote Marcus Aurelius again?"

"Hopefully," Kayl said. "I am studying him. Did I get it right?"

"Yes," Genji said. "It's a partial quote, but yes. Kiss me. Right now."

"What?"

"Kiss me. Now."

It was his turn to stare. "Selene, we're both in uniform!"

"So?" Genji said. "Isn't it sort of a tradition with us to put on public displays of affection in uniform while we're on Mars? Doesn't tradition mean anything to you, Lieutenant Owen?"

"It does, Lieutenant Genji," he said. Partially unstrapping his seat harness, Kayl leaned over to kiss her.

He held it longer than she expected.

As Kayl settled back into his seat and refastened his harness, Genji heard a soft chorus of throat clearing behind them. At least it sounded amused rather than disapproving, or even repulsed at the sight of a full human and an alloy kissing.

"Okay?" Kayl said.

"That was more than okay," Genji replied. "It exceeded expectations," she added, using a common term in military performance evaluations.

He laughed. "Is that going to be your reaction whenever I quote Marcus Aurelius to you?"

"Maybe. Keeping learning more and see what happens."

"That is a very strong motivator," Kayl said.

"Seriously, Kayl, you were a lot more hesitant when we first met. Like, you knew what you should do, but expected to get hammered for it. It made you cautious."

"Earth Guard had beaten me down." He smiled. "I guess someone changed me, though. She gave me back everything I'd lost and then some."

"What's her name?" Genji demanded. "I want to hunt her down."

"Just find me," Kayl said. "I'll be beside her."

"Do you think we've made a real difference, Kayl?"

He nodded toward her uniform. "I'd say that's a certainty. Exactly what difference is harder to be sure of. But to the sailors on the *Yamanaka*, you're not an alloy any longer, Selene. You're Lieutenant Genji. That could be a huge thing, if it snowballs and impacts how everyone sees aliens. And that does seem to be happening on Earth."

"There'll always be people who see someone who's different and fear that," Genji muttered.

"Yes," Kayl agreed. "But the fewer like that, the better. If the Spear of Humanity is more like a letter opener in the new future, that's a big improvement, right?"

"I find it very hard to joke about the Spear," Genji told him. "But, yes, if it's a lot smaller, that would be a wonderful thing."

The lifter trembled slightly as it headed down into atmosphere.

"We've got escorts!" the pilot called out happily on the lifter's intercom.

Kayl turned to look at the panels displaying information. "Aerospace fighters and police."

"Just like old times," Genji muttered. So much for a happy mood, when she had to worry one of those escort pilots might be another enemy intent on killing the alien.

Kayl reached over to hold her hand as the boat fell through the Martian atmosphere.

"I liked it better when you were driving," Genji said to distract herself from her worries. "That was one hell of a ride."

"I'm glad you liked it," Kayl said. "So far, so—"

"Do *not* say that!"

The lifter settled onto the landing field.

As Kayl helped her out of her harness and onto her feet, Genji looked at the panels showing the outside view. Showing lifters lined up on the field. Her leg was protesting supporting weight even in Martian gravity. "If this goes really bad, I am not in any shape for another run," she told Kayl.

"I'll carry you," he said.

No one had to get into suits to reach the nearest air lock. A vehicle rolled out onto the field, its rear mating to the air lock on the lifter. Everyone walked through into comfortable seats, the vehicle air lock sealed, and it rolled toward a large, open air lock waiting at the entrance to the colony.

Kayl had kept hold of her hand through much of that, reading her nervousness. Genji tightened her grip on him, unable to shake her worries based on a lifetime of experience as an alloy, and knowing how, physically, she wasn't ready for a fight or flight if anything bad happened.

The vehicle stopped inside the big air lock, the outer door closing, atmospheric pressure rising, the main door on one side of the vehicle finally opening.

Cerise Camacho and her staff led the way. Genji stood with Kayl's assistance, following the others across a short stretch to where the inner doors stood open. Damn, her leg did not like this.

As she stepped out into the Martian street, Genji involuntarily flinched as a roar went up from the crowds lining the route.

19

THEY WERE CHEERING.

There were banners of blue waving above many of the people watching. She stared, seeing that not only did the blue match that of her never-existed-now uniform and the civilian coveralls that had replaced it, but the banners also had a single stripe of gold along the top, matching the gold trim on her Unified Fleet uniform. "How the hell . . . ? Do they remember my uniform?"

A familiar voice answered her. "Which uniform is that?"

Genji and Kayl turned to see Captain Yusuke Yesenski, the commander of Earth Guard forces on Mars. "The uniform of a fleet that may never exist, sir," Genji said, trying to use the exact same words she had employed when Yesenski had first seen her Unified Fleet uniform.

He didn't show any recognition of the words, though. "If you're asking about the colors of the banners, the blue is based on the coveralls you wore for your speech on the commons. The gold stripe just felt right."

"It felt right?" Kayl asked.

"No one knows why," Yesenski said. "Come along, you two. Mars is waiting for you."

Kayl helped Genji limp to a waiting, open-topped vehicle, where beaming civilians and more officers in uniform awaited them: the governor of Mars, the vice-governor, the new commander of the Martian Planetary Defense Forces, and the chair of the Martian parliament.

"Welcome back to Mars!" the governor cried loudly, his words amplified, the crowd responding with cheers.

Kayl looked around as they took seats in the back of the

vehicle, his stunned expression matching how Genji felt. "Things are a little different this time."

"What's going on?" Genji said to him. "What is this?"

The governor heard her. "This is a welcome for someone the Martians see as one of their own! The hero of the resistance to the Forty-Eight-Hour Martial Law. The defender of the people and of the mother world, Earth itself. You, Lieutenant Genji."

Did her bafflement show on her face? Bewildered, Genji forced a smile and stared as the vehicle surged into motion and rolled slowly down the street, the crowds waving and cheering as they passed, Martian Planetary Defense Force soldiers standing sentry to hold back the crowds.

She couldn't help noticing that none of the MPDF soldiers were armed. At least someone had thought that through. Had any of the soldiers she could see been among those who had tried to shoot her the last time she was on Mars?

Genji leaned close to Kayl. "Am I hallucinating under sedation?"

"No," Kayl said. "This is real."

"How can it be real?" She noticed signs among some of the people they were passing, teenagers by the look of them. "Kayl, they're cheering you, too. See? Lieutenant Owen! Why are they also calling you Duke?"

"I told them that nickname," Kayl said, smiling and waving in greeting. "If Ed sees this, he's going to be very unhappy."

"Good! I hope it still hurts when he moves." Genji felt her smile become more natural as she also waved. "Kayl, what is that thing with the banners? The gold stripe just felt right?"

"Yeah," he said. "That's weird. Maybe somewhere in their subconscious memories there's still some trace of your Unified Fleet outfit, so their banners still show that. I guess in a way, they might still remember, too."

A ray of happiness forced its way through the bafflement and worry filling her mind. Genji smiled again, this time a fully genuine smile.

"We're going to the command center," Captain Yesenski told them. "Your quarters will be right off of it, and there's some work to do."

"We wanted to hold a banquet," the governor of Mars called back to them. "But the negotiators are very eager for you to help iron out some problems, and we understand your injuries are still healing. We've got the welcoming banquet scheduled for four days from now."

"They expect me to solve everything in four days or less?" Genji murmured in Kayl's ear. "I am hallucinating, aren't I?"

"No, you're really not," Kayl said as the car came to a stop outside the main entrance to the Earth Guard command center. "Either that or I am, too."

"We did some remodeling," Captain Yesenski said. "The negotiators are in a new bloc of rooms attached directly to the command center."

As Genji and Kayl left the ground vehicle, another roar of applause sounded.

Genji, trying to favor her leg more, looked over at Kayl. "Lieutenant Owen, as much as I hate to admit it, I'm going to need more assistance walking. It's not a public display of affection if you're rendering physical assistance to a wounded comrade."

He grinned, leaning in close so she could put a lot of weight on his arm.

The guards at the entrance stood at attention as she and Kayl passed.

Inside, officers and sailors and civilian employees stood to applaud her, as Genji looked about, once more unable to believe this. Not everyone stood. Not everyone applauded. There were still looks of worry, looks of unwelcome. But those were a distinct minority.

She saw Jeyssi among those standing and offered a small, stiff wave with her injured left arm. "Lieutenant Arronax!"

On the other side, Genji saw Kayl nodding to Lieutenant Hector Thanh.

The command center seemed to be a lot larger than she remembered, every step a little more difficult. But eventually they reached the far side, where a new entrance to the negotiator offices was crowded with men and women. Genji recognized some of them, both the majority smiling, and a few watching with continued suspicion.

"We know you'll need time to rest," one of the women began.

"I've been resting," Genji said. "I'm ready to work."

The quiet hallways of the negotiator offices were a welcome respite. She didn't mind showing her need for Kayl's help walking here where much fewer people could see.

None of this felt real, Genji thought. This was not how alloys were welcomed. What had she done to the world she had known?

They reached a large room, dominated at one end by a big panel, rows of chairs allowing many observers to easily watch and hear everything it displayed.

Genji sat down in front of the panel as one of the negotiators tapped a control.

"This will let the Tramontine know we wish to talk," the negotiator said. "Here's a list of the matters we've been stuck on."

"Okay," she said, skimming the list. "I should be able to help." Looking over to Kayl, she smiled again. "Thank you, love. I can take it from here. You don't have to hang around. Get some rest."

He nodded, smiling as well, but his eyes were still concerned. "I want to hang around," Kayl said.

The panel lit up, showing several Tramontine seated facing her. "Greetings, Ones who share," she said in Tramontine, initiating the conversation as the junior speaker should. "I am Lieutenant Selene Genji, the one to who you graciously shared the name Sister, returned to assist in any way I can. Permit me to help with understanding?"

The lips of the Tramontine in the image tightened into lines, looking to humans as if they were angry. But Genji knew the expressions were the equivalent of human smiles.

"One we call Sister, you have returned!" a Tramontine onemale said. "You are on the planet?"

"Yes. I sit here upon the surface of the planet humans call Mars. We can speak without delays."

"Permit us to be very pleased! We watched reports among the humans of your injury. Did we understand correctly? You were harmed?"

"I was harmed," Genji said. "I was also protected. I will recover in full. Those who called for harm have been removed from power. The humans wish me to once again help them speak with you. Permit me to assist in this task?"

"Tell us, first, please, how the humans view those like us. Those such as you. Some among us are concerned, given recent harm to you. Some reports implied you were close to learning final answer."

It was a Tramontine way of saying she had nearly died. Genji paused to consider her words. "I was hurt, but other humans ensured I would not learn that answer. The humans feared you as they at first fear all who are different. But they have accepted me." She couldn't have honestly said that before now, before being cheered on Mars. "I am here because they accept me. They will, I am certain, accept Tramontine. This is new for them. Beyond their experience. Most desire to know more of the Tramontine, to have pleasant relations, to share. A few remain frightened. In time, their numbers will decline. This I believe."

"This is not how it happened? Not how the events you once knew became unfortunate history?"

"This is not how it happened," Genji confirmed. "This is very different. Much has been changed."

"Enough? Has enough been changed?"

"I do not know. I dare to hope it might be so. I dare to

hope I will prove some theories wrong, find new answers, and create new questions."

That generated another wave of Tramontine smiles. "Sister to us you are. Your news brings us joy. You will discuss specifics of your actions and changes?"

"Later, if that is permitted," Genji said. "I have a duty first to assist in matters of mutual understanding. If that is acceptable."

The Tramontine all made the hand gesture that meant the same thing as a human nod. "It is acceptable, eager as we are to hear of those things. Your assistance in these matters of understanding is welcomed. We have tried to discuss our desires regarding natural resources in the asteroid belt of this solar system. Please explain what humans mean by 'absentee owner'? How does one share or take if one is not present?"

Genji looked over to where Kayl was standing and watching. She smiled and waved. "I'm good! Get some rest! I've got some explaining to do!"

OWEN GRINNED AND WAVED back, watching as Selene turned to speak again in Tramontine.

He'd seen how puzzled she was by their reception on Mars. And understood how she felt. This was so different, it felt unreal.

"How are you doing, Lieutenant Owen?" Captain Yesenski asked as he walked up. "Lieutenant Genji is getting a lot of attention."

"She deserves it, sir," Owen said. "I'm fine. Knowing that she's fine. If that makes sense."

"It does." Yesenski watched Selene speaking rapidly in Tramontine. "I should have guessed last time you were here that she'd come from the future. Lieutenant Genji knew too much, knew things no one should be able to know. Like that language. When did you learn the truth about her?"

"My second conversation with her," Owen said. "It didn't come up in the first conversation because it didn't occur to me to ask her what year she thought it was."

"That was never a secret between you?"

"No, sir."

"You did a great job of protecting her and her secret," Captain Yesenski said. "Hopefully you'll get credit for that in the histories."

Owen shook his head. "All that matters is that those histories are different from the ones Selene learned and experienced."

"How bad did it get? Can you tell me?"

Selene had told the Earth Cooperation Council. Surely Captain Yesenski could also be trusted with the full truth. "On June twelfth, 2180, Earth will be destroyed."

Yesenski stared at him. "Destroyed? As in gone?"

"Yes, sir."

"Holy . . ." Captain Yesenski gazed at Selene. "Because of those wars? Is that still going to happen?"

Owen shrugged helplessly. "There's no way to be sure, but Lieutenant Genji has caused a lot of changes. Earth Guard won't collapse now, I think. That should have a huge impact. And what she's done in regard to First Contact. Selene said in her history it was a prolonged mess leading to a lot of fear and misunderstandings."

"That's not hard to believe," Yesenski said. "I was speaking with some of the negotiators yesterday. They were all of the opinion that if not for Lieutenant Genji, we'd still be trying to figure out what the Tramontine meant by that first image they sent. We'd be tearing our hair out in frustration, and everyone else would be getting more and more nervous and fearful of what the aliens wanted. Have you ever read the *Rubáiyát of Omar Khayyám*, Lieutenant Owen?"

"No, sir. If it's anything like Marcus Aurelius's *Meditations*, I'm sure Lieutenant Genji will be pushing me to read it, though."

"It's not exactly the *Meditations*," Yesenski said, smiling for a moment. "Perhaps the most famous passage in Khayyam's work is this one: 'The Moving Finger writes; and, having writ, Moves on: nor all thy Piety nor Wit Shall lure it back to cancel half a Line, Nor all thy Tears wash out a Word of it.'" Captain Yesenski glanced at Owen again. "But, this once at least, Lieutenant Genji seems to have proven Omar Khayyam to be wrong. She's changing what was written, isn't she?"

"You deserve credit for that as well, sir," Owen said. "Your actions the last time we were on Mars made a huge difference."

"I did my job, Lieutenant," Yesenski said. "The best I could as I saw it. Just like you did on the *Lifeguard*."

"I was just trying to save Lieutenant Genji's life, sir."

"You did more than that," Yesenski said. "You forced a lot of people to confront the question of what they were doing and why. It's easy to forget why when you're caught up in day-to-day work and the only important goal seems to be making it through to tomorrow. Too many people end up thinking holding on to their job is what matters, when what really matters is doing their job." He watched Selene for a few moments. "I guess that event in 2180 would wipe out humanity. Or nearly so. Humanity got a do-over, thanks to . . . Who sent her back, Lieutenant Owen? Those Tramontine?"

"No, sir," Owen said. "As far as Selene knows, it was an accident caused by the shock wave from Earth's death."

"An accident?" Yesenski shook his head. "That was one hell of a lucky accident for humanity, then, wasn't it? Are you a religious believer, Lieutenant Owen?"

"Spiritual, I guess," Owen said. "It's hard to look at the universe from space and not feel . . . Something."

"Same here," Captain Yesenski said. "Maybe that Something thought humanity deserved a second chance. I hope we do deserve it despite our all-too-frequent tendency to repeat mistakes over and over again. If we'd managed to kill you and Lieutenant Genji, we would've answered that with a big no. But, somehow, you two made it through."

"We didn't do it alone," Owen said. "A lot of people, including you, sir, helped us at critical points. Lieutenant Genji feared she'd have to do it alone, or maybe just with me, because her experiences as an alloy in the 2160s and 2170s weren't happy ones. She's still having trouble accepting that . . . well, people are accepting her in the 2140s."

"I think people like Lieutenant Genji make their own roads if other people give them half a chance," Yesenski said. "But I imagine you don't need me telling you how exceptional she is."

Owen grinned. "No, sir, I do not."

"Lieutenant Owen, I hope you'll remain in Earth Guard once this all shakes out. And convince Lieutenant Genji to stay in as well, not just as an honorable position, though I'm not sure any institution can handle both of you at the same time. I know Vice Admiral Tecumseh wants to get her hands on Genji for her staff, but so far the Security Committee is fending her off and holding on to Lieutenant Genji."

"Thank you, sir. We really haven't gotten past realizing that we're still alive and the number of people trying to kill us has dramatically dwindled. Whatever we do, we're going to do it together."

"Somehow I never doubted that." Captain Yesenski turned and beckoned. "I've assigned Lieutenant Arronax to be your personal assistant for at least the next week. She'll show you where your rooms are. VIP Quarters, Lieutenant Owen. A nice step up from that grungy apartment you two were staying in last time."

Jeyssi walked up as Yesenski headed off. "How may I assist you, Lieutenant Owen?"

"Very funny, Jeyssi," Owen said. "You didn't get in any trouble after last time we were here, did you? Selene and I were worried about people like you and Hector Thanh."

She grinned. "Things were a bit tense at times, but Captain Yesenski mysteriously lost some records, and some complaints and reports got misfiled. In some quarters I was a pariah, and in others I was a rock star for helping you. In other words, nothing happened that wasn't worth it. In particular, because of it all, I just might have gotten to know a lot better someone who has potential to be the someone I've been looking for. So, thanks."

He smiled at her. "You finally found someone you have chemistry with?"

"Let's just say when we're combined, the reaction generates a lot of heat," Jeyssi said. "Let's get back to you. I was informed that you shouldn't push yourself too hard since you are officially still convalescing."

"I'm okay. I wasn't hurt nearly as badly as Selene was." He looked over at Selene, engrossed in her conversation with the Tramontine. "I should go and get some rest. But I don't want to leave her."

"You act like a lot of people have been trying to kill you two for months. I'll get you a chair. Oh, by the way, your old roommate Joe says hi, and well done, and can he have the stuff you left behind on *Vigilant*?"

Owen laughed. "Sure. Except for the personal items."

"All your personal items got swept up by Earth Guard security. You'll have to pry your stuff out of their hands. Oh, and Sabita Awerdin rather tearfully asked me to pass on her best wishes for you and your alien."

"My alien?" Owen asked. "Sabita called her that?"

"Give her time, Kayl. Losing you to Selene was hard on her."

"She never had me! I like Sabita as a friend, she's a great person, but that was it."

"Where have I heard that 'I like you as a friend' thing before?" Jeyssi said.

"When you told me that," Owen said, "I accepted it and moved on."

"You did mope a bit."

"I did not mope."

"You totally moped. I felt bad!" She smiled. "But you did accept it. And I'm glad you did. Given the sorts of things Selene can do, I'm happy not to be an ex-girlfriend she might see as a rival."

Owen shook his head. "No offense, Jeyssi, but Selene has no rivals. How did I end up with her?"

"Beats me." Jeyssi grinned. "Maybe you earned it."

GENJI STIFLED A YAWN, realizing how long she'd been talking to the Tramontine and the human negotiators.

The lead negotiator noticed. "Lieutenant Genji, you've done marvels already today. Please get some rest."

Genji hesitated. "Is it all right if I have a private discussion with the Tramontine? About me?"

The negotiators present exchanged looks. "I don't see why not. Does this pertain to First Contact?"

"No. It's questions about me. Things they might understand concerning the whole 'being in a different time' thing. If what I learn impinges on First Contact, I will pass it on."

"We're already trusting her with everything else," another negotiator pointed out.

"People can stay if they want," Genji said.

"When we can only understand a few words of the conversation?" the lead negotiator said. "Never mind. Get your personal business done. We'll see you tomorrow."

Genji turned back to face the Tramontine, hesitant to discuss what she had to bring up. "May Sister ask questions of personal concern? New questions?"

The reply came immediately. "New questions are always welcome, Sister."

"May I ask, do you have memories of me in uniform when I visited the ship?"

"Uniform? Clothing such as that worn by Lieutenant Owen? Such as you wear now?"

"Yes," Genji said. "But a darker blue, and with gold trim instead of silver."

A long pause followed. "It is unusual," the Tramontine finally replied. "One says she remembers this without certainty, she who spent most time with you. Others do not. Images from records show clothing different from that of Lieutenant Owen. Darker, but also not similar in design. Here is sample."

The image that appeared showed her in civilian coveralls. Genji sighed. "Permit me to explain." She described what had happened at the end of the fight aboard the *Lifeguard*, and what she had learned afterwards.

She had never seen the Tramontine so excited.

"Remarkable! Proof of changes in time to come! What was to be will yield to sufficient cause. A great gift you have given, Sister!"

"Is this proof," another Tramontine asked, "when proof cannot be verified? When it exists only in the mind of one?"

"The one who shares my life also remembers my Unified Fleet uniform," Genji said. "And there is the matter of the banners on Mars." She explained those things as well.

The Tramontine discussed it among themselves for what felt like a long time before addressing her again. "Remarkable. Proof cannot be verified except in recollections, but we have no reason to doubt your information. It confirms suggestions made earlier, that universe seeks to conserve what was."

"How so?" Genji asked. "It changed."

"Universe made smallest possible change, correct? Style of clothing. Color remained same. All else same. Conservation of effort even in adapting to changes in events. Exciting answer! Minimum necessary changes to accommodate alteration to future. Yet memory remains of before change in you and in one very close to you. Implies consciousness resists even external changes to what was and will be. May mean consciousness itself helps keep you in existence as you are."

"'I think, therefore I am'?" Genji said, quoting the ancient philosopher.

"Yes. Could well be so."

"That's . . . astounding," Genji said. "I have questions regarding consciousness as well, regarding an observer of events." She explained her thinking about Kayl.

"Ah," the Tramontine said. "Master of Flight knows Sister based on close observation. He could well . . . reinforce? Make stronger, your existence. If Sister ceases to exist, how does universe compensate? It cannot simply change to another human as it changed clothing with uniform. Lieutenant Owen would know. Lieutenant Owen would lack causation you provided. If large change in you, how to explain all else? How to replace? Likely impossible. He is additional tether tying you to this you and this universe."

"But," Genji said, uncertain how she was feeling about all this, "also impossible for me to exist if I haven't been born."

"Impossible? Evidence so far argues not impossible. Conservation of effort. You see? Keeping you here, you existing, may be smallest possible accommodation to changes. All alternatives harder. Any alternative must explain actions, changes, caused by you in this time. Exact changes, made at exact times, by exact person. What else would do this?"

Genji inhaled slowly as she thought. "So we're back to the argument that I must exist now because of the impact I've had on events in 2140."

"How else to explain such events?" the Tramontine asked. "Uniform cannot exist? Change type of clothing. Easy. Minimal effort. Lieutenant Selene Genji cannot exist? Impossible. Must have existed now, even if not born in future. Better if not born in future, because if never exist in future, time travel not needed to bring you to now. Too hard otherwise, perhaps impossible to resolve paradox."

"Then where do I come from?" Genji demanded. "How did I originate?"

"Amazing question! So difficult!" The Tramontine sounded as happy as she had ever heard any of them. "Consciousness does not yield easily. Perhaps answer lies there. You will permit us to examine theories, possibilities? This is private matter for you, but also with huge implications for all."

"I will gladly permit you to think on this," Genji said. "It seems the more who are thinking about me, the more 'me' is likely to exist."

"Excellent formulation of thought. Sister you are to us."

"Sister I am to you," Genji said, feeling again that strange-for-her sensation of belonging. Tied into that was growing dread, though. "But . . . if the universe seeks to conserve what was, does that not mean the Earth is still doomed to die? That the universe will make the smallest changes it can to ensure larger things remain the same?"

More discussion. "Events must be consistent with causes," the Tramontine finally said. "Uniform changes, but event on what you call Martian Commons still happens. Tipping point must come, where maintaining future event requires more effort than yielding to change. As in Unified Fleet finally ceasing to have ever been, and your uniform then never having been. Unified Fleet not existing is major event, yes? Yet point came where changes you made resulted in keeping that fleet more difficult than future changing so it never will exist. In same way, if you achieve tipping point for doom of Earth, the universe will yield to change that requires least, and your Earth will not be doomed. Look at causes for that event. If those change enough, maintaining event becomes too hard. Universe yields to easier, different outcome.

"Must emphasize again we see no imaginable tipping point for you not being in 2140. You have created conditions in which every alternative to you being here requires much more effort, perhaps impossible effort."

"*I* have created conditions?" Genji asked, unable to believe what she'd just heard.

"Yes! By willingness to change events, to create major risk to your own existence, you caused changes that now require your existence. This sounds like paradox, but is not. Sister, must emphasize that new consensus is you *must* exist. Nothing else explains. You can cease to live, but must have been in this now."

"How will I know?" Genji asked, amazed at the certainty of the Tramontine. "Stopping Earth's doom. How would I know if I'd succeeded?"

"Cannot know, but can . . . feel? Perhaps proper word. You know, in ways no other can, conditions that led to doom. You observed event. When you see changes strong enough they add up to tipping point, you will recognize, we think. It will feel different. What you saw. You do not feel changes so far are enough to tip?"

"No," Genji said. "I do . . . feel . . . that something very big is close to tipping. I can't explain why. It's probably just wishful thinking."

"No one can know," the Tramontine said. "Only you can sense. You believe you have addressed causes, not symptoms, that led to doom of Earth? This means tipping point may come. What is most important cause remaining?"

"Most important?" Genji said, thinking. "If Earth Guard recovers, if other institutions are starting to address the things that led to failures that led to wars, I guess the most important thing left is fear. Does that grow and strengthen as people look for someone else to blame? Someone different from them?"

"Is this changing?" the Tramontine asked. "Or same?"

"It's . . . different," Genji said. She looked at her hand, the skin shiny in the lights overhead. "I . . . People touch me. Full humans. They're not . . . scared of that. Not most of them. Not the way they were, I mean, will be, in the 2160s and 2170s. I . . . They cheered me. Me. The people on Mars did that.

I . . . I don't understand it. There's still some . . . reserve in some people. Still clear suspicion in others. But . . . so many almost seem to . . . not mind that I'm different. I don't understand how that can be possible."

"If you observe these things, they must be possible, even if understanding still requires work."

"Thank you for accepting me as you have," Genji said. "I am not one of you, but you treat me as if I were. This brings me great happiness."

Flat Tramontine smiles answered her. "It is our honor to share happiness with you."

The call ended, and Genji stretched, wincing as her aches and newly healed injuries protested the movement.

"All done?" Kayl called.

She looked over, seeing him seated off to one side. "Have you been there all this time? I told you to get some rest."

Kayl stood up and walked to her. "I've never made any secret about the problems I sometimes have following directions. Come on, Lieutenant Genji. Lean on me."

"You are the only person I would accept that offer from," Genji said as she stood despite the protests in her leg and most of the rest of her body. "How far do we have to go?"

"It's only a few hundred meters," a familiar voice replied. "Some people can run that distance almost unprotected on the surface of Mars."

"I can't run that far today," Genji said with a laugh. "Hi, Jeyssi. It's nice to see you, but why are you here?"

"I've been assigned to you two," she said. "Escort, helper, whatever. Come on. I'll show you to your VIP Quarters."

"VIP Quarters?" Genji said. "Why?"

"Don't ask why, just go with it." She led the way, slowing her pace to accommodate Genji's. "You're both hungry, right? I can order something delivered."

"What's available?" Kayl asked.

"Umm . . . do you like ramen?"

"Of course we like ramen," Genji said.

"There's a place that delivers to the command center and has ramen as good as any in Tokyo," Jeyssi said. "Honest. It's good."

"That sounds like just the thing," Kayl said.

"And tea, right? No coffee for our new lieutenant. Congratulations on that, by the way, Lieutenant Genji. Welcome to Earth Guard."

"I'm still getting used to the idea," Genji said as they reached a door. "No guards?"

Kayl shook his head. "Camacho and Yesenski talked it over. They thought it would be important to show we have confidence while among Earth Guard personnel. There are security sensors watching this area, and guards monitoring them."

Genji considered that, finally nodding. "Okay."

Inside, the quarters were very nice. "This is how they put up lieutenants in 2140?" Genji said, looking around at the furnishings.

"I told you, don't fight it," Jeyssi replied. "Ah, here comes dinner. If you don't mind, I have a date who has been very patient but would really like to see me tonight. Do you require anything else, Lieutenant Owen, Lieutenant Genji?"

"A date?" Genji asked. "Have fun. I prefer it when Kayl's former girlfriends are committed to someone else."

"Not a former girlfriend!" Jeyssi said as she left.

Food delivered, Kayl helped Genji to the table. She sat down carefully, favoring her injured leg, before uncovering the large bowl in front of her, steam wafting up. "It smells great. Takes me back to Shibuya."

"And sencha green tea," Kayl added, setting the mug in front of her before sitting down opposite Genji.

"Are you trying to spoil me, Lieutenant Owen?" She took a drink, sighing. "If only we also had some sake."

"Junmai okay?" Kayl held up a bottle. "Jeyssi looked out for us."

"Hit me." Genji tried the sake, uttering another sigh of happiness. "Let's eat, and drink, then discuss life, the universe, and everything, and probably drink some more."

Eventually her bowl was empty, her having to raise it with one hand to drain the last drops. "More sake, please. These glasses are too small."

Kayl topped her off. "What was it you want to talk about?"

"That last conversation with the Tramontine, I asked them about what we're doing and what's happened," Genji said. "They think what happened to my uniform is proof the universe will put in the minimum possible effort to reflect changes."

"The universe is a slacker?" Kayl asked, looking amused as well as skeptical.

"The universe has a lot of things to deal with," Genji said. "Which means maybe it follows the path of least effort whenever it can. Conservation of effort. The Tramontine also think our own consciousness may act as an anchor on reality as we know it, fighting any effort to change. I asked them about the impact of an observer in sustaining an event or a thing. Specifically, when it comes to me, whether the fact that I've been observed doing things in 2140 is an important factor in my being here as me, along with the need for the universe to have a cause for the effects that are taking place."

"Um . . . what?" Kayl said. He was leaning back, relaxed, looking content but also puzzled.

"Whether the fact that you know me, whether the fact that you have watched me do these things, is something that helps sustain my existence," Genji said. "And the Tramontine thought that was possible. That it might be an important factor. The universe needs a cause, but did that cause need to be me? If I'm observed doing the things I cause, then that reinforces that I have to be the cause. My consciousness may help anchor me here, but so does your consciousness. Do you see?" To her surprise, Kayl seemed to be trying very hard not to smile. "What is funny about this?"

"I'm sorry," Kayl said. "It's just . . . did you just tell me that I'm the reason for your existence?"

She stared at him for a long moment, trying desperately not to laugh, before giving up and letting it out. "That is what you got from what I said?" Genji finally managed to say after she'd stopped laughing. "That even I am all about you?"

"I'm sorry, but you said it, not me."

"Maybe you still exist because of me," Genji said.

"Okay, we happen to know that's true, because if not for you, I would have died seven times already."

"Eight times," Genji said. "It's eight times now. Not that I'm keeping count."

"Okay, eight times. So, yes," Kayl said, still smiling, "you are the reason why I still exist."

"I'll have to inform the Tramontine of that," Genji said. "Anyway, you're likely stuck with me. Why is my glass empty?"

"I'm glad to hear you're not going anywhere," Kayl said, lifting the sake bottle to fill her glass again. His reply was interrupted by an alert. "There's a news item from Earth. It's . . . Wow." He sat up, suddenly sober and attentive.

"What?" Genji asked warily.

"'In light of the serious issues raised,'" Kayl quoted, "'the World Court has issued an expedited ruling that Lieutenant Selene Genji, and the alien beings calling themselves the Tramontine, are persons in all legal senses of the term.'"

Genji felt her jaw drop in shock. "That's impossible."

"You keep using that word," Kayl said, smiling at her.

"It's not even 2141 yet! The final ruling that alloys were human wasn't going to happen until 2169!" Genji sat back, trying to control her breathing. "How are people reacting? How big are the protests?"

"Only minor protests, apparently. But mostly widespread praise," Kayl said, smiling wider.

"You're making that up."

"No. You can read it yourself. Even some of the opponents to the ruling say they're happy someone like you can now be held legally accountable for her actions."

Genji shook her head, her mind filled with confusion. "None of this makes sense. It's . . . it's . . . I'm an alloy. Alloys are shunned by so many people. Even people who accept us don't really *accept* us. How could . . . ? How can . . . ?"

"Selene," Kayl said, reaching over to grasp her hand, "you changed all that. You fell into 2140, before anyone knew what they were supposed to think about alloys. Before anyone knew how they were supposed to react to your appearance. Once fear and hate get deeply rooted, it's very hard to dig them out. Even the greatest people have trouble making much progress against them. But by showing up in this time, you appeared before everything focused on real aliens had time to take root. Which means you haven't been judged because you're an alloy. Alloys have been judged because of you. And you have caused a lot of people to think someone like you is pretty great, or at least as much a person as they are."

He paused, his eyes on her. "You've been allowed to define yourself before others could try to define you. I don't know how many people in human history would have given anything for that chance. You got it, and just maybe, the example of you will make at least some of those who prejudge others rethink what they're doing. If a part alien can be seen as a person, then maybe humanity will finally start seeing all other full humans as persons, too. Maybe we needed to encounter real aliens to realize that we're all human. Which means you have flipped what happened in your history. Meeting aliens didn't have to result in all that anger and fear."

"They kept trying to kill me, Kayl," Genji said. "Remember? You were there. Some of the bullets intended for me hit you."

"But we're alive because of all of the people who didn't buy into that. All of the people who judged you by your actions, who listened to your words. I'm not saying that battle is over.

But you've proven to a lot of people that an alloy is a person. We've got the high ground, and we're going to hold it. Together."

Genji stared at him, trying to accept that such a thing could be possible. That this world, unlike the one she had seen destroyed in 2180, could accept her. Where were the huge protests that had followed the decision in 2169? The governments vowing to never accept the ruling?

What was this feeling inside her? Of something . . . something . . .

Tipping.

"Selene?"

No. It couldn't have happened. She called up her memories of that awful day, June twelfth, 2180. Watching the Earth be destroyed.

And realized those memories *felt* different, *looked* different in her mind. Not with the details of an observed event. Not accompanied by the remembered feelings of horror and shock. Everything blurred. Uncertain. Not like something seen firsthand, something experienced. More like something . . . imagined.

"Ohmigod," Genji managed to say, finding it hard to breathe.

"Selene?" Kayl asked, his voice filled with urgency and concern. "Are you okay? What's wrong?"

She stared at him, knowing how wide her eyes must be. "Nothing. Nothing."

"What?"

"Nothing is wrong." Genji managed to take a deep breath. "We did it, Kayl." She felt herself start to laugh at the same moment as tears came.

"We did it?" he asked, watching her in confusion. "What . . . what did we do?"

"We've changed the Earth's fate, Kayl," Genji said, hearing her voice break. "The Tramontine told me I might know, that my memories of Earth's doom might change. And they did, Kayl. It's not going to happen. Not that day. Not like that. We did it."

His expression had changed to shock. "You're sure?"

"As sure as I can be. *Kayl, we did it!*"

He came around the table in a rush, bending to kiss her and hold it for a long time. "*You* did it," Kayl said when he finally broke the kiss, his face still close to hers, their breath mingling.

As their lives now mingled, intertwined.

"We," Genji said in a whisper. "Not me. Not you. Always we."

In that moment she realized she had a different answer to something she had once thought decided for all time. "Kayl, I'm going to have my implant removed."

"What implant?" he asked, stepping back slightly and straightening up.

"My contraceptive implant. What other implant would I be talking about?"

His gaze on her grew dumbfounded. "But, I thought—"

"I couldn't raise my child in the world I came from," Genji said, getting up and moving closer to him again, the pain in her leg barely noticeable. "Or in a world doomed to die in forty years. But I want to raise *our* daughter in *this* world. Okay with you?"

"Hell, yes."

"I mean, not right away," Genji added. "I'll have the implant removed in a few years. There's a lot to do, yet, before we take on that extra responsibility. And I'd like a little more time to see how my own genome works out. But . . . then. Okay?"

"In a few years," Kayl said, smiling.

"You'd agree with anything I said right now, wouldn't you?"

"Yeah, I would."

"Hey," Genji added, feeling giddy from the combination of the sake and the amazing realization of what they had done, "as long as you're being so agreeable, why stop at one? Or, two, since we've already got Krysta. Oh, I forgot, this means the adoption can go forward. How about three or four daughters?"

"Counting Krysta?" Kayl seemed to be the one having trouble breathing now. "I think that would be wonderful."

"And now that I'm legally a person, we can get married. We do not have to wait a few years for that. But I'm willing to wait until your family can get to Mars for the ceremony. Am I going to be planning a wedding? *I'm* going to have a wedding? Do we need anything else? What else could we need? Are you happy?" Genji said.

Kayl wrapped his arms about her. "Yes. I can't imagine ever being happier."

"Oh, just wait until those other daughters start showing up. I thought happiness would forever be out of my reach. I was wrong. It took a little work, it took saving the world, but I was wrong." Genji held him as tightly as she could with her right arm, trying to imagine a world in which she didn't know the outlines of the future. A world in which institutions wouldn't collapse, fanaticism wouldn't flourish, a world in which terrible battles and wars wouldn't be fought as a result, a world in which countless lives wouldn't senselessly perish. A world in which an alloy, and an alloy's children, could belong.

A world in which the Earth would not be destroyed on the twelfth of June, 2180.

There would be plenty of battles ahead. Battles to be accepted as herself, battles against fear of the different, battles to keep institutions on the right path, and battles to curb the barely hidden corruption that fed public distrust. Not to mention worries about how her own genome might affect her in years to come. But she wouldn't be fighting those battles alone.

"Hey, Lieutenant Owen."

"Yes, Lieutenant Genji?"

"We're going to need to choose another hill."

ACKNOWLEDGMENTS

I remain indebted to my agent, Joshua Bilmes, for his ever-inspired suggestions and assistance. Thanks also to Robert Chase, Kelly Dwyer, Carolyn Ives Gilman, the spirit of J. G. (Huck) Huckenpohler, Simcha Kuritzky, Michael LaViolette, the spirit of Aly Parsons, Bud Sparhawk, Mary Thompson, and Constance A. Warner for their suggestions, comments, and recommendations.

The quotes from Marcus Aurelius are taken from the Penguin Classics edition of *Meditations*, translated by Martin Hammond.

ABOUT THE AUTHOR

Jack Campbell is the pen name of John G. Hemry, a retired U.S. Navy officer. His books, including the bestselling Lost Fleet series, have been translated into fifteen languages and sold four million copies worldwide.

John's father (LCDR Jack M. Hemry, USN ret.) is a mustang (an officer who was promoted through the enlisted ranks), so John grew up living everywhere from Pensacola, Florida to San Diego, California, including an especially memorable few years on Midway Island. He graduated from Lyons High School in Lyons, Kansas in 1974, then attended the U.S. Naval Academy (Class of '78), where he was labeled "the un-Midshipman" by his roommates. His active duty assignments in the U.S. Navy included: *USS Spruance* (DD963) (Navigator, Gunnery Officer); Defense Intelligence Agency (Production Control Officer); Navy Anti-Terrorism Alert Center (Watch Officer, Operations Officer); Amphibious Squadron Five (Staff Intelligence Officer/N2); Navy Operational Intelligence Center (Readiness Division); and Chief of Naval Operations Staff N3/N5 (Plans, Policy and Operations).

John speaks the remnants of Russian painstakingly pounded into him by Professor Vladimir Tolstoy (yes, he was related to *that* Tolstoy).

He lives in Maryland with a wife who is too good for him and three great kids.

Find John on *www.jack-campbell.com* or follow him on X @JohnGHemry.

«« ALSO AVAILABLE FROM TITAN BOOKS »»

THE DOOMED EARTH: IN OUR STARS

When the destruction of Earth causes a time rift, one ship is thrust back in time to decades prior. The semi-disgraced naval officer Kayl Owen is sent from the Earth Guard ship *Vigilant* to investigate. He finds one person alive, one person whose DNA analysis reveals some non-human DNA, a person who his superiors say isn't human.

That's not how Kayl Owen sees it. He thinks Lieutenant Genji of the near future Unified Fleet—the future successor of Earth Guard—is every bit a person. And what's more, the knowledge she brings from the future might hold the key to saving Earth from destruction.

Owen, Genji and everything they know is deeply threatening to a lot of people, and the two of them need to survive each day to get to the next and save the future for everyone. But will changing Earth's future erase Genji?

"Campbell juggles a lot here, with military cover-ups, alien first encounters, and ruminations on what it means to be human studding the sprawling plot...This series is off to a good start."
—*Publisher's Weekly*

"Sometimes it's nice to read a book that just focusses on telling a good tale. This is one of them, told by someone who knows how to write an engaging story."
—*SFF World*

"Jack Campbell's *In Our Stars* is a wonderful, engaging, often uplifting adventure about caring and doing what's right, no matter the odds or the cost. And the soul of it all is honestly reminiscent of Heinlein at his best."
— Taylor Anderson, *New York Times*-bestselling author

«« ALSO AVAILABLE FROM TITAN BOOKS »»

THE LOST FLEET: OUTLANDS – BOUNDLESS

The master of military science fiction returns.

Admiral John 'Black Jack' Geary carries evidence of crimes which could destroy the Alliance he has fought so hard to save. Now his battle-weary fleet returns to Unity, the seat of the Alliance government.

But instead of a hero's welcome, he faces assassination attempts and political threats. His arrival ignites a furious Senate trial, and Geary must use all his guile to ensure the guilty are brought to justice, without himself becoming judge and jury. All the while forces lurk in the shadows, poised to strike at any moment.

Unsure of who he can trust, Geary is sent on a dangerous mission to lead his fleet through the shattered Syndicate Worlds, and beyond to alien-controlled space. As the Alliance faces the failures of its past, Black Jack must confront its legacy – distrust and rebellion.

Praise for Jack Campbell's The Lost Fleet series:

"An excellent blend of real science and space action."
—Brandon Sanderson, #1 *New York Times*-bestselling author

"Black Jack is an excellent character, and this series is the best military SF I've read in some time."
—*Wired*

"The Lost Fleet series is a must-read for fans of military scifi. Packed with complex characters and even more complex deep-space naval battles, it's the ultimate saga of human perseverance and the will to survive."
—Zac Topping, author of *Wake of War*

"Campbell combines the best parts of military SF and grand space opera … plenty of exciting discoveries and escapades.
—*Publishers Weekly*

TITANBOOKS.COM

«« ALSO AVAILABLE FROM TITAN BOOKS »»

THE GENESIS FLEET: VANGUARD

The Saga of the Genesis Fleet begins…

Earth is no longer the centre of the universe. After the invention of the faster-than-light jump drive, humanity is rapidly establishing new colonies. But the vast distances of space mean that the protection of Earth's laws no longer exists. When a nearby world attacks, the new colony of Glenlyon turns to Robert Geary, a former junior fleet officer, and Mele Darcy, once an enlisted Marine. They must face down warships with nothing but improvised weapons and a few volunteers – or die trying.

The only hope for lasting peace lies with Carmen Ochoa, a "Red" from anarchic Mars, and Lochan Nakamura, a failed politician, and their plan for a mutual alliance. But if their efforts don't succeed, space could become a battlefield between the first interstellar empires…

"Jack Campbell's *Vanguard* starts a new series with a bang. Honestly, it reads like first rate, action-packed, historical fiction--only this history is set hundreds of years in an all too believable future."
—Taylor Anderson, *New York Times*-bestselling author

"*Vanguard* is the book Campbell's Lost Fleet readers have been waiting for, whether they knew it or not. From the moment the young Robert Geary takes his first breath of air on a new planet, the story grabbed me by the throat and didn't let go."
—Elizabeth Moon, *New York Times*-bestselling author of the Vatta's War series

"Launching a trilogy in his Lost Fleet universe, the always reliable Campbell delivers an exciting tale of interstellar adventure… Campbell's skilfully constructed tale keeps a riveting pace, making each character's personal stakes into fundamental threads woven into a high-energy whole."
—*Publishers Weekly*

TITANBOOKS.COM

«« ALSO AVAILABLE FROM TITAN BOOKS »»

INFINITE STARS

The seductive thrill of uncharted worlds, of distant galaxies… and the unknown threats that lurk in the vastness of the cosmos. From *Foundation* to Lensman, *Star Wars* to *Guardians of the Galaxy*, space opera continues to exert its magnetic pull on us all.

This is the definitive collection of original short stories by many of space opera's finest authors, writing brand new adventures set in their most famous series. Herein lie canonical tales of the Honorverse, the Lost Fleet, *Dune*, Vatta's War, Ender Wiggin, the *Legion of the Damned*, the *Imperium*, and more.

Also included are past masterpieces by authors whose works defined the genre. Nebula and Hugo Award winners, *New York Times* bestsellers, and Science Fiction Grand Masters—these authors take us to the farthest regions of space.

The modern masters of space opera and military science fiction, with 14 brand new stories set in their most famous universes— exclusive to this volume!

"*Infinite Stars* presents a neat mix of truly classic older Space Opera and brand-new stories, by writers both justly familiar and quite new to me, introducing the reader to some of the best ongoing Space Opera series."
—Rich Horton, *Locus*

"A stellar cast of authors with some of the finest short stories ever written in the genre. What in the world are you waiting for? This is a no-brainer. Buy it!"
—David Farland, *New York Times*-bestselling author of *Dunelords* and *Star Wars: The Courtship of Princess Leia*

TITANBOOKS.COM

For more fantastic fiction, author events,
exclusive excerpts, competitions, limited editions and more

VISIT OUR WEBSITE
titanbooks.com

LIKE US ON FACEBOOK
facebook.com/titanbooks

FOLLOW US ON TWITTER AND INSTAGRAM
@TitanBooks

EMAIL US
readerfeedback@titanemail.com